nightfall
STEPHEN LEATHER

Published by 47North
P.O. Box 400818
Las Vegas, NV 89140

ISBN-13: 9781612182292
ISBN-10: 1612182291

nightfall

by

STEPHEN LEATHER

47NORTH

CHAPTER

1

Jack Nightingale didn't intend to kill anyone when he woke up that chilly November morning. He shaved, showered, and dressed, made himself coffee and a bacon sandwich, and at no point did he even contemplate the taking of a human life even though he had spent the last five years training to do just that. As a serving member of the Metropolitan Police's elite CO19 armed response unit he was more than capable of putting a bullet in a man's head or chest if it was necessary and provided he had been given the necessary authorization by a senior officer.

His cell phone rang just as he was pouring the coffee from his pot. It was the coordinator of the Metropolitan Police's negotiating team. "Jack, I've just had a call from the duty officer at Fulham. They have a person in crisis down at Chelsea Harbour. Can you get there?"

"No problem," said Nightingale. After two courses at the Met's Bramshill Officer Training College he was now one of several dozen officers qualified to talk to hostage-takers and potential suicides.

"I'm told it's a jumper on a ledge and that's all I have. I'm trying to get backup for you but we've got four guys tied up with a domestic in Brixton."

"Give me the address," said Nightingale, reaching for a pen.

He ate his bacon sandwich as he drove his MGB Roadster to Chelsea Harbour. During the three years he had worked as a negotiator he had been called to more than forty attempted suicides, but on only three occasions had he seen someone take their own life. In his experience, people either wanted to kill themselves, or they wanted to talk. They rarely wanted to do both. Suicide was a relatively easy matter. You climbed to the top of a high building or a bridge and you jumped. Or you swallowed a lot of tablets. Or you tied a rope around your neck and stepped off a chair. Or you took a razor blade and made deep cuts in your wrist or throat. If you were lucky enough to have a gun you put it in your mouth or against your temple and pulled the trigger. What you didn't do if you really wanted to kill yourself was say you were going to do it and then wait for a trained police negotiator to arrive. People who did that usually just wanted to talk, to have someone listen to their problems and reassure them that their lives were worth living. Once they'd got whatever was worrying them off their chests they came down from the ledge or put down the gun or lowered the knife and everyone cheered and patted Nightingale on the back and told him "job well done."

When he reached the address that the duty officer had given him, his way was blocked by a police car and two community support officers in police-type uniforms and yellow fluorescent jackets. One of them pointed the way Nightingale had come and told him to turn around in a tone that suggested his motivation for becoming a CSO had more to do with wielding power than helping his fellow citizens. Nightingale wound down the window and showed them his warrant card. "Inspector Nightingale," he said. "I'm the negotiator."

"Sorry, sir," said the CSO, suddenly all sweetness and light. He pointed over at a parked ambulance. "You can leave your car there, I'll keep an eye on it."

The two CSOs moved to the side to allow him to drive through. He parked behind the ambulance and climbed out, stretching and yawning. If you'd asked Nightingale what he was expecting that chilly November morning, he'd probably have shrugged carelessly and said that jumpers tended to be either men the worse for drink, women the worse for antidepressants, or druggies the worse for their Class A drug of choice, generally cocaine or amphetamines. Nightingale's drug of choice while working was nicotine, and he lit himself a Marlboro and blew smoke up at the cloudless sky.

A uniformed inspector hurried over, holding a transceiver. "I'm glad it's you, Jack," he said.

"And I'm glad it's you, Colin." He'd known Colin Duggan for almost a decade. He was old-school—a good, reliable cop who like Nightingale was a smoker. Nightingale offered the inspector a Marlboro and lit it for him, even though smoking in uniform was a disciplinary offence.

"It's a kid, Jack," said Duggan, scratching his fleshy neck.

"Gangbanger? Drug deal gone wrong?" Nightingale inhaled and held the smoke deep in his lungs.

"A *kid* kid," said Duggan. "Nine-year-old girl."

Nightingale frowned as he blew a tight plume of smoke. Nine-year-old girls didn't kill themselves. They played with their PlayStations or Wiis or they went rollerblading, and sometimes they were kidnapped and raped by pedophiles, but they never, ever killed themselves.

Duggan pointed up at a luxury tower block overlooking the Thames. "Her name's Sophie, she's locked herself on the thirteenth-floor balcony, and she's sitting there talking to her doll."

"Where are the parents?" said Nightingale. There was a cold feeling of dread in the pit of his stomach.

"Father's at work, mother's shopping, the girl was left in the care of the au pair." Duggan gestured with his cigarette at an anorexic blonde who was sitting on a bench, sobbing, as a uniformed WPC tried to comfort her. "Polish girl. She was ironing, then saw Sophie on the balcony. She banged on the window but Sophie had locked it from the outside."

"And what makes her think Sophie wants to jump?"

"She's talking to her doll, won't look at anyone. We sent up two WPCs but she won't talk to them."

"You're supposed to wait for me, Colin," said Nightingale. He dropped his cigarette onto the floor and crushed it with his heel. "Amateurs only complicate matters, you know that."

"She's a kid on a balcony," said Duggan. "We couldn't just wait."

"You're sure she's a potential jumper?"

"She's sitting on the edge, Jack. A gust of wind and she could blow right off. We're trying to get an airbag brought out but no one seems to know where to get one."

"How close can I get to her?"

"You could talk to her through the balcony window."

Nightingale shook his head. "I need to see her face, to see how she's reacting. And I don't want to be shouting."

"Then there are two possibilities," said Duggan. "She's too high to use a ladder, so we can either lower you down from the roof or we can get you into the apartment next door."

"Lower me?"

"We can put you in a harness and the Fire Brigade boys will drop you down."

"And I talk to her hanging from a string like a bloody puppet? Come on, Colin. I'm a negotiator, not a bloody marionette."

"The other balcony it is then," said Duggan. He flicked his butt away. "Let's get to it, then." He waved over a uniformed constable and told him to escort Nightingale up to the thirteenth floor. "Except it isn't the thirteenth, it's the fourteenth," said Duggan.

"What?"

"It's a superstitious thing. Don't ask me why. It is the thirteenth floor, but the lift says fourteen. It goes from twelve to fourteen. No thirteen."

"That's ridiculous," said Nightingale.

"Tell the developer, not me," said Duggan. "Besides, you're talking to the wrong person. You won't catch me walking under a ladder or breaking a mirror. I can understand people not wanting to live on the thirteenth floor." He grinned at Nightingale. "Break a leg, yeah?"

"Yeah," said Nightingale. He nodded at the uniformed constable, a lanky specimen whose uniform seemed a couple of sizes too small for him. "Lead on, McDuff."

The constable frowned. "My name's not McDuff," he said.

Nightingale patted him on the back. "Let's go," he said. "But first I want a word with the au pair."

The constable and Nightingale went over to the sobbing woman who was still being comforted by the uniformed WPC. Over fifty people had gathered to stare up at the little girl. There were pensioners huddled together like penguins on an ice floe, mothers with toddlers in strollers, teenagers chewing gum and sniggering, a girl in goth clothing with a collie dog who grinned at Nightingale as he walked by, workmen in overalls who were shouting at the police to do something, and a group of waitresses from a nearby pizza restaurant.

"Why aren't you up there, getting her down?" shouted a bald man holding a metal toolbox. He pointed at Nightingale and the young constable. "You should do something instead of pissing about down here."

"Can't you Taser him?" asked Nightingale.

"We're not issued with Tasers, sir," said the constable.

"Use your truncheon then."

"We're not…" He grimaced as he realized that Nightingale was joking.

They went to the au pair, who was blowing her nose into a large white handkerchief. He nodded at the WPC. "I'm the negotiator," he said.

"Yes, sir," she said.

Nightingale smiled at the au pair. "Hi, what's your name?" he asked.

"Inga," sniffed the girl, dabbing at her eyes with the handkerchief. "Are you a policeman?"

"I'm Jack Nightingale," he said, showing her his warrant card. "I'll be the one who's going to talk to Sophie."

"Am I in trouble?"

"No, of course you're not," said Nightingale. "You did the right thing, calling the police."

"Her parents will kill me," said the au pair.

"They won't," said Nightingale.

"They'll send me back to Poland."

"They can't do that, Poland is in the EU. You have every right to be here."

"They'll send me to prison, I know they will."

Nightingale felt his heart harden. The au pair seemed more concerned about her own future than what was happening thirteen stories up. "They won't," he said. "Tell me, Inga, why isn't Sophie at school today?"

"She said she had a stomachache. She didn't feel well. Her mother said she could stay home."

"Her mother's shopping?"

The au pair nodded. "I phoned her and she's coming back now. Her father's cell phone is switched off so I left a message on his voicemail."

"Where does he work?"

"A bank in Canary Wharf." Still sniffing, she took a wallet out of the back pocket of her jeans and fished out a business card. She gave it to Nightingale. "This is him." Nightingale looked at the card. Simon Underwood was a vice president at a large American bank.

"Inga, has Sophie done anything like his before?"

The au pair shook her head fiercely. "Never. She's a quiet child. As good as gold."

"Tell me what happened. How did she come to be on the balcony?"

"I don't know," said the au pair. "I was ironing. She was watching a Hannah Montana video. Then when I looked up she was on the balcony and she'd locked the door."

"You can lock it from the outside?"

"There's only one key and she had it. I shouted at her to open the door but it was like she couldn't hear me. I banged on the window but she didn't look at me. That's when I called the police."

"And she wasn't sad this morning? Or angry? Or upset at something? Or somebody?"

"She was quiet," said the au pair. "She's always quiet."

"You didn't argue with her? Or fight with her about something?"

The au pair's eyes flashed. "You're going to blame me, aren't you? You're going to send me to prison?" She began to wail.

"No one's blaming you, Inga."

The au pair buried her face in her handkerchief and sobbed.

Nightingale nodded at the constable. "Let's go," he said.

"What will you do?" the constable asked as they walked by the crowd of onlookers.

"Talk to her. See if I can find out what's troubling her, see what it is she wants."

"She wants something?"

"They always want something. If they didn't want something then they'd just go ahead and do it. The key is to find out what it is they want."

"Wankers!" shouted the bald man with the toolbox.

Nightingale stopped and glared at the man. "What's your problem, pal?"

"My problem is that there's a little girl up there and you tossers aren't doing anything about it."

"And what exactly are you doing? Gawping in case she takes a dive off the balcony? Is that what you want? You want to see her slap into the ground, do you? You want to hear her bones break and her skull smash and see her blood splatter over the concrete? Because that's the only reason you could have for standing there. You're sure as hell not helping by shouting abuse and making an ass of yourself. I'm here to help, you're here on the off chance you might see a child die, so I'd say that makes you the tosser. I'm going up there now to see how I can help her, and if you're still here when I get down I'll shove your tools so far up your arse that you'll be coughing up wrenches for months. Are we clear, tosser?"

The bald man looked away, his face reddening. Nightingale sneered at him and started walking to the entrance again. The constable hurried after him.

The reception area was plush with overstuffed sofas and a large coffee table covered with glossy magazines. A doorman in a green uniform was talking to two uniformed PCs. "Where are the stairs?" asked Nightingale.

The doorman pointed to three elevator doors. "The elevators are there, sir," he said.

"I need the stairs," said Nightingale.

"It's thirteen floors, sir," said the constable at his side.

"I know it's thirteen floors, McDuff," said Nightingale. He jerked his chin at the doorman. "Stairs?"

The doorman pointed to the left. "Around the side there, sir," he said.

Nightingale hurried toward the stairs, followed by the constable. He pushed through the doors and started up the concrete stairs, taking them two at a time. The number of each floor was painted on the white wall in green letters, and by the time they'd reached the tenth floor both men were panting like dogs. "Why can't we use the elevator, sir?" gasped the constable. "Is it procedure with jumpers?"

"It's because I hate elevators," said Nightingale.

"Claustrophobia?"

"Nothing to do with confined spaces," said Nightingale. "I just don't like dangling over nothing."

"So it's fear of heights?"

"It's fear of elevators," said Nightingale. "I'm fine with heights. As you're about to find out."

They reached the twelfth floor. The policeman had taken off his helmet and unbuttoned his tunic. Nightingale had taken off his overcoat and draped it over his shoulder.

They reached the thirteenth floor though the number stenciled by the door was fourteen. Nightingale pulled open the door and went through into the corridor. "What number is her apartment?" he asked.

"Fourteen C," said the constable. "We can get into Fourteen D. A Mr. and Mrs. Jackson live there and they've agreed to give us access."

"Okay, when we get in there keep the Jacksons away from the balcony. The girl mustn't see them and she sure as hell mustn't see you. Nothing personal, but the uniform could spook her."

"Got you," said the policeman.

"You'll be just fine, McDuff," said Nightingale. He knocked on the door of Fourteen D. It was opened by a man in his early sixties, gray-haired and slightly stooped. Nightingale flashed his warrant card. "Mr. Jackson, I'm Jack Nightingale. I gather you're happy for me to go out on your balcony."

"I wouldn't exactly say that I was happy, but we need to get that little girl back inside."

He opened the door wide and Nightingale walked in, followed by the constable. The man's wife was sitting on a flower-print sofa, her hands in her lap. She was also gray-haired, and when she stood up to greet Nightingale he saw that she had the same curved spine. "Please don't get up, Mrs. Jackson," he said.

"What's going to happen?" she said anxiously. Like her husband she was well-spoken, with an accent that would do credit to a BBC announcer. They were good, middle-class people, the sort that would rarely cross paths with a policeman, and Nightingale could sense their unease at having him and the uniformed constable in their home.

"I'm just going to talk to her, Mrs. Jackson, that's all."

"Would you like a cup of tea?" she asked.

Nightingale smiled. More often than not, as a member of CO19 he was treated with contempt if not open hostility, and the Jacksons were a breath of fresh air.

"You could certainly put the kettle on, Mrs. Jackson," he said. "Now, do you know Sophie?"

"We say hello to her, but she's a shy little thing, wouldn't say boo to a goose."

"A happy girl?"

"I wouldn't say happy," said Mrs. Jackson.

"She cries sometimes," said her husband quietly. "At night."

"What sort of crying?" asked Nightingale. "Screaming?"

"Sobbing," said Mr. Jackson. Her bedroom is next to our bathroom, and sometimes when I'm getting ready for bed I can hear her sobbing."

"We've both heard her," agreed Mrs. Jackson. Her husband walked over to her and put his arm around her, and for a brief moment Nightingale flashed back to his own parents. His father had been equally protective with his mother, never scared to hold her hand in public or to demonstrate his affection in other ways. His last memory of them was the two of them standing at the door of their house in Manchester, his arm around her shoulders, as they waved him off to start his second year at university. His mother had looked up at Nightingale's father with the same adoration that he saw in Mrs. Jackson's eyes.

"Any idea why she'd be unhappy?" asked Nightingale. "Did you see her with her parents?"

"Rarely," said Mr. Jackson. "They've been here what, five years?" he asked, looking at his wife.

"Six," she said.

"Six years, and I can count on the fingers of one hand the number of times I've seen her with her mother or father. It's always an au pair she's with, and they seem to change them every six months or so." He looked at his wife and she nodded imperceptibly. "The thing is," he continued, "one doesn't like to talk out of turn, but they didn't seem to be the most attentive of parents."

"I understand," he said. He took his cigarette lighter and cigarettes from the pocket of his overcoat and gave the coat to the constable. "Why don't you just take a seat while I go out and talk to her," he said to the Jacksons.

Mr. Jackson helped his wife onto the sofa while Nightingale went over to the glass door that led onto the balcony. The balcony was actually a terrace, with terra-cotta tiles and space for a small circular white metal table and four chairs, and several pots of flowering shrubs. The terrace was surrounded by a waist-high wall.

The door slid to the side and Nightingale could hear traffic off in the distance and the crackle of police radios. He stepped slowly onto the terrace and then looked to the right.

The girl was sitting on the wall of the balcony next door. She was holding a Barbie doll and seemed to be whispering to it. She was wearing a white sweatshirt with a blue cotton skirt and silver trainers with blue stars on them. She had porcelain-white skin and shoulder-length blonde hair that she'd tucked behind her ears.

There was a gap of about six feet between the terrace where he was and the one where the girl was sitting. Nightingale figured that he could just about jump across, but that would be a last resort. He walked slowly over to the side of the terrace and stood next to a tall, thin conifer in a concrete pot. In the distance he could see the River Thames and far off to his left was the London Eye. The girl didn't seem to have noticed him, but Nightingale knew that she must have heard the door slide open. "Hi," he said.

Sophie looked across at Nightingale but didn't say anything. Nightingale stared out over the Thames as he slid a cigarette between his lips and flicked his lighter.

"Cigarettes are bad for you," said Sophie.

"I know," said Nightingale. He lit his cigarette and inhaled deeply.

"You can get cancer," said Sophie.

Nightingale tilted his head back and blew two perfect rings of smoke. "I know that too," he said.

"How do you do that?" she asked.

"Do what?"

"Blow smoke rings."

Nightingale shrugged. "You just blow and stick your tongue out a bit," he said. He grinned amiably and held out the cigarette. "Do you want to try?"

She shook her head solemnly. "I'm a child and children can't smoke, and even if I could smoke I wouldn't because it gives you cancer."

Nightingale shrugged again and took another drag on the cigarette. "It's a beautiful day, isn't it?" he said, looking out over the river again.

"Who are you?" Sophie asked.

"My name's Jack."

"Like Jack and the beanstalk?"

"Yeah, but I don't have my beanstalk with me today. I had to use the stairs."

"Why didn't you use the elevator?"

"I don't like elevators."

Sophie put the doll to her ear and frowned as if she were listening intently. Then she nodded. "Jessica doesn't like elevators, either."

"That's a nice name, Jessica."

"Jessica Lovely, that's her full name. What's your full name?"

"Nightingale. Jack Nightingale."

"Like the bird?"

"That's right. Like the bird."

"I wish I was a bird." She cuddled the doll as she stared across the river with unseeing eyes. "I wish I could fly."

Nightingale blew two more smoke rings. This time they held together for less than a second before the wind whipped them apart. "It's not so much fun, being a bird. They can't watch TV, they can't play video games or play with dolls, and they have to eat off the floor."

Down below a siren kicked into life and Sophie flinched as if she'd been struck. "It's okay," said Nightingale. "It's a fire engine."

"I thought it was the police."

"The police siren sounds different." Nightingale made the *woo-woo-woo* sound of a police siren and Sophie giggled. Nightingale leaned against the wall of the balcony. He had set his phone to vibrate and he felt it judder in his inside pocket. He took it out and looked at the screen. It was Robbie Hoyle, one of his negotiator colleagues. He'd known Hoyle for more than a decade. He was a sergeant with the Territorial Support Group, the force's heavy mob who went in with riot shields, truncheons, and Tasers when necessary. Hoyle was a big man, well over six feet tall with the build of a rugby player, but he had a soft voice and was one of the Met's most able negotiators. "I'm going to have to take this call, Sophie, I'm sorry," he said. He pressed the green button. "Hi, Robbie."

"I've just arrived, do you want me up there?"

"I'm not sure that's a good idea," said Nightingale. Whenever possible the negotiators preferred to act in teams of three, one doing the talking, one actively listening, and one gathering intelligence, but Nightingale figured that too many men on the balcony would only spook the little girl.

"How's it going?" asked Hoyle.

"Calm," said Nightingale. "I'll get back to you, okay? Try to get rid of the onlookers, but softly, softly." He ended the call and put the phone away.

"You're a policeman, aren't you?" said Sophie.

Nightingale smiled. "How did you know?"

Sophie pointed down at Colin Duggan, who was staring up at them, shielding his eyes from the sun with his hand. Robbie Hoyle was standing next to him. "That policeman there spoke to you when you got out of your car."

"You saw me arrive, yeah?"

"I like sports cars," she said. "It's an MGB, right?"

"That's right," said Nightingale. "It's an old one. How old are you?"

"Nine," she said.

"Well my car is twenty-six years old, how about that?"

"That's old," she said. "That's very old."

"There's another thing that birds can't do," said Nightingale. "When was the last time you saw a bird driving a car? They can't do it. No hands."

Sophie pressed the doll next to her ear as if she were listening to it, then took it away and looked across at Nightingale. "Am I in trouble?" she said.

Nightingale shook his head. "No, you're not in trouble, Sophie. We just want to be sure that you're okay."

Sophie shuddered as if a lump of ice had been drawn along her spine.

"The girl who looks after you, what's her name?" asked Nightingale.

"Inga. She's from Poland."

"She's worried about you."

"She's stupid."

"Why do you say that?"

"She can't even use the microwave properly."

Nightingale shrugged. "I have trouble getting my video recorder to work."

"Videoplus," said Sophie.

"What?"

"Videoplus. You just put in the number from the newspaper. The machine does it for you. Everyone knows that."

"I didn't." A gust of wind blew across from the river and Sophie put a hand onto her skirt to stop it billowing around her leg. Nightingale caught a glimpse of a dark bruise above her knee. "What happened to your leg?" he asked.

"Nothing," she said quickly. Too quickly, Nightingale realized. He blew smoke and avoided looking at the girl. "Why didn't you go to school today?"

"Mummy said I didn't have to."

"Are you sick?"

"Not really." She bit down on her lower lip and cuddled her doll. "I am in trouble, aren't I?"

"No, you're not," said Nightingale. He made the sign of the cross over his heart. "Cross my heart, you're not."

Sophie forced a smile. "Do you have children?"

Nightingale dropped the butt of his cigarette and ground it with his heel. "I'm not married."

"You don't have to be married to have children." Tears began to run down her cheeks and she turned her face away.

"What's wrong, Sophie?"

"Nothing." She sniffed and wiped her eyes with her doll.

"Sophie, let's go inside. It's cold out here."

She sniffed again but didn't look at him. Nightingale started to pull himself up onto the balcony wall but his foot scraped against the concrete and she flinched. "Don't come near me," she said.

"I just wanted to sit like you," said Nightingale. "I'm tired of standing."

She glared at him. "You were going to jump over," she said. "You were going to try to grab me."

"I wasn't, I swear," lied Nightingale. He sat down, swinging his legs as if he didn't have a care in the world but in fact his heart was pounding and his stomach churning. "Sophie, whatever's wrong, maybe I can help you."

Sophie sniffed. "No one can help me."

"I can try."

"He said I mustn't tell anyone."

"Why? Why can't you tell anyone?"

"He said they'd take me away. Put me in a home."

"Your father?"

Sophie pressed her doll to her face. "He said they'd blame me. He said they'd take me away and make me live in a home and that everyone would say it was my fault."

The wind whipped up her skirt again. The bruise was a good six inches long. "Did he do that?" said Nightingale, nodding at the mark.

Sophie pushed her skirt down and nodded as she sniffed.

"Let's go inside, Sophie, we can talk to your mummy."

Sophie closed her eyes. "She already knows."

Nightingale's stomach lurched. He had his hands palms down, his fingers gripping into the concrete, but he felt as if something were pushing him in the small of his back.

"I can help you, Sophie. Just come inside and we'll talk about it. I can help you, honestly I can. Cross my heart."

"You can't help me," she said, her voice a dull monotone. "No one can help me." She lifted her doll, kissed it gently on the top of its head, and then slid off the balcony without making a sound.

Nightingale stared in horror as the little girl dropped, her skirt billowing up around her waist. He leaned forward and reached out with his right hand even though he knew there was nothing he could do. "Sophie!" he screamed. Her golden hair was whipping around in the wind as she dropped straight down, her arms still hugging the doll. "Sophie!" he screamed again. He closed his eyes at the last second but he couldn't blot out the sound she made as she hit the ground, a dull wet thud as if a wall had been slapped with a wet blanket. Nightingale turned and slid down the balcony wall. He lit a cigarette with trembling hands and smoked it as he crouched on the balcony, his back against the concrete, his legs drawn up against his stomach.

The uniformed constable who had escorted Nightingale up the stairs appeared at the balcony door. "Are you okay, sir?"

Nightingale ignored him.

"Sir, are you okay?" The constable's radio crackled and a female voice asked him for a situation report.

Nightingale stood up and pushed him out of the way.

"Sir, your coat!" the constable called after him.

The elderly couple were standing in the middle of the living room, holding each other. They looked at Nightingale expectantly but he said nothing to them as he rushed past. He took the stairs three at a time, his fingers brushing the handrail as he hurtled down the stairwell, his footsteps echoing off the concrete walls.

There were a two paramedics and half a dozen uniformed officers in the reception area, all talking into the radios. Duggan was there and he opened his mouth to speak, but Nightingale silenced him with a pointed finger and walked right by him.

Two female paramedics were crouched over the little girl's body. The younger of the two was crying. Four firemen in bulky fluorescent jackets were standing behind the paramedics. One of them was wiping tears from his eyes with the back of one of his gloves. Nightingale knew there was nothing any of them could do. No one survived a fall from thirteen floors. Nightingale saw glistening blood pooling around the body and he turned away.

Hoyle was standing next to a uniformed PC, frowning as he spoke into his cell. He put the phone away as Nightingale walked out of the building. "Superintendent Chalmers wants you in his office, Jack," said Hoyle. "Now."

Nightingale said nothing. He brushed past Hoyle and headed for his MGB.

"Now, Jack. He wants to see you now."

"I'm busy," said Nightingale.

"He'll want you to see the shrink, too," said Hoyle, hurrying after him. It was standard procedure when there was a death.

"I don't need to see the shrink," said Nightingale.

Hoyle put a hand on Nightingale's shoulder. "It wasn't your fault, Jack. It's natural to feel guilty, to feel that you've failed."

Nightingale glared at him. "Don't try to empathize with me and don't sympathize, I don't need it, Robbie. I don't need any of it."

"And what do I tell Chalmers?"

"Tell him whatever you want," said Nightingale, twisting out of Hoyle's grip. He climbed into his MGB and drove off.

CHAPTER

What happened later that chilly November morning really depends on who you talk to. Jack Nightingale never spoke about it and refused to answer any questions put to him by the two investigators assigned to the case. They were from the Metropolitan Police's Professional Standards Department, and they questioned him for more than eighteen hours over three days. During that time he said not one word to them about what had happened. If you'd asked the two detectives they'd have said they were pretty sure that Nightingale had thrown Simon Underwood through the window. If they'd been speaking off the record, they would probably have said they had every sympathy with Nightingale and that given the chance they would probably have done the same. Like policemen the world over they knew that pedophiles never stopped offending. You could put them in prison so that they couldn't get near children, or you could kill them, but you could never change their natures.

The postmortem on the little girl had shown signs of sexual activity and there were bruises and bite marks on her legs and stomach. A forensic dentistry expert was able to match two of the clearer marks to the father's dental records. And a swab of the little girl's vagina showed up the father's sperm. The evidence was conclusive: he had been raping her over a long period, over several years according to the coroner. The investigating officers presented the evidence to the mother, but she denied all knowledge of any abuse. The investigating officers didn't believe her.

Underwood had been in a meeting with six employees from the bank's marketing department when Nightingale walked out of the stairwell on the twentieth floor of the bank building in Canary Wharf. He had shown his warrant card to a young receptionist and demanded to be told where Underwood was. The receptionist later told investigators that Nightingale had a strange look in his eyes. "Manic," she told them. "He was manic." The receptionist had pointed down the corridor to Underwood's office and he had walked away. She had called security but by the time they had reached the twentieth floor it was all over.

Nightingale had burst into Underwood's office, but he wasn't in, and his terrified secretary told him that her boss was down the corridor. She later told the investigators that Nightingale had been icy cold and there had been no emotion in his voice. "It was as if he were a robot, or on autopilot or something," she said.

There were differing descriptions from the six witnesses who were in the meeting room with Underwood. One said he looked crazed, two repeated the secretary's assertion that he was icy cold, two woman said he seemed confused, and the senior marketing manager said that he reminded her of the Terminator in the second movie, the one that Arnold Schwarzenegger was trying to kill. The investigators knew that personal recollections were the most unreliable of evidence, but the one thing that all the witnesses agreed on was that Nightingale had told everyone to leave, that he had closed the door behind them, and that a few seconds later there was an almighty crash as Simon Underwood exited through the window.

Was he pushed? Did he trip? Did Nightingale hit him and he fell accidentally? Was Underwood so stricken by guilt that he threw himself through the window? The investigators put every possible scenario to Nightingale, and threw in a few impossible ones for good measure, but Nightingale refused to say anything. He didn't even say, "No comment." He just sat staring at the investigators with a look of bored indifference on his face. They asked him several times if he wanted the services of his Police Federation representative, but Nightingale shook his head. The only time he did speak was to ask to go to the toilet or to go outside to smoke a cigarette.

For the first couple of days the newspapers were after Nightingale's blood, crying police brutality, but then a sympathetic clerk in the coroner's office leaked the postmortem details to a journalist on the *Sunday Times*, and once it became known that Underwood had been molesting his daughter, the tide turned and the tabloids starting calling for Nightingale to be honored rather than persecuted.

The Independent Police Complaints Commission sent two more investigators to talk to Nightingale, but he was as uncommunicative with them as he had been with the PSD detectives. The IPCC officers offered Nightingale a deal: if he told them that Underwood had jumped then there would be no charges. If he told them that Underwood had slipped and fallen through the window, there would be no charges. All they wanted was to be able to close the file on the man's death. Nightingale said nothing.

There were those in the Met who said that Nightingale had his head screwed on right, that the IPCC and the PSD were lying sons of bitches and that no matter what he said they would hang him out to dry. There were others in the job who said that Nightingale was an honorable man, that he'd killed Underwood and he wasn't prepared to lie about what he'd done. Whatever the reason, whatever had happened to Underwood, Nightingale simply refused to talk about it, and after a week the investigators gave up.

Nightingale went to Sophie's funeral but kept his distance, not wanting to intrude on the family's grief. A photographer from one of the Sunday tabloids tried to take his picture, but Nightingale grabbed his camera and smashed it against a gravestone. Nightingale left before Sophie's coffin was lowered into the cold, damp soil.

There were two reports into Mr. Underwood's death, one by the PSD and one from the IPCC. Both were inconclusive and both criticized Nightingale for refusing to cooperate. Without Nightingale's statement, there was no way that anyone would know what had happened in the meeting room that day. There were two eyewitnesses who saw the body fall and slap into the tarmac, close enough to hear Sophie's father shout, "No!" all the way down, but not close enough to see if he had jumped or if he had been pushed. There was CCTV footage of the reception area which clearly showed Nightingale arriving and leaving, but there were no coverage of the room and no CCTV cameras covering the area where Underwood hit the ground. Both reports went to the Crown Prosecution Service's offices at Ludgate, and they decided there wasn't enough evidence to prosecute Nightingale.

He had been on suspension until the reports were published, but once they had been released he was called into the office of his superintendent, who told him that his career was over and the best thing for everyone concerned would be for him to resign. Superintendent Chalmers had a letter of resignation already typed out, and Nightingale signed it there and then before handing over his warrant card and walking out of New Scotland Yard, never to return.

Sophie's mother killed herself two weeks after the funeral. She swallowed a bottle of sleeping tablets and a bottle of paracetamol and she left a note saying that she was so, so, sorry she hadn't been a better mother.

CHAPTER

3

--=TWO YEARS LATER=--

Nightingale knew he was dreaming, but there was nothing he could do to stop it. He knew that he wasn't really climbing the stairs to the twentieth floor of the tower block in Canary Wharf where Simon Underwood worked. He was moving too slowly, for a start, and there was no exertion, no sweat, no shortness of breath. He walked out of the stairwell and showed his warrant card to a faceless receptionist who shook her head but didn't say anything and then he moved silently down a corridor to Underwood's office even though he knew that the banker wasn't there. Then he was moving down another corridor, the sound of his heartbeat echoing off the walls, toward a set of double doors. Then the doors burst open and Underwood was there, standing in front of a group of suits. Underwood's mouth moved but made no sound. Nightingale pointed at the doorway and the suits hurried out, leaving Nightingale alone with the banker. "You're going to hell, Jack Nightingale," said Underwood, his eyes blazing with hatred. Then in slow motion he turned to the floor-to-ceiling window behind him.

Nightingale opened his mouth to shout at Underwood but then his alarm went off and he awoke, bathed in sweat. He lay on his bed, staring up at the ceiling. He'd been having the nightmare at least once a week ever since the day that Simon Underwood had gone through the window and fallen to his death. He groped for his pack of Marlboros and smoked one all the way down to the filter before getting up and showering.

His apartment was a third-floor walk-up in Bayswater, two bedrooms and one bathroom and a kitchen that he hardly ever used. On the ground floor was a Chinese restaurant that did a great bowl of duck noodles, and it was a short walk to the nearest Tube station. Nightingale had bought the apartment when he'd been promoted to inspector, and in another twenty-one years he'd own it outright. He liked Bayswater. It was lively, there were always people around and shops open, it was buzzing day and night. And on the days when he felt like jogging, Hyde Park was only a few minutes away. Not that he felt much like jogging these days. He went downstairs, bought himself a cup of Costa coffee, then walked around to the lockup where he kept his MGB and drove to the office of Nightingale Investigations. His office was in South Kensington, another walk-up but this time above a hairdresser's that offered him a fifty percent discount on haircuts provided he allowed a trainee to cut his hair.

Nightingale arrived at his office shortly after nine o'clock and his secretary was already at her desk. Jenny McLean was in her midtwenties, with short blonde hair and blue eyes that always reminded Nightingale of Cameron Diaz. Jenny was shorter than the actress and smarter, educated at Cheltenham Ladies College and Cambridge and fluent in German, French, and Japanese. Her family owned a country mansion with five hundred bedrooms and twelve acres, or vice versa, and chased foxes and shot wild birds on the weekend. Nightingale had absolutely no idea why she worked for

him. He'd placed an advert in the local paper and she'd walked off
the street with her CV and told him that she'd always wanted to work
for a private investigator and that she could type and knew her way
around Microsoft Office. He'd wondered at first if she was an under-
cover agent for the Inland Revenue checking on his tax returns, but
she'd worked for him for more than a year, and now he didn't know
how he'd manage without her. She smiled brightly and nodded at the
door to his office. "Mrs. Brierley's already here," she said.

"Can't wait to hear the bad news, huh?" said Nightingale. He
didn't like doing divorce work. He didn't like following unfaithful
husbands or wayward wives, and he didn't like breaking bad news
to women who cried or men who threatened violence. He didn't
like it, but it paid the bills, and he had a lot of bills that needed
paying.

"Can I get you a coffee or a tea, Mrs. Brierley?" he asked as he
walked into his office.

Joan Brierley was in her early fifties, a heavyset woman with
dyed blonde hair, too much makeup, and lines around her mouth
from years of smoking. She shook her head and held up a pack of
Benson and Hedges. "Do you mind if I...?" she said.

Nightingale lifted his own pack of Marlboros. "I'm a smoker
too," he said.

"There aren't many of us left," she said.

"Strictly speaking, this is my workplace so I should fine myself a thousand pounds every time I light up," said Nightingale.
He reached over and lit her cigarette with a disposable lighter and
then lit his own.

"On the phone you said you had bad news," said Mrs. Brierley.
"So he's been cheating, has he?"

"I'm afraid so," said Nightingale.

"I knew it," she said, her voice shaking. "When money started
disappearing from our joint account, I knew it."

"I filmed them," said Nightingale. "So you could see for yourself. I followed them to a hotel, but he has also visited her house when her husband is away."

"She's married?"

Nightingale nodded.

"Why would a married woman want to steal another woman's husband?" said Mrs. Brierley.

It wasn't a question that Nightingale could answer. "I've got his cell phone records. He calls her three or four times a day and sends her text messages." He slid over a stack of photocopied sheets. "The messages say it all, pretty much."

Mrs. Brierley picked up the phone records. "How did you get these?"

"Trade secret, I'm afraid," said Nightingale. He had contacts working for most of the cell phone companies, who would give him anything he wanted, for a price.

She sneered as she scanned them. "He loves her?" she hissed. "He's been married to me for twenty-four years and he loves her?"

Nightingale went over to his DVD player and slotted in a disc. He sat down again as Mrs. Brierley turned to look at the screen. The camerawork wasn't great but Nightingale had been hired to do surveillance, not produce a Hollywood movie. He'd taken the first shot from behind a tree. Brierley arrived in his dark blue Toyota, a nondescript man in a nondescript car. Brierley had a spring in his step as he walked into the hotel's reception and was holding a shopping bag from a local liquor store. Nightingale had managed to get closer to the hotel entrance and had filmed Brierley signing in and being given a key.

The next shot was of the woman arriving. He'd managed to get a good shot of her parking her BMW and had followed her to the entrance of the hotel. Like Brierley, she didn't look around and clearly wasn't worried about being followed.

Mrs. Brierley stared at the screen, her mouth a tight line.

The final shot was of Mr. Brierley and the woman leaving the hotel together. He walked her to her car, kissed her, and then went over to his Toyota.

Nightingale pressed the remote control to switch off the DVD player. "Your husband paid in cash but I have a copy of the receipt." He slid a photocopied sheet of paper across the desk toward Mrs. Brierley, but she was still staring at the blank television screen, the cigarette burning between her fingers. "The woman's name is Brenda Lynch, she is…"

"I know who she is," said Mrs. Brierley, her voice a dull monotone.

"You know her?"

"She's my sister."

Nightingale's jaw dropped. "Your sister?"

"Didn't you know? said Mrs. Brierley. She forced a smile. "Some detective you are. Lynch was my maiden name." She took a long drag on her cigarette, held it deep in her lungs, and then exhaled slowly.

"I'm sorry," said Nightingale.

She waved away his apology as if it were an annoying insect. "How much do I owe you, Mr. Nightingale?"

"Miss McLean outside has your bill," said Nightingale.

Mrs. Brierley leaned over his desk and stubbed out what remained of her cigarette.

"I'm sorry," said Nightingale again.

"There's nothing for you to be sorry about," she said. She stood up. "You did a very professional job, Mr. Nightingale." There were tears in her eyes but she forced a smile. "Thank you."

Nightingale opened his door for her. "Mrs. Brierley would like her bill, Jenny," said Nightingale.

"I have it here," she said, handing a sheet of paper to Mrs. Brierley. Mrs. Brierley took out her checkbook and wrote a check while Nightingale went back into his office. He flopped down into his chair and stubbed out the remains of his cigarette. He didn't enjoy breaking bad news to people, but that was part of the job. If a husband or a wife suspected that their spouse was up to no good, ninety-nine times out of a hundred they were right. In Mrs. Brierley's case it had been unexpected withdrawals from their current account, late nights supposedly at the office, and a new brand of aftershave in the bathroom. He saw the phone records by his feet and the photocopy of the hotel receipt and realized that Mrs. Brierley had left them behind. He thought about going after her but decided against it, figuring that she had deliberately not taken them with her. He wondered what she would do now that she knew the truth. She would almost certainly divorce her husband, and probably split up her sister's family as well. She had three children and two of them still lived at home, so she'd probably keep the house and Mr. Brierley would end up in a rented apartment somewhere either with or without his sister-in-law for company.

Nightingale went back to his desk and started reading the Metro free newspaper that Jenny had brought with her. Shortly afterwards he heard Mrs. Brierley leave. There was a soft knock on his door and Jenny pushed it open. She was holding a full pot of coffee. "You read my mind," he said.

"It's not difficult," she said. "You don't ask much from life. Curries, cigarettes, coffee."

"The breakfast of champions," he said.

She poured coffee into his mug. "She took it quite well, didn't she?"

Nightingale shrugged. "She cried, which is a good sign. It's when they go quiet that I start thinking about knives and hammers and things that go bump in the night."

"I gave her the card of a good divorce lawyer."

"Very thoughtful of you." Nightingale sipped his coffee. Jenny made great coffee. She brought the beans from a shop in Mayfair and ground them herself.

"I felt sorry for her," said Jenny, sitting on the edge of his desk.

"There are two sides to every case," said Nightingale. "We only get to hear the side that pays us."

"Even so…" said Jenny.

Nightingale sipped his coffee again. "Maybe she made his life a misery. Maybe the sister was kind to him. Maybe she let him wear her stockings and suspenders and the wife wouldn't."

"Jack…" said Jenny, shaking her head.

"I'm just saying, you can't go feeling sorry for the clients. They're just jobs."

"Speaking of which, a solicitor down in Surrey wants to see you." She handed him a scribbled note.

Nightingale frowned as he studied the piece of paper. "Can't he just e-mail us the info?"

"He said he wants to see you in his office. He's got gout so he has trouble getting about. I figured you wouldn't mind as you don't have much on at the moment."

Nightingale flashed her a tight smile. He didn't need reminding how light his caseload was. "This place, Hamdale. Never heard of it."

"I've got the postcode, you can use the GPS on your phone."

"You know I can never get it to work."

Jenny grinned and held out her hand. "I'll do it for you, you luddite." Nightingale gave her his Nokia and she programmed in the location. "You'll be fine," she said.

"And how do I get back?"

"Leave a trail of breadcrumbs," she said, sliding off the desk. "If you leave now you should be there by two o'clock."

CHAPTER

4

Nightingale cursed as he squinted at his phone's GPS display. The autumn sun was glinting off the screen and he couldn't make out which way he was supposed to go. He peered through the windscreen and saw a signpost ahead of him. He braked. It said "Hamdale, 5 Miles" and pointed to the left.

He followed the sign and slid his phone into his pocket. Hamdale was a tiny village, a cluster of houses around a thatched pub and a row of half a dozen shops. The solicitor's office was wedged between a cake shop and a post office. There were double yellow lines along both sides of the road so Nightingale did a U-turn and left the MGB in the pub's car park.

When Nightingale pushed open the door, a bell dinged and a gray-haired secretary looked up from an electric typewriter and peered at him over the top of her gold-framed spectacles. "Can I help you?" she asked.

"Jack Nightingale," said Nightingale. He looked at the piece of paper that Jenny had given him. "I'm here to see a Mr. Turtledove."

"Ah, he's expecting you," said the woman. "I'll tell him you're here. Would you like a cup of tea?"

"I'm fine, thanks."

The woman placed both hands on the top of her desk and grunted as she pushed herself up, but a door to the inner office opened and she relaxed and dropped back down into her chair. "I was just going to show Mr. Nightingale in," she said.

The man who had opened the door was in his sixties, almost bald with heavy jowls and watery eyes. He was wearing a heavy tweed suit and leaning on a wooden walking stick. He was a good head shorter than Nightingale and he looked up at him and smiled, showing yellowing teeth as he held out his hand. Nightingale shook the proffered hand gently, afraid that he might break the man's hand, but Turtledove's grip was deceptively strong. "Come in, please," he said.

Turtledove's office was little more than a box with a small window overlooking a backyard. The room was lined from floor to ceiling with legal books, and there was a damp, dusty smell that reminded Nightingale of the shed that he'd used as a den when he was a kid. There were two chairs in front of the desk and they were both buried under piles of dusty files, all tied up with red ribbon. "Please just put the files on the floor," said the solicitor as he limped around his desk and sat down in his own high-backed leather chair. He placed his stick against the windowsill behind him then turned and looked somberly at Nightingale. "First let me say how sorry I am for your loss," he said.

Nightingale put a stack of files on the floor and sat down on one of the chairs. "My loss?" he said.

"Your father."

"My father?" Nightingale shook his head in bewilderment. He had no idea what the elderly solicitor was talking about. He took out his wallet and gave Turtledove one of his business cards. "I'm Jack Nightingale. I'm here about a job."

Turtledove frowned, looked around for his spectacles, and then sighed as he realized that they were perched on top of his head. He pushed them down and read the card, then smiled amiably at Nightingale. "There's no job, Mr. Nightingale, I'm sorry about the confusion. I'm the executor of your late father's will."

Nightingale raised his eyebrows. Now he was even more confused. "My parents' estate was finalized more than a decade ago."

Turtledove made a tutting sound and rifled through a stack of files on his desk and then pulled one out. "Your father passed away three weeks ago," he said.

"My parents died in a car crash a couple of days after my nineteenth birthday," said Nightingale. It had been a senseless accident. They had stopped at a red traffic light and a truck had ploughed into the back of them. The car was crushed and burst into flames, and according to the young constable who had broken the news to Nightingale, they had died instantly. Over the years, he'd come to realize that the constable was only saying that to make the news more bearable. In all probability they had died in the flames, screaming in agony. Policemen had to lie when they broke bad news, or at least bend the truth to make it less painful. He knew from experience that people rarely died instantly in accidents. There was, more often than not, a lot of pain and blood and screaming involved.

"Your adoptive parents," said Turtledove, nodding sagely. "Bill and Irene Nightingale."

"I wasn't adopted," said Nightingale. "I've seen my birth certificate. They're my parents. Their names are on the certificate. And they never said that I was adopted."

"That may well be, but they were not your biological parents." He opened the file and slid out a sheet of paper which he passed across the desk. "These are your details, aren't they? Correct date of birth, national insurance number, schools attended, your university?"

Nightingale scanned the sheet and nodded. "That's me," he said.

"Then your father was Ainsley Gosling, and it has fallen on me to administer his last will and testament." He smiled and peered over the top of his spectacles. "It's just occurred to me that I'm a Turtledove, you're a Nightingale, and your father was a Gosling. What a coincidence that is."

"Isn't it," said Nightingale. "But I've never heard of this Ainsley Gosling. And I'm damn sure I wasn't adopted."

"You were adopted at birth, which is why I assume your adoptive parents' names went down on the certificate. It would never happen these days of course."

"Bullshit," said Nightingale.

Turtledove's lips tightened. "There's no need for profanity, Mr. Nightingale. I can understand that this might well come as a shock to you, but I am only the messenger. I was never given to understand that you were not aware that Mr. Gosling was your biological father."

"I apologize," said Nightingale. "If he's my father, then who is my mother?"

"I'm not privy to that information, I'm afraid."

Nightingale fished his pack of Marlboros out. "Can I smoke?"

"I'm afraid not," said Turtledove. "It's against the law, you know, to smoke in a place of employment."

"Yes, I know," said Nightingale. He put away the cigarettes. "How did he die, this Gosling?"

"I don't know," said Turtledove. "The case came to me from another lawyer, a firm in the City. I was told that Mr. Gosling had passed away and that I was to act as executor to the will."

"That's a bit unusual, isn't it?"

"Very," said Turtledove. "I had no dealings with Mr. Gosling, and I never met the man. I was merely sent his last will and testament and your details and told to contact you as his sole heir and beneficiary."

"But usually wouldn't the solicitor who drew up the will also administer it?"

"Of course," said Turtledove. "But I suppose the fact that I was local meant it would be easier for me to deal with the house. But as you say, it is unusual."

"House? What house?"

Turtledove took the will out of the file and gave it to Nightingale. "There isn't much in the way of money, I'm afraid. But there is a substantial property. A country house, by the name of Gosling Manor. It's about six miles outside Hamdale. I assume that's why I was asked to execute the will." He opened a drawer and gave Nightingale a key ring with two keys on it. "I've some paperwork for you to sign, then the house is all yours. And I've a map here with the house marked on it."

"Burglar alarm code?"

The solicitor shook his head. "I assume there isn't one."

Nightingale put the key and the map into his coat pocket. "You said there was cash?"

"A few hundred pounds," said Turtledove. "We're going to need to get the house valued in case there are inheritance tax issues."

"You mean I'm going to have to pay for the house?"

"It depends on its value. But once your inheritance tax liability has been assessed, yes, you will most certainly have to pay it. Death and taxes are the only two certainties in life, as Mark Twain once said. Or was it Benjamin Franklin?" He put a hand up to his forehead. "My memory just isn't what it was."

"You don't know what the house is worth?"

The solicitor looked over the top of his glasses at Nightingale. "I'm just the middleman, I haven't seen the house or met with the deceased. I was just told that the property is substantial."

"Mr. Turtledove, this is all very unusual, isn't it?"

"Mr. Nightingale," said the solicitor, "I've never had a case like it."

CHAPTER

Nightingale drove slowly down the narrow country road. The sky had darkened while he had been in the solicitor's office, and it was starting to rain. He switched on the MGB's wipers and they swished back and forth, leaving greasy streaks on the glass. He looked down at the map that Turtledove had given him. When he looked up he saw a tractor pulling out in front of him and he jammed on his brakes. The tires couldn't grip the wet road and the car slid to the right. Nightingale took his foot off the brake pedal and then pumped it and brought the skid under control, managing to stop just inches from the back of the tractor. The driver was wearing headphones and was bobbing his head to and fro in time to whatever music he was listening to, totally oblivious to how close he'd come to killing Nightingale. As Nightingale sat with his hand gripping the steering wheel, his heart pounding, the tractor roared off down the road, leaving a plume of black smoke behind it. He realized that his mind hadn't been on the road, he'd been too busy thinking about his meeting with the solicitor. It didn't make any sense. Nightingale had never even suspected that Bill and Irene Nightingale weren't his real parents. Even the phrase "real parents" sounded wrong. Of course they were his real parents. Every childhood memory he had, they were there. His mum teaching him the alphabet, his father helping him read his bike for the first time, clapping as he blew out birthday candles, the look of pride on their faces when he told them that he'd been accepted by King's College, London. There had been tears in his father's eyes when he told Nightingale that he was the first member of his family ever to go to college. Nightingale was sure that if he really had been adopted, his parents would have said something.

Nightingale took deep breaths to steady himself, then put the car into first gear and headed along the road. To the right was a field that had been recently ploughed, to the left a six-foot-high stone wall. Ahead of him he saw a break in the wall and a large circular metal mirror attached to a tree. He slowed the car. He saw metal gates and a sign. Gosling Manor. He pulled up alongside the gates and climbed out of the MGB. On the other side of the gates a narrow paved road curved to the right through thick woodland, mainly deciduous trees that had lost most of their leaves, their bare branches outlined like skeletons against the gray November sky. There was a thick chain linking the two gates and a brass padlock. Nightingale took out the keys that Turtledove had given him. One was heavy and made of brass and it fitted the padlock. Nightingale unraveled the chain, pushed open the gates and got back into his car.

He drove slowly through the gates. The road curved to the right, then to the left, then the trees began to thin out and ahead of him he saw the house. Nightingale brought the car to a halt. It was a stunning mansion, the sort of grand house that you'd see on the cover of *Country Life* magazine, or on a box of chocolates that you'd give to an elderly relative at Christmas. The main part of the house was built of sandstone with upper façades of weathered bricks. It was two stories high topped by a steepled tile roof almost the same color as the bricks and with four towering chimney stacks, giving it the impression of an oceangoing liner. Vibrant green ivy had been trained to climb the walls, reaching from the ground to the slate roof, with the main vines as thick as a man's wrist. The main entrance was shrouded in ivy around a massive oak door with ornate black hinges. The window frames were all painted white, and to the left of the main building was a single brick block with four garage doors, also painted white, with a matching tiled roof. To the left of the house was a magnificent conservatory that looked as if it had been added as an afterthought, and there was a wing beyond the conservatory that was at right angles to the main building as if it too had been added later. The house gave the appearance of having grown out of the ground rather than having being built by man, as if it had pushed itself out of the earth as a living, breathing thing.

He drove slowly toward the house. The paved road merged into a parking area large enough for several dozen vehicles, now littered with dead leaves, and in the middle stood a massive stone fountain. There was no water in the fountain, the centerpiece of which was a weathered stone mermaid surrounded by dolphins and fish. Nightingale parked the MGB and climbed out. He looked back down the road that disappeared into the woodland. There was no sign of the main road, no sounds other than the birds in the woodland and the occasional bark of a far-off dog. He turned back to look at the house. "And it's mine, all mine," he muttered to himself. When Turtledove had given him the keys, Nightingale had assumed that there had been some mistake, but as he stood looking at the grand house he realized that mistakes like that didn't happen—people weren't accidentally handed multi-million-pound mansions. Checks would have been carried out, assurances given, and the only way that the house could be his was if Ainsley Gosling really was his father.

The thought that his parents had lied to him so completely made his head spin. If he really had been adopted, then his parents couldn't have kept the secret to themselves, surely? Other members of the family must have known, babies didn't just appear from nowhere. He took out his cell phone and scrolled through his address book and called his Uncle Tommy. He hadn't spoken to him since the previous Christmas, when he'd driven up to spend the day with his aunt and uncle.

It was his aunt who answered the phone. "Aunty Linda? It's Jack."

There was a moment's hesitation as if she wasn't sure who Jack was, then she almost yelped. "Jack!"

"Hi, Aunty Linda, how's things?"

"Jack, it's so good to hear from you. Is everything okay?"

"Everything's fine. And Uncle Tommy, he's okay?" He looked around as he talked, and he frowned when he saw a CCTV camera half-hidden in the ivy over the front door.

"He's taken the dog out for a walk. He'll be so sorry that he missed you. How's work? Are you married yet?"

"No, I'm not married yet," laughed Jack. "Look, I know this is a strange thing to ask out of the blue, Aunty Linda, but do you by any chance know if I was adopted?" There was another CCTV camera on the side of one of the chimneys, and another atop the conservatory. There was a long silence and Nightingale thought for a moment that he'd lost the connection. "Aunty Linda, did you hear me?"

"What a question, Jack. We don't hear from you for almost a year and you ask a question like that."

"I know, I'm sorry, but something very strange has happened. You'd know, wouldn't you? You'd know if I was adopted."

"Jack, I can't…"

"You can't what, Aunty Linda?"

There was another long silence.

"Aunty Linda?"

"Jack, this is really something you'd have to talk to your uncle Tommy about."

"Why can't you tell me?"

"Because Uncle Tommy is your father's brother, he's blood. I'm just Tommy's wife. You have to talk to him."

"Aunty Linda?"

"I have to go, Jack. I'll get your uncle Tommy to call you. Good-bye now." The line went dead.

Nightingale frowned as he put the phone away. She'd sounded nervous, scared even, and he'd never known his aunt to be scared of anything before. He stood back and carefully scrutinized the front of the house. He spotted another three CCTV cameras. He took out the keys that Turtledove had given him and walked up to the door. There were two locks and they both opened with the same key. The door creaked as he pushed it open. He stepped into a hallway with wood-paneled walls and a marble floor, dominated by a massive chandelier hanging from the ceiling. Nightingale looked around for a burglar alarm console but couldn't see one, and there was no beeping to suggest that an alarm system was working. There was no furniture and no pictures or mirrors on the wall. The house had been cleared but he had no way of knowing if it had been professional burglars or a removal firm that had taken everything away. There was a light switch by the door but nothing happened when Nightingale flicked it. He walked across the hallway, his black leather shoes squeaking on the marble floor, and tried another light switch, but that didn't work either.

There were three oak doors leading off the hallway. Nightingale pushed open one and stepped into a room the size of a basketball court with a vaulted ceiling and a massive white marble fireplace. The room was also devoid of furniture, and the carpets had been taken up to reveal oak floorboards. There were patches of underlay stuck to the boards like flaking skin and around the edge, close to the skirting board, metal tacks that had been used to keep the carpet in place. Whoever had lifted the carpets had simply ripped them up.

Along one wall was a line of windows that looked over ornamental gardens with bushes that had been trained into the shapes of exotic animals. Nightingale saw a giraffe and an elephant and a line of horses and beyond them what looked like a hedge maze. The curtains had been removed but the brass rods from which they had hung were still in place. Nightingale frowned as he saw a small CCTV camera in one corner of the room, aimed at the windows. He could understand the need for security on the exterior of the building but having them inside seemed like overkill.

He realized that there was something on top of the mantelpiece and he walked over to it, the floorboards creaking underfoot. It was an envelope, and as he got closer he saw his name was printed on it in slightly uneven typing. As he reached for it he heard a bang upstairs and he flinched. He listened intently but heard nothing. He picked up the envelope. Something shifted inside. He was just about to open it when he heard a noise from the upper floor, this time a scratching sound that lasted a second or two. He put the envelope into his jacket pocket and then walked on tiptoe to the door. He listened at the door but heard nothing.

The staircase that curved upwards was marble and he made no sound as he crept upstairs. He put his hand on the wooden banister as he craned his neck to look around the curving staircase. The wall to the left of the staircase was paneled and there were brass picture hooks from which large pictures had once hung.

The stairway opened into a large hallway which ran the length of the building. There were small chandeliers hanging every twelve feet or so, miniature replicas of the one in the downstairs hallway. Nightingale saw a light switch but it wasn't working. The hallway to the left was over the large room downstairs so that was where he headed, still on tiptoe. There were CCTV cameras at either end of the hallway and doors to the left and the right. He eased open the first door on the left. It was empty, and as in the rooms downstairs the curtains had been removed. He gently closed the door then opened the door on the opposite side of the hallway. It too was empty.

He pulled the door closed and moved silently down the corridor. He listened carefully at the next door before he put his hand on the brass handle and turned it. There was furniture in the room in the form of a large four-poster bed and a green leather winged armchair, and there were dark green curtains on the window, tied back with gold ropes. The bed was made and didn't appear to have been slept in, and the bathroom was spotless.

He checked another nine bedrooms but all were empty. He went back downstairs and checked the downstairs rooms. There was a large dining room, a study, another reception room, a huge kitchen from which all the appliances had been removed, and a walk-in pantry with bare shelves. Even the conservatory had been stripped of its contents. Nightingale looked out across a sweeping lawn and beyond it a small lake. To the left of the lake was a stable building next to a large paddock. Nightingale shivered. There were cast-iron radiators dotted around the house but the heating system wasn't working.

He tried opening the conservatory door but it was locked. The solicitor had only given Nightingale two keys, one for the padlock at the gates and the other for the front door. He walked slowly back through the kitchen and into the main hallway. He heard a soft scratching upstairs. "If you want to get out before I lock up, now's the time," he called upstairs. The scratching stopped immediately. "Stupid cat," Nightingale muttered under his breath. He pulled open the front door and gasped when he saw two men standing there. He took a step back as the two men stepped toward him.

They were wearing uniforms, he realized, police uniforms. The younger of the two policemen grabbed him by the arm. "What are you doing here?" he asked. Nightingale was too surprised to speak and he just shook his head. The policeman tightened his grip on the arm. "Right, come on, in the car."

"It's my house," said Nightingale.

The policeman let go of him. He was in his early twenties, skinny, with a rash of acne across his forehead. "What's your name?" he asked.

"Jack Nightingale," he said. "Look, I used to be in the job, now I'm a private investigator."

"Let's see your ID then."

Nightingale took out his wallet and showed them his license, and gave them one of his business cards. He patted his chest and sighed. "You scared the shit out of me," he said.

"The house has been locked up since Old Man Gosling died," said the older policeman. He had gray hair and broken veins across his cheeks and an old scar under his chin that looked as if it had been done with a broken bottle. "We were told the house was going up for auction."

"He left it to me," said Nightingale. "A solicitor in Hamdale is handling the probate or whatever they call it. I'm the sole heir."

"Are you a relative?"

"Apparently," said Nightingale. "If you don't mind me asking, how did you know I was here? The power's off so I assume the alarm's not working."

"There's no alarm link to our station," said the policeman. "Gosling had his own security arrangements. We saw the gate open as we were driving past, that's all. What's the name of the solicitor?"

"A guy called Turtledove." He pulled the solicitor's business card from his wallet and showed it to them. "You guys are local?"

"Depends what you mean by local," said the older policeman. "There used to be a police house in Hamdale but that went in the seventies. The nearest station now is Hastings. But we took the call when it happened. Well, I did anyway. He killed himself. Blew his head off with a shotgun in the master bedroom."

"There's no doubt that it was suicide?" asked Nightingale.

"Shotgun was still in his hands. And there was some weird stuff in the room that suggested he was a bit not right in the head, if you get my drift."

"I don't," said Nightingale. "What do you mean?"

"There were lots of candles burning. And he was in some sort of magic circle, one of those star things. He killed himself in the middle of the circle."

"There's no sign of that now," said Nightingale.

"A team of cleaners went in. Crime-scene cleaners. They do a good job, those guys. You wouldn't get me doing it for love nor money."

"How did you get in the house?" asked Nightingale. "Security seems pretty tight."

"Gosling's driver found the body. He let us in."

"But there was no note?"

The older policeman shook his head. "They don't always leave notes."

"They usually do," said Nightingale. "They want to explain themselves, maybe ask for forgiveness."

"You know a lot about suicides then?" said the younger PC.

"I was a negotiator, back in the day," said Nightingale.

The older policeman frowned. "Jack Nightingale? Aren't you the guy who killed that pedophile?"

"Allegedly," said Nightingale. He took out his pack of Marlboros. The younger PC shook his head as if Nightingale were trying to sell him a wrap of heroin, but the older one nodded and took one. Nightingale lit the man's cigarette and one for himself.

"Mr. Nightingale here's a bit of a legend," said the older cop. "Threw a banker out of a window down Canary Wharf."

"Allegedly," said Nightingale. He took a long drag on his cigarette and then blew smoke into sky.

"The bastard was fiddling with his daughter," said the sergeant. "She topped herself, right?"

"Right," said Nightingale. He shivered and took another drag on his cigarette.

"The bastard had what was coming to him," said the older policeman, flicking ash to the ground.

"Allegedly," said Nightingale.

"So, are you going to be moving in?" asked the younger policeman.

Nightingale laughed and looked up at the imposing façade of the house. "You've got to be joking," he said, "I'd rattle around in a place this big."

"Must be worth a fortune. What do you think, Sarge?"

"Five million, six maybe."

"Before the property crash, maybe."

"What happened to all the furniture and stuff?" asked Nightingale. "Who took it away?"

The older policeman shrugged. "It was gone when we got there. The only room that had furniture was the bedroom where he died."

His radio crackled and he walked away, talking into his microphone.

"You're going to hell, Jack Nightingale," said the younger policeman, his voice dull and lifeless, almost robotic.

Nightingale turned to look at him. "What?" he said.

"I said are you going to sell up, is that the plan?"

Nightingale frowned, wondering if he'd simply misheard the man.

"You could make even more money dividing it up into rental units."

"I guess so," said Nightingale. He was sure he hadn't misheard. But the policeman didn't appear to be messing with him, he was smiling good-naturedly, just making conversation with a former cop while he waited for his colleague to finish on the radio. "I haven't really had time to think about it."

"Was he a close relative, Old Man Gosling?" He had an Essex accent, with long vowels and clipped consonants, slightly high-pitched as if his voice hadn't fully broken, and nothing like the voice that had told Nightingale that he was going to hell.

"Not really," said Nightingale. "He was my father. Allegedly."

The older policeman walked back. "Landlord of the Fox and Goose has got a problem with gypsies," he said. He grinned at Nightingale. "Not that we can call them gypsies these days. Citizens of no fixed abode is probably the politically correct term. Anyway, one of them has just glassed a waitress so we've got to get over there. Good luck with the house." He reached into his pocket and gave Nightingale a Neighborhood Watch card. "My number's on there, give me a call if you need anything."

Nightingale studied the card. Sergeant Harry Wilde. "Thanks," said. "Look, something I don't understand. The house is old, right? More than a hundred years old, I'd guess."

"A lot more," said the policeman. "The main part of the house dates back to the sixteenth century, but there were a lot of additions made during the nineteen-thirties. Then the family that sold it to Gosling were into horses so they built the stable yard and paddocks."

"So why's it called Gosling Manor? Has it been in the family for generations?"

The sergeant shook his head. "Mr. Gosling bought it in the eighties, cash on the nail, they say. Used to be called Willborough Manor, after the family who built it. They were the local squires here for a couple of hundred years. Mr. Gosling put a few noses out of joint by renaming it, and there's a lot of folk around here still call it by its old name. They've got a point. Houses are like boats, you only bring bad luck by renaming them."

"Yeah, well, it was certainly unlucky for Gosling," said Nightingale.

Wilde's radio crackled again. "We've got to go," said the sergeant. He stuck out his hand and Nightingale shook it. "What you did back then, fair play to you. You did the right thing."

Nightingale smiled thinly and nodded but he didn't say anything. He had long since given up trying to justify to himself what he'd done that November morning and he'd never, ever, tried justifying it to anyone else.

He watched the two policemen walk over to their patrol car before climbing into his MGB. He took the envelope out of his pocket. Inside there was a key and the business card of a safe-deposit box company in South Kensington. "The plot thickens," he muttered to himself. He looked at the envelope again. Other than his name there was nothing on it, no indication of who had left it for him in the house. He doubted that Ainsley Gosling had left the envelope on the mantelpiece, because if had been there when the police had entered they'd have opened it in case it had been his suicide note. That meant that someone else had been in the house, after the police had taken away the body.

CHAPTER

6

The safe-deposit company was in Mayfair, and Nightingale went by Tube because he figured it would be a nightmare trying to park his MGB. He went straight from home after phoning Jenny to say that he would be late in. Jenny was full of questions about his visit to the Hamdale solicitor but Nightingale said it would have to wait until he was back in the office.

The company's office was discreet with just a small brass plate on a black door and a single brass doorbell. He pressed the bell and looked up at a CCTV camera. The door buzzed and Nightingale pushed his way in. The reception area was equally discreet, gray walls and carpet and glass and metal furniture and no inkling of what services were on offer. Nightingale told a receptionist why he was there, and two minutes later a female clerk in a gray suit was leading him down a steel staircase to a large room lined with metal doors of varying sizes. The clerk took Nightingale's key and used it and a key of her own to open the two locks on one of the larger doors. She pulled out a metal box and placed it on a table, had him sign a form attached to a clipboard, then went back upstairs. Nightingale stared at the metal box, wondering what it contained. The clerk hadn't strained as she'd lifted it so if there was cash inside there wouldn't be much. Diamonds would be nice, he decided. Or a few Krugerrands. Or maybe even an explanation of who Ainsley Gosling was and why he had given up his son for adoption and never made any attempt to contact him until after he'd blown off his head with a shotgun. He took a deep breath and pulled open the lid. It was empty. Nightingale groaned. What was the point of leaving him the key if there was nothing in the box? Was someone playing a sick trick on him? He started to close the lid but stopped as he realized there was something on the bottom of the box. A brown envelope. He took it out and opened it. Inside was a single DVD.

CHAPTER

Jenny was on the phone when Nightingale opened the door to his office. "I'm sure that the check was sent out on Tuesday and it's only Thursday today so it could still be in the post," she said, wagging a warning finger at him as he went over to the DVD player. "He isn't in at the moment, but as soon as he gets in I'll tell him to call you."

Nightingale slotted in the DVD and turned on the television. "Remote?" he mouthed at Jenny.

She pointed at his desk. "Absolutely," she said into the phone. "Good-bye." She replaced the receiver and wagged her finger at him again. "You can't mess around with Customs and Excise like this," she said. "They send people to jail for not paying their VAT."

"I know, while they let murderers and rapists roam the streets," he said, picking up the remote control. "You should write a letter to the editor of the *Daily Mail.*"

"How did it go yesterday? What's the job?"

"There's no job," said Nightingale. "But I do have a house. A bloody big house. And a father I never knew that I had."

"Jack, what on earth are you talking about?"

"Get me a coffee and I'll tell you," he said. As Jenny made coffee, Nightingale filled her in on the events of the past twenty-four hours.

"A mansion?" she said when he'd finished.

"Right out of *Country Life*," he said. "Land as far as the eye can see, a stables, a conservatory, more bedrooms than you can shake a stick at."

"And it's yours?"

"Seems to be. Unless there's a hidden camera somewhere and this is all some *Candid Camera* stunt."

"And this Gosling, he's your father?"

"According to the solicitor, yes. My biological father. I was adopted at birth. He killed himself a few weeks ago. I've asked Robbie to get me the case file."

He pointed the remote at the DVD player and pressed "PLAY." "He left me this, in a safe-deposit box."

The screen flickered into life. A bald, elderly man, his scalp flecked with liver spots and scabs, was frowning and cursing as he adjusted the lens of the camera, then he walked over and sat down on a bed. It was the bed in the master bedroom of Gosling Manor, Nightingale realized. The bedroom where Ainsley Gosling had killed himself.

The man was overweight, with heavy jowls and a swollen belly that strained at the crimson dressing gown he was wearing. He adjusted the gown and Nightingale caught a glimpse of milky-white skin, blue-veined like a ripe Stilton. There were dark patches under his eyes as if he hadn't slept in days. He took a deep breath to compose himself before forcing a smile and beginning to speak. "Hello, Jack," he said, his voice a deep wheezy growl. "I wish this could have been under more fortuitous circumstances, but…" He shrugged. "As you probably have already realized I'm Ainsley Gosling, your father." He shrugged again and adjusted the dressing gown. "Your biological father, that is." Gosling sighed. "I've not been much of a father, obviously. And there's not much I can do to rectify that now." He held up his hands. "Mea culpa, Jack. It's all my fault."

"What's his fault?" asked Jenny. "What's he talking about?"

Nightingale didn't answer but motioned for her to be quiet as he stared intently at the screen. Gosling was in his seventies and grossly overweight but he had Nightingale's slightly hooked nose and the same frown lines across his forehead.

Gosling sighed again, then coughed. Nightingale recognized a smoker's cough and he smiled. His parents, his adopted parents, had never smoked and they could never understand why their son had taken up the habit. Maybe Gosling really was his father and smoking was in his genes.

"So, to business," Gosling continued. "The fact that you're watching this means that I'm already dead. And that you've been to the house. Nothing that I can say will ever make up for what I've condemned you to."

"What does he mean, Jack?" said Jenny.

"Shhh," hissed Nightingale.

"But you must believe me, Jack," Gosling continued. "I do regret my actions, and if I could turn back time…" He shrugged. "But even I can't do that. What's done is done." Gosling took a deep breath, then coughed. The cough turned into a splutter and he sat on the bed, his belly trembling and his shoulders shaking as he fought to control himself. "I'm your father, Jack. I assume that's already been explained to you. Not that being your father means anything, not in the traditional sense. I've given you nothing over the last thirty-three years. Not even your name."

Gosling bent down. When he straightened up he was holding a bottle of brandy and he took a swig before wiping his fleshy mouth with the back of his hand. "I gave you away when you were a few hours old, Jack. I gave you to a man who gave you to the Nightingales. He knew they were good people and that they were so desperate for a baby that they'd take you, no questions asked." He took another swig at the bottle, then cleared his throat before continuing. "So where do I start?" he said, looking at the bottle in his hand as if seeing it for the first time. "At the beginning or at the end? Do I tell you what's happened, or what's going to happen?" He shrugged and took another slug of brandy, then closed his eyes. He shuddered, then opened his eyes again and looked straight into the lens of the camera. He took a deep breath and licked his lips.

"Get on with it," Nightingale muttered.

"On your thirty-third birthday, Jack, a demon from hell is coming to claim your soul." Gosling closed his eyes, took a deep breath, and sighed. When he opened his eyes they were burning with a fierce intensity and he began speaking faster. "I did a deal with a devil, thirty-three years ago. Not THE devil. A devil. One of his minions. A nasty piece of work."

"This is a joke, right?" said Jenny. "Somebody's messing with you?"

"The deal was simple enough," continued Gosling. "I got power, almost unlimited power. Power over women, power to amass money, more money than a man could spend in a dozen lifetimes. The only thing I couldn't get was immortality. That wasn't up for negotiation." He forced a smile showing uneven yellowed teeth. "Even a newborn's soul wouldn't buy me that."

"He's insane," said Jenny. "Look how his hands are shaking. Look at his eyes. He's mad as a hatter, Jack."

Nightingale ignored her and blew smoke at the television screen.

"In exchange for your immortal soul, I got the keys to the kingdom here on Earth. And now it's time to pay the piper." He took another swig of brandy and then looked at his wristwatch. "I've tried to put this right, Jack. I've tried to renegotiate but there's nothing I can do. What's done is done. Your soul and your sister's soul are forfeit."

Jenny frowned in confusion. "You don't have a sister," she said. She turned to look at him. "Do you?"

"Not that I know of," said Nightingale. "But I'm getting a lot of surprises this week."

"You said you were an only child."

"I am."

"Your sister was born two years after you," growled Gosling, almost as if he was answering Jenny's question. "Another child, another deal. Another soul. I tried to trace her but she's vanished." Gosling tried to smile at the camera but it came across as a snarl, the snarl of an animal that knew it was trapped. "I just wanted you to know that I'm sorry, Jack. Sorry for what I did, sorry for what happened, and sorry for what's going to happen to you." Gosling shrugged and got to his feet unsteadily. His dressing gown flapped open and he grabbed at it with his free hand as he lurched over to the camera, still clutching the bottle of brandy. His swollen belly filled the screen and then it went blank.

"Jack, what the hell is going on?"

Nightingale put his hands behind his neck. "I have absolutely no idea," he said. And that was the truth. Jack Nightingale didn't believe that he had a soul, and he certainly didn't believe that a soul was something that could be bartered or traded like a sack of beans. He reached for his pack of cigarettes.

"You smoke too much," admonished Jenny.

"Can't argue with you there," said Nightingale, taking out a cigarette and lighting it.

"Your birthday's the week after next, isn't it?" she said.

"Friday the twenty-seventh," he said. "What is it today?"

"Thursday the fifth."

"Three weeks then. But you don't need to get me anything."

"I wasn't planning to," she said. "What are you going to do?"

"Few beers and a curry," said Nightingale. "Same as I do every year. Birthdays are no big deal."

Jenny jerked a finger at the DVD player. "You know what I mean."

"It's a prank, Jenny. Some sort of practical joke."

"He left you his house. And his money. He made you his sole heir, that's what the solicitor said."

"So?"

"So why would he do that unless you were his son?"

"Maybe he is my father, maybe he isn't. I'll talk to Robbie, see if he can run a DNA check for me. But even if he is my biological father…" He gestured at the television. "Even if that's true, this, what he just said, that's just nonsense." He flicked ash into his ashtray. "Did you hear what he said? He sold my soul for the keys to the kingdom. He's mad, Jenny. Deranged." He looked at his watch. "Tell you what, can you mind the fort, I'm going to have a chat with Turtledove."

Turtledove was dipping a digestive biscuit into a cup of tea when Nightingale burst into his office. Turtledove's jaw dropped and a chunk of biscuit fell into his tea.

"Mr. Turtledove, I need you to tell me what's going on," said Nightingale.

Turtledove's glasses were perched on top of his head but they fell down onto his nose as he stared at Nightingale. "Excuse me?" he said.

Turtledove's secretary appeared at Nightingale's shoulder. "I'm so sorry, Mr. Turtledove, I said you were busy but he barged right by me."

"You didn't even get out of your chair," said Nightingale, not looking at her. He closed the door on her and sat down. "I don't think you've told me everything, Mr. Turtledove."

"I've told you all I know," said Turtledove, putting the remains of his biscuit on his saucer.

"Just who is Ainsley Gosling?"

"I told you yesterday, he's your genetic father."

"What did he do for a living? How did he make his money? How could he afford that house? Have you seen it? It's a mansion, Mr. Turtledove, a huge mansion."

"I never met Mr. Gosling and I never visited the house," said the solicitor. "I told you that already."

Nightingale took out his cigarettes. Turtledove opened his mouth to protest but closed it when Nightingale glared at him. Nightingale lit a cigarette and blew smoke, trying to calm himself down.

"I understand how stressful it must be, losing your father," began Turtledove, but Nightingale cut him short with a wave of his hand.

"Please don't try to empathize with me," said Nightingale. "I've been trained to empathize and I can spot a fake a mile off. Now you said you never met Gosling. How can that be if you're the executor of his will?"

"I didn't draw up the will, it was delivered to me, by courier," said the solicitor. "After he died."

"So you didn't witness the signature?"

"Mr. Nightingale, how many times do you want me to repeat myself? I never went to the house, and I never met Mr. Gosling. I was simply asked to execute the will."

"So you have no idea if the will is genuine or not?"

"I assume the firm that drew up the will made all the necessary checks," said Turtledove. "My understanding is that he was a client of theirs for many years."

Nightingale flicked ash onto the floor. "Who is he? What did Gosling do for a living?"

"I have absolutely no idea," said the solicitor. "Obviously being local I had heard of him, but I gather that he kept to himself. He was a very private man."

"He died three weeks ago," said Nightingale. "Why did it take you so long to contact me?"

"I was only sent the file on Monday," said the solicitor. "On Wednesday I called your office."

"Did you know that he committed suicide?"

Turtledove's jaw dropped.

"I assume from the look on your face that you didn't," said Nightingale.

"Good Lord, what happened?"

"He blew his head off with a shotgun," said Nightingale. "I don't suppose he left a note with you, did he, anything that you were supposed to give me?"

"There was nothing," said the solicitor. "He killed himself, you say? That's terrible. That's simply terrible."

"Did he leave a note with you?"

"No," said Turtledove. "Nothing."

"So you never went to Gosling Manor?"

"Never."

"And you didn't leave an envelope on the mantelpiece?"

The solicitor frowned. "I'm sorry, I don't understand."

Nightingale waved his cigarette dismissively. "It doesn't matter," he said. "You're being paid for your work, I assume. You're not doing this out of the goodness of your own heart."

"Of course I'm being paid," said Turtledove.

"By whom?"

"A bank in Brighton."

"Specifically," said Nightingale. "I want a name."

Turtledove flicked through a case containing business cards. He took one out, squinted at it, and handed it to Nightingale. "This is the gentleman who handled your father's finances, he's the manager of a bank in Brighton."

"But you haven't met him?"

"No. He sent me a retainer and a promise to pay my bill in full once the will has been executed."

"Why are you being paid by a bank in Brighton and not by the lawyer who sent you the file?"

Turtledove looked pained. "I'm afraid I can't answer that, Mr. Nightingale. As I keep telling you, everything about this matter has been irregular, and frankly I'm starting to wish that I'd never heard of Ainsley Gosling."

"You and me both, Mr. Turtledove," said Nightingale.

CHAPTER

9

The bank manager was a middle-aged man in a dark blue pin-striped suit that appeared to be a size too large for him. His office was a windowless cube in a featureless block a stone's throw from the Brighton seafront. He extended his arm to shake hands with Nightingale and his sleeve still covered his wrist and most of his thumb. "My name's Mr. Collinson," he said. "I'm the manager here but I'm not sure how I can help you."

Nightingale never trusted men who introduced themselves as "Mister." It suggested that they wanted to impose their authority on a relationship from the start. There was a brass nameplate on the manager's desk that announced his full name—Phillip Collinson—but even that was preceded by a "Mr." Collinson waved Nightingale to a chair. It was a small, uncomfortable plastic chair with metal legs while the one that Collinson dropped into was a massive leather executive model with large arms and a high back, the type favored by shaven-headed villains in James Bond films.

The bank manager was balding but had artfully combed his hair across the top of his head and used hair gel to keep it in place. He leaned back in his chair and pursed his thin lips as he scrutinized Nightingale's business card. "The thing is, Mr. Nightingale, if you are Ainsley Gosling's son, why the different surname?"

"I was adopted, apparently," said Nightingale. "But surely you know that, weren't you the one who instructed Turtledove?"

"I didn't actually instruct him," said Collinson, placing the card on his desk and steepling his fingers under his chin. "The instructions regarding the execution of the will came from a law firm in the City. I'll be paying Mr. Turtledove for his work, but that's the end of my involvement with the will."

"But you met Mr. Gosling?"

"Of course, several times. He was a valued customer."

"Did he come here or did you go out to Gosling Manor?"

"We went to his house," said Collinson. "Mr. Gosling was reluctant to travel so either I or the deputy manager would go to see him."

"Do you do that for all your customers?" asked Nightingale. "My bank manager won't even see me to talk about my overdraft."

Collinson smiled without warmth. "As I said, Mr. Gosling was a valued customer."

"Rich, you mean?"

"Rich is relative," said Collinson. "But let's just say that it was worth our while to keep Mr. Gosling happy. But I don't understand why you're here now, Mr. Nightingale. Mr. Turtledove will be handling the will and the distribution of assets, it's nothing to do with the bank."

"Did he ever mention me?"

"No, he didn't."

"He didn't mention that he had a son?"

"Never."

"You said he was a valued customer," said Nightingale. "Exactly how much was he worth?"

Collinson sat back in his executive chair and patted his hair as if checking that the comb-over was still in place. "That's confidential, I'm afraid. I can't reveal details of a client's account."

Nightingale reached into his jacket pocket and took out a photocopy of Ainsley Gosling's will and gave it to the bank manager. "I'm his sole beneficiary, so anything he has will come to me."

Collinson licked his upper lip as he studied the document, then he put it on the desk and leaned back in his chair again. "To be honest, Mr. Nightingale, I don't think that there will be much coming your way. During the last years of his life, Mr. Gosling spent most of his funds."

"On what?"

Collinson chuckled. "We don't ask our customers what they spend their money on," he said.

"The house is worth a lot."

"It's heavily mortgaged," said the bank manager.

"But you said Gosling was rich."

"That's what you inferred, Mr. Nightingale," said Collinson.

"All right, valued customer you said. But you're saying he died penniless?"

"Not penniless, no," said Collinson. "But last year he took out a large mortgage on the house, and during the two years prior to that he withdrew the bulk of the funds he was holding with us. The credit crunch didn't help, of course, the house fell in value as did his stock portfolio."

"There was no furniture in the house, did you know that?"

Collinson shook his head. "It was fully furnished the last time I visited," he said. "Beautiful furniture, most of it antiques. And a very valuable collection of paintings."

"Well, it's all gone now," said Nightingale. "How much money did he have with you before he started withdrawing it?"

"I wouldn't be able to get the figure without looking at his file," said the bank manager. "I'm not sure that I could do that, even with you being his sole heir."

"Approximately," said Nightingale. "Ballpark figure."

"Ballpark?" Collinson frowned and stared up at the ceiling as if the numbers were written there. "I'd say twelve million pounds in cash. A million or so in Krugerrands and gold bullion. A stock portfolio amounting to some fifteen million pounds, give or take." He looked back at Nightingale and shrugged. "I'd say somewhere in the region of twenty-eight million pounds."

"And the mortgage?"

"Two million," said Collinson.

"So you're saying that in just a few years Ainsley Gosling spent thirty million pounds and you've no idea what he spent it on?"

"More than that, I'm afraid," said the bank manager. "We only handled his UK assets. My understanding is that there were funds in the United States, Central Europe, and Asia, notably Hong Kong and Singapore."

"Amounting to how much exactly?"

Collinson shrugged. "I don't have exact figures for his overseas assets, but it would certainly be in excess of one hundred million pounds."

Nightingale sat stunned. "A hundred million?"

"In excess of."

"And it's all gone?"

"I'm afraid so, yes."

"There's no suggestion that he was being blackmailed or had a drug or gambling problem?"

"We don't make a habit of prying into the private lives of our clients, Mr. Nightingale," said Collinson disdainfully, as if Nightingale had just accused him of shoplifting.

"Just so long as you have their money?"

"Exactly," said the bank manager, totally missing Nightingale's attempt at sarcasm.

CHAPTER

10

Nightingale wanted a drink and time to think. He drove back to London and left his MGB in the multistory car park close to his office, then slipped into one of his favorite local pubs. It was a gloomy inn that had yet to be given a corporate makeover— no fruit machine, no olde worlde menu with microwaved lamb shanks and chili con carne, just a long bar and a few tables and a grizzled old barman who didn't look at Nightingale or try to start a conversation. As he walked over to the bar he called Jenny on his cell. "I'm in the Nag's Head," he said. "I need some thinking time."

"Yeah, alcohol is renowned for helping the thought process," she said acidly.

"Come and join me."

"I'm trying to sort out our accounts due," said Jenny. "If we don't get our cash flow sorted we won't be able to pay our VAT."

"Now you're making me feel guilty," said Nightingale.

"I doubt that," she said. "Keep your cell on, if anything crops up I'll give you a call."

She ended the call. Nightingale ordered a bottle of Corona and sat at the bar. If what Gosling had said was true, then his parents had lied to him, lied to him virtually from the day that he was born. There had never been so much as a hint from them that he wasn't their child. There had been two boys in his class at primary school who had been adopted, and it was something that he had talked to his mother about, and she had never given any indication that she wasn't his biological mother. Nightingale couldn't understand why they hadn't told him that he was adopted. There was no shame in it, and he wouldn't have loved them any the less, but now they were dead and gone and the truth had come out but he wasn't able to ask them why they had lied. Or was it all a massive confidence trick? Was Turtledove part of some elaborate con? Was the idea to convince Nightingale that the house was his, then to ask him to put money up front? He smiled to himself. If it was a con, it would be a waste of time because Nightingale had little in the way of cash to be parted from.

He sipped his Corona beer. He was drinking it from the bottle with a slice of lime shoved down the neck. Someone had told him once that the lime was there to keep away the flies, but Nightingale liked the bite that it gave to the beer.

A hand fell on his shoulder and Nightingale jumped. Beer sloshed over his hand and he cursed and turned to see Robbie Hoyle grinning at him. "Screw you, Robbie, do you have to creep up on me like that?"

Hoyle slid onto the bar stool next to Nightingale. "Jumpy…" he said.

"I'm not jumpy, I just don't like being crept up on, that's all. How did you know I was here?"

"The lovely Jenny said you were drowning your sorrows." He took a manila envelope from his inside pocket and waved it in front of Nightingale's face. "I was going to drop the stuff you wanted but then I figured I could do with a drink myself. I didn't realize you were so skittish."

"What do you want, Robbie?" asked Nightingale.

"A Porsche, a villa in Malaga, a mistress with huge tits, and a dad who owns a brewery, all the normal sort of crap."

"To drink, you soft bastard. What do you want to drink?"

Hoyle nodded at the barman. "I'll have a red wine, preferably one from a bottle with a cork." He slid the envelope across the bar to Nightingale. "Here's the info about the Gosling suicide," he said. "It was a strange one and no mistake. You were right about the magic circle. It's called a pentangle and it's supposed to offer you protection against things that go bump in the night. That's what the report says, anyway. They ran it by an occult expert. Apparently quite a few people who dabble in the occult end up topping themselves."

Nightingale opened the envelope and slid out four large photographs. It was the bedroom in Gosling Manor, but not the way that he'd seen it when he went to the house. The bed was there, and the chair, but sprawled between the two was the bloated body of the man in the DVD, his head a bloody mess, a shotgun across the legs. The bed, the chair, and the body were surrounded by a five-pointed white star that seemed to have been drawn on the floor, and at the points of the star were large church candles. Wax had dripped down the candles and solidified in pools around their brass holders. Inside the pentangle were brass bowls containing what looked like ashes.

One of the photographs was of the wall near the window, showing a spray of blood across the wallpaper. There was dried blood on the windows, too, and on the ceiling. A lot of blood.

"None of that spooky stuff is there now, I take it?" said Hoyle.

"The cops said that a crime-scene clean-up crew was in," said Nightingale. "And they did a hell of a job. I didn't see any blood splatter or anything."

"So what's the story, morning glory?"

"You won't believe it," said Nightingale. "I'm not sure I believe it myself."

The barman gave Hoyle a glass of red wine. He sniffed it and nodded his thanks. "So tell me."

Nightingale told him. He told him about the meeting with Turtledove, about Gosling Manor, the safe-deposit box, and the DVD. "What I can't work out is why my parents lied," said Nightingale. "Why didn't they just tell me?"

"If you were adopted at birth, and your biological parents didn't want to see you again, then what would be the point?"

Nightingale frowned at Hoyle. "What?"

"If your real parents, your biological parents, weren't going to see you, then there'd be no point in telling you."

"Bullshit," said Nightingale. "There's all sorts of reasons for needing to know that you're adopted."

"For instance?"

Nightingale shrugged. "I don't know. Blood groups maybe. Inherited disorders. I don't have their DNA, Robbie. I deserved to know that." He sipped his beer. "He was bald."

"Who was bald?"

"Gosling. My biological father. Bald as a cue ball. My dad, the man that I thought was my dad, had a great head of hair. I always thought I'd inherited my hair from him, but now I find out that my dad was a bald guy."

Hoyle laughed. "Is that what's got you all riled up? The fact that you might be bald one day?"

"It's not about baldness, it's about me not being who I thought I was. Robbie, my biological father made a DVD saying that he had sold my soul to the devil and then he blew his head off with a shotgun, which suggests if nothing else that he might have had a few sanity issues. What if I take after him, Robbie? Nature and nurture, right? We're a combination of our genes and our environment, and now I've found out that my genes have come from a nutter."

"A bald nutter, to boot."

"Exactly," said Nightingale.

Hoyle sipped his wine. "It's a joke, right? Some sort of sick practical joke?"

"I'm just telling you what happened," said Nightingale.

"I mean this Gosling character, he's just playing with you."

"He killed himself, Robbie. Blew his head off with a shotgun. Bit extreme for a prank, don't you think?" He pulled out some photocopied sheets from the envelope. The police report and a copy of the conclusions of the inquest which had been held a week after the death. The verdict was suicide. "Just a thought, there's no doubt that it was Gosling that died, is there? Shotgun blasts don't leave much to identify."

"It's all in there," said Hoyle. "His fingerprints matched the ones in the house. Nothing useful dental-wise so they did a DNA match. It's definitely him."

"Can you do me a favor?"

"Within limits," said Hoyle cautiously.

"I want to know if I really am his son, Robbie. Can you check my DNA against his?"

"Shouldn't be a problem," said Hoyle. He grinned. "Do you want to give me a sample now?"

Nightingale took a small plastic bag from his jacket. Inside were half a dozen hairs that he'd plucked from his scalp, the roots intact.

Hoyle took the bag. "I was hoping for blood," he said. He slid the bag into his jacket pocket. "It might take a day or two," he said. "I'll have to wait until there's a friendly face in the lab."

"I can't believe the way my parents lied to me," said Nightingale. "And my uncle and aunt. They must have known too."

"Have you spoken to them?"

"My aunt was all jittery, and my uncle, he's going to call me back."

"What about other family?"

"That's it, pretty much. Mum was an only child, all my grandparents died years ago, and Uncle Tommy and Aunt Linda never had kids. Linda has a few relatives but I hardly know them." He looked up from the papers he was reading. "What happened to the body?"

"Cremated." Hoyle rubbed his finger around the rim of his wine glass. "You're not taking this selling your soul to the devil thing seriously, are you? People don't sell their souls to the devil."

"He didn't say he sold his soul. He said he sold my soul. And my sister's."

"You don't have a sister, Jack. You were an only child, remember? Which, incidentally, explains a lot."

"What?"

"Only kids tend to be self-centered, used to getting their own way, have difficulty in forming lasting friendships."

"Screw you."

"See? That proves my point. Now me, one of four kids, you couldn't wish for a more sociable fellow."

"I say again, screw you. And the rest of the Waltons."

"Easy enough to check if you had a sister," said Hoyle. "There'd be a birth certificate."

"Gosling's not down on my certificate," said Nightingale. "Just my mum and dad. If Gosling did have a daughter, she'd be almost impossible to trace."

"It's bollocks, the whole thing."

"Yeah, maybe," said Nightingale. He drained his bottle of Corona.

"You know it's bollocks, right?" said Hoyle. "There's no such thing as the devil."

"Not THE devil. A devil. He was very clear on that."

"So now you believe in devils?"

"I'm not saying that. If there was a devil then there'd be a God, and I've seen nothing over the past thirty-two years that's convinced me there's a God. No God, no devil, end of story."

"There you go, then. It's bollocks."

"He's left me a huge bloody house in the sticks, Robbie. A mansion."

"So you're going up in the world."

"Why would he do that if I wasn't his flesh and blood? It's one hell of an expensive joke, don't you think?"

"Okay, show it to me."

"What?"

"The house. Spooky Towers."

"At night?"

"You are jumpy." Hoyle grinned and finished his wine, then motioned at the barman for the bill.

"The power's off, Old Man Gosling stopped paying his bills a month before he died."

"I've got flashlights in the car. You scared?"

"Don't be stupid. And it's not in the least bit spooky. It's bloody gorgeous in fact."

"I double dare you," said Hoyle, grinning. He waggled his fingers and made a ghostly wailing sound.

"Screw you, Robbie," said Nightingale.

It was just before nine o'clock when they pulled up in front of Gosling Manor in Hoyle's Ford Mondeo. Hoyle climbed out of the car and looked up at the house. "Wow, Jack, it's huge. It's got to be worth millions."

"It would have been worth a lot more before the property crash," said Nightingale. "And it's mortgaged to the hilt apparently."

"How many bedrooms?"

"A lot."

"And four garages. How cool is that?" Hoyle walked around to the trunk of the car, his feet squelching on dead leaves. He opened it, took out two flashlights, and tossed one to Nightingale. "Come on, show me around then."

Nightingale took out his key and opened the front door. "Wipe your feet," said Nightingale.

"You sound just like Anna," said Hoyle.

"I just don't want you walking dead leaves around my house," said Nightingale.

"Now you definitely sound like her," laughed Hoyle. He wiped his feet on a large mat in front of the door. "Happy now?"

They walked inside, playing their flashlight beams around the hallway. Nightingale led the way through to the huge drawing room and pointed his light at the massive fireplace. "That's where the envelope was," he said. "It wasn't there when the cops came so someone else must have a key."

"Where's all the furniture?" asked Hoyle.

"He must have sold it," said Nightingale. "I'm guessing that he sold everything before he died, except for the furniture in the bedroom."

Hoyle played the beam of his flashlight around the room. "You could have some great parties in here."

"You could have a half-decent game of five-a-side soccer," said Nightingale.

Something scraped across the floor upstairs and both men jumped. "What the hell's that?" said Hoyle.

"Probably a cat," said Nightingale. "There was a cat upstairs last time I was here."

"Didn't sound like a cat," said Hoyle.

"Do you want to leave?"

"Hell no, we're here now," said Hoyle. "Show me where he offed himself."

Nightingale led Hoyle back into the hallway and up the staircase. "What are you going to do with the place?" asked Hoyle.

"Sell it, I guess," said Nightingale. "Pay off the mortgage, see what's left. Why, do you want to make me an offer?"

"You could think about developing it," said Hoyle. "Turn it into apartments. There's a big market for these old buildings when they're done right."

"It'd be sacrilege to split it into apartments, a beautiful house like this," said Nightingale. "I don't know how hard it would be to find a buyer."

"The rich are always rich," said Hoyle. "Recession or boom, they always have money. You're right, sell it to Russian oligarch or a Saudi prince and let them enjoy it."

"I was thinking, back in the bar, it might be a con."

"A con?"

"They're setting me up for something. Telling me that the house is mine, then hitting me for money somehow."

"Have you got money?"

Nightingale laughed. "No," he said. "But maybe they don't know that. Can you do me a favor and check out the solicitor for me? His name's Ernest Turtledove. He's based in a village called Hamdale."

Something screamed out in the fields and both men stopped dead. "Fox?" said Hoyle hopefully.

"I hope so," said Nightingale. He played the beam of his flashlight along the landing. "This way." He headed down the corridor toward the master bedroom.

Hoyle ran his beam along the ceiling, the light making the miniature chandeliers sparkle. He stopped when he saw the CCTV camera at the end of the corridor. "Smile," he said. "We're on *Candid Camera*."

"They're all over the place," said Nightingale. "But no alarms from what I can see. Just the cameras."

"Which means what, do you think?"

The two men stopped in the middle of the hall, both their flashlight beams pointing at the camera. "Which means he wasn't worried about burglars. It was more about watching the house, inside and out."

"Maybe not," said Hoyle. "If you've got comprehensive CCTV coverage then you don't need an alarm. Any burglar worth his salt would know that he would be filmed and give the place a wide berth."

"Unless they wore masks," said Nightingale. "You're missing the point, Robbie. He was scared of someone, but it wasn't burglars. And whoever he was scared of wouldn't be put off by an alarm."

Hoyle walked down the corridor to take a closer look at the camera. He played the beam of the light around the camera unit. "It's not working," said Hoyle.

"Why would it be?" said Nightingale. "The power's off." Nightingale went to stand next to Hoyle. There was a small red light on the side of the unit but it wasn't glowing.

Hoyle shone his light along the ceiling and down the wall. "I don't see any wiring," he said. "Could be a wireless system. I wonder where the monitors are?"

"I didn't see any downstairs. And there was nothing in the bedroom."

"Must be somewhere," said Hoyle. "They wouldn't take them away and leave the cameras behind."

Nightingale walked back to the door leading to the master bedroom and opened it. "This is where he killed himself."

Hoyle played his light along the ceiling. "No CCTV cameras in here," he said. He walked into the bedroom and moved the beam of his flashlight around the walls and across the ceiling. "They've done of a hell of a good job of cleaning this up, haven't they?"

"The cops said it was a professional clean-up crew," said Nightingale, following him into the room.

"If ever I kill anyone, I'll use them to clean up afterwards," said Hoyle. "They've got rid of all the splatter." He traced his light along the floor. "And there's no staining on the floor at all." He frowned. "What about the pentangle?"

"I guess that was chalk, they just rubbed it off," he said. "I think this is where he lived, during his last few days. There was no furniture anywhere else in the house. This was the nerve center, I guess."

"So why no monitors?" said Hoyle. "If he was holed up here, he'd need the monitors close by. Otherwise they'd be useless."

"What are you thinking, Robbie? He was here under siege, waiting for somebody?"

Hoyle grinned. "Somebody," he said. "Or something." He made a ghostly face, waggled his hands in the air, and moaned.

"A man died here, Robbie, let's not forget that."

"He killed himself," said Hoyle, suddenly serious. "And anyone who does that loses any sympathy I might have had. Killing yourself is the coward's way out, Jack, because it leaves the living to clear up the mess they've made."

"You don't know the facts," said Nightingale.

"I know that he's dumped a whole load of grief on you," said Hoyle. "He claims to be your father but doesn't have the decency to tell you face-to-face. He could have at least had a sit-down with you, answered any questions that you had, and then gone ahead and done the dirty deed."

"Yeah, maybe."

"There's no maybe about it," said Hoyle. "Only cowards commit suicide."

"Sometimes it takes guts," said Nightingale quietly. "Sometimes it's the only way out."

"Well there's no way I'd off myself and leave my girls wondering why," said Hoyle.

"He did explain," said Nightingale. "That's what the DVD was for."

"You're not buying this, are you?" said Hoyle scornfully. "You don't really think that on your birthday a demon is going to come and take your soul?"

Nightingale scowled. "Of course not."

"There you are then. The DVD is a load of crap. He was a nutter, and genetic father or not he's just trying to screw with your mind from beyond the grave."

"Because?"

"He was a nutter, Jack. There's no because with a nutter." He nodded at the door. "Come on, let's have a look downstairs."

Nightingale followed Hoyle down the staircase. Hoyle ran his hands along the paneled wall. "This is quality workmanship," he said. "No Polish builders here, this is the real thing. The wood alone is worth thousands. How old do you think it is?"

"The cops said sixteenth century," said Nightingale. "It was called something else then, named after the local squires."

"Hey, do you think owning this makes you the new squire? Maybe you'll get to deflower the local virgins. Any idea how much land it has?"

"I didn't ask," said Nightingale.

"Could turn it into a golf course, maybe," said Hoyle. "This would make a great clubhouse."

They went through to the kitchen. Hoyle opened a door to find a pantry lined with empty shelves while Nightingale opened another door to reveal a tiled room that had been plumbed in for washing machines and dryers but which had been stripped bare. Beyond the pantry were three small rooms. There were marks on the walls where posters and pictures had once been and Nightingale figured they were staff quarters. A door led to the back garden. There were three locks and two bolts and there was a CCTV camera aimed at it. "That one's not wireless," said Hoyle, aiming his torch beam at the camera. "See the wire there?"

Nightingale squinted up at the camera. A black wire at the rear of the camera unit burrowed into the plaster. "Which means what?" asked Nightingale.

"Which means that the monitors are somewhere downstairs, probably," said Hoyle. "Have you checked all the rooms?"

"Not yet," said Nightingale.

"Let's have a look-see," said Hoyle. They went back to the main room, then along a corridor that led to a large room lined with teak bookshelves and cabinets. "The library?" said Hoyle.

"Looks like it," said Nightingale.

Beyond the library was another drawing room with a huge fireplace, and beyond that a smaller room that must have once contained a snooker table because the wooden scoreboard was still on one wall and a rectangular light fitting hung from the center of the ceiling. There was a CCTV camera over the door.

Hoyle went back into the corridor and played the beam of his flashlight along the ceiling. "The house is old, so the cameras must have gone in after the panelling, right?"

"Obviously," said Nightingale.

Hoyle turned his flashlight on Nightingale, and Nightingale held up his hand to shield his eyes. "So I don't think they could have pulled the paneling away without damaging the wood, do you?" he ran his flashlight along the pristine walnut panels. "This is all quality joinery," he said. "You can't just pull them off and stick them back."

"So?"

"So I don't think they can be running the wires from the downstairs cameras along the hallway. They couldn't do that without damaging the paneling."

Nightingale frowned. "Okay, so wireless upstairs and wired downstairs. But the wires don't run along the corridor." Realization dawned. "There's a basement," he said.

"Exactly," said Hoyle. "They ran the wiring straight down."

They went back to the main hallway. "If there were stairs to the basement, wouldn't they be here?" asked Nightingale.

Hoyle walked along the panelling, tapping it every few feet. Each tap produced the same dull thudding sound.

"Are you looking for a secret panel?" asked Nightingale.

"Have you got any better ideas?" Hoyle carried on tapping.

"Why would he need to hide the entrance to his own basement?"

"Who knows what was going through his head? We've already decided that he was a nutter, right?" He carried on tapping the paneling.

"We don't even know if there is a basement," said Nightingale.

"Old place like this, it's bound to have one," said Hoyle. "They used to build their foundations really deep." He moved along the hallway and tapped again. This time the blow sounded hollow rather than the flat thud he'd been getting earlier. Hoyle grinned and tapped the wood with his knuckles again. There was definitely a different timbre to the sound, almost an echo.

"You've got to be kidding me," said Nightingale. He tapped the wall near him. It was a dull thud. Hoyle tapped again. The hollow, echoing sound.

Hoyle ran the tips of his fingers around the panelling, then pushed. Nothing moved.

"Try pulling," said Nightingale.

Hoyle gripped the panelling and pulled. There was a click and a section of the wall swung open. "Open sesame," he whispered. He grinned at Nightingale in triumph. "What would you do without me, Jack?" he asked.

CHAPTER

Nightingale followed Hoyle down the staircase to the basement. The stairs were wooden and there was a brass banister on the left. He kept his hand on the banister and he felt for each stair with his foot before trusting his weight on it. The beams of their flashlights picked out books, shelves and shelves of them, mostly leather-bound.

"Why did he put his library down here?" said Nightingale.

"Because he was a nutter," said Hoyle. "Nutters do nutty things."

They stopped halfway down the staircase and shone their lights around. The basement appeared to run the full length of one of the wings of the house. The walls were lined with bookshelves, and running down the center of the space were two lines of display cabinets. There was a sitting area with two large red leather Chesterfield sofas and a coffee table piled high with books, and a huge desk which was covered in newspapers. There was an antique globe that was almost four feet high and a massive oak table with more than a dozen candles on it. Molten wax had dripped from the candles down the legs of the table and pooled along the floor.

"This is just weird," said Nightingale.

"It looks like he spent a lot of time down here," said Hoyle. "Come on, let's have a look around."

Hoyle headed down the stairs. Nightingale wrinkled his nose. There was a musty smell in the air that left a nasty taste in his mouth. It wasn't just the smell of old books or soot from the candles, it was bitter and acrid, and when he swallowed his stomach lurched and he had to fight to stop himself from throwing up.

Hoyle reached the bottom of the stairs and walked between the two rows of cabinets. "Jack, you've got to see this," he called, shining the beam of his light around one of the cabinets.

Nightingale reached the bottom of the stairs and walked around the candle-covered table to where Hoyle was standing. The cabinet that Hoyle was standing next to was glass-sided, about four feet tall. The glass shelves inside the cabinet were filled with human skulls of different sizes, some so small that they could have only come from infants, others adult size, yellowed with age, the teeth stained brown and ground down from years of wear and tear.

"How sick is this?" said Hoyle. "He collected skulls."

Nightingale bent down and peered into the display case. Most of the skulls had small irregular holes in the back as if they had been pierced with a chisel or smashed with a hammer. "They didn't die of natural causes," he said.

"Could have been done postmortem," said Hoyle.

"I hope so," said Nightingale.

They walked along to the next cabinet. It was filled with knives. Knives with curved blades, knives with handles carved in the form of exotic creatures, knives with twin blades, knives made of wood, of ivory, of every sort of metal. Some of the knives had what appeared to be dried blood on their blades, others were chipped and scratched, some were covered with strange writing. "Most of these are illegal, antiques or not," said Nightingale.

Hoyle went over to the next cabinet. It was full of crystal balls of different sizes. He shone his flashlight into the case and the light refracted into a dozen rainbows. Nightingale walked over to the wall and ran his flashlight beam across the books. Most were bound with aged leather and only a few had titles on their spines. He pulled out a book at random. There was a title etched into the front cover. *Sacrifice and Self-Mutilation.* He opened the book. It had been printed in 1816 in Edinburgh. He flicked through it. There were illustration plates that made his stomach turn, black-and-white drawings of people being tortured and butchered. He put the book back and took out the one next to it. It was in Spanish, and bound in what looked like lizard skin. He couldn't make sense of what the book was about, but the illustrations inside were of strange and mythical creatures, winged dragons and twin-headed snakes. Nightingale pulled out books at random. All were old, their pages well-thumbed and creased, and many had hand-written notes in the margins. Most were concerned with witchcraft or black magic.

Nightingale flinched as something crashed behind him. He whirled around, dropping the book that he'd been holding. Hoyle was standing looking down at dozens of bits of broken glass. "Come on, Robbie, what are you playing at?" Hoyle didn't reply. Nightingale put the book back on the shelf and went over to him. "What was it?" he asked, looking down at the glass shards.

"It was one of the crystal balls," said Hoyle. "I dropped it."

"Yeah, I can see that," said Nightingale. He picked up one of the smaller balls and weighed it in the palm of his hand. "But these are solid crystal," he said. "They shouldn't shatter."

"That one was different," he said. "It was weird, full of smoke or mist, like it was moving all the time."

"Are you okay, Robbie?" asked Nightingale.

"I saw something," said Hoyle quietly. "In the mist."

"What? What did you see?"

Hoyle shook his head. He prodded one of the curved shards with his shoe.

"Robbie, what did you see?"

"It's stupid. Nothing."

"Robbie?"

Hoyle swallowed. "I saw myself."

"Your reflection?"

"No, like I was inside the glass. In the mist. I was standing in the middle of a road…"

"Come on, Robbie, you're winding me up."

Hoyle shook his head. "I was standing in the middle of the road and a taxi hit me. A black cab."

"Robbie…"

Hoyle looked at him earnestly. "I'm serious, Jack. The cab went right over me."

"It's dark down here, Robbie. You were shining the torch on it, the light must have played tricks on you."

"I know what I saw," said Hoyle.

"Crystal balls are mumbo jumbo nonsense," said Nightingale. He stared at the ball he was holding. "Show me the future, oh magic ball," he moaned. "Tell me what lies ahead." He ran his flashlight beam across the ball and the light fragmented into a rainbow. "Nothing," he said. "Maybe I should try another channel." He grinned at Hoyle. "Do you think I could get Sky Sports on this?" Hoyle tried to smile, but Nightingale could see that his friend was unsettled. He put the small crystal ball back in the display case. He ran the beam of his light along the bookcases that lined the basement. "How many books do you think there are here? Thousands? Tens of thousands?"

"A lot," said Hoyle.

"He can't have read them all, surely."

"Maybe he was a speed reader," said Hoyle. "Maybe they're investments. Maybe he bought them by the yard and never read them."

They walked along the display cases. "He was a collector, that's for sure," said Nightingale. There was a case full of what appeared to be shrunken heads, leathery fist-sized lumps with straggly hair and pig-like noses. In the case next to it were chunks of rock. Nightingale played his beam along the rocks and realized that they were fossils. He peered closer. They looked like birds but they had long claws and teeth.

"Vampire bats?" asked Hoyle, only half joking.

"I don't know what they hell they are," said Nightingale. "They're fossils so they've got to be old. But I don't think birds ever had teeth, did they?"

"They look more like lizards than birds," said Hoyle. He played the beam of his torch down the basement, to the end furthest from the stairs. "That looks like the security system down there," he said. There were half a dozen LCD screens on the wall in two banks of three.

The two men walked through the display cases toward the screens. As they got closer they saw that there was a black wooden desk with a straight-backed chair in front of them, and on the desk was a large stainless-steel console dotted with labeled buttons. Nightingale ran his finger along the console. "This picks up the feeds from the CCTV cameras," he said. "Look at this, there's what, twenty-four cameras?"

"Twenty-eight," said Hoyle. "Overkill, wouldn't you say?"

"He'd sit down here watching the cameras. But watching for what?"

"Scared that someone would rip off his collection?"

"I don't think he was scared," said Nightingale. "I think he just wanted to know what was going on in the house. He couldn't have been alone. He'd have needed a staff: cleaners, gardeners, a driver, an estate manager. Maybe he didn't trust them. Maybe he didn't trust anybody."

"But when he died, he was alone in the house," said Hoyle. "That's what it said in the file."

"He must have let the staff go," said Nightingale.

Hoyle waved a hand at the rows of display cases behind them. "And what is this place? What was Gosling doing down here? It's not a display or an exhibition, he kept it all hidden away."

"You know what it is," said Nightingale. "It's Witchcraft'R'Us, that's what it is. A shrine to black magic. Ainsley Gosling was a Satanist and this is where he plied his trade."

"There's no such thing as magic," said Hoyle. "Smoke and mirrors and superstition, that's all there is. This is the twenty-first century, Jack. The third millennium. Magic belongs back in the Dark Ages."

"You got the heebie-jeebies over that crystal ball, didn't you?"

"That was different. That wasn't magic, that was…" He paused, lost for words. "I don't know what that was. Maybe you were right, maybe it was the light playing tricks with my reflection."

"Okay, but you got married in a church, didn't you?"

"So?"

"So that was a religious ceremony, before God."

"That's different," said Hoyle, rubbing his wedding band.

"No, it's the same. What you did in church with Anna was a ceremony with all the paraphernalia of religion. And remember Sarah's christening? I had to renounce Satan and all his works."

"They're just words, Jack. Everyone says until death do us part, but most marriages end in divorce. They're words, not spells." He waved his arm at the shelves full of books. "This is bollocks. All of it. And you know it's bollocks."

"I'm not saying it's not bollocks," said Nightingale. "I'm just saying that Gosling obviously believed in it, that's all. And maybe that belief is what drove him to kill himself." He nodded at the stairs. "Come on, let's get the hell out of here. We can't see anything with the flashlights, I'll get the power switched back on and we'll come back."

They walked past an oak desk on the way to the stairs. Unlike the other desks in the basement it wasn't piled high with books or papers, there was just a single leather-bound volume open with a Mont Blanc fountain pen next to it. The pages were filled with a handwritten scrawl but Nightingale couldn't read it with the flashlight. He picked it up and took it with him.

CHAPTER

13

Robbie Hoyle lived in a neat semidetached house in Raynes Park that he'd bought a couple of years before property prices crashed and which was now worth less than the mortgage he'd taken out to pay for it. His wife's black VW Golf was already in the driveway so Hoyle parked in the street.

"Maybe we should sell this place and move into Chez Nightingale," said Hoyle as they walked down the driveway to the house.

"I don't think you could afford the rent, mate."

"You could cut me a deal," said Hoyle. They walked down the driveway and Hoyle unlocked the door. "We're going to need a bigger place, we bought it before we knew we were having twins."

"Twin girls, they can share a room," said Nightingale.

"Spoken like an only child," said Hoyle, pushing the front door open. "Trust me, kids need their own space."

Anna Hoyle came out of the kitchen, holding a bottle of red wine. "Keep the noise down, boys. I've only just got the twins to sleep and Sarah's got an exam tomorrow."

"I love you too," said Hoyle. He pecked her on the cheek.

"I'm serious," said Anna. She smiled at Nightingale and held up the wine bottle. "Hi, Jack. Red okay?" Nightingale and Robbie had met Anna at the same time ten years earlier. She had been a probationer at the South London station they were working at and they had both asked her out. She'd actually said yes to Nightingale first, but on the evening they were due to go out he'd been called away on an armed siege at a bank in Clapham, and the following evening she'd gone for a drink with Robbie and things had gone so well that they had married six months later. Three children later and she was still a stunner, with shoulder-length blonde hair and a trim figure and green eyes that always seemed to be amused.

"Red's fine. Sorry I kept your man out," said Nightingale, taking off his raincoat. He dropped it on the back of an armchair and gave her a brotherly peck on the cheek. He'd long ago come to terms with the fact that she'd never be more than a friend, though he still caught himself looking at her legs whenever she left the room.

"I'll get the glasses," said Hoyle. "You sit yourself down. I know you gumshoes spend all your day pounding the streets."

"Great," said Nightingale. He sat down on the sofa and stretched out his legs.

"How's business?" asked Anna, sitting down opposite him.

"Getting by," he said, trying not to look at her cleavage. "The divorce rate always goes up during a recession. More arguments about money, I guess."

"And Jenny?"

"She's fine."

"Asked her out yet?"

Nightingale groaned. "Anna, she's an employee. She's staff. Start anything with a staff member these days and you end up in an industrial tribunal."

"She fancies you something rotten, Jack. It's as plain as the nose on your face. Why else do you think she works for you?"

Nightingale grinned. "We're a dynamic company with growth prospects," he said.

Hoyle returned from the kitchen with three glasses. He put them on the coffee table and flopped down in an armchair while Anna poured the wine. "So did Jack tell you he's a man of property now?"

"Really?" said Anna. "Property?"

"I've been left a house."

"A mansion," said Hoyle. "It's fantastic, babe. You have to see it to believe it. Dozens of bedrooms, a library, the kitchen alone is the size of this place."

"Lucky you," said Anna. "How come?"

"A relative died," said Nightingale.

"Close?" asked Anna.

"My father."

Anna's eyebrows shot skywards. "Jack!"

"Okay, somebody claiming to be my father."

Hoyle sipped his wine. "Some sort of Satanist, apparently."

"A devil worshiper?" said Anna. "This is a joke, right?"

"I don't know about devil worship, but he was definitely disturbed. He blew his head off with a shotgun."

Anna drew her legs up underneath her and held the wine glass with both hands. "I thought your parents died years ago," she said.

"They did. But apparently I was adopted and Gosling was my genetic father."

"But you'd know if you were adopted, surely."

"It happened at birth. I was given to the Nightingales and it was registered as if I were their natural child. Anyway, it might all be bollocks. It might just be some sort of scam."

"You should be able to prove if he was your father or not. DNA, right?"

"I'm on the case," said Robbie.

"We could ask him now, if you like," said Anna.

Nightingale and Hoyle both looked at her in amazement. "What?" said Nightingale. "What on earth are you talking about?"

"What was his name? Your father?"

"My genetic father. Gosling. Ainsley Gosling."

"Well, let's ask Mr. Gosling. Let's go right to the source."

"Anna, what's going on?" asked her husband.

"Let's have a séance." She held up the glass she was holding. "Hands on a glass. Talking to the dead, the spirits." She waved her glass at Hoyle. "Robbie and I used to do it years ago."

"It was a joke, a party game," said Hoyle.

"We had some pretty weird messages."

"There's always someone pushing the glass," said Hoyle.

"Anna, you don't really believe that you can talk to the dead," said Nightingale.

"It works, I can't explain why it works, but you can get messages from people who've passed over."

Nightingale frowned. "You're serious?"

"I'm just saying, it's worth a try. And they say that spirits that have passed over violently, like when they've been murdered or committed suicide, tend to hang around. I suppose because there's unfinished business."

"Well, Jack is certainly that," said Hoyle.

Anna smiled brightly at Nightingale. "Want to give it a go?"

CHAPTER

Nightingale, Hoyle, and Anna sat at the dining table. Anna had written the letters of the alphabet on squares of paper along with the words "YES" and "NO." She placed the letters in a circle with the "A" at the top, and put the "YES" and "NO" inside the circle. Hoyle fetched another wine glass from the kitchen and placed it upside down inside the circle. "Now what?" asked Nightingale. "We stare at it and make spooky sounds?"

"We have to place our right index fingers on the bottom of the glass," said Anna. "But first we have to cleanse our auras."

"We have to what?" said Nightingale.

"I think she's saying you need a shower," said Hoyle.

"It's about making the area safe and comfortable for spirits," said Anna, ignoring her husband's sarcasm. She went over to the fireplace and lit three candles there, and carried one over to the sideboard, close to the dining table. Then she switched off the lights. "The spirits feel more comfortable in the shadows," she said.

"Don't we all," said Nightingale. "Why can't I have my wine?"

"There must be no alcohol at the table, no cigarettes, no impurities," said Anna.

"Because?"

"Because impurities attract the bad spirits," she said.

"Where do you pick up this stuff?" asked Nightingale.

"She reads," said Hoyle.

Anna took her seat and held out her hands. "Now we form a circle and say the Lord's Prayer," she said.

"Strictly speaking, it's a triangle," said Nightingale.

"Don't quibble," said Anna. "Now hold my hands and close your eyes."

The two men did as they were told. As they sat holding hands, Anna led them through the Lord's Prayer. It had been a long time since Nightingale had said the prayer, and he stumbled twice, mumbling over the words that he'd forgotten. When they'd finished they opened their eyes. Anna kept hold of their hands. "Let all spirits here within know that we mean you no harm and that we are here solely to do God's will," she said.

"Amen," said Hoyle.

"Good grief," said Nightingale.

Anna looked at him disapprovingly. "You have to take this seriously," she said. "Now place the index finger of your right hand on the bottom of the glass." She touched the bottom of the glass gently and the two men did the same. "Right, here we go," she said. "Is there anybody there?" They sat in silence for ten seconds. "Is there anybody there?" Anna repeated.

"You're mad, you know that," said Nightingale.

"I'd be careful if I were you," said Hoyle. "The last person who said she's mad is buried out in our back garden."

Anna glared at her husband and he fell silent. "Is there anybody there?" she said, her voice lower this time.

Hoyle grinned across at Nightingale and waggled his eyebrows. Nightingale tried not to laugh. Their smiles vanished as the glass jerked under their fingers.

"Is there anyone there?" repeated Anna.

Slowly but surely the glass scraped across the table top, heading for the piece of paper with "YES" written on it.

"No way," said Nightingale under his breath.

"Shhh!" hissed Anna.

The glass stopped next to the YES. Then it slowly moved back to the middle of the circle. Nightingale looked at Hoyle, frowning. Hoyle shook his head as if to say that he wasn't pushing the glass.

"What was your father's name again?" whispered Anna.

"Ainsley Gosling," said Nightingale, staring at the glass.

"We want to speak with Ainsley Gosling," said Anna. She tilted her head back so that she was looking up at the ceiling. "Is Ainsley Gosling there?"

The glass jerked again, then began to move inexorably toward the YES. It stopped halfway, but then a few seconds later it began to move again until it nudged the piece of paper with YES on it.

"I don't believe this," whispered Nightingale. "Someone's pushing it."

"Jack, shhh!" hissed Anna. "The spirits sense negativity." The glass moved across the table, back to the center of the table. Nightingale stared at it. He certainly wasn't applying any pressure to it and it didn't feel as if either Anna or her husband were pushing or pulling it. "Do you have a message for us?" asked Anna, and even before she had finished the question the glass shot across to YES, then slowly slid back to the center.

"This is amazing," whispered Hoyle. He looked across at Nightingale. "You're not pissing around are you, Jack?"

Nightingale shook his head. His finger was aching but he didn't want to take it off the glass, afraid that he would put a stop to whatever was happening. "Now what, Anna?" he said.

Anna ignored him. She was still staring up at the ceiling. "What is it you want to say to us?" she said. The glass didn't move. Nightingale stared at it, willing it to do something, but it stayed defiantly where it was. "You are among friends," said Anna softly. "We only want to hear what it is you have to say."

The glass started to move quickly and in quick succession touched the letters J, A, C, and K.

"Jack!" said Hoyle excitedly. "It spelled out JACK."

"We can all read, honey," said Anna. "You don't have to spell it out for us." She took a deep breath. "Yes, Jack is here with us. Do you have a message for Jack?"

The glass moved slowly toward YES, touched the piece of paper, and then drifted back to the middle of the table.

The glass began to move in small circles, slowly at first and then faster, so fast that Nightingale's finger almost slipped off it. Then it shot off to the letter I and stayed here for several seconds before sliding back to the center. Almost immediately it went to the opposite side of the circle and nudged the letter W. Slowly it spelled out I-W-A-N-T. Then it stopped.

"I WANT," said Hoyle. "Did you see that? It spelled out I WANT."

"What do you want?" asked Anna. "Please tell us, what is it that you want."

The glass began to move again. It slid over to the letter Y, then O, and slowly spelled out "YOU TO…"

The glass stopped. "What?" said Hoyle, staring at the glass. "What is it you want Jack to do?"

The glass began to move again in a series of jerky movements, and in rapid succession it picked out N-A-I-L-J-E-N-N.

"Nail Jenn…" said Nightingale, then realization dawned and he cursed and took his finger off the glass. Anna and her husband burst out laughing.

"You two are a couple of kids," said Nightingale, folding his arms and leaning back in his chair.

"Your face," said Hoyle.

"Come on, admit it, we had you going," said Anna.

"It's not funny," said Nightingale.

"It is from where we're sitting," said Hoyle. "I want you to nail Jenny," he said in a spooky voice, waggling his fingers. "That's what we want in the spirit world, we want Jack Nightingale to get laid." He stood, retrieved his wine, and flopped down onto the sofa. "You bought it, hook, line, and sinker."

"Only because I trusted you," said Nightingale. "Which isn't a mistake I'll make again."

Anna gathered up the pieces of paper and screwed them into a ball, then threw it at Nightingale. It bounced off his head and fell onto the floor. "I'm going home," said Nightingale.

"Don't sulk," said Anna.

Nightingale laughed as he stood up. He held out his arms and hugged Anna. "Bitch," he said.

"Sticks and stones," said Anna.

Nightingale kissed her on the cheek and waved good-bye to Hoyle. "I will get you back, you know that," said Nightingale.

"I wouldn't have it any other way," said Hoyle, raising his glass of wine in salute.

CHAPTER

15

Nightingale woke up early on Friday morning with Simon Underwood's words ringing in his ears. It was the second night in a row he'd had the dream. He sat up and ran his hands through his hair and caught sight of his reflection in the mirrored door of the closet on the far wall. His face was bathed in sweat and there were dark patches under his eyes as if he hadn't slept for a week. He groaned and lit a cigarette, smoked it all the way down, then showered and padded to the kitchen naked to make himself a black coffee. As he sipped his coffee he phoned his uncle Tommy. It was just after six thirty but both his aunt and uncle had always been early risers. His aunt answered again but she didn't say anything to him, just called for her husband. Uncle Tommy sounded hesitant. "Yes, Jack, how's things?"

"Everything's fine, Uncle Tommy. I called you a couple of days ago."

"Aye, I'm sorry, lad, I've been busy."

"I need to talk to you, Uncle Tommy. About Mum and Dad."

"Aye, Linda said. But it's complicated, and I'm not sure that your dad would want me talking about it."

"He's dead, Uncle Tommy, so I can't ask him or Mum. I have to know the truth. You can understand that, can't you?"

Uncle Tommy sighed but didn't answer.

"We have to talk about this, Uncle Tommy," said Nightingale.

"Aye, lad. I guess so."

"How about I drive up to Altrincham on Sunday? About ten? Ten in the morning?"

Uncle Tommy put his hand over the receiver and said something to his wife. "Linda says come for lunch, Jack. She'll do one of her roasts."

"Lunch it is."

"Jack, look…I'm sorry about all this."

"Let's talk on Sunday, Uncle Tommy. It'll be easier face-to-face."

Nightingale was already at his desk when Jenny McLean walked in. She waved through the doorway as she dropped her bag onto her desk and slipped off her trainers and changed into a pair of Chanel high heels with pretty bows on the back. "The early worm," she said.

He was studying the book that he'd taken from the basement in Gosling Manor, and he looked disapprovingly over the top of it. "A bit of respect would be nice," he said. "Me being management and all. I couldn't sleep. Came back to watch the DVD again."

"Are you worrying about it?"

"My father tells me he's sold my soul to a devil and then blows his head off with a shotgun? Don't you think I should be a bit concerned?"

"He was probably mad. Deranged."

"And I'm his offspring. So what if it's hereditary?"

"What if what's hereditary?"

"He went mad. Maybe he was schizophrenic. Manic depressive. I don't know. But if he was my father then maybe I'll go crazy too."

Jenny nodded at the dirty mugs on his desk. "I think you might be suffering from an excess of caffeine, Jack."

"It's not the coffee," said Nightingale. "I look at the man in the video, and the more I look the more I see myself in him."

"That's ridiculous," said Jenny.

"It's the eyes. I look into his eyes and it's like looking into a mirror."

"He doesn't look anything like you."

"You don't know what I'll look like when I'm his age."

"He was fat, he looked like he'd spent a lifetime boozing and taking God-knows-what drugs, and he looked sick."

"And bald," said Nightingale.

"And bald," repeated Jenny. "Though I don't see what that's got to do with it."

"Gosling was bald. That means I'll go bald, too."

Jenny grinned. "No it doesn't," she said. "The baldness gene crosses the sexes. Didn't you do biology at school?"

"I must have been off the day we did bald. How does it go again?"

Jenny sighed and picked up the dirty coffee mugs. "You'll inherit the hair of your mother's father," she said.

"Are you sure?"

"I'm sure," she said. "Do you have any idea who your real mum might be? If what Gosling said is true, you have a mum out there."

"I know," said Nightingale. "But I wouldn't have the first idea how to find her. I doubt that he went through an agency."

"We could try hospital records for the day you were born. That would be a start."

"If Gosling was doing this secretively, he wouldn't have used a hospital," said Nightingale. "For all we know, I could have been born in Gosling Manor. Oh, yeah, while I remember, how much is in the company account?"

"Not much."

"I'm going to use the credit card to pay the electricity bill at Gosling Manor. Just under a grand. Can we cover it?"

"Barely," said Jenny. "You know we dipped into the red again last month."

"We've got an overdraft facility of five hundred quid, right?"

"We used that then went into the red," said Jenny.

"Mrs. Brierley's check should clear tomorrow."

"Assuming it doesn't bounce like last time," said Jenny.

"That was because her shit of a husband emptied the account," said Nightingale. "The new check was on her own account. It'll be fine."

"You're not planning to live there, are you?"

Nightingale laughed. "If you'd seen the size of the place, you wouldn't even ask," he said. "It's huge. It's a couple of hundred yards from the kitchen to the main bedroom."

"Gosling lived there alone, didn't he?"

"I'm not sure. I think he must have had staff living in, for cleaning if nothing else. And it would need a team of gardeners. That's another reason I couldn't live there—I couldn't afford the upkeep."

"So why have the power connected?"

"Robbie and I found a basement and I want to give it another going-over. It was hard going by flashlight. And the estate agents will need the electricity on when they start showing people around."

"That's the plan? Sell it?"

"I'm going to have to because there's going to be inheritance tax to pay. Turtledove doesn't know how much it'll be, but it'll be a lot."

Jenny looked at the clock on the wall. "You didn't forget Mr. McBride did you?"

"McBride?"

"The gentleman whose wife is having an affair with her boss, remember?"

Nightingale looked at his watch. "What time's he due?"

"Ten," she said.

"Time for another coffee, then," he said.

"What are you reading?" asked Jenny as she went over to the coffee machine. She put down the dirty mugs and picked up a clean one.

"A book," said Nightingale. "And I'm not reading it. I'm staring at it trying to make sense of the letters, which isn't the same thing."

"What are you talking about?" said Jenny. She poured him a cup of coffee and carried it through to his office.

Nightingale handed the book to her. "See for yourself," he said.

Jenny took the book and opened it. It was full of handwritten scrawl, some of it in dark blue ink, some in black, and some in what looked disconcertingly like dried blood. Dotted among the text were sketches of various circles and pentangles. Jenny tried reading a sentence at random but she couldn't make any sense of it. It certainly wasn't English, or any other language that she recognized.

"At first I thought I might have caught dyslexia," said Nightingale. He sipped his coffee, then reached for the bottle of whisky. Jenny moved the bottle out of his reach without taking her eyes off the book.

"You don't catch dyslexia," Jenny said, frowning as she tried to make sense of the spidery writing. "Where did you get this from?"

"I got it from the house last night," said Nightingale. "Old Man Gosling has a basement packed with books and stuff. Weird stuff. I thought that might have been his diary but I can't make head nor tale of it. I think it's written backwards, but even if you read it from right to left it still doesn't make sense."

Jenny smiled and looked up from the book. "I've got it," she said.

"The suspense is killing me," said Nightingale. "What have you got?"

"It's not written backwards, it's mirror writing. There's a difference."

"So you have to read it in a mirror? How did he write it, then?"

"You can teach yourself to write that way. Leonard da Vinci used to do it, so that no one could read his papers."

Nightingale took the book from here and stared at one of the pages. Then he shook his head. "It still doesn't make any sense."

Jenny fetched a small mirror from her bag, then sat down opposite Nightingale and placed it on the book. "It's not English, that's why," she said.

Nightingale took the mirror from her and tried reading the reflection of a sentence. "What is it, Italian?"

"Latin."

"My education was a bit light on dead languages," said Nightingale. "Can you translate it?"

Jenny rolled her eyes. "Didn't you read my CV when you hired me?"

"I was too busy looking at your legs," said Nightingale. "Can you tell me what it says?"

"Eventually," said Jenny.

A sudden knock at the door startled them both. Jenny hurried over and opened it. A middle-aged man in a wheelchair looked up at her. He was in his late forties with lank brown hair flecked with gray that kept falling into his eyes. He was wearing a scarlet windbreaker and black leather gloves with the fingers cut off, and had bulging arm muscles that Nightingale figured were the result of pushing himself around. His name was Joel McBride and Nightingale had bad news for him. "I'm sorry I'm early but the taxi got the pickup time wrong so here I am," said McBride.

"No problem, Mr. McBride," said Nightingale, getting up from his chair. "As my lovely assistant just reminded me, the early worm catches the bird. There's something we need to talk about."

"About my wife?" said McBride.

"I'm afraid so," said Nightingale.

CHAPTER 16

Nightingale ordered another Corona, his third, and wondered whether it was worth going outside the wine bar for a cigarette, but decided that on balance he'd prefer to continue to watch a recording of an Manchester United–Liverpool match on a big LCD TV with the sound turned down. Nightingale's father, his real father, the man that had brought him up, had been a big Manchester United fan and had taken him to hundreds of games over the years. William Nightingale had been a season ticket holder for as long as he could remember, and Jack's yearly birthday present from the age of ten had been his own season ticket. It was father and son time, and going to the Manchester United games had marked some of the happiest times of his childhood. His father had helped Nightingale collect autographs of the first team players, standing with him in all weathers outside the players' entrance, passing the time by testing each other on the names of all the squads going back to the early fifties. Nightingale had gone once or twice after his parents had died, but it had never felt the same and he hadn't renewed his ticket. "I knew I'd find you here," said a voice at his shoulder. It was Jenny.

"I wasn't exactly hiding, and it is the closest bar to the office," he said. He looked at his watch. It was just before eight o'clock. "Why aren't you home?"

She held up the Waitrose shopping bag in her hand. "I was in the office, reading the Gosling diary," she said. "I got caught up in it." She put the bag down on the bar and ordered a glass of white wine from the barman. "Can we sit at a table?" she asked Nightingale. "I always feel like a lush standing at the bar."

"I feel like a lush too, but where am I going to find one at this time of night?" said Nightingale. He grinned and waved at an empty table. "You grab yourself a seat and I'll get your wine."

Jenny threaded her way through the tables and sat down. She put the bag down in front of her and helped herself to a breadstick. Nightingale took Jenny's white wine and his bottle of Corona over to the table and sat down opposite her.

"Are you okay?" she asked.

"Of course I'm okay. Why wouldn't I be?"

"You've been quiet, that's all."

"I've been working."

"How many beers have you had?"

Nightingale grinned again. "What are you, the alcohol police?"

"You're not driving, are you?"

Nightingale raised his glass. "No, Jenny, I'm not driving."

"And you're sure you're okay?"

He sipped his beer. "I'm fine," he said. "Fine and dandy." He nodded at the Waitrose bag. "Have you managed to make sense of that?"

Four women in power suits burst into laughter at the table next to them. They were all in their early thirties, wearing too much makeup and too much jewelry, and while they were laughing noisily they were weighing each other up with humorless eyes. Nightingale had them pegged as office colleagues and not friends. He made eye contact with one and she sneered at him dismissively. Nightingale smiled to himself and sipped his beer again, unfazed by the woman's look of contempt.

"What are you grinning at?" asked Jenny.

He turned to look at her. "I'm just happy that you're the way you are and not like those harpies over there."

"Harpies?"

"The hard-faced bitches in their power suits, drinking bubbly and baring their fangs."

"That sounds a tad misogynistic," said Jenny.

"I love women," said Nightingale.

"That's so not true," said Jenny. "You like some women, you tolerate most of them."

"I open doors for them, I give up my seat on buses."

"On behalf of womankind, thank you so very much." She sipped her wine. The women on the other table laughed out loud and one of them shouted at a waiter to bring over another bottle of champagne. "Having said that, I do see what you mean," she said. She put down her wine glass and took the book out of the bag. "So, here's the scoop. This wasn't written by Ainsley Gosling. He would have been reading it, not writing it."

Nightingale raised one eyebrow. "So who did write it if it wasn't him?"

"Far as I can tell it's a diary, written by somebody called Sebastian Mitchell. The first entry is 1946. The most recent was twelve years ago. There are notes in the margin which aren't in mirror Latin so I'm guessing that Gosling wrote them." She put the book down on the table. "I've only read bits, it's going to take forever to read the whole thing. My Latin's rusty and it's a pain having to read it in the mirror. But I can tell you that this guy Mitchell was some sort of Satanist. A devil worshiper. You've heard of Aleister Crowley, right?"

"Vaguely."

"He was a big-time Satanist, died over fifty years ago. Mitchell studied under him. Crowley died in 1947, the year after Mitchell started writing his diary. But whereas Crowley enjoyed his infamy, Mitchell preferred to hide his light under a bushel, and this was never meant for publication."

"It says all that in the diary?"

"It mentions Crowley, yes. But the diary isn't about him. The diary is about how Mitchell was trying to summon demons. A sort of 'how to' book, detailing what Mitchell did, the pitfalls and the perils, what worked and what didn't."

"This just keeps getting better and better, doesn't it?"

"Just because it's written down doesn't mean it's true. I kept a diary until I was fifteen, full of adolescent ramblings."

"Now that I'd like to read," said Nightingale. He sipped his beer. "Gosling was using this book. It was open on his desk, it might well have been the last thing he read. I need to know what he was thinking about before he killed himself." He ran his hand through his hair. "Is there stuff in there about selling souls?"

"Jack, you know that's nonsense."

"I need to know what he believed," said Nightingale. "It doesn't matter whether or not it's nonsense, what matters is what he believed. Is there stuff in there about selling the souls of children?"

"It's a handwritten diary, Jack. Mitchell could have been as crazy as…" She left the sentence unfinished and reached for her glass.

"As my genetic father, you were going to say."

Jenny avoided his eyes. "I'm not saying he was crazy. But he did kill himself, there's no getting away from that."

"What does it say about selling souls, Jenny?"

Jenny sighed and looked back at him. "You have to summon a devil," she said. "Not THE devil, but one of his minions. In the book, Mitchell describes the different sorts of devils and what they do. So if you want to sell a soul you have to summon one of his minions."

"How do you know which devil to summon?"

"You're not taking this seriously, are you?"

"Just tell me what the book says."

Jenny nodded slowly. "Okay. According to Mitchell there are 66 princes under the devil, each commanding 6,666 legions. And each legion is made up of 6,666 devils."

Nightingale frowned as he struggled to do the calculation in his head.

"Just under three billion," said Jenny.

"There are three billion devils in hell?"

"It's a big place," said Jenny. "Look Jack, Mitchell was delusional, the book's proof of that. No one in their right mind believes in a hell full of devils."

Nightingale sighed. "I know." He drained his beer and waved for a waitress to bring over another bottle. "Here's the thing, Jenny. There are two possibilities the way that I see it. One, he sold my soul to a devil and on my thirty-third birthday my life as I know it is over."

"Which is nonsense."

Nightingale raised his bottle to her. "Which is nonsense," he agreed. "Two, he was as mad as a hatter. There was something wrong with him, paranoid schizophrenia, early Alzheimer's, bipolar, I don't know." He tapped the side of his head. "A few bricks short of a wall."

"You're still worrying about that hereditary thing, is that it?"

"And you think I shouldn't be?"

"I think it's obvious that he was having problems," said Jenny. "That doesn't mean that you will."

"Mental problems, Jenny. And mental problems can be hereditary. My father was mad, so far all I know, I could be headed that way too." He pointed at the book in front of her. "Anyone who wrote that must be crazy, and anyone who believed in it must have been crazier. My dad blew his head off with a shotgun, Jenny. Maybe..." His voice trailed off. He shook his head and drained his bottle.

"What, Jack? What is it?"

"I was a negotiator, you know that. Everyone thinks that negotiators are like they are on TV, you run around talking to hostage-takers, talking villains out of banks and getting them to hand over their guns before anyone gets hurt. But it's not like that. Most of the time it's domestics that have gotten out of hand or it's sad buggers wanting to kill themselves. Or to be talked out of killing themselves." He took a long pull on his beer. "Christ, I want a cigarette."

"That's the beauty of the legislation," said Jenny, "you're only allowed one pleasure at a time."

"Sometimes they just want someone to talk to," said Nightingale. "There was one woman out in Tower Hamlets, every time she had a fight with her husband she'd pick up a knife and sit in her garden and threaten to cut herself. A negotiating team would go out, and after an hour or two and a few cigarettes she'd give us the knife and she'd start crying and saying that she loved her husband even though he belted her every time he had a few drinks inside him."

"She wasn't really suicidal?"

"She just wanted someone to talk to, and by threatening to harm herself, she got that. I saw her three times over the years. Knew what brand of smokes to take her and what buttons to press when I got there. Emma, her name was. She's probably still at it." He sipped his beer then took another long pull at it. "It wasn't hard to empathize with Emma. She was trapped in a life that she hated, with a man who showed emotion by using violence, she'd had half a dozen miscarriages that were probably because of the drink and the drugs and the smoking. You could understand what was upsetting her. And once you understand you can negotiate, you know? You can tell them what they want to hear."

"And she wanted someone to care, is that it?"

"That's all she wanted. Someone to listen to her, to prove that she mattered, that her life amounted to something."

"And did you really care? Or were you faking it?"

"I cared. Of course I cared. She was a human being in pain, how could I not care?" He finished his Corona and waved at the waitress for another. "But the ones who really want to kill themselves, they're a different ball game. You could look into their eyes and you'd know, you'd just know, that there was something not right there. You'd know without a shadow of a doubt that they were going to do it, and that the only reason you were here is because they wanted an audience."

"Why? Why would they want an audience?"

Nightingale shrugged. "Who knows? There's no logic to what a crazy person does, that's what crazy is."

"Crazy is as crazy does?" said Jenny. "Very Forrest Gump."

"Yeah, life is a box of chocolates," said Nightingale. "In my father's case, Black Magic."

"That's funny," said Jenny. "Good to see you haven't lost your sense of humor."

The waitress brought over another bottle of beer. Jenny's wine glass was still half-full.

"Some people just want to kill themselves and they do it in private," said Nightingale. "It's easy enough to do. You swallow a bottle of sleeping tablets or hang yourself with a rope or jump off a very tall building when no one's looking. But sometimes they want an audience, they want a reaction, so they'll throw themselves in front of a train or they'll stand on a ledge and wait for a crowd to gather. They're the really sick ones."

"You've seen a lot of people kill themselves?"

Nightingale grimaced. "Not too many, but enough," he said. "But the one thing they had in common was the look they had, the look in their eyes. Once you've seen it, you never forget it. And I can see it in Gosling's eyes when I look at that DVD. I can see it, Jenny."

"Jack…"

Nightingale stood up.

"Jack, are you okay?"

"I just need some fresh air."

"You mean you need a cigarette, right?"

Nightingale shook his head. "I need to walk for a while, clear my head."

"Do you want company?"

"Thanks, but I need to be on my own for a bit." He nodded at the book. "Can you keep a hold of that for me, see if you can turn up anything else I should know."

"You're not going to drive, are you?"

He waved a hand dismissively. "Of course not," he said.

"You've been drinking, Jack."

"I know I've been drinking. And I'm not going to drive. I just need some air."

Nightingale lit a cigarette as he walked down the street. He passed a dozen or so shops, three of which had gone out of business while the rest were desperately trying to drum up trade by offering sales of up to ninety percent off and free credit. The only shops that seemed to be thriving were the charity shops offering secondhand clothes, household goods, and toys. A cold wind blew at his back and he raised the collar of his raincoat.

"Hey, mister, got a cigarette?"

There was a girl sitting in the doorway of an Oxfam shop, a sleeping bag wrapped around her legs. She was dressed in goth black and had thick mascara and black eye shadow, her dyed black hair was unkempt, and there were chunky silver rings on all of her fingers. A black-and-white border collie lay on the ground next to her. The girl grinned up at him and mimed smoking a cigarette just in case he'd missed the question.

Nightingale held up his burning cigarette. "You know these things'll give you cancer?" he said.

"Everybody dies," said the girl. She couldn't have been more than twenty-five, thought Nightingale. "Sooner or later."

"But some sooner than others," agreed Nightingale. He took out his packet of Marlboros and offered her one. "Don't say I didn't warn you."

She took one and smiled up at him. "Got a light?"

Nightingale held out his lighter and flicked a flame. She cupped it with her left hand as she lit her cigarette. One of her rings was a strange cross, curved into a loop at the top.

"You're going to hell, Jack Nightingale," said the girl, her hand touching his.

Nightingale jerked his hand back. The dog flinched and then looked at Nightingale mournfully, its tail twitching from side to side. "What did you say?"

"It opens the gates of hell," she said. "The ring. It's an ankh. The symbol of eternal life. Do you want to buy it? You can give it to your girlfriend."

"I don't have a girlfriend."

"Boyfriend then."

"I'm not gay."

"Just lonely?"

Nightingale straightened up and looked at her as he took a long drag on his cigarette. "I'm not that lonely that I need a dog for company," he said.

The girl stroked the collie. "He's not company, he's protection," she said.

"He doesn't look that fierce," said Nightingale.

"You'd be surprised," she said. "Things aren't always the way they seem. Where are you going?"

Nightingale shrugged. "I don't know."

"Don't know, or won't tell?"

Nightingale flicked ash onto the floor. "I've a lot on my mind," he said.

"You can think too much, you know," she said. "Sometimes you've just got to go with the flow. Que sera, sera. Whatever will be, will be."

Nightingale took out his wallet. "You sleep rough?" he asked.

"I don't sleep much, really," she said. Nightingale handed her a twenty-pound note but she shook her head. "I'm not begging," she said.

"Buy the dog something. A bone. Whatever."

The dog's tail twitched as if he understood what Nightingale was saying. "He's not begging, either." The girl flashed him a grin and grabbed the note. "But there's no point in looking a gift horse in the mouth, is there?" The note disappeared into her leather jacket.

"I never understood that saying," said Nightingale.

"It's about checking teeth, to see if the horse you've been given is a good one or not. It'd be like me checking to see if the money you've just given me was fake or not. That'd be looking a gift horse in the mouth." She stroked the dog as she talked. Her fingernails were painted black, and they were long and pointed, almost talons. She saw him looking at them and she held up her right hand. "You like?"

"They're distinctive."

She curled her fingertips and admired the nails. "Do you want me to scratch you?" she said.

"What?"

"That's what guys say when they see my nails. They say they wonder what it would be like to have their backs scratched by them. Is that what you were thinking?"

It was exactly what Nightingale had been thinking, but he shook his head.

"Why is it do you think that guys really want girls to hurt them?"

"I'm not sure that's true," said Nightingale.

"It is, believe me," said the girl. She started stroking the dog again. "I think guys like to be treated like dogs. You stroke them, you feed them and exercise them, but then you have to punish them every now and again to show them who's the boss."

Nightingale chuckled. "Well, good luck with that philosophy," he said. He waved and walked on.

"You take care," she called after him.

"You too," said Nightingale. He smoked his Marlboro as he walked away, deep in thought. That was twice now he thought he'd heard someone tell him that he was going to hell. The constable at Gosling Manor, and now the girl with the dog. Was he imagining it? It was what Simon Underwood screamed in the dream, just before he went through the window. But that was a dream, or a nightmare, and now he was wide awake, albeit a bit drunk. He smiled to himself. "Maybe I'm just going crazy," he muttered to himself.

"We're all crazy," said a gruff voice.

Nightingale jumped. There was homeless man sitting in the doorway of a hardware shop, nursing a bottle of cider. He was in his sixties with long gray hair and a straggly beard dotted with crumbs, and he had wads of newspaper tied around his legs with string.

"The whole world's gone crazy," said the man, waving his cider bottle at Nightingale. "God's abandoned us and the Lord Jesus doesn't care anymore. They're letting us wallow in our sins until the end of days."

"Sounds about right," said Nightingale. He took out his wallet, gave the man a ten-pound note, and carried on down the road.

Nightingale hadn't lied when he'd told Jenny McLean that he wasn't going to drive. And he'd meant what he'd said about wanting some fresh air, even though the first thing he'd done after he'd left the wine bar was to light a cigarette. Nor had he been lying when he'd told the girl in the shop doorway that he didn't know where he was going. So far as he was concerned, he was doing just as he'd promised, taking a walk while he collected his thoughts. But his subconscious had other plans for him, and his walk took him to his car and thirty minutes later he was driving through East London and ten minutes after that he was parking outside the graveyard where his parents were buried and wondering why he had never visited their graves since the day of the funeral.

He climbed out of his MGB and locked the door, then stuck his hands into the pockets of his raincoat and walked toward the ivy-covered stone arch that led to the churchyard. The house where Nightingale had been brought up as a child was a mile from the weathered gray stone church but the only time he had been there was on the day of his parents' funeral. They had never shown any interest in religion and Nightingale had been surprised to find that they had bought the twin burial plot just three years before their untimely death, crushed in their car by a fuel tanker driver who later swore that he hadn't seen the red traffic lights and hadn't seen their car. He hadn't been drinking and he tested negative for drugs and his tachometer showed that he'd only been driving for four hours before the accident. The coroner put it down to a fatal lapse in concentration and the driver ended up serving two years in prison for causing death by careless driving. It was just one of those things, everyone had said at the funeral and the reception afterwards—they had just been in the wrong place at the wrong time.

There was a wooden gate set into the arch and it creaked as Nightingale pushed it open. A black painted sign topped by a cross announced the name of the church and that the vicar was the Reverend T. Smith and that there would be a bring-and-buy sale in aid of the church roof restoration fund the following Wednesday.

It was starting to get dark and there were no lights on inside the church. As Nightingale followed the path around to the right of the building, a halogen security light clicked on, illuminating the graves to his right. A second light clicked on as he continued to walk, and elongated shadows writhed over the gravestones. The stained-glass windows were covered over with wire mesh and there was anti-climbing paint on the drainpipes. Nightingale suspected that local thieves had more to do with the need for restoring the roof than simple wear and tear.

The graves he was looking for were at the far end of the graveyard, close to the boundary wall and shaded by a spreading willow tree. There was a single black marble headstone with the names William and Irene Nightingale, their dates of birth and the date they'd died, and above them, optimistically, Living Together In

Eternity. It was the first time that Nightingale had seen the gravestone. On the day of the funeral there had just been a hole in the ground and the Astroturf strips covering the mud and a pile of earth ready to be shoveled back in. Nightingale remembered little about the service. He was nineteen years old and if he'd been asked back then whether he believed in God he'd have laughed scornfully and probably refused even to answer. If he'd been asked the same question now, fourteen years later, the laugh would have been more ironic and he still probably wouldn't have bothered to answer. He looked down at the grave. "Funny old world, innit?" he said out loud. Off in the distance an owl hooted. The two security lights clicked off. There was an almost full moon overhead and the sky was clear of clouds so there was enough light to see by. A cold breeze from behind made him shiver so he turned up the collar of his coat and put his hands back in his pockets. His right hand found his cigarette lighter and he held it like a talisman. "Why did you never tell me that you weren't my real parents?" he said softly, directing his words at the gravestone. His breath feathered in the cold night air. "I wouldn't have loved you any less. You'll always be Mum and Dad to me. No matter what."

The owl hooted again. Nightingale sighed. What he was doing made no sense to him. He didn't believe in ghosts, he didn't believe in an afterlife, and he sure as hell didn't believe that he could talk to his long-dead parents.

"This is crazy," he said. "I'm crazy. The whole thing is crazy." He took out his lighter and his pack of Marlboros and lit a cigarette. "I know, I smoke too much," he said. "And I drink. I'm a big boy now." He took a deep lungful of smoke, held it, and then exhaled slowly, aiming it at the marble headstone. "Did you know Gosling? Did you know he was my real father? Is that why you never said anything? Is that why you never told me that I was adopted?"

Nightingale felt his neck stiffen and he pushed his head back and looked up at the sky. High overhead a passenger jet was moving across the night sky, its red and green navigation lights flashing. Nightingale rubbed the back of his neck with his left hand. He could feel the tension in the muscles, the tendons as taut as steel cables.

"Can I help you?" asked a voice.

Nightingale jumped, his left foot slipped on the grass, and he fell sideways. His arms flailed as he fought to keep his balance and he cursed loudly. He turned to see a middle-aged vicar in a long clerical robe and a brass cross around his neck who seemed as shocked as Nightingale was. "You scared the life out of me," said Nightingale, patting himself in the chest.

"I'm sorry," said the vicar. "I thought you'd heard me walking along the path. I wasn't exactly on tiptoe." He had the look of an ex-boxer, with a squarish jaw and a slightly flattened nose, and while he was a good six inches shorter than Nightingale he was heavyset and had thick forearms that bulged through his clerical garb. His light brown hair was flecked with gray and receding, and while he studied Nightingale with unflinching pale blue eyes he had the smile of a kindly uncle.

"I was…deep in thought," said Nightingale. "Miles away."

"I saw the lights go on, and we've had a lot of problems recently," said the vicar. "When times are good, we have vandalism most weekends, when times are bad it's all we can do to keep the lead on the roof."

"I'm sorry, I guess I shouldn't be here," said Nightingale. He pointed at the grave. "My parents. I wanted to…" He shrugged. "Actually I'm not sure what I wanted."

"You're not a regular at my church, are you?"

"I'm afraid not. Sorry. A lost sheep."

"No one is ever truly lost," said the vicar. "The shepherd will always welcome you back." He extended his hand. "Timothy. Timothy Smith."

Nightingale shook hands with the vicar. "Jack." He nodded at the stone. "Jack Nightingale. My parents."

The vicar looked at the headstone. "Fourteen years ago," he said. "How time passes."

Nightingale looked at the vicar, but the face wasn't familiar. He didn't remember much about the funeral. He remembered sitting on a hard pew next to his aunt and uncle, and he remembered Uncle Tommy telling him how to drop a handful of earth into the grave, and he remembered how muddy it was and how he hadn't been able to bring himself to clean his shoes for at least a month after the funeral. But he didn't remember the face of the man who had conducted the service, or anything that he'd said at the time. "You knew my parents?"

"Of course," said the vicar. "They were regular churchgoers."

"Not while I was at home," said Nightingale. "I never remember them taking me."

The vicar nodded. "They had only been coming for about a year before they died."

"I would have been at university," said Nightingale. "It's funny, I never knew that they were religious."

"People do turn more to religion as they get older," said the vicar. "As they become more aware of their own mortality, they start looking for solutions."

"Lifelines?" said Nightingale.

"Perhaps," said the vicar. "We take our converts where we can."

Nightingale held up his cigarette. "Is it okay to smoke?"

The vicar smiled. "Of course." He gestured at the church. "But not inside, we're covered by Health and Safety regulations these days." He looked wistfully at the cigarette in Nightingale's hand.

"You smoke?" asked Nightingale.

"I try not to," said the vicar. "And every year I give it up for Lent." Nightingale offered the pack to the vicar. He took one and Nightingale lit it for him. "They always make me feel like a cowboy, Marlboros," the vicar said.

"It was the pack that got me started on them," said Nightingale. "Took me a while to get used to the smoke."

The two men inhaled and blew smoke up at the moon.

"Can I ask you a question?" said Nightingale.

"Of course," said the vicar. "Anything but geography. I was always bad at geography. How's anyone supposed to remember all those capital cities?"

Nightingale chuckled. "It's a bit more esoteric than that," he said. "I wanted to ask you if you believed in the devil."

The vicar frowned. "If one believes in the Lord, you have to believe in the devil. The two come as a package deal, if you like."

"Horns and a forked tail and a pitchfork?"

"Not necessarily," said the vicar. "But who can doubt that there is evil in the world?"

"I believe in evil. But is it evil within men, or is evil an outside force that corrupts?"

"When there was only Adam and Eve there was no evil. Evil came from without."

"Because Satan introduced the serpent into Paradise? You believe in all that?"

"It's not my faith that needs examining, is it? What exactly is it that's troubling you, Jack?"

Nightingale smiled ruefully. "You don't want to go there."

"Try me," said the vicar. "One smoker to another."

Nightingale shrugged. "I'm not sure I know what's going on. What's real and what's an irrational fear." He took a drag on his cigarette and blew smoke. "Is it possible to sell your soul?"

"To the devil?"

Nightingale nodded. The vicar took a long drag on his cigarette. "Tough question," he said. "Tougher than geography."

"Is that your way of saying you don't have an answer?"

"I'll have a stab at it," said the vicar, flicking ash onto the path. He took a deep breath. "We talk of giving one's life to Christ, so there must also be misguided individuals who give themselves over to evil."

"And would such a deal be irrevocable?"

"A person can always change his mind. The history of the Church is filled with conversions." He took a drag on his cigarette. "Looks like I'm a smoker again."

"Once a smoker, always a smoker," said Nightingale. "What if there was a contract? A contract with the devil."

The vicar looked pained. "It's more a case of coming to believe that Jesus Christ is our Lord the Savior."

"I understand that, but I'm not talking about a contract with Christ. I'm talking about doing a deal with the other side. The dark side. What if your soul is promised to the devil?"

"I think you're being too literal, Jack," said the vicar. "One no more signs a contract with the devil than one does with Jesus. It's not a matter of signing on the dotted line. It's a matter of belief." He dropped his cigarette butt onto the path and squashed it with his foot.

"And do you believe in hell?"

"As a concept?"

"As a place."

The vicar chuckled. "There, you see now, I told you not to go asking me about geography."

"You've very good at avoiding questions," said Nightingale. "You'd be a nightmare to interrogate."

"You're a police officer?" asked the vicar.

"In a previous life," said Nightingale. "So is there a hell, or not? And if there is, where is it?"

"Scripture doesn't give us an exact location," said the vicar. "It's a place of real torment that may or may not have a physical location in this universe. A black hole maybe. Or it might be in another dimension, a place we move to after death."

"You believe that?"

"I believe in God, of course. It'd be difficult to do this job if I didn't. And I believe that we go from this life to be with God."

"But where?" asked Nightingale. "Where do we go?"

"Heaven," said the vicar. "That's what the Bible says."

"But where is heaven?"

The vicar smiled. "There you go," he said. "Geography again." He put a hand on Nightingale's shoulder. "I'm sorry I can't answer all your questions, I know how frustrating that can be. So far as I'm concerned, as a Christian, it's less important where heaven is than it is to know that one day I'll be there."

"I suppose so," said Nightingale. He realized that there was no way the vicar could answer his question. No one could.

"The Church doesn't have all the answers," said the vicar. "There has to be faith. Belief is about faith."

"And that's the problem," said Nightingale. "I'm a bit short of both at the moment."

CHAPTER

19

Nightingale lit a cigarette as he steered the MGB with one hand. The vicar hadn't been much help but then Nightingale hadn't expected that he would be. He hadn't gone to the graveyard for spiritual guidance. Truth be told, he had no idea why he'd gone. The questions he needed answering could only be answered by his parents, and they were dead. Dead and buried.

He wound down his window and blew smoke as he drove. There was no proof that he was adopted. It could all turn out to be some perverse mistake, that Ainsley Gosling had been mistaken or had chosen Nightingale to be the victim of some beyond-the-grave hoax. Fathers didn't sell the souls of their children to the devil, not in the twentieth century or the twenty-first. Not in any century. But until Robbie came back with the results of the DNA analysis, Nightingale had no way of knowing whether Gosling really was his biological father.

A blue light flashed in his rearview mirror. Nightingale looked up and swore when he saw the police car behind him. He hadn't been speeding but the car had weaved a little while he was lighting the cigarette. The siren blipped and Nightingale swore again. He indicated, pulled over, and switched off the engine. The police car pulled up behind him and two constables got out. Nightingale gritted his teeth and stubbed out his cigarette. They'd smell the alcohol on his breath, without a shadow of a doubt. He leaned over and flicked open the glove compartment and groped around for the pack of Wrigleys chewing gum that he always kept there. He unwrapped two sticks and slotted them into his mouth, then opened the door and climbed out of the car, keeping his hands where the policemen could see them. "Sorry, guys, I wasn't speeding was I?"

The younger of the two men was in his midtwenties and holding a Breathalyzer machine. The older constable did the talking. "Have you been drinking, sir?" he asked.

"A few beers, a few hours ago," said Nightingale. Even with the spearmint gum he knew he wouldn't get away with a complete denial. He took out his wallet and showed them his private investigator identification. "Guys, I know this won't cut me any slack, but I used to be in the job."

"If you were in the job, you'd know that there's no slack to be cut," said the policeman. "We're going to need a sample of your breath to ascertain if you have been drinking. If you are unable or unwilling to provide such a sample we will take you to the station where a blood or urine sample will be taken."

Nightingale raised his hands in surrender. He knew there was no point in arguing. "No problem," he said.

The younger policeman handed him the Breathalyzer unit and showed him what to do. Nightingale took a deep breath, then blew slowly into the tube. The red light winked on accusingly and the policeman grinned in triumph.

The older policeman told Nightingale that he was being arrested but Nightingale wasn't listening. It was his own fault, no one had forced him to drink and drive, he'd made the choice and now he was going to have to pay the penalty for his stupidity.

"You're going to hell, Jack Nightingale," said the younger policeman, putting a hand on his shoulder. His voice was cold and flat, devoid of all emotion.

"What?" said Nightingale.

"I said we'll secure your car and drive you to the station, Sir. Please give me the keys." His voice had returned to normal.

Nightingale shook his head. "What did you say, just then?"

The younger constable looked over at his colleague. "Drunk as a skunk," he said.

"I'm not drunk," said Nightingale. "I've been drinking but I'm not drunk. Now what did you say about me going to hell?"

"There's no need for offensive language, sir," said the older policeman, taking hold of Nightingale's left arm.

"I wasn't being offensive," said Nightingale. "I just want to know what he said."

"He said we're going to have to secure your vehicle. You can come back and get it once we've done the paperwork back at the station and you're fit to drive. Now please don't give us any more trouble." The policeman tightened his grip on Nightingale's arm.

Nightingale said nothing. He handed over his keys and let them lead him to the police car.

20

A bored custody sergeant made Nightingale empty his pockets, checked his driving license, and then asked him if he suffered from any medical problems. "I'm fine," said Nightingale. The sergeant went through a list of diseases and illnesses, methodically ticking them off as Nightingale shook his head. "Do you think you might self-harm?" asked the sergeant. He was in his late forties, with thick graying hair and a wide jaw.

"Do I what?" asked Nightingale.

"Do you think you might hurt yourself?" He tapped the form. "I have to ask."

"What if I said I yes? What if I said I was going to hurt myself?"

"Then we'll have to leave the cell door open and I'll have to get a constable to sit outside and watch you."

"All night?"

"For as long as you're in custody."

"That's crazy, isn't it?"

"It's the rule," said the sergeant. "We've only got CCTV in two of the cells and they're both taken."

"I don't see why you need to keep me here in the first place. Can't you just bail me and send me on my way?"

"We have to be sure that you won't go back and drive your vehicle while still intoxicated."

"What if I crossed my heart and swore to God that I'll go right home?"

The sergeant shook his head. "You'll be here for a few hours," he said. "It's procedure. You were showing at twice the legal limit."

"I tell you what," said Nightingale. "If you let me keep my cigarettes and get me a cup of coffee, I'll promise not to self-harm."

"No cigarettes in the cell, but I can let you have a smoke in the yard when you want one," said the sergeant. "The coffee isn't a problem, but I warn you now it tastes like dishwater."

"So long as it's got caffeine in it, I'll be happy. And so long as I'm happy, I won't be self-harming."

Both men turned as they heard a commotion at the entrance to the custody suite. Three uniformed officers were half dragging, half carrying a man who was cursing and shouting. The man was in his twenties, wearing faded jeans, trainers, and a torn T-shirt that was flecked with blood. He was struggling with the three policeman and while they were all much bigger than him they were clearly having trouble keeping him under control. "The devil made me do it!" shouted the man, spittle spraying from his lips. "Don't you see? Don't you understand?"

"What's the story, lads?" asked the custody sergeant.

"Assault with a deadly weapon, Sarge," said one of the constables. "He was charging down the High Street with a samurai sword, hitting anyone he saw. Cut three women and almost took the arm off a pub doorman."

"Where's the sword now?" asked the sergeant.

"In the van," said the oldest of the three constables. He was wearing a stab-proof vest and black gloves. There was a cut across his cheek.

"Did he do that to you?" asked the sergeant.

The constable nodded. "With his nails, after we took the sword off him."

The man struggled and swore and the three officers wrestled him to the floor. Two held him by the arms while the third lay across his legs.

"Has he been drinking?" asked the custody sergeant.

"Can't smell it on his breath," said the constable who was holding his legs.

"Must be drugs then," said the sergeant. "Either that or just plain crazy." He walked over and stood looking down at the man. "What have you taken?" he asked. "Amphetamines? Cocaine? Tell us and we can help you."

"Fuck you!" screamed the man. He spat at the sergeant and phlegm flecked across his tunic. The sergeant took a step back. "Put him in number three," he said. "And use restraints until he's calmed down."

Two of the constables lifted the man up, holding an arm each, while the third kept a tight grip on his legs. "Just calm down and you walk under your own steam, right?" said the officer holding the man's legs. "But you keep struggling like this and we'll have to Taser you, okay? For your own safety. You keep fighting us and you're the only one who'll get hurt."

The man ignored the officer. He stared at Nightingale and grinned manically. "You understand, don't you?"

Nightingale stared back at the man. His eyes were red and watering and burning with a fierce intensity.

"You believe in the devil, don't you? You know what he can do. Tell them. Tell them that the devils are here, making us do their work for them!"

Nightingale looked away.

"Tell them!" screamed the man, lunging at Nightingale. "Tell them, you bastard!"

The three constables grappled the man, lifted him off his feet, and carried him, still screaming, toward the cells.

"It's a full moon in a few days," said the custody sergeant, using a tissue to wipe the phlegm off his tunic. "It always brings out the crazies. They might not sprout claws and fangs but the moon sure does do something to them."

"Tell me about it," said Nightingale. "When I was a negotiator we always had a higher workload when the moon was full. More assaults, more rapes, more suicides, more everything."

The sergeant picked up Nightingale's driving license and frowned at it. "You're not *the* Jack Nightingale, are you?" he said.

"I'm *a* Jack Nightingale."

"Inspector, right?"

"In another life, yeah," said Nightingale. "Have we met?"

"You came out to a wannabe jumper when I was on the beat in Kilburn," said the sergeant, handing back the license. "Asylum seeker who said he'd kill himself if he wasn't given leave to remain. You spent the best part of five hours talking him down. You were a big smoker then, I remember. I was sent out to buy you a pack of Marlboros."

"Thanks for that," said Nightingale.

The older of the two policemen who had arrested Nightingale walked into the custody suite. The custody sergeant waved him over. "Hey, Bill, did you know that Mr. Nightingale here was a celebrity?"

The officer shrugged carelessly. "He said he used to be in the job, yeah."

"He was a negotiator, one of the best," said the custody sergeant. He nodded at Nightingale. "And CO19, right?"

"For my sins, yeah."

"He's the one who threw the pedophile banker out of the window in Canary Wharf," said the custody sergeant.

"Allegedly," said Nightingale.

"Are you serious?" said the officer, suddenly interested.

"He was fiddling with his daughter," said the custody sergeant.

"More than fiddling," said Nightingale. "He'd been raping her for years."

"Bastard," said the officer.

"The mother knew what was going on, didn't she?" asked the custody sergeant.

"I think so," said Nightingale.

"How could a mother let that happen to her kid?" asked the custody sergeant.

Nightingale shook his head. "It's beyond me," he said.

"What happened to the little girl?" asked the officer.

"She died," said Nightingale flatly.

"Offed herself," said the custody sergeant. "Poor little thing." He pushed Nightingale's cigarettes and lighter across the counter. "I've a lot of respect for what you did, Jack," he said. "That bastard deserved it."

Nightingale pocketed the pack of Marlboros and slid the lighter into his trouser pocket. "Thanks," he said.

"I'll get you a coffee sent in and we'll have you out of here as soon as possible."

"Thanks, Sergeant."

True to his word, the custody sergeant brought Nightingale a cup of coffee about half an hour after he'd been placed in a cell. "I sent one of the lads out for Starbucks," said the sergeant. "Thought I'd save you the canteen rubbish."

"I appreciate it," said Nightingale, taking the cup from him.

"Probably your first time on this side of a cell door," said the sergeant.

Nightingale nodded. "That's true enough." He was sitting on the bed, a concrete block on which there was a blue plastic mattress. To the right of the door was a toilet without a seat.

"Do you want a blanket or something?"

"I'm fine," said Nightingale.

The sergeant started to leave, then he stopped. Nightingale could see that he wanted to say something. "After the guy went through the window...?" said the sergeant.

"Yes?"

"There were no...ramifications?"

"I left the Force," said Nightingale.

"But you weren't charged?"

Nightingale shrugged. "There was no evidence. No witnesses, no CCTV. And I said nothing."

The sergeant smiled. "Always the best way," he said. "Especially when dealing with the rubber heels." Rubber heels was the nickname of the Professional Standards Department, the cops who investigated other cops. "And now you're a private investigator? Pays well, does it?"

"Pays okay," said Nightingale. "But there's no pension and not much in the way of perks."

"You miss the job?"

Nightingale sipped his coffee before answering. "I miss the job, but I don't miss all the crap I had to wade through to do it."

"A lot of the guys, they're saying they wish they had the balls to do what you did."

Nightingale shrugged but didn't say anything.

The sergeant looked as if he wanted to say more, but he just nodded and left. Nightingale sat on the bed and stared at the wall as he drank his coffee.

It was just after half past five in the morning when the custody sergeant unlocked the cell door again. He gave Nightingale a printed sheet informing him of his court date and told him that he was free to go. "Are you going home?" he asked.

"I thought I'd go get my car," said Nightingale.

"Why don't you have another puff in the Breathalyzer first," said the sergeant. "I wouldn't want you picked up again. They'd probably blame me for letting you out too soon."

Nightingale gave another breath sample, and this time he was below the limit. "Is there a minicab firm I can use?" asked Nightingale.

The sergeant nodded at a row of orange plastic seats. "Sit yourself down, I'll see if I can arrange something," he said. He went over to his counter and spent a few minutes on the phone, then he called Nightingale over. "Two of our guys will run you out," he said. Nightingale thanked him. "All part of the service, Jack," he said.

CHAPTER

Nightingale got home just after eight o'clock in the morning. He let himself into the house, made himself a cup of coffee, and phoned Robbie Hoyle. "What's wrong?" said Hoyle.

"Maybe I just wanted a chat.""

"It's Saturday morning. Early Saturday morning. My day of rest. Yours too. So I'm guessing there's something wrong."

"You should be a detective," said Nightingale.

"Yeah, so should you," said Hoyle. "Now what's wrong?"

"I was pulled in for drunk driving last night."

"Oh shit," said Hoyle. "Did you hit anyone?"

"No, nothing like that. I had a few beers and they Breathalyzed me."

"You stupid bastard," said Hoyle.

"I know, I know," said Nightingale.

"You'll lose your license, you know that?"

"That's why I'm calling, Robbie."

"Come on, Jack, you know there's nothing I can do if you're in the system. Not these days."

"I wasn't asking you to pull strings," said Nightingale. "I need a brief, a good one. Who's hot on drunk driving right now? There's got to be something that could sway the court. Former officer of the law, under a lot of stress, father just committed suicide, I'm thinking mitigating circumstances."

"I'll ask around," said Hoyle. "Are you okay?"

"I'm fine, just kicking myself."

"Do you want to come around tomorrow? Anna's doing a roast."

"Maybe, mate. Let me see how my hangover shapes up."

"If you need anything, let me know," said Hoyle.

"Just get me that lawyer, mate," said Nightingale. "If I lose my license I'll be well screwed."

CHAPTER

22

Nightingale spent most of Saturday asleep. He woke up at six o'clock in the evening, cooked himself eggs and bacon, and made himself a coffee, then watched Sky News as he ate. A large computer company had sacked two thousand workers, two High Street retailers had gone into receivership, and unemployment was heading toward four million. The pound was continuing to slump, the stock market was in the doldrums, and the tame economist that Sky had wheeled out said things would get worse before they improved.

When he'd finished eating he sat with his feet on the coffee table, flicking through his hundred or so cable channels but unable to find anything that held his attention. He switched off his television and stared at the sideboard. There were a dozen photographs in various-sized frames standing on top. There was his graduation picture, wearing a robe and mortar board, his passing out picture at Hendon Police College, a photograph of Robbie and Annie on their wedding day, and standing to the right in a small group, three photographs of his parents. He stared at the family portraits. The middle one of the three was a wedding photograph, his mother all in white and holding a spray of flowers, his father in a gray suit, his arm around her waist. He was thirty-two when he married, and Nightingale's mother had just turned twenty-five. She was pretty, with curly black hair and green eyes that suggested Irish ancestry and a sprinkling of freckles across her upturned nose. She was smiling up at her husband in the same way that Nightingale had seen her look at him all the way through his childhood. There had never been any doubt that she had loved her husband with all her heart. The photograph to the right of that one was a little smaller and set into a silver frame. It was the first picture of Nightingale as a baby, wrapped in a soft white blanket, his cheeks red and his eyes closed, held by his mother, who in turn was being held by his father, the two of them looking down at him with love and pride in their eyes. It was, Nightingale now realized, the start of the lie. He wasn't their child, he had been given to them. On the day that the photograph had been taken, they were strangers with no connection to him, no family link, no DNA, just a man and a woman who had been given a baby. The baby they were holding could have been anybody's. It just happened to be Nightingale. Everything that had happened to Nightingale after that day, everything that he had become, was all based on a lie.

The third photograph was taken outside Manchester United's Old Trafford stadium. Nightingale was just twelve years old, and he was flanked by his father and his uncle, all three of them sporting red-and-white scarves. They were on their way into the stadium to take their place in the stands. It was a few years before the stadium had been made all seating and Nightingale's father had always preferred to watch his football on his feet. A fellow supporter had taken the photograph with a camera that Nightingale's father had given him the previous Christmas.

Nightingale stared at the picture. His uncle must have known. Good old Uncle Tommy. Laughing, joking Uncle Tommy, who always turned up with a present and a card and a bear-hug every birthday and Christmas, and who'd slipped him an envelope with a thousand pounds the day Nightingale headed off to university. Good old Uncle Tommy, who must have known about the lie right from the start. And Aunty Linda. They must have both known because they'd have seen that his mother had never been pregnant and that Nightingale had appeared from nowhere. They must have both known that Nightingale was adopted, and they had never let on, not even at the funeral. They had both been there, of course, standing either side of Nightingale as the two coffins were lowered into the ground. And neither of them had ever said anything about him being adopted, not then and not since.

He stared at the photograph of the three football fans. A father, his son, and the uncle. Except that Jack Nightingale wasn't William Nightingale's son and Tommy wasn't his uncle. They were both party to the lie, and so was Nightingale's mother. Until Nightingale found out the truth, he would never be able to look at them the same way again.

CHAPTER

23

Nightingale parked his MGB in the street in front of his uncle's house, a neat three-bedroom semidetached in a tidy, predominantly middle-class area of Altrincham, to the south of Manchester. It had taken him the best part of three hours to drive from London. He climbed out, stretched, and lit a cigarette. His aunt and uncle were both ex-smokers, had been for twenty years, and refused to allow anyone else to light up anywhere near them. Uncle Tommy's black Renault Megane was parked in the driveway. Nightingale locked his MGB and walked slowly down the path to the front door, knowing that he would have to extinguish the cigarette before ringing the doorbell. The garden was well-tended, with two large rhododendron bushes on either side of a neatly mown lawn, and there was a small water feature with a quaint stone wishing well and a bearded gnome holding a fishing rod. The gnome had been there for as long as Nightingale could remember and as a child he'd always been a little scared of it, half-convinced that it was moving whenever he took his eyes off it. Nightingale flicked ash at the gnome. "How are they biting?" he asked. The gnome stared fixedly ahead at the hook on the end of its line. "Maybe you should try somewhere else." He tossed the remains of his cigarette into a flower bed, then went up to the front door and reached out to press the doorbell. He heard a rustling noise behind him and his heart raced as his childhood fears flooded back. He turned around half expecting to see the gnome coming up behind him, but it was only Walter, his aunt's black-and-white cat. The cat brushed itself against the back of Nightingale's legs and meowed. Nightingale leaned down and rubbed it behind its ears. "Long time no see, Walter," he said. The cat arched its back and purred loudly.

Nightingale straightened up and rang the doorbell. He heard a chime inside the house. Walter continued to purr and run himself against Nightingale's legs. "What's wrong, Walter, you starved of affection?" asked Nightingale. After thirty seconds he rang the bell again but no one came to answer the door. "Where are they, Walter?" said Nightingale. "Are they in the back garden, is that it?"

Nightingale walked around the side of the house and opened a wooden gate that led to the rear of the house. That was where Uncle Tommy had his vegetable patch and where he grew his prize-winning roses. As Nightingale closed the gate behind him, he noticed a red smudge on his hand. He held the hand up to his face, frowning. It looked like blood. There was no cut, just a smear of red. He checked both hands, and then the latch on the gate, but there was only the one smudge.

He walked down the path to the garden. "Uncle Tommy?" he called. "Are you out here?"

There was no answer. He knocked on the kitchen door. "Aunty Linda, it's me, Jack!"

Walter meowed and looked up at Nightingale. Nightingale knelt down and stroked the back of the cat's neck. "What's going on, Walter?" he said. There was a glistening red smudge on the cat's nose. A sudden panic gripped Nightingale and his heart began to race. He looked across at the kitchen door. Set into the bottom was a cat flap which Walter used to get in and out of the house. There were red smudges on the bottom of the flap.

Nightingale stood up and banged on the kitchen door. "Aunty Linda! Uncle Tommy! Are you in there?" He pressed his ear to the wooden door but heard nothing. He hit the door again with the flat of his hand.

He moved over to the kitchen window and stood on tiptoe as he peered through. Beyond the sink he could see a bare leg, a shattered plate, and a pool of blood. Nightingale banged on the window. "Aunty Linda! Aunty Linda!"

He looked around, wondering what he should do. He saw his uncle's shed and he ran to it, throwing open the door and grabbing a spade. He dashed back to the house and used the spade to smash the window and knock the glass out of the frame, then he climbed inside. His aunt was on the kitchen floor, her head smashed open, brains and blood congealing on the tile-patterned lino. Her mouth was wide open and her eyes stared glassily up at the ceiling. Nightingale knew immediately that there was no point in checking for signs of life.

He walked carefully around the pool of blood. There was no sign of a murder weapon and the back door had been locked, which meant that the attacker had either left by the front door or was still in the house. There was a knife block by the fridge and Nightingale pulled out a large wood-handled carving knife.

"Uncle Tommy, are you in the house?" he shouted.

He went through to the sitting room. There was an unopened copy of the *Sunday Mirror* on the coffee table, and an untouched cup of tea. Nightingale went over to the table and touched the cup. It was cold and there was a thick scum on the surface of the tea.

He moved slowly back into the hallway, listening intently. He started up the stairs, taking them one at time, craning to look up at the landing above. Halfway up the stairs was an axe, the blade covered in blood. Nightingale didn't touch it but stepped carefully over it. As he reached the top of the stairs he heard a soft creaking sound and he froze, the knife out in front of him. He took another step. There was something moving on the landing. Something just out of sight. He crept up, his mouth bone-dry, his heart pounding. He stopped again when he heard another gentle creak and then he saw something move. It was a foot. A naked foot, suspended in the air. Nightingale took another step and saw two feet, and then pajama bottoms and then as he reached the top of the stairs he saw his uncle, hanging from the trapdoor that led to the attic. There was a rope around his neck and from the unnatural angle of the head it was obvious that the neck had snapped. Nightingale realized that Uncle Tommy must have sat in the trapdoor and dropped. He was naked from the waist up and there were flecks of blood across his chest. There were no wounds on him so the blood could only have been his wife's. He must have battered his wife to death in the kitchen and then come upstairs and killed himself.

The rope creaked as the body moved slightly. He was dead but the fluids within the body were shifting as the organs settled. The pajama bottoms were wet around the groin and there was a pool of urine on the floor. Nightingale took out his cell phone and dialed emergency. As he waited for the operator to answer, he turned around. The bathroom door was wide open and through the doorway Nightingale saw the mirror above the sink. Scrawled across it in bloody capital letters were seven words. YOU ARE GOING TO HELL, JACK NIGHTINGALE.

24

Jenny was sitting at her desk, using a small mirror to read the handwritten diary, when Nightingale walked in. He opened the door to his office. "Coffee would be nice," he said. He flopped down onto his chair and put his feet up on the desk. He leaned back and stared at the ceiling. A small spider had set up home in the corner by the window and there was a layer of dust on the blinds. "When's the cleaner in next?" he called.

"She was here Friday morning," Jenny replied as she poured him coffee. "And she'll be in again tomorrow."

"Then she's doing a shit job," said Nightingale. "She's Polish, right?"

"Romanian," said Jenny. "I'll talk to her."

"Tell her to give the blinds a wipe, too."

"I hear and obey," said Jenny, appearing at the door with a mug of steaming coffee. She held it up. "Just like your women—hot and black."

Nightingale frowned. "What?"

stephen leather

"I was joking," she said, putting the mug on his desk and sitting down opposite him. "Trying to lighten the moment."

"But I've never had a black girlfriend," said Nightingale, reaching for the mug.

"That's what makes it funny. What's wrong, Jack? You look like…"

"Like I've seen a ghost?"

"Well, yes, actually."

Nightingale sipped his coffee. "My uncle killed himself yesterday. Killed himself and murdered his wife. My aunt."

Jenny's jaw dropped. "What?"

"My uncle Tommy. He hanged himself."

"Why?"

Nightingale shrugged. "He didn't leave a note. I spoke to my uncle during the week and said I'd drive up to Altrincham for Sunday lunch so they were expecting me. He sounded fine then. But when I got there, they were dead."

"Jack, that's terrible. That's…" She sat down. "I don't…it doesn't…" She shook her head. "This is unreal."

"It's real all right," said Nightingale. "I spent all yesterday talking to the Manchester cops."

"The cops?"

"It was a murder-suicide, Jenny. The cops have to investigate, but it's open and shut. My aunt's blood was all over him and she'd scratched his face. There was no one else involved."

"But why? Why would he kill his wife?"

"I've no idea. I told them I wanted to talk about my parents, whether I was adopted or not."

"And they were okay on the phone?"

"They sounded a bit nervous, but they invited me around for lunch."

"I can't believe this," said Jenny.

"I'm having trouble coming to terms with it myself," said Nightingale.

"They weren't having problems or anything?"

"I don't think so."

"Jack, you don't think this is connected to Gosling, do you?"

"It didn't occur to me, Jenny." Actually that was a lie because as soon as Nightingale had seen the bloody letters on Uncle Tommy's bathroom mirror he had known that he was in some way connected to the death of his aunt and uncle. But what he couldn't figure out was what that connection was. When he'd first seen the words scrawled in blood he'd thought that he was dreaming. He'd stared at the message in horror, imagining that at any minute he'd be in Underwood's office and the man would crash through the window and fall to his death. But it was no dream, he didn't wake up, the words were real, and his uncle and aunt were dead. Nightingale had no idea why he was hearing people telling him that he was going to hell, and he had no idea why his uncle would write the phrase on the bathroom wall before killing himself. But until he had worked out what was going on, he didn't intend to worry Jenny.

"Did you tell the police about Gosling?" Jenny asked.

"I thought it would just make a complicated situation even more complicated." Nightingale swung his legs onto his desk. "It was one hell of a weekend," he said. "I spent Friday night in the cells."

"You what?"

Nightingale sipped his coffee. "I was done for drunk driving on Friday night."

"Oh, Jack…"

"I know, I know."

"You said you weren't going to drive."

"And I wasn't. Swear to God, when I left the wine bar I had no intentions of getting behind the wheel. I don't know what came over me."

"So now what happens?"

Nightingale took another sip of his coffee. "I didn't hit anyone so I'm hoping it'll just be a fine and I'll avoid a ban. But if they do ban me I'll need to find somewhere to keep the MGB."

"I'll look after it for you," said Jenny.

"Have you got a garage?"

"I can leave it with my parents. My dad can drive it every week, keep the battery charged. Those old cars seize up if you don't drive them."

Nightingale smiled. "We call them classics rather than old cars," he said. "Does he know what he's doing?"

"He's got two old Jags and a frog-eyed Sprite. Sorry, classic Jags. And a Jensen-Healey."

"You never told me that."

"You never asked, Jack. My dad used to work for Jaguar. He was an accountant and before he retired he was on the board."

Nightingale put down his coffee mug. "You constantly amaze me," he said.

"Mutual," said Jenny.

"How goes the translation?"

Jenny shuddered. "It's full of some very weird stuff."

"How weird?"

Jenny leaned forward. "Have you got a tattoo?"

"A tattoo? What, 'I love Mum,' that sort of thing?"

"A pentangle. Either a tattoo or a mark that looks like a pentangle." She sat back in her chair. "I know, it sounds ridiculous. But according to Mitchell's diary, anyone whose soul belongs to the devil has a mark. A pentangle. Hidden somewhere on the body."

"You're right, it sounds ridiculous," said Nightingale. "I'm thirty-two years old, if I had a tattoo I'd know about it."

"So you've nothing to worry about then," said Jenny. She started to get up but Nightingale waved for her to sit back down.

"Whoa, Nellie," he said. "Are you saying that if I do have a mark then I should worry?"

"You said you haven't."

"But if I had. Do you think I'd have something to worry about?"

"I think I'm reading the ramblings of a deeply disturbed mind. A sad bastard with too much time on his hands."

Nightingale raised his coffee mug in salute. "That's my girl," he said. "You had me worried for a moment."

"Worried about what?"

"That you were starting to take this nonsense seriously." He took another sip of coffee. "Do you still have that pal at the Department for Work and Pensions?"

"Sure. Why?"

"Can you get her to run a check and see if Sebastian Mitchell is still alive and kicking?"

"If he is, he'll be in his eighties. Maybe older."

"Be nice to know if he's still around, that's all. Or if he met a sticky end, too."

CHAPTER

25

Nightingale unlocked the front door of Gosling Manor and flicked the light switch. The massive chandelier glowed with more than two dozen bulbs. He had paid the bill on Friday and the electricity company had promised to have the power reconnected over the weekend. "Excellent," he said. He switched the light off again. It wasn't yet noon and the hallway was flooded with natural light from a skylight in the double-height ceiling. He walked through to the main living room and flicked the light switches there to check that they were working, then he went back into the hall and looked up at the CCTV camera that covered the main entrance. The small red light on the side glowed weakly.

He went back into the main room and looked through the window. Something moved by the trees, a small shadow that slipped behind a massive oak tree. Nightingale stared at the tree, wondering what he'd seen. It was too tall to have been a dog or a fox, too small to have been a man. It could have been a child, but what would a child be doing on the grounds? He lit a cigarette and continued to stare at the tree. The grounds of Gosling Manor would be a magnet for local kids, he realized. Lots of trees to climb, places to build dens, and with the house empty there'd be no one to chase them off. If the house had been in the city it would have been vandalized already, the windows smashed and graffiti sprayed across the doors and walls. Even though country children were different from their inner-city counterparts, Nightingale knew that it would only be a matter of time before someone broke in. An empty house was just too tempting a target, even when it was in the middle of nowhere. He needed some sort of security at the house, either a night watchman or a security company making regular visits. If the house was vandalized or squatters moved in, it would be that much harder to sell. The grounds needed maintaining, too. The lawns were still in immaculate condition, but grass grew and it would need cutting before too long. And someone would have to rake up all the dead leaves.

Nightingale sighed. It was going to cost him a small fortune to carry out even basic maintenance on the huge house, and it was money that he didn't have. And there was bound to be a sizeable inheritance tax bill. Even if he were to sell the house quickly, once he'd paid off the mortgage and the taxman and the estate agent, he reckoned he'd be lucky to see more than a few thousand pounds. He blew smoke and for a brief moment considered setting fire to the building and claiming on the insurance. Except that there probably wasn't any insurance. Gosling hadn't taken out insurance on his mortgage payments, so Nightingale figured he almost certainly hadn't insured the house against fire.

There was no further movement around the oak tree and Nightingale turned away from the window. He went back into the hall and pulled open the panel that led down into the basement. He flicked the light switch at the top of the stairs and the fluorescent lights kicked into life. Nightingale heard a scratching sound upstairs and he froze, his hand still on the switch. For a few seconds there was only the sound of his own breathing, then he heard a meow and more scratching. "Hey, cat, get down here and I'll let you out!" shouted Nightingale. His voice echoed in the hallway. The scratching stopped. Nightingale had never been a fan of cats. He didn't like the way cats stared at people, the disdainful way they looked down their noses at human beings as if there were no doubt in their minds that cats were the superior species. Nightingale had always figured that if cats were so smart, they would be able to open their own cans of food. "Or you can stay up there and starve, the choice is yours," shouted Nightingale. Starvation wasn't an option, Nightingale knew, as there would almost certainly be a large rodent population calling Gosling Manor their home. Cats, unlike human beings, were natural survivors.

Nightingale went slowly down the stairs. The basement didn't look quite so large now that the lights were on, but it was still bigger than most small-town libraries. Unlike in the rooms upstairs, the lighting in the basement was purely functional, fluorescent tubes hanging from chains.

The exhibits in the display cases didn't look quite so eerie under the stark lights. For the first time Nightingale noticed the bare brick walls and the slightly uneven tiled floor.

The six LCD screens at the far end of the basement were blank, but as Nightingale got closer he could see small green lights showing that they were switched on. He sat down on the chair and looked at the stainless-steel console. He pushed the button labeled "MAIN ENTRANCE" but nothing happened. He tried "STUDY" but that too didn't work. Nightingale frowned. Then he noticed that there were six buttons on the top right of the console, numbered one through six. He pressed them and one by one the screens flickered into life. The two screens in the middle showed full-screen views while the others were divided into four, giving a total of eighteen shots of the house and exterior.

The lower of two main screens showed one of the upstairs corridors while the upper one showed the master bedroom. Nightingale pressed the "STUDY" button again and the master bedroom was replaced by the study. He methodically worked his way through all twenty-eight cameras. There was no sign of the cat.

There was a cupboard to the left of the desk and Nightingale opened it. Inside was a computer with slots for six DVDs. He pressed the eject button but all six were empty. If there had ever been recordings made of the CCTV feeds, they weren't there now.

Nightingale pressed the button for the view of the master bedroom and leaned back in the chair. He could just about make out the rusty-colored stain where Gosling's body had lain after he'd pulled the trigger. Had there been anyone in the basement when Gosling had killed himself? Probably not, Nightingale decided. Gosling wouldn't have wanted any witnesses. A shotgun in the mouth wasn't a cry for help, he wasn't looking for someone to talk him out of it. He just wanted to end it all. He must have dismissed the staff before killing himself.

Nightingale stared at the bed, and the chair, and the candles surrounding the circle. The circle was presumably some sort of magical protection, Gosling must have believed that he was safe if he stayed inside it and that implied that he had to be inside it all the time. But there was no food in the room, and no way of getting to the bathroom without leaving the circle. So if Gosling had been inside the circle for any length of time he must have had someone in the house to help him, to bring him food and to deal with his waste. He took out his wallet and flicked through it until he found the Neighborhood Watch card given to him by the policeman he'd met the first time he came to the house. He tapped out the number on his cell and the policeman answered on the third ring.

"Sergeant Wilde? This is Jack Nightingale, I own Gosling Manor. You were around with your colleague earlier this week."

"You can call me Harry, Jack. You outranked me when you were in the job, so it's only fair."

"Can you talk?"

"I just got home and my wife's burning my dinner as we speak, so yes, fire away. How can I help you?"

"You said that Gosling's driver let you into the house. After he found the body."

"That's right."

"Was there anyone else in the house?"

"At the time he killed himself? No. He'd sent what staff there was home the night before."

"So there were people still working there? Even though the furniture had all gone?"

"There was a skeleton staff, I think. An old woman who did the cooking and a bit of cleaning, and her husband tidied up the garden. And the driver. He doubled as a butler."

"I don't suppose you've got their phone numbers, have you?"

"Why, is there a problem?"

"No, I just need someone to keep the place clean, I thought the old staff might be the best bet," lied Nightingale. "I'm not that handy with the old mop and brush, to be honest."

"You and me both," laughed the policeman. "Look, let me have a look through my old notes. I can call you on this number?"

"Day or night," said Nightingale. He thanked the policeman and ended the call.

He wandered past the bookshelves, running his fingers along the spines of the books. He stopped at one titled *The Devil and His Works* and pulled it out. It was a large leather-bound volume published in 1924 and written by Sir Nicholas Weatherby. Nightingale wondered what a peer of the realm was doing writing a book about the devil. He flicked through to the index. There were four references to summoning the devil. The first was in the second chapter but was just a passing reference, the second and third were in the fifth chapter and were quotes about Satan in the Bible. But the fourth took up half a dozen pages in the final chapter. Nightingale took the book over to Gosling's desk and sat down to read the final chapter.

Sir Nicholas began the chapter with a stern warning about the dangers of any sort of interaction with Satanic forces. Many who tried ended up dead or deranged, and only highly experienced Satanists should ever attempt to make contact with the devil or his demons. Nightingale laughed out loud at the flowery language used by the author, a style of writing more suitable to a Barbara Cartland romance than a serious treatise on the Dark Arts.

Having warned his readers of the dire consequences of attempting to contact the devil, Sir Nicholas then gave a spell which he said guaranteed an appearance by Satan himself. "It is," said Sir Nicholas, "only to be used by a Level Nine Satanist with the protection of a Magic Circle fortified by Holy Water blessed by the Holy See himself."

Nightingale shook his head and smiled. He couldn't see how repeating a few words, none of which made any apparent sense, could achieve anything, let alone summon the devil. He stood up and in a loud voice slowly recited the first sentence. "Bagabi laca bachabe Lamc cahi achababe Karrelyos," he said. He stopped and listened but all was still. He smiled to himself. What did he expect? The stench of brimstone? A flash of lightning? It was a nonsense. "Lamac lamec Bachalyas," he continued. He paused again. He looked around the basement. Nothing had changed. It hadn't got colder, or hotter, lighter or darker. There was no sign that the words were having any effect at all. He could feel his heart racing and his mouth had gone dry even though he knew it was all a charade. He kept his finger on the page so that he wouldn't lose his place, and continued to read. "Cabahagy sabalyos Baryolas Lagoz atha cabyolas Samahac et famyolas Harrahya." When he reached the end he put down the book and stood up. "Is there anybody there?" he said. His voice echoed around the basement. "Anybody?" He grinned. "I thought not. The whole thing is bollocks." He held the book up above his head. "If it isn't bollocks, and if there really is a devil, then strike me down now, do your worst. Come on! Come on, you bastard! Do your worst!"

He caught sight of himself in an ornate gilt mirror and realized how ridiculous he was being to even entertain the idea that a few mumbled words would summon a demon from hell. He winked at his reflection. "Only joking," he said. He turned away from the mirror and walked down to the bank of surveillance monitors. Something moved on one of the small screens. A car at the entrance to the estate. Nightingale leaned over the console and pressed the button to bring up the picture on one of the big screens. He doubted that the devil would be turning up in a Ford Mondeo.

He watched Robbie Hoyle climb out of his car and walk over to the speakerphone. A handset on the left of the console buzzed and Nightingale picked it up. "Hi, Robbie," said Nightingale. "What's up?"

"How did you know it was me?" said Hoyle.

"Smile, you're on *Candid Camera*."

Hoyle looked around until he spotted the camera and he waved. "Are you going to let me in or what?"

"You're not trying to sell me something?"

"No."

"And you're not a Mormon or a Jehovah's Witness?"

"Definitely not."

"You're not the devil, are you?"

"What?"

"The devil. Can you prove that you really are Robbie Hoyle and you're not the devil in disguise."

"Don't be a prick, Jack. Jenny told me you were here, she said we should talk."

"I'll take that as a no."

Nightingale looked at the console but couldn't see a button that operated the gates. He took the handset away from his head. There was a single button below the mouthpiece and he pushed it. On the screen the gates began to open. "Thank you so much," said Hoyle, and he walked back to the car. Nightingale replaced the handset and went back up the stairs.

Hoyle was still just halfway down the drive when Nightingale opened the front door. Hoyle parked the car in front of the house next to Nightingale's MGB and climbed out. "Are you okay?" asked Hoyle.

"What did the lovely Miss McLean tell you?"

"That your uncle killed his wife then offed himself."

"That's pretty much it."

"Bloody hell, Jack. What happened?"

Nightingale shrugged. "I've no idea. I spoke to them on the phone and they were okay. I drove up on Sunday and she was dead in the kitchen and he was hanging from the attic."

Hoyle walked into the hall. "Jack, you look like shit."

"Thanks." Nightingale shut the door behind them. "There was something weird, Robbie. Something I didn't tell Jenny." Nightingale sighed. "My uncle wrote something on the bathroom mirror before he killed himself. In blood."

"You're serious?"

"Do I look like I'm joking?" He took a deep breath. "He wrote that I'd be going to hell."

"You, specifically?"

"'You are going to hell, Jack Nightingale.' That's what he wrote."

"In blood?"

"In blood," repeated Nightingale. "In my aunt's blood. His wife."

"He wrote that in blood and then hanged himself?"

Nightingale nodded.

"That's sick."

"The whole thing is sick," said Nightingale.

"Why would he write that?"

"I don't know, Robbie. But…"

"But what?"

Nightingale shook his head. He had been about to tell his friend about the dreams he'd been having and that the words written in blood were Simon Underwood's last words before he went through the window of his office, but he knew how crazy that would sound so he bit his tongue. "Nothing," he said.

"And what did the police say about what he wrote?"

Nightingale shrugged. "They didn't see it."

"What?"

"I cleaned the mirror before they got there."

"Are you mad? Tampering with evidence in a murder case. They'll throw away the key."

"Only if they find out. And you're the only person I've told. No one else knows."

"Even so, Jack. You can't do that. It's evidence."

"He killed her, Robbie, there's no doubt about that. The axe was on the stairs and there was blood spatter all over his chest, and he was a big man so I don't see that anyone else could have hung him from the attic. The message on the mirror would just muddy the waters, that's all." He nodded at the entrance to the basement.

"Come on, let's go downstairs." Nightingale headed down into the basement and Hoyle followed.

They reached the bottom of the stairs and Hoyle stood with his hands on his hips as he looked around. "It's a lot less intimidating with the lights on, isn't it?"

"Yeah, and the CCTV is running too so you can check out every room without leaving your seat. You still haven't said why you're here, Robbie."

"Don't get all paranoid, mate. Jenny said you were coming out here so I said I'd swing by and see what you were up to. Check that you were all right. Oh, and the DNA results came back," said Hoyle. "Ainsley Gosling is definitely your father."

"Terrific," said Nightingale.

"Is that good news or bad?"

"I'd put it at about fifty-fifty," said Nightingale. "Why would my uncle kill himself, Robbie? And why would he batter his wife to death? He loved her. They were peas in a pod, joined at the hip. Same as my parents." He grimaced. "I suppose I should start saying 'adopted parents,' now that I know Gosling was my real father."

"What did the Manchester cops say?"

"Murder-suicide, which is obviously what it was. The doors were locked, her blood was on the axe along with his fingerprints, and there was blood splatter all over him. Open and shut."

"Except no motive."

"They reckon he just snapped. It happens."

"And what about what he wrote?"

Nightingale ran his hands through his hair. "I don't know, Robbie. I just don't know."

"He must have written it for a reason," said Hoyle. "I understand why you didn't want the cops to see it, but you can't pretend it wasn't there."

"I don't know why he would have written it. He was fine when I last spoke to him."

"And why are you here? Jenny said you've a couple of cases that need work."

"Nothing that can't wait a day or two," said Nightingale. "I'm trying to find my mother. My real mother. My birth mother. I wanted to talk to my uncle about the adoption, but that avenue's been closed, so I thought I'd try to track down my birth mother. Ainsley Gosling is my genetic father, so he must have known who my birth mother was. Is." He shrugged. "See, I don't know if she's even alive anymore." He sat down on one of the sofas. "In a way, she might be the only family I've got left. And maybe she can tell me what's going on."

Hoyle looked around. "I don't suppose there's a coffee machine down here, is there?"

"Everything but," said Nightingale.

"There must be adoption records, right? If your parents adopted you there'd have to be paperwork."

"My birth certificate has Bill and Irene Nightingale down as the parents, there's nothing to say that I was adopted. And according to the DVD that Gosling left me, I was given to them at birth. I don't think there was any agency involved."

"That's illegal."

"It was thirty-three years ago, I don't think everything was as computerized as it is now. And I get the feeling that Gosling wasn't too concerned about the legality of what he was doing. I think he just got the baby, his baby, and gave it to the Nightingales and they passed it off as their own." He waved his arm around the basement. "I think the answer is somewhere here. Gosling must have kept records, and this is his hidey hole, so I want to see what I can find." He pointed to the middle of the basement. "I'm going to start with those filing cabinets there but I'll go through every single book in this place if I have to."

"Looking for what, exactly?"

"I don't know, Robbie. But he was a rich man so he must have kept track of what he was spending. Everyone does, right? You keep receipts and bank statements and bills."

"Anna looks after the finances," said Hoyle. "But yeah, I know what you mean."

"So I think Gosling must have paid someone to help him with the adoption. He couldn't have done the whole thing himself. If I can find his records for the year when I was born, I might find a clue as to who my real mother was." He smiled ruefully. "I keep saying that. Real mum. As if Irene Nightingale was some sort of fake. She wasn't, she was my mum and she'll always be my mum, no matter how this pans out." He flicked ash onto the floor. "Shouldn't you be at work?"

"Late shift," said Hoyle.

"Do you want to make yourself useful?"

Hoyle nodded. "That's why I'm here."

CHAPTER

26

Nightingale found Ainsley Gosling's financial records in six beech filing cabinets between a display case full of ivory carvings and a seaman's chest with a lock that had gone rusty with age and which defied all his attempts to open it. Gosling had been methodical with his record-keeping with separate files for each quarter going back to 1936. Nightingale pulled out the three most recent files and took them over to a desk where Hoyle was pouring over a leather-bound book the size of a small coffee table which been filled with newspaper clippings. Hoyle looked up. "He was interested in serial killers," said Hoyle. "Fred West, the Yorkshire Ripper, Harold Shipman, he followed all their cases."

"Everyone should have a hobby," said Nightingale, dropping the files onto the desk. "These are his most recent financial records, can you see what he was up to in the months before he died?"

Hoyle closed the massive scrapbook and picked up one of the files as Nightingale went back to the filing cabinets. The records for the year he was born were in the third cabinet. He pulled out the four files and took them over to the desk.

"He was buying books, big time," said Hoyle, holding up a receipt from a Hamburg book store. "He paid a million and a half euros for something called *The Formicarius* in January."

"A million and a half euros for a book? It's no wonder all his money went."

"Published in 1435, according to this. But that's just one book. There's another receipt here for six hundred thousand dollars, another for a quarter of a million pounds. A stack of receipts from China that I can't read. And from the look of it, they were all about witchcraft or demonology. Occult stuff." Hoyle pointed at the bookshelves. "That's where all his money went. He spent millions putting this library together."

Nightingale put the files on the desk. "He wasn't building a library. He was buying information."

"I don't follow you," said Hoyle.

"He didn't care about the books, he wanted the information in them." Nightingale sat down in a leather winged chair. "Here's what I think. He did a deal with the devil when I was born. Or at least he thought he did a deal."

"Jack…"

Nightingale held up a hand to silence his friend. "Whether he did or he didn't isn't the issue, what matters is what was going through his mind. And so far as he was concerned, he'd gone and sold my soul. Then as he said on the DVD, he had a change of heart. He wanted out of the deal, but for that he needed information." He waved at the bookshelves. "So that's what he bought. Information. He thought the answer lay somewhere in those books."

"You're not starting to believe this mumbo jumbo, are you?"

"I'm trying to empathize with Gosling," said Nightingale. "I'm trying to think the way he was thinking. If I can get inside his head, maybe I can make sense of this. Maybe I can work out why he killed himself."

"What does it matter why he killed himself?"

Nightingale shrugged. "He was my father."

"In name only," said Hoyle. "You never knew him. Why does it matter? And why are you looking for your genetic mother?"

Nightingale didn't reply.

"You think this all might be true, don't you?" asked Hoyle quietly.

"Don't be soppy," said Nightingale.

"You want to ask her, that's what this is all about. You want to ask her if Ainsley Gosling sold your soul to the devil."

Nightingale shook his head and opened one of the files. It was full of bank statements, used checkbooks, and receipts. "I don't think he sold my soul. But I think he believed that he did. There's a difference. Besides, I haven't got a mark."

"What do you mean, a mark?"

Nightingale sighed. "They say that if your soul belongs to the devil, you carry a mark. Like a tattoo."

"They? Who the hell is they?"

"The people who believe in this crap," said Nightingale. "It was in that book that I took with me last time. It was written by some top Satanist. In the book he says that if the devil has your soul, you have a pentangle tattoo somewhere on your body. And I haven't. You've seen me in the changing rooms enough time."

"That's true. Not a pretty sight, it has to be said."

"But no pentangle. So it's all bollocks." He flicked through one of the checkbooks. The dates in it were from the year that Nightingale was born.

"Damn right, it's bollocks," said Hoyle. He held up another receipt. "He bought a dozen books from a shop in New Orleans, for a total of half a million dollars. All of them about Voodoo. You know, you should be able to sell these books, you'd make a fortune."

"Assuming I can find someone crazy enough to buy them," said Nightingale. He handed the checkbook across the desk to Hoyle. "Thirty-three years ago, Ainsley Gosling paid twenty thousand pounds to a woman called Rebecca Keeley."

Hoyle studied a check. "That was a lot of money back then."

"It's a lot of money now," said Nightingale.

"What do you think the going rate for a baby was back then?"

Nightingale nodded. "Twenty grand sounds about right to me. I'll see if I can track her down."

Hoyle tapped the file that he'd been working his way through. "What I don't see in these files are his household accounts. Utility bills and payments to staff. It's all big payments, he must have left the small stuff up to a manager."

"His driver, maybe," said Nightingale. "He only had three people working for him toward the end."

Hoyle pulled a piece of paper out of the file that he was reading. "You know he had a Bentley?"

Nightingale shook his head.

"An Arnage," said Hoyle. "Nice motor."

"But nothing here for the driver?"

"No pay slips, no National Insurance, no tax details."

"He probably didn't want his staff down here, so the household accounts must be somewhere else."

Hoyle looked at his watch. "I'm going to head off," he said. "Gotta be in the factory by six. You're sure you're okay?"

"I keep flashing back to my uncle's house. And I keep thinking that maybe if I'd gone straight around to see them…" He shrugged. "Yeah, I'm fine. I'm leaving now, myself. I'm on a case this evening."

Hoyle stood up. "Anything interesting?"

"Divorce. Wife fooling around. Makes a change, usually I'm following the husband." He nodded at the file that Hoyle was holding. "Are you going to take that with you?"

"Thought I might, yeah. If I find anything interesting I can run the names through the PNC."

"Go ahead, knock yourself out," said Nightingale.

They went up the stairs together and Nightingale switched off the lights and pulled the panel shut behind them. He locked the front door and the two of them stood looking up at the building.

"It's an awesome place, Jack," said Hoyle. "Be a great place to raise a family."

"Bloody hell, Robbie, can you imagine the upkeep? Not to mention the mortgage. I'll have to sell it, pay whatever taxes they hit me with, pay off the mortgage, and if I'm lucky I'll have enough left to buy a pack of smokes."

"I'm just saying, it must be nice to be rich."

"No argument there."

"How did Old Man Gosling make his money?"

Nightingale shrugged. "No idea," he said. "Maybe we'll find out somewhere in his records."

"Are you okay?" asked Hoyle.

Nightingale shrugged. "I guess so."

"I never said I was sorry, about your dad dying."

"No great loss," said Nightingale. "I didn't know him. Never met him. He was nothing to me, so there's no grieving to be done. I did that when my parents died. Then I did grieve, for a long time. With Gosling it's confusion more than grief. I just don't understand what was going through his mind, why he gave me up for adoption. Why he did what he did."

Hoyle held up the file he was holding. "Maybe we'll find the answer in these files."

Nightingale nodded. "Yeah, I hope so," he said. "I really hope so."

CHAPTER

27

The problem with divorce work, as Nightingale knew all too well, was that the deceived spouse always wanted proof. It wasn't enough just to say that he saw a man and woman enter a hotel and that they stayed there for an hour. The client wanted photographs or a video, hard evidence that could be waved in the face of the guilty party. The problem with photographs was that good cameras were bulky, and that for decent shots a telephoto lens was necessary, and hotels, even cheap ones, didn't take kindly to men in raincoats skulking around their reception areas with cameras.

Nightingale's green MGB was too conspicuous for surveillance work and the company credit card was close to its limit, so Nightingale had borrowed Jenny McLean's Audi A4. He wasn't sure how his assistant managed to afford a car like the A4, but he couldn't bring himself to ask her directly in case she mistook his curiosity for jealousy. He'd parked outside the hotel and listened to a radio discussion program while he waited for Mrs. McBride to arrive for her assignation. She was as regular as clockwork, using the same hotel on the second and last Monday of each month. She always parked in a multistory car park a short walk from the hotel, driving there with her lover. She would walk to the hotel first, check in, and get the key to the room before phoning her lover on his cell. Nightingale had watched them two weeks earlier but Joel McBride wouldn't take his word for it and was insisting on photographic evidence.

Nightingale saw Mrs. McBride coming around the corner and he switched off the radio. He climbed out of the Audi and locked it. He was holding a black leather attaché case and he pointed it in Mrs. McBride's direction as he pressed a hidden button in the handle. There was a small lens, less than the size of a penny, in the side of the briefcase connected to a digital video recorder inside the case.

Mrs. McBride was smiling as she talked into her cell phone, her high heels clicking on the sidewalk. She was an attractive blonde in her thirties, about five feet six with good legs. She was so engrossed in her phone call that she didn't give Nightingale a second look as she walked past him. The briefcase recorded sound and vision and he managed to get close enough to hear her say "darling" and tell whoever it was that she would see him soon.

She pushed through the double doors into reception and Nightingale followed her. As she walked up to the desk, Nightingale moved across to a sofa and sat down, keeping the lens pointed at Mrs. McBride. She handed over her credit card and filled out her details, then took her room key and headed for the elevators. Nightingale got up and walked slowly after her, pretending to have a conversation into his own cell phone. He waited until she had got into the elevator and the doors were just about to close before stepping in. "I'm just getting into the elevator," he said into his phone. "I'll call you back." He put the phone into his raincoat pocket and looked at the floor button she'd pressed. He smiled. "Same floor," he said. He took a deep breath, trying to calm his racing heart. He hated elevators with a vengeance but on this occasion he had no choice other than to follow her inside.

She flashed him an uninterested smile and looked up at the floor numbers as they winked on and off. When they reached the floor she walked quickly down the corridor. Nightingale followed, keeping well back. She was in a room in the middle of the corridor so he walked by her, tilting the case to keep her in the camera's view. He heard her unlock the door and then close it. Nightingale walked to the end of the corridor, turned, and stepped around the corner, keeping the briefcase aimed at the room where Mrs. McBride was. He didn't have to wait long. He heard the elevator doors open and he took out his phone, holding it against his ear with his left hand while keeping the attaché case aimed down the corridor with his right.

Mrs. McBride's lover walked briskly down the corridor, tapping a copy of the *Evening Standard* against his leg. He was wearing a dark blue pinstripe suit that had the look of Savile Row and a cashmere overcoat over one arm.

Nightingale walked slowly, muttering into his phone, keeping the case pointing toward the man as he knocked on Mrs. McBride's door. She opened it and kissed him, then dragged him inside just as Nightingale drew level with the door. His timing was perfect.

He went back outside and sat in the Audi. Two hours later he videoed the man leaving on his own, walking down the street toward the Tube station, and five minutes after that he got a nice shot of Mrs. McBride walking out of the hotel, looking like the cat that had got the cream.

CHAPTER

Jenny looked up from her computer when Nightingale walked in, swinging his attaché case. "How did it go?" she asked.

"Perfect," said Nightingale. He put the case on her desk, clicked the double locks, and opened it. Inside was a small digital video camera wired to the lens in the case. Nightingale removed the memory card from the side of the camera and gave it to Jenny. "Run off a couple of DVDs, might need a bit of editing."

"No problem," said Jenny. "How's my car, by the way?"

"Oh yeah, I had a bit of a run-in with a delivery van, scraped the side a bit."

"You did not!"

Nightingale grinned. "Joke," he said. "Would I take any risks with your pride and joy? Now, did you get the credit card records? They were obviously regulars at the Hilton. Be handy to show how often they go there."

"Yes, but my contact's asking for more money."

"Because?"

"Because he says they're clamping down. Data Protection Act and all that. Now he wants three hundred a go."

"There's enough in petty cash, right?" said Nightingale, lighting a cigarette.

Jenny flashed him a sarcastic smile. "We haven't had any petty cash for the last three months. I paid him myself."

"Put it on Mr. McBride's bill," he said.

"My DWP pal wants more too."

"What is it with these people?" sighed Nightingale. "They shouldn't even be selling us information in the first place."

"I think that's why the price keeps going up," said Jenny.

"But she came through, did she?"

"She managed to track down Rebecca Keeley. She's in a nursing home, apparently. But nothing on Mitchell. Mitchell isn't on any of the databases, apparently. Never paid tax, never been on the electoral roll, never seen a doctor. The original invisible man."

"Well, I hope we're not paying for that," said Nightingale.

"We're paying for the checks, Jack, not the results."

"So what's the story on Keeley? It's an old folks home, is it?"

"Hardly," said Jenny. "She's only just turned fifty."

Nightingale's brow furrowed. "Fifty? That means she was seventeen when she gave birth."

"You're assuming that she is your mother, Jack. And that's a very big assumption. All you have is the fact that Gosling gave her a large sum of money at about the time you were born."

"Twenty thousand pounds was a lot of money back then," said Nightingale. "He must have been paying her for something important."

"She could have sold him a painting. Or a piece of furniture."

"He was very methodical with his records. Every other check stub was filled in with either a reference number or a description of what he'd paid for. But the one for Keeley just had the amount with no explanation."

"I'm just saying, don't get too excited, it might turn out to be nothing."

"Message received and understood," said Nightingale. "So why is she in a home anyway if she's only fifty?"

"I don't know, but I've got an address," she said, handing him a sheet of paper. "Shall I get Mr. McBride in so that you can give him the bad news? And his bill."

"Might as well," said Nightingale, studying the paper she'd given him. The Hillingdon Home was in Hampshire, and there was no indication what sort of home it was. Underneath the address was a phone number and the name of the administrator of the home, a Mrs. Elizabeth Fraser.

"His wife paid for the hotel room, did you know that?"

"Yeah, I saw her handing over her card. Unbelievable, isn't it. She sleeps with her boss and she pays for it. What's he got that I haven't?"

"Charm for a start," said Jenny.

CHAPTER

29

"Go on, number five!" screamed Nightingale, waving his betting slip in the air. "Go on, my son!"

"His name's Red Rover," said Hoyle at his shoulder.

"He doesn't know his name," said Nightingale. "Go on, number five!"

The greyhounds reached the second bend in a tight pack with number five somewhere in the middle. Nightingale had put twenty pounds to win on number five for no other reason than he'd liked the way the dog seemed to be smiling as it was walked around by its trainer.

Robbie Hoyle had put fifty pounds on number six and as the dogs sped into the final stretch he cursed as he saw that number six was bringing up the rear.

"Come on, number five!" shouted Nightingale.

A black dog, its tongue lolling out of the side of its mouth, seemed to hit a second wind and it hurtled into the lead. It crossed the finishing line just yards behind the mechanical rabbit. Number five came in third. Nightingale screwed up his betting slip and dropped it on the floor. They were in Wimbledon Stadium in South London. It had been Hoyle's idea; he had been a regular visitor before he was married but since he had become a husband and father he barely managed to get in two or three evenings a year. "Who do you fancy in the next race?" asked Nightingale, studying his form sheet.

"Old Kentucky," said Hoyle.

"I think having the word 'old' in the name isn't a great start," said Nightingale.

"Won his last four races," said Hoyle. "Come on, drinks are on me if he loses."

They joined a queue to place their bets. "I got an address for that woman, the one that Gosling gave twenty grand to," said Nightingale. "Some sort of home in Hampshire."

"You really think she might be your mother?"

"She's the only lead I've got."

"Are you going to see her?

"I've got to, Robbie."

"You don't have to, you could let sleeping dogs lie." He grinned. "No pun intended."

Nightingale shrugged and kept his eyes on the list of runners that he was holding.

"Are you going to see her because she's your mother? Or because of this devil's contract thing?" asked Hoyle, lowering his voice to a whisper.

"I just want to meet her."

"What if she doesn't want to meet you?"

Nightingale turned to look at Hoyle, frowning. "What do you mean?"

"She gave you up for adoption thirty-three years ago. She hasn't made any attempt to contact you during that time, and the last thing she's going to expect is you turning up on her doorstep."

Nightingale reached the front of the queue and he handed a twenty-pound note to the cashier, a rotund woman in her fifties with blue-rinsed hair and green eye shadow. "Old Kentucky in the next race," he said.

The woman smiled at him through the Perspex protective screen. "You're going to hell, Jack Nightingale."

"What?" said Nightingale, his fingers gripping the list of runners so tightly that his knuckles whitened. "What did you say?" He knew what she'd said, he'd heard her quite distinctly. There was no mistake.

"Win or place?" said the woman.

Nightingale ran his hand through his hair. He was sure he'd heard her right the first time, she hadn't mumbled or whispered, she'd looked him right in the eye as she'd spoken, and her voice had been flat and cold, the voice of something not quite alive. But like everyone else who had told him that he was going to hell, she didn't seem to be aware of having said it.

"Win or place, young man?" said the cashier. "I don't have all day."

"Win," said Nightingale. He stared at the woman. Had he simply imagined it? Was it his subconscious playing tricks with him? It had started with the dreams, the dreams of Simon Underwood falling to his death, but maybe now his subconscious had decided that the dreams weren't enough, that it wanted to torment him while he was awake. Or maybe it was simply that he was going crazy.

The cashier handed him a betting slip and Nightingale walked away.

"Jack, are you okay?" Hoyle called after him.

Nightingale shook his head and reached for his pack of cigarettes. No, he wasn't okay. He was a long, long way from being okay. He lit a cigarette but had only taken one drag when an officious man in a blazer tapped him on the shoulder and told him that smoking wasn't allowed.

"But we're outside," he said, waving up at the sky.

"It's a place of work," said the man. "Health and Safety."

"It's a bloody nonsense," said Nightingale.

"It's the law," said the man. He had short wiry hair and its dark brown hue was so uniform that it could only be dyed. His cheeks were threaded with burst veins and he had the look of a former sergeant major who hankered for the days when he could make life a misery for men who couldn't answer back. "Don't give me a hard time, sonny."

"You're not going to tell me I'm going to hell, are you?"

"I don't have to use bad language," said the man, holding up a small transceiver. "All I have to do is call security."

Nightingale dropped the cigarette onto the ground, stamped on it, and headed for the bar. He was about to order a beer but then changed his mind and asked for a whisky instead. It had just arrived when Hoyle appeared at his shoulder. Nightingale handed the barman a ten-pound note and ordered Hoyle a glass of red wine.

"What's wrong, mate?" asked Hoyle.

"Nothing's wrong," said Nightingale. He downed his whisky in one gulp and when the barman returned with Hoyle's wine, he pointed at his empty glass and asked for a refill.

"Clearly," said Hoyle. "Since when you have been knocking back the whisky like that?"

"What the hell's happening to me, Robbie? My bloody life's turned upside down in less than a week. My parents aren't my parents. The man who is my father claims that he sold my soul to the devil. And my uncle kills my aunt and himself and…" He shook his head and picked up his glass.

"And what?"

"That message, the one that my uncle wrote in blood. People keep saying it to me."

"They what?"

"I keep hearing people tell me that I'm going to hell."

"You're under a lot of stress, that's all. Have you heard me say it?"

"No."

"That's a relief." His face went blank and he stared at Nightingale. "You're going to hell," he said, his voice a low whisper.

"Screw you, Robbie. It's not like that."

Hoyle's face broke into a grin. "Just trying to lighten the moment," he said.

"Cheers, mate." Nightingale drained his glass.

"But seriously, you should lay off the booze," said Hoyle. "You were never a big drinker. Strictly amateur."

"I can drink you under the table," said Nightingale. "And look who's talking, you're a bloody wine drinker."

Hoyle grinned and picked up his wine. "You're just upset because you thought you were a Nightingale, but you turned out to be a Gosling," he said. "How the mighty have fallen."

"It's not funny," said Nightingale. "My whole life has been a lie, Robbie. My parents lied to me from the day I was born. My uncle and aunt lied. Probably everyone I knew as a kid knew the truth and lied to my face."

"They didn't lie to you, they just didn't tell you the whole truth, there's a difference," said Hoyle.

"That's a lie by omission," said Nightingale. "Which is still a lie."

"You were adopted, loads of parents adopt and don't tell their kids. It's just…simpler."

"Simpler? Or do you think the fact that they bought me from a Satanist might have had something to do with their reticence?"

Hoyle shrugged but didn't answer. "Anyway, can we change the subject?" said Nightingale. "I've had it up to here with Ainsley bloody Gosling."

Hoyle sipped his wine. "Jenny said business hasn't been so good recently."

Nightingale looked across at him. "She did, did she?"

"She said it was a bit quiet, yeah."

"It's a bit of a dry spell, that's all," said Nightingale. "It happens. Peaks and troughs. Swings and roundabouts. Everyone's cutting back because of recession, so the corporate side is down. But divorce work is up. We're doing okay."

"I don't know why you're bothering with all that marital strife stuff. You're better than that, Jack."

"Like I've got a choice." Nightingale sipped his whisky.

"You were a great negotiator. The best. You should be working for one of the kidnapping insurance firms. Or in-house security for one of the multinationals."

"The last guy I negotiated with exited through a twenty-story window, let's not forget," said Nightingale. "That doesn't look great on the old CV."

"I'm serious," said Hoyle. "You're better than this. You know you are. Two years in the wilderness is enough. It's time to come back in."

"Maybe."

Hoyle slapped Nightingale on the back. "You know I'm right, mate. Oh, one bit of good news for you. Your man Turtledove is the real McCoy, he's been a solicitor for getting on forty years and there's never been a complaint against him. So whatever's going on, it's not a con game. Now come on, the next race is about to start."

"Do you believe in hell, Robbie?"

"Who was it who said that hell is other people?"

"I'm serious," said Nightingale. "Do you believe in a place called hell?"

"I've been to Southall, mate. That's as close to hell as I ever want to go." Hoyle put his arm around Nightingale's shoulders. "No, Jack, there is no such place as hell. You can trust me on that."

Nightingale nodded and finished his whisky. "Let's go see these dogs run," he said.

30

Joel McBride had thought long and hard before deciding to kill himself. He had no children, his own parents were long dead, and most of the friends he had were friends of his wife and he was sure that they would side with her. McBride loved his wife and had done since the day they'd met, when she was a salesman for a children's book publisher and he had been working in the Trafalgar Square branch of Waterstones. She'd walked in wearing a short skirt and a low-cut top ready to extol the merits of her firm's three new children's authors and within an hour they were having coffee in the Starbucks over the road and two nights later they were in Leicester Square and the night after that they were in bed together.

They had been married less than six months when McBride had injured himself. They had been on a riding holiday in Spain. His wife was a keen rider but it had been his first time on a horse. His first time and his last. They had gone trekking through sand dunes, six holidaymakers and two girls from the stable, and they had rounded off the afternoon with a gallop along the beach. The stable girls knew that McBride was a novice and told him to hold back, but he'd wanted to show off to his wife so he'd given the horse its head. It was a combination of bad luck and bad judgment; the rein had snapped and McBride had fallen and the horse had stamped down on him at the same time as he had hit the sand. His spine had snapped and the spinal cord severed. His holiday insurance paid for the hospital in Spain and the flight back to London, but he never walked again and never would.

Things had changed after the accident, obviously. He could get himself in and out of his wheelchair and he could manage the toilet himself, and he was able to drive a specially-adapted car, but he was still a cripple, and worse than that, he was a cripple who couldn't get an erection.

Sex was out of the question, at least the sort of sex that they'd enjoyed before the accident. He did the best he could to please her with his hands and with his tongue but he knew that it was never enough. He knew that one day she would take a lover but he had hoped that she'd be honest enough to tell him, and to reassure him that she still loved him, that she was his wife and would be forever.

He'd suspected for weeks that she had embarked on an affair, but she denied it when he raised it with her. But he knew, in his heart he knew, and he knew too that she was planning to leave him. She might have stayed for a few more weeks, maybe months, but there had been a growing coldness in her eyes and long silences in front of the television, and that was when he had asked Jack Nightingale to check up on her.

McBride had confronted her with the evidence, with the phone records and the video of her checking in to the hotel and leaving, and he'd asked her if she was going to leave him, but she hadn't said anything, she'd simply put on her coat and walked out of their house. He had waited all evening and all night and she hadn't returned, and she'd switched off her cell phone. McBride knew that he couldn't bear to live without her.

His house, their house, the house they'd lived in for more than six years, was just a mile from the canal. The canal was the best way, he'd decided. He had painkillers but he'd checked on the Internet and an overdose wouldn't kill him straightaway. He'd die, but he'd die from liver failure and it would be a long, lingering death over several days. He could probably get sleeping pills from his doctor but it usually took at least three days to get an appointment with his local GP. He thought of cutting his wrists but the idea of slicing through his flesh with a knife made him physically sick. The canal would be simple and quick.

McBride's wheelchair wasn't powered, he used his hands to propel it along the sidewalk. He hadn't bothered putting on the fingerless leather gloves that he used to protect his hands and his palms were soon muddy and sore. It had rained earlier that evening and the wheels made a swishing sound as he rolled along. The canal wasn't deep, McBride knew. Five feet at most. It would be impossible for most adults to drown in but standing up wasn't an option for him. He'd found a long length of chain in his garage, left there by the man who had sold them the house. It was heavy, the links the thickness of his thumb, and he had wrapped it around his waist and fastened it with a padlock, just in case he changed his mind at the last minute.

There was a concrete ramp leading from the sidewalk up to the towpath, steep but not so steep that he couldn't roll the wheelchair up. He rolled slowly along the muddy path. To his left were banks of nettles and beyond them a tall hedge threaded with blackberry bushes. The canal was on his right. There was a canal boat moored there, dark blue with circular brass windows and skylights. The canal curved to the left and McBride kept going until the boat was out of sight, then he pulled the chair around so that he was facing the water. He closed his eyes and swallowed. "Our Father, who art in heaven," he whispered. He hadn't been inside a church since the day of his wedding, and he had never thought of himself as being religious, but he knew that he wanted to die with the Lord's Prayer on his lips. He continued to mumble the prayer as he grabbed the muddy wheels and propelled himself forward. He had to push hard to get the wheels over the edge but he rocked himself back and forth and then he pitched headfirst into the cold, dark water.

McBride thought that he was alone when he died, but there was one witness. Two if you counted her dog, which would be reasonable because the dog did watch as McBride wheeled himself to the edge of the canal and into the water. The girl was wearing goth black and had upside-down black crosses dangling from her ears and an Egyptian ankh hanging around her neck. She wore a black leather motorcycle jacket and black leather jeans and black high-heeled boots. The dog woofed and looked up at his mistress. She smiled down at him and stroked his head, concentrating on the spot he liked, just behind his ear. "Not one of ours," she said. The dog panted and dribble dripped from his fleshy tongue. He was wearing a black leather collar with a silver buckle and studs, and hanging from it was a small silver pentangle.

CHAPTER

31

The Hillingdon Home sounded grand but it wasn't. It was a six-ties-built concrete block with rusted metal-framed windows and graffiti spray-painted across the doors. As Nightingale finished his cigarette, he looked up at the upper floors. Blank faces stared from some of the windows, white smudges behind the glass. It was a local authority home on the outskirts of Basingstoke, about fifty miles south of London. The car park was full so Nightingale had left his MGB in the street, a short walk away. In his left hand Nightingale was carrying a bunch of flowers. He had decided that he ought to bring something and decided that flowers were the best bet. He dropped the butt of his cigarette onto the floor and pushed open the double doors that led to the reception area.

He'd phoned ahead to let the home know that he was coming and an overweight West Indian lady in a flower pattern dress took him along to the administrator's office. The administrator was a fifty-year-old woman, stick-thin with chestnut-brown dyed hair and thick-lensed spectacles perched on the end of her nose. She sat behind a large desk on which was an old-fashioned computer and a plastic nameplate—Elizabeth Fraser. "I have to say, it was a bolt from the blue when you called," said Mrs. Fraser. "Miss Keeley hasn't had a visitor in the ten years that she's been here."

"We lost touch," said Nightingale.

"I'll say," said Mrs. Fraser. She tapped on the keyboard of her computer and frowned when she read what was on her screen. "The thing is, Mr. Nightingale, we don't have anyone down as her next of kin."

"As I said, we've been out of touch."

She peered at him over the top of her glasses. "And the different surname is a concern," she said.

"I was adopted," said Nightingale. "I think that she gave me up for adoption when I was born."

"I see," said Mrs. Fraser. "Would you have any paperwork to substantiate that?"

Nightingale shrugged. "I'm afraid not, it was a private adoption."

"I have to say, Mr. Nightingale, I'm a little reluctant to allow you access to Mrs. Fraser without some sort of evidence that you are a family member."

Nightingale took out his wallet and removed his driving license. He gave it to the administrator. "This proves who I am, Mrs. Fraser," he said. "As to proving that I'm her son, other than a DNA test I'm not sure how I'd go about doing that. But I'm guessing the fact that she's in a local authority home suggests that she doesn't have any money, so it's not as if I'm here to rip her off, is it? I have to be honest and say that I don't have any proof that she is my mother. But I was hoping that if I talked to her..." He shrugged. "I don't know, Mrs. Fraser. My life has been pretty much turned upside down over the last week and I just want some answers. I'm hoping that I might get them from Miss Keeley."

Mrs. Fraser smiled. "You're correct about the money," she said. "Miss Keeley doesn't have a penny to her name." She fed Nightingale's details into the computer and then gave the driving license back to him. "I don't see why you shouldn't see her, but I must warn you not to expect too much from this visit," she said. "Miss Keeley was in a mental institution before she came here, and while she isn't what we'd classify as mentally ill now, she is very uncommunicative. In fact, she hasn't said a word since she was brought here. From what we were told, she didn't speak in her last institution either. Not a word. The reason she was moved here is because there was no suitable medical treatment available and she was no longer considered a danger to herself or others."

"How long has she been in care?" asked Nightingale.

"She's been here for a little under ten years. She was in a mental institution for six years before coming here, but her records are patchy prior to that. There was a fire in the home she was in before the mental institution, apparently."

"So she could have been institutionalized her whole life," said Nightingale.

"That's a definite possibility," said Mrs. Fraser. She stood up. "I think you'll understand once you've seen her."

The administrator led Nightingale out of her office and down a corridor to the stairs and they walked up to the third floor where a male nurse was sitting at desk reading a copy of the *Daily Express*. He nodded at Mrs. Fraser.

"Everything okay, Darren?" she asked.

"No worries, Mrs. Fraser," said the man. He had an Australian accent. He was a big man in his late twenties, well over six feet tall, with wavy blond hair and a fading suntan and a small diamond earring in his right ear.

"We're here to see Miss Keeley, is she okay?"

The man smiled. "She never changes," he said. "I wish they were all as amenable."

Mrs. Fraser took Nightingale down the corridor and stopped outside a door on which there was a clear plastic box containing a white card. Mrs. Fraser looked at the card then put it back in the box and knocked on the door. She opened it. "It's only me, Miss Keeley," she said. "I have a visitor for you."

As the administrator opened the door wider, Nightingale saw a hospital bed, neatly made, and a bedside table with a water glass and a paperback book. It was the New English Bible, he realized, and it was well-thumbed.

"This is Jack Nightingale," said Mrs. Fraser. "He's come to have a chat with you. That's nice, isn't it?

The woman was sitting in an armchair by the widow. Her hair was gray and long and tied back in a ponytail, and she was wearing a shapeless, pale-blue linen dress and fluffy pink slippers. She had her hands clasped together in her lap and was staring out of the window, her lips pursed as if she was about to blow a kiss.

Nightingale stepped into the room and Mrs. Fraser closed the door. "He's just come to say hello, and he's brought you some flowers," said Mrs. Fraser.

Nightingale held out the bunch of flowers but the woman didn't react. Her face was lined and there were dark patches under her eyes and the hands in her lap were wrinkled and hooked, like claws. "She's only fifty, right?" said Nightingale.

"That's right," said Mrs. Fraser.

Nightingale lowered his voice to a whisper. "But she looks so...so old."

"The drugs can have that effect, I'm afraid."

"Drugs?"

"She's had a lifetime of tranquilizers, antidepressants, and anti-schizophrenia medication."

"But she's not on medication now?"

"She's still on antidepressants. And she has developed diabetes so she has to have regular insulin injections. There's also a high-cholesterol problem and she has to take medication for her low blood pressure." She patted the woman on her arm. "I'll leave you alone with Jack for a while, Miss Keeley," she said. She smiled at Nightingale. "I did warn you not to expect too much," she said. "They'll bring her meal at four o'clock, you're welcome to stay until then. Just let Darren know that you're leaving."

"Thank you," said Nightingale. Mrs. Fraser let herself out and Nightingale put the flowers onto the bed. He went to the foot of the bed and sat there, facing the woman. She continued to look out of the window, across the road to the discount carpet warehouse opposite. "Do you know who I am?" he asked quietly.

The woman showed no sign of having heard him.

"My name's Jack. Jack Nightingale." He smiled. "Though my name probably won't mean anything to you."

The woman continued to stare through the window, as if she was alone in the room.

"Rebecca, did you have a baby thirty-three years ago? Did you? Because if you did, then I'm your son, Rebecca. I'm the baby that you gave away." Nightingale smiled again, but this time it was more of a grimace. "Or sold. Did you sell me, Rebecca? Did you sell me for twenty thousand pounds?"

The woman's hands moved slightly in her lap. She scratched her left wrist with the yellowed fingernail of her right index finger. Nightingale could hear the sound, a dry rasp like two sticks being rubbed together.

Nightingale stared at her, trying to see some sort of resemblance to his own face. She had a tight, pinched face and a sharp, almost pointed nose, and she looked nothing like him.

"Are you my mother?" he asked. "Just answer me that? Did you give birth to me, thirty-three years ago?" He smiled. "It's Friday," he said. "Friday the thirteenth. That's funny isn't it, that of all the days I should come to see you, it's Friday the thirteenth. And two weeks today I'll be thirty-three years old. Do you know what's supposed to happen to me on my thirty-third birthday, Rebecca? Do you?"

She stared at him with unseeing eyes. He couldn't even tell if she'd heard a single word that he'd said to her. He stood up and walked over to the door. He grabbed the handle, but before he pulled the door open he turned to look at her.

"Can't you even say good-bye to me?" he said.

The woman didn't move.

"Mum?" The word felt strange on his lips. "If you are my mum, can't you even say good-bye? This will be the last time you ever see me." He thought he saw a slight movement of her head, but then she was perfectly still again. He went over to her chair and squatted down so that his head was level with hers. For the first time he noticed that she was wearing a small gold crucifix around her neck on a fine gold chain. "Mum, can you hear me?"

Her eyes were glistening with tears but her cheeks were dry, as dry and wrinkled as old parchment.

"Why did you do it? Why did you sell me to Ainsley Gosling? I know he gave you twenty thousand pounds. Was it to buy me?"

The woman's right hand twitched and her eyes widened. It was the first reaction she'd shown since he'd walked into the room. Her mouth opened and he saw that she had no teeth, just ulcerated gums.

"Ainsley Gosling, you know that name, don't you?"

The woman's mouth opened wider. Her tongue was coated with white fur and he could smell her breath, sour and vinegary like stale vomit.

"Ainsley Gosling," repeated Nightingale. "He was the man you sold me to, wasn't he? Tell me."

The woman's hands bunched into arthritic fists and her eyes widened as she stared at Nightingale, seeing him for the first time. She took a deep breath and opened her mouth and then began to scream as if she were being burned at the stake.

CHAPTER

Robbie Hoyle sipped his coffee and flicked through the file that he had taken from the basement of Gosling Manor. Ainsley Gosling had been a methodical man and seemed never to have thrown away a single receipt or invoice. There were travel inventories that showed he traveled the world, and invoices from antiques shops and auction houses that showed he was an avid collector. Hoyle saw an invoice with a Harley Street address, written in an almost illegible scrawl. He screwed up his eyes as he tried to make sense of the handwriting. He could make out some of the words but not all, but it was clearly an invoice for treatment at a private clinic. And one of the words was quite clear—ultrasound.

Hoyle looked at the heading again. The doctor's name was there—Dr. Geoffrey Griffith—and underneath was typed his specialty. He was a pediatrician. Hoyle grinned as he looked at the date. It was twenty months after Nightingale had been born. "Got you," whispered Hoyle. He couldn't see the name of the patient on the invoice but he was fairly sure that it involved Nightingale's missing sister. He took out his cell phone and scrolled through the address book until he found Nightingale's number. The call connected but after half a dozen rings it went through to voicemail. Hoyle looked at his watch. His shift was due to start in fifteen minutes so he drained his cup, paid his bill, and headed out of the coffee shop. The Starbucks was across the road from the police station. He looked left and right. A double-decker bus drove by, then an *Evening Standard* delivery van. Cars rushed by on both sides of the road. He pressed the redial button but the call went straight through to Nightingale's voicemail again. A Tesco truck drove by, then a motorcycle courier, then a line of cars bumper-to-bumper. "Jack, it's Robbie. I'm just heading into work but I've found something in Gosling's file about your sister." There was a gap in the traffic and Hoyle tucked the file under his arm and stepped off the sidewalk. "I'll give you a call when my shift's over..."

The girl in the goth clothes was standing in the doorway of a florist's. Her collie dog was sitting next to her, its ears pricked up. The girl ran a hand through her spiky jet-black hair and arched her back as she watched Hoyle step off the sidewalk.

"Hey, Robbie!" she shouted. Her voice cut through the hum of the traffic and Hoyle stopped in his tracks. "Hey, Robbie, have you got a light?" she called.

Hoyle turned, frowning, the phone still against her ear. The girl waved and then blew him a kiss. Hoyle took a step toward her, then the black cab hit him full on at thirty-five miles an hour, breaking his legs, hip, and spine, bursting his spleen, and splintering his ribs which then punctured his lungs. The taxi driver later said that he'd been distracted by something in the back of his cab, which was empty at the time. Something had been fluttering around like a trapped bird, he told police, but when he'd turned around there was nothing there. That was when the cab had ploughed into Hoyle. The cabbie hadn't even had time to brake before the impact.

Hoyle bled out quickly as he lay on the tarmac, and he was dead before the paramedics arrived. The contents of the file were scattered across the road. The wind picked them up and blew them in all directions. The invoice from the pediatrician got caught in an updraft and it spun into the air, then slapped against a lamppost. The wind caught it again and it swirled back into the road. It blew under a parked car and settled in a puddle of oily water.

The young girl and the dog stood and watched as Hoyle's life ebbed away, then they turned and left through the crowds pouring out of nearby shops, some staring in horror, others reaching for their cell phones to photograph and video Hoyle as he lay dying in the road.

CHAPTER

33

The male nurse straightened the quilt over Rebecca Keeley, took the thermometer from her mouth, and looked at it. "I'm not sure you should still be here," he said to Nightingale. He put the thermometer into the top pocket of his tunic. "I think it'd be better if you left now."

"It wasn't anything I did," said Nightingale. The woman had only screamed once, but the mournful wail had gone on for more than a minute and it was only when she ran out of breath that she finally stopped. Her hands had tensed into fists and her eyes were wide and staring as she screamed, but after she'd finished she grabbed her crucifix in her right hand and held it in front of her as if she were warding off a vampire.

The nurse had burst into the room expecting the worst, but the woman had remained in her chair even when she was screaming. When she stopped the nurse helped her onto the bed and draped the quilt around her. Nightingale tried to help but the nurse pushed him away. Nightingale's cell phone had started to ring while the nurse was comforting his mother, but he had reached into his pocket and switched it off.

The nurse took his stethoscope from around his neck and listened to her chest, then took her pulse before turning to Nightingale again. "I really think you should go," he said.

"We were just talking and she started to scream," said Nightingale. "I didn't do anything."

"Miss Keeley doesn't talk," said the nurse. "I've been here eighteen months and she's not said one word to me." He stood up and faced Nightingale with his hands on his hips. "It would be better if you left now."

"She's never done that before? Screamed like that?"

The nurse shook his head. "She's normally as good as gold. What did you say to her?"

"Nothing," lied Nightingale. "I just said who I was and showed her the flowers. Are you sure she isn't in pain or something?"

"No, she's fine."

"Look, I'd really like to sit with her for a while," said Nightingale.

"She needs rest," said the nurse. "I think she'd be better off sleeping."

"If it's a question of money," said Nightingale, taking out his wallet.

The nurse held up a hand. "It isn't," he said. "It's a question of my patient's well-being. She needs her rest, Mr. Nightingale. You can come and see her tomorrow."

Nightingale could see that the nurse was adamant, so he thanked the man for his help and left. As he left the room he picked up a hairbrush off the dressing table and slipped it into his pocket.

34

Jenny looked up and smiled as Nightingale walked into the office. "How did it go?" she asked.

Nightingale shrugged. "Difficult to say."

"Was she pleased to see you?"

"Not really," said Nightingale. He went over and made himself a coffee. "Want one?" he asked Jenny.

"I'm okay," she said. "Come on, Jack, tell me what happened. Is she your mother or not? What did she say?"

"Not much," said Nightingale. "She's been on all sorts of anti-depressants for years. She's in a hell of a state."

"But she's your mother. There's no doubt?"

"I don't know," said Nightingale. "She screamed like a banshee when I mentioned Gosling, but all in all I couldn't get much sense out of her." He pulled a Ziploc bag from the pocket of his coat. Inside was the hairbrush he'd taken from the room. "But I did get a DNA sample."

"You stole her brush?"

"I borrowed it," said Nightingale. "She can have it back when I'm done with it. You remember that private forensic laboratory we used on that paternity case? The one out by the airport?"

"Applied Forensics," she said, taking the bag from him.

"Courier the brush over. I'll give you a few of my hairs, too. Get them to run a comparison on the DNA to see if we're related. Ask them to do a rush job."

"You have to pay double for their forty-eight-hour service," said Jenny.

"Then let's do it," he said. "The sooner I know, the better."

"Okay, but remember that today's Friday. Even if I get it to them today, it'll be Tuesday at the earliest before we get the results back."

"I need to know quickly," said Nightingale. He perched on the corner of her desk. "If she really is my mother then I have to go back and see her again."

"Was she pleased to see you?"

"Horrified, more like." He sipped his coffee. "Screamed the place down actually. They threw me out."

"Why?"

"Well, they were quite nice about it, but I had to leave." The door to the office opened. There were two men in raincoats standing there and before they even opened their mouths Nightingale knew that they were cops.

"Jack Nightingale?" said the older of the two.

"That's what it says on the door."

The one who had spoken produced his warrant card. "I'm Inspector Dan Evans. This is DC Neil Derbyshire." Derbyshire also held out his warrant card.

"Is this about my aunt and uncle?" asked Nightingale, putting down his coffee and standing up.

Evans frowned. "I'm sorry, I don't understand."

"Tommy Nightingale. And Linda. Up in Altrincham."

"It's a Jack Nightingale we're here to see," said Evans.

"That's me," said Nightingale. "What's it about?"

"Do you know Inspector Robert Hoyle?" asked Evans.

"Robbie? Sure."

"In what capacity?"

"He's a friend. And a former colleague. What's happened?"

"I'm sorry, Mr. Nightingale. Inspector Hoyle died this morning."

The news hit Nightingale like a punch to the solar plexus. "He what?"

"RTA, just after eleven o'clock. He was crossing the road, got hit by a taxi."

Nightingale sat down heavily. "My God. Oh my God."

"It was an accident," said Derbyshire. "He stepped off the sidewalk and the taxi ploughed into him."

"We got your name and number off his cell," said Evans, frowning at the detective constable. "Yours was the last number he called."

"Had the driver been drinking?" asked Nightingale.

"Stone-cold sober. Says he was distracted by something in the cab but that Inspector Hoyle had just stopped in the middle of the road."

Nightingale fumbled for a cigarette.

"Can I get you coffee or tea or something?" Jenny asked the detectives, getting up from her chair. She put a hand on Nightingale's shoulder.

"We're fine, thank you," said Evans.

"What's happening about Anna? Who's telling Anna?" said Nightingale.

"Superintendent Chalmers is around there now," said Evans.

"Chalmers?" said Nightingale. "She hates Chalmers."

"You used to work in hostage negotiation, right?" asked Derbyshire.

"In another life," said Nightingale sourly.

"You're the one who killed the pedophile, right? The banker that was molesting his daughter?"

"Allegedly," said Nightingale.

"They said you threw him out of a ten-story window," said Derbyshire.

"They?" echoed Nightingale.

"Hey, I'd have done the same in your place," said Derbyshire.

"Most of us would," agreed Evans. "If we had the balls. I'm a dad myself. Two girls. If anyone touched them..."

Nightingale straightened up. "Is there anything else, guys? Anything you need from me."

"We're just clearing up loose ends," said Evans.

"But there's nothing untoward, right? It was an accident, pure and simple?"

"Is there something else, something we should know about?" asked Evans.

Nightingale shrugged but didn't say anything.

"Was he doing something on the side for you?" asked Evans.

"Robbie was a straight arrow," said Nightingale.

"We all do favors for our friends, especially those who used to be in the job," said Derbyshire.

"I never asked him for favors like that. I didn't have to."

"No offence," said Evans.

"None taken," said Nightingale. "Thanks for..." He left the sentence unfinished. There was no reason to thank the two detectives, they were just doing their job.

The two detectives left and Nightingale went through to his office and pulled open the bottom drawer of his desk. He kept a bottle of brandy there for those clients that needed a stiff drink after hearing bad news. Nightingale took out the brandy and waved it at Jenny. "Do you want one?" he asked.

Jenny nodded. She sat down and ran her hands through her hair. "I don't believe this," she said.

Nightingale sloshed brandy into two glasses and gave one to Jenny. "I've got to go and see Anna," he said.

"God, she must be in pieces. Three children. Oh, those poor kids." She gulped down some brandy with a shaking hand. "This doesn't feel real."

It never did, Nightingale knew. As a police officer he'd broken news of fatalities to families more than a dozen times, and rarely was the news greeted with anything but disbelief. Mothers, fathers, children, it didn't matter who he told, the first reaction was always complete denial. Their loved one couldn't be dead, they'd only just seen them, talked to them, they were on their way home, they had just left for work. Then once they had acknowledged the death, came the questions—how, why, when—as if understanding would lead to acceptance. More often than not it didn't. Acceptance only came with time.

It was two young policemen who had broken the news to Nightingale that his parents had died. They had turned up at his university dorm with one of his lecturers, asked him to sit down, and told him that they had bad news about his parents. Even when they had explained what had happened, Nightingale had still called home to check because he hadn't wanted to believe that his mum and dad were dead. Then when he went back home and stood in the empty house, he still half thought that they would be back at any moment, that he'd hear their car in the driveway and they would come rushing in, laughing and saying that it had all been a terrible mistake and they weren't the ones who had died in the accident. Even at the funeral it hadn't seemed real, the coffins were closed and part of him kept clinging to the hope that it was someone else inside the wooden boxes and that his parents were still alive somewhere.

"Why, Jack?" she asked. "Why Robbie?"

"There's no reason," said Nightingale. "Wrong place, wrong time. A stupid accident. And accidents happen." He smiled thinly. "It's Friday the thirteenth, remember. Shit happens on Friday the thirteenth."

"But why to Robbie?"

Nightingale sipped his brandy. It wasn't a question that he could answer. Bad things happened to good people sometimes. That was the way of the world. He stood up and went over to his raincoat and took out his cell phone, then sat down at his desk and switched it on. "I was the last number he called, but my phone was off while I was with my mother," he said. He looked at the phone's screen. He had a voicemail message. He pressed the button to get the message and put the phone to his ear. "Jack, it's Robbie. I'm just heading into work but I've found something in Gosling's file about your sister." Nightingale could hear traffic in the background. "I'll give you a call when my shift's over..." There was more traffic noise, then a girl's voice in the distance. "Hey, Robbie!" And a second or two later: "Hey, Robbie, have you got a light?" Then there was a sickening thud and then silence. Nightingale took the phone away from his ear and stared at it in horror.

"What's wrong?" asked Jenny.

"I think I just heard Robbie being run over," he said.

"No way," said Jenny.

"He was calling to say he had some information for me, and then some girl called his name and then..."

Jenny held out her hand. "Can I?"

"I don't think you should, kid," said Nightingale.

"Please. I want to."

Nightingale gave her the phone and she listened to the message. "Who's the girl?" she asked. "Did you recognize her voice?"

Nightingale shook his head. "I don't think so."

"She knew Robbie, she called him by name."

"I guess so."

"But if she knew him, why did she ask him for a light? She must have known that Robbie didn't smoke."

Nightingale took the phone from her. "I don't know," he said. "Maybe she was calling someone else and he thought she was talking to him." He took another sip of brandy. "I'll go and see Anna."

"Can I come?"

Nightingale opened his mouth to say that she should stay and mind the office, but knew that it was the wrong thing to say. She had known Robbie well, and had been around to his home and met Anna and the kids. "Of course," he said. "Just leave a note on the door saying we'll be shut for a couple of hours." He put the bottle of brandy back into his bottom drawer. "On second thought, let's just close up for the day. If it's important they can call me on my cell."

There were a dozen large nondescript salon cars parked outside the Hoyle house and a single police patrol car. Nightingale found a parking space about a hundred yards from the house. It was starting to rain but Jenny had brought an umbrella with her so they both sheltered under it as they walked along the sidewalk. "What do you say to someone whose husband has died?" she said.

"There's nothing you can say," said Nightingale. "You've just got to show that you're there for them."

"Will she be all right, you know, financially?"

"Sure, he'd have had insurance on the mortgage so the house will be paid for, and there'll be a pension. The job will have people helping her."

"Poor Anna. Poor, poor Anna."

"Has anyone close to you died, Jenny?"

Jenny shook her head. "Touch wood, I've been lucky so far," she said. "My granddad passed away a few years ago but he was ninety-seven. My family live forever pretty much."

"You're lucky," said Nightingale.

Jenny put her arm through his. "Sorry," she said. "I wasn't thinking."

"You don't have to walk on eggshells with me," said Nightingale. "I was a cop for almost ten years, I've seen more than my share of dead bodies. I'm well over my parents, and Gosling, well, he was just a name. My aunt and uncle..." He shrugged. "I don't know. That still hasn't really hit me. I think it's because I was in London and they were up in Altrincham, I didn't get to see them that much, so in a way nothing has changed. I mean, I know they're dead..." He shrugged again. "It's difficult to explain. I was just about coming to terms with it but now this, now Robbie's dead too."

"Are you okay?" Jenny asked.

"You don't have to keep asking if I'm okay," said Nightingale. "You're as bad as Robbie..." He groaned. "God, listen to me. Talking as if he were still..." Nightingale shook his head and swore savagely.

Jenny squeezed his arm. "Do you want to go for a walk? We can come back later."

"No, we have to go in, we have to see her now."

They walked up the path to the front door and Nightingale rang the bell. Anna's older sister, Marie, opened the door. Her cheeks were wet from crying but she forced a smile when she saw Nightingale. "Jack, hello."

"I'm so sorry, Marie," said Nightingale. He hugged her and gave her a light peck on each cheek. "This is Jenny, she works with me."

Marie smiled at Jenny. "Come on in, let me take your coats. Anna is in the sitting room."

Anna was sitting on the sofa, her arm around her eight-year-old daughter, Sarah. There were a dozen people in the room, standing drinking tea and making small talk. An elderly woman who Nightingale didn't recognize was walking around with a plate of chocolate biscuits. Superintendent Chalmers was standing by the window in conversation with Hoyle's immediate superior, a chief inspector whom Nightingale had met a couple of times. Both men nodded at Nightingale and carried on talking to each other. Anna wiped her eyes with a handkerchief but she started sobbing again when she saw Nightingale. She whispered to her daughter and then hurried over to him.

"I'm so sorry, Anna," he said. "If there's anything...you know... just ask."

Anna hugged him and rested her head on his shoulder. "I still haven't told the twins," she sobbed. "I don't know what to tell them."

"They're too young to understand," said Nightingale.

"They're asking for him, last time I said he was at work. They're asleep now." She put her hands on his chest and looked tearfully into his eyes. "What do I say, Jack? How do I tell them that they'll never see their father again?"

Nightingale bit his lower lip. He was finding it difficult enough to come to terms with Robbie Hoyle's death, he couldn't imagine how two three-year-olds were going to react. "I don't know, Anna. All you can say is that Robbie loved them more than anything and that he's in heaven looking down on them."

"Do you believe that, Jack? Do you believe he's up there somewhere, watching us?"

"I'd really like to think so, Anna," said Nightingale, but he could hear the uncertainty in his voice. "But kids believe, and that's what's important."

"I can't live without him, Jack."

"Yes, you can, Anna. We're all here for you. We'll get through this."

Tears rolled down Anna's cheek and she wiped her face with her handkerchief. She smiled when she realized that Jenny was standing next to Nightingale. "Oh, Jenny, thanks for coming."

"If there's anything I can do, Anna, if you need help taking care of the kids or shopping or if you need driving anywhere," she said, giving her a hug.

"Thanks so much," said Anna. She nodded at the woman taking around the chocolate biscuits. "Robbie's mum was straight round and she's staying with me until…" She wiped her eyes again. "Until, I don't know…"

"Are you okay for money, love?" asked Nightingale.

Anna nodded quickly. "There's a really nice man from the Police Federation gave me his card, he said he'll handle everything. Robbie's pension, any money we need to tide us over, he'll take care of it."

"That's good," said Nightingale.

"Robbie didn't even have a will, did you know that?"

"Who does?" said Nightingale. "I haven't."

"Me neither," agreed Jenny. "You just don't think about it, do you?"

"I did ask him, loads of times," said Anna. "But he said that writing your will was just tempting fate, that he had no intention of…" She faltered, then blew her nose on her handkerchief. "Stupid, stupid bastard," she said. She touched Nightingale on the arm. "I've got to get back to Sarah. She's been so calm, so collected, so together, but I don't think it's really hit her yet."

"She's in shock," said Jenny. "We all are."

Anna nodded and wiped her eyes, then went back to the sofa and sat down next to her daughter. Sarah held her mother's hand and smiled bravely, her lower lip trembling.

"I can't believe this is happening," said Jenny. "I keep thinking I'm going to wake up, it just doesn't feel real."

Nightingale looked around. "Can you see any whisky? I need a drink."

"Jack..." said Jenny.

"Come on, Robbie would understand," he said. "If it were me, I'd expect Robbie to have a drink." He smiled ruefully. "But then again, if it was me, there wouldn't be this many people grieving." He nodded over at the superintendent. "Bloody Chalmers wouldn't be here, for a start."

"It's good that he came, Jack," said Jenny.

"He hated Robbie. And vice versa."

"Which makes it all the more decent of him to have come," said Jenny.

Nightingale shrugged. "Yeah, maybe," he admitted.

Marie appeared at Jenny's shoulder. "Would you like a coffee or tea?" she asked them.

"Coffee, please," said Jenny.

"Me too," said Nightingale.

"I'll put a drop of something in yours, Jack, shall I? A drop of brandy, maybe? Or whisky."

"You read my mind, Marie, thanks. Whisky would be great."

"It's not mind reading," she said. "Every cop in the room has got brandy or whisky in their coffee. Even the superintendent over there."

Jenny smiled at Nightingale as Marie went off to the kitchen. "See, Jack, he is human after all."

CHAPTER

36

"When did you eat last?" asked Jenny, as they walked toward Nightingale's MGB. It had stopped raining but there were still pools of water on the road. They had stayed in Anna's house for almost two hours, during which time more than a hundred police officers had called to pay their respects. Robbie Hoyle had been well-liked, but even if he had been the most unpopular man on the Met, they would still have come. Police officers were a tight family and they always closed ranks when one of their own died.

"Does whisky count as one of the major food groups?" asked Nightingale.

"No, it doesn't," said Jenny.

Nightingale shrugged. "Yesterday."

"You didn't have breakfast?"

"Who has breakfast these days?" said Nightingale. "No one has the time."

Jenny put her arm through his. "Come on, we're going to eat," she said. "My treat."

"Your treat? Am I paying you too much?"

"You haven't paid me at all this month," she laughed. "How does Chinese sound?"

"If you're paying, we'll eat whatever you want," he said. They reached the MGB and climbed in. Nightingale headed north to London. Jenny knew a Chinese restaurant around the corner from her home in Chelsea where she was greeted like a long-lost cousin. Nightingale asked her to order and she did so in what sounded like fairly fluent Cantonese, much to Nightingale's surprise.

"I didn't know you spoke Chinese," he said.

"I sometimes wonder if you even looked at my CV," she said. "It did say that I spent four years in Hong Kong when I was a kid."

"Yeah, I probably didn't get that far down it," said Nightingale. "You had shorthand and typing and a good phone voice."

Two Tsingtao beers arrived. "I'm serious, Jack. Sometimes you're a bit on the self-centered side."

"I'm all I've got," said Nightingale. "I guess that comes from having my parents die when I was a teenager."

"Maybe, but you should try opening up more."

He raised his glass to her. "Okay, I will."

"No, you won't," she said. She clinked her glass against his.

"I'll try," he said.

Their food arrived. Half a Peking duck, scallops fried with celery, chicken with cashew nuts, bok choy in oyster sauce, and rice. An old Chinese lady with her hair held up in a bun with two scarlet chopsticks came over and spoke to Jenny in Chinese and walked away cackling.

"What's the joke?" asked Nightingale, struggling to cope with his chopsticks.

"She wanted to know if you were my husband."

Rice tumbled from Nightingale's chopsticks and fell onto his lap. "And what did you say?"

"I told her you were my father."

"What? I'm only ..." He frowned. "How much older than you am I?"

"You really didn't read my CV, did you? I'm twenty-five. And you'll be thirty-three next week. Which makes you...?"

"Eight years older. Which hardly makes me father material, does it?"

"Jack, I was joking. And would you like a knife and fork?"

"I can manage, thanks," said Nightingale. He picked up a piece of chicken and managed to get it halfway to his mouth before it slipped from his chopsticks and splattered onto the tablecloth.

"There's nothing to be ashamed of in not being able to handle chopsticks," she said, deftly picking up a cashew nut with hers and popping it into her mouth.

"Yeah, well you're half-Chinese, apparently," said Nightingale.

"I said I lived in Hong Kong for a few years, I wasn't born there," she said. "Daddy was working for one of the trading firms."

A scallop slipped from between his chopsticks and fell into the bok choy. He held the chopsticks up in front of her face. "So my question to the Chinese expert is, now that they know how great knives and forks are, why don't they stop using these bloody things?"

"Tradition," she said.

"Well they've changed other traditions, haven't they? They stopped using rickshaws and wearing those Mao outfits, and they replaced donkeys with cars easily enough, so why not do the sensible thing and replace chopsticks with more user-friendly utensils?"

Jenny laughed and Nightingale waved for the waitress to bring them two more beers. They laughed and argued and ate and discussed everything but the one thing that they were both thinking about—Robbie Hoyle.

When they had finished their meal a waitress placed a saucer onto the table. On it was the bill and two fortune cookies. Nightingale picked up one of the cookies and held it up between his finger and thumb. "This had better be good luck," he said.

"Lottery numbers would be nice," said Jenny.

Nightingale grinned. He crushed the cookie and let the pieces fall to the tablecloth. He unrolled the slip of paper and looked at the typewritten sentence. The smile froze on his face. It was as if time had stopped dead and his whole world was focused on the seven words in front of him. YOU ARE GOING TO HELL, JACK NIGHTINGALE.

"Jack, what's wrong?" asked Jenny, leaning across the table toward him.

Nightingale couldn't take his eyes from the printed fortune and he was holding it so tightly that his finger and thumb had gone white.

"Jack?" said Jenny. She reached over and pulled the slip away from him. Nightingale sagged in his seat, his arms folded across his chest. She read the fortune, and smiled. "It's not so bad," she said. "Never take a stranger at his word, but remember that friends can also lie." She shrugged. "Good advice, if you ask me."

Nightingale snatched the piece of paper from her and reread it. NEVER TAKE A STRANGER AT HIS WORD, BUT REMEMBER THAT FRIENDS CAN ALSO LIE. Nightingale wiped his face with his left hand, blinked his eyes several times, and read it again.

"Jack, what's wrong?"

Nightingale turned the slip of paper over. The back was blank.

"You look like you've seen a ghost."

He tossed the fortune onto the table. "I'm just tired," he said. "My eyes are playing tricks on me."

"What do you think it said?"

"Nothing."

"Don't lie to me, Jack."

Nightingale massaged the bridge of his nose. "I'm just tired, kid."

"Don't 'kid' me," she said. She picked up the fortune and waved it in front of him. "This is the normal sort of fortune rubbish you find in every cookie. But when you looked at it, it was as if you were reading your death warrant."

"It was nothing," said Nightingale. "I'm just tired."

"I'm serious, Jack. Don't you dare lie to me. "

"It's a long story."

"I'm not going anywhere."

Nightingale sighed. "Okay. I thought it said that I was going to hell. That's what it said the first time I read it."

"That you were going to hell?"

"That's right. That I, Jack Nightingale, was going to hell."

"So you misread it. No big deal." She frowned. "Those words mean something, don't they?"

"My uncle wrote them before he died. In blood. In his bathroom. The very same words."

Jenny gasped. "What? Why didn't you tell me that before?"

"Because...I don't know, Jenny. I thought maybe I'd imagined it. Like I imagined it just now, when I read the fortune."

"Why would your uncle tell you that you were going to hell?"

Nightingale shrugged. "I've no idea. But the words, they keep cropping up."

"Since when?"

"Like I said, it's a long story."

"Jack..."

"Okay, okay," said Nightingale. He sighed and put his head in his hands. He had never told Jenny about Sophie Underwood, or what had happened to her father. It wasn't something that he wanted to talk about, but as he sat in the Chinese restaurant and stared at the tablecloth stained from all the food that had slipped from his chopsticks, he told her everything that had happened on that chilly November morning. Or at least as much as he could remember.

"Hand on heart, Jenny, I don't remember what happened to the father. I don't remember if he jumped or if I pushed him. There's a gap in my memory, just a few seconds, but no matter how many times I replay it in my mind, I can't remember what happened. It feels like I pushed him, I know I wanted to and I know he deserved to die the way Sophie died, but I can't remember doing it. But the one thing I can remember is what he said to me. Or screamed at me, more like." He looked at her and forced a smile. "I remember him yelling at me that I was going to hell. Not a curse, not an insult, but like he knew it was a fact."

"It's an expression, Jack."

Nightingale shook his head. "He meant it. And I remember him saying it as clear as if he were standing here right now. But I don't remember what happened after that. The next thing I remember I was downstairs, heading toward my car. He said it and I saw it just then, on the fortune that came out of my cookie."

Jenny held up the slip of paper. "But it doesn't say that, Jack."

"Not now it doesn't. But it did when I looked at it. It did, Jenny. I swear."

"Maybe it's your subconscious playing tricks with you. You heard about Robbie, it made you think about sudden death, and that made you think about Underwood, and your subconscious started replaying what happened two years ago and muddled things up."

"Since when were you a psychiatrist?"

"It's common sense, that's all. We're both under stress, after we found out what had happened to Robbie. And stress does funny things to people."

Nightingale nodded, then drank the rest of his beer. "I still can't believe Robbie's dead. You know, I've known him almost ten years. We were at Hendon together."

"He was a nice guy," said Jenny.

"He was a better cop than me," said Nightingale. "A better human being, too. A husband, a father. He didn't deserve to die like that."

"It was just a stupid accident."

"He was leaving a message for me when he was hit by the cab," said Nightingale. "Maybe if I'd answered the phone it wouldn't have happened." He ran a hand through his hair. "Do you want another beer? One for the road?"

Jenny shook her head. "I'm fine," she said. "It was an accident, Jack. You have to stop blaming yourself. And at least it was quick. He didn't suffer."

"That's bollocks," said Nightingale. "They always say that. 'At least he didn't suffer. At least it was quick.' That's bollocks. One moment they're there, then they're gone. Bang. Thank you and good night."

"But isn't that better than lying in a hospital bed wired up to a life-support machine?"

"There's too much unfinished business. There's no time to prepare yourself, or to prepare the people you care for. Sudden death just rips people away. It leaves too many unanswered questions." Nightingale stood up, opened his wallet, and dropped three twenty-pound notes onto the saucer. "I need a smoke," he said. "And don't worry, I won't be driving."

Jenny picked up the money and gave it to him. "My treat, remember?"

"Thanks." He put the notes back in his wallet.

"I'll come with you."

"Secondhand smoke kills," he said. "I wouldn't want you on my conscience."

Jenny opened her mouth to argue but Nightingale shook his head and held up his hand to silence her. "I just want to be on my own," he said. "I'm sorry. I need to think."

"And you can't think when I'm around? Jack, you can't always push people away like this."

"I'm not pushing anyone away," he said.

"No, you're running away, and that's worse. You can't solve your problems by running away from them."

Nightingale turned and headed for the door. "Watch me," he said.

CHAPTER

The forensic lab phoned Jenny with the results of the DNA test first thing on Tuesday morning. She hurried into Nightingale's office. "The lab came back with the results," she said. "Rebecca Keeley's your mother."

"There's no doubt?" said Nightingale.

"Only that one in six billion nonsense," said Jenny. "She's your birth mother, no question of it. They're sending me a fax over right now. And their bill."

"Will petty cash cover it?" asked Nightingale hopefully.

"It would if we had any petty cash," said Jenny. "We'll need a check."

Jenny's computer beeped to tell her that she had received an e-mail. She went over to her desk while Nightingale phoned Hillingdon Home and spoke to Mrs. Fraser. The administrator said that his mother had slept through the night and now seemed much calmer. Nightingale explained that following a DNA test he was now sure that Rebecca Keeley was his mother, but he thought it better not to tell her that he'd stolen the hairbrush. Mrs. Fraser said she had no objections to Nightingale visiting again. This time Nightingale didn't take flowers, but he had with him an old photograph album. The male nurse met him in reception and explained that his mother was sitting out in the garden. It wasn't so much a garden as a patch of grass at the back of the building with a couple of wooden benches, a rockery filled with heathers of various hues, and a stone birdbath covered in sparrow droppings. Nightingale's mother was sitting on one of the benches, wearing a tweed coat and a purple headscarf. She was staring at the birdbath and stroking the crucifix around her neck.

"I like her to get some fresh air now and again," said the nurse. He looked at the plastic watch on his wrist. "I'll take her back inside in half an hour. He pointed at a large picture window overlooking the garden. Three old women were sitting in armchairs, staring blankly through the window. "I'll be in the residents' lounge," he said. "If she starts getting agitated again, I'll have to bring an end to the visit."

"I understand," said Nightingale.

Nightingale went over to the bench and sat down next her, unbuttoning his raincoat. He sat with the photograph album on his lap and said hello but she ignored him.

"It's me, Jack," he said. "I've come back to see you."

There was no reaction, no sign that she was even aware that he was there. He opened the album. The first picture was of Nightingale only a few days old, wrapped in a white cloth, his eyes wide open. "This is me, not long after I was born," he said. He pushed the album toward her. "Do you remember me as a baby? Did you see me when I was born or did he take me away from you straightaway? I know you're my mother, Rebecca. I checked. There's no doubt. I'm your son."

The woman looked down at the picture and she frowned, still rubbing the crucifix between her thumb and first finger.

"Do you recognize me, Rebecca? Do you recognize the baby in this picture?"

"Edward?" she whispered.

"Edward? Is that the name you gave me? Is that what you called me? My name's Jack now, Jack Nightingale." He turned the page. There were six photographs spread over two pages, different views of his parents holding him. "These are the people who took care of me, Rebecca. William and Irene Nightingale. My parents."

She reached out and gently touched the photographs one by one with her left hand, holding the crucifix tightly in her right.

"Do you remember, Rebecca?" asked Nightingale, his voice a soft whisper. "Do you remember holding me when I was born? Did you hold me? Did you kiss me?"

He turned the page. The next set of photographs was of Nightingale when he was two weeks old, still small and defenseless. He flicked through the pages and showed her one of him smiling. He'd always been a happy baby, according to his mother. Happy and smiling and as good as gold.

A single tear trickled down Rebecca Keeley's left cheek.

Nightingale reached across and held her left hand. "Why did you give me away?" he asked.

She frowned and shook her head slowly. Nightingale wasn't sure if she didn't understand the question or if she was denying what he'd said.

"What was the money for? The twenty thousand pounds?"

She shook her head slowly from side to side. "Are you a ghost?" she whispered.

"A ghost?" repeated Nightingale. "Why do you think I'm a ghost?"

"You died," she whispered. "You died when you were born."

Nightingale froze. "Is that what he told you? Is that what Ainsley Gosling told you?"

"You were stillborn, he said. The doctor wouldn't even let me see you. They took you away and said that they'd bury you but I never saw a grave." She stared at him with tear-filled eyes. "Why have you come back?"

"I didn't die," said Nightingale. "I didn't know about you. I didn't even know you existed. Gosling gave me to the Nightingales and they brought me up."

The woman's brow furrowed even more. "You're not a ghost?"

Nightingale stroked her wrinkled hand. "No, I'm flesh and blood."

"And Ainsley?"

"He died," said Nightingale. "A few days ago."

"What happened?"

"He got sick and died," said Nightingale. He had no compunction about lying to the woman. He didn't think she would react well to the news that that Gosling had blown his head off with a shotgun.

"Is he a ghost now? Will he come to see me?"

"I don't think so," said Nightingale.

"I loved him," said the woman, her hands trembling.

"What was the money for?" asked Nightingale. "The twenty thousand pounds he paid you?"

"He said I needed a holiday. He said he'd join me and he gave me the money and a train ticket to Blackpool and I never saw him again. I always wanted to see Blackpool. I wanted to climb the tower and walk on the pier." She blinked her watery eyes. "What's your name?" she asked.

"Jack."

"That's a nice name. I was going to call you Edward."

"That's a good name," said Nightingale. He smiled. "You know, I never really felt like a Jack. But Edward? I'd never thought of Edward. Eddie? Ed?"

"Never Eddie," she said primly. "Edward."

"You can call me Edward, if you like," said Nightingale. "Rebecca, do you know if he had any other children? A daughter maybe?"

"I stayed in the hospital for two days afterwards and then I went to Blackpool and the last time I saw him was at the station. He said he'd come to see me in Blackpool. But he never did." A tear rolled down her left cheek. "Why did he tell me that you'd died?"

"I don't know. I'm sorry."

She sniffed. "I'm sorry too," she said. "How old are you?"

"Thirty-three next week," he said. "On Friday. Friday the twenty-seventh."

She gasped and clutched at the crucifix. "My God."

Nightingale stared at her. "What?"

She avoided his gaze and stared at the birdbath. "Nothing," she whispered, rubbing the crucifix between her finger and thumb. "Nothing, nothing, nothing, nothing." She repeated the word like a mantra.

Nightingale narrowed his eyes, "You know, don't you?"

She bit her lip and shook her head.

"You do. You know what he did, why he took me away from you when I was born."

"I don't, I don't, I don't," she murmured. She kissed the crucifix with her thin bloodless lips and carried on rubbing it. "I don't, I don't, I don't."

"You know what's going to happen on my thirty-third birthday, don't you? On Friday next week."

The woman didn't answer but she squeezed the crucifix harder.

"You know, don't you? You have to tell me. You owe me that much."

Tears rolled down both her cheeks. "He told me you died," she muttered. "That's what he told me."

"But you knew what he was, didn't you? You knew he was a Satanist?"

She shook her head. "Not at first. I just thought he was a man who liked me, who cared about me."

Nightingale took a deep breath. He wasn't getting anywhere by asking her directly. She was confused, and clearly damaged by the years of medication. He forced himself to smile and he gently stroked her hand. He knew from his years of negotiating that sometimes you had to come in from the side, to slip through the defensive barriers that people put up to protect themselves. "I bet he was a handsome man," he said quietly.

"Oh yes," she said. "The first time I met him, he took my breath away."

"Where did you meet him?"

"Church," she said.

"Church?" repeated Nightingale. That didn't make sense because the last place a Satanist would go would be to a place of worship. "Which church?"

"A spiritualist church in Islington," she said. "I wanted to contact my parents. They died when I was young and I was in care. I used to go to the church trying to get a message from them."

"And did you?"

"No." She trembled. "Not at the church, but later, with Ainsley, they spoke to me."

"Ainsley helped you contact your parents?"

"He helped them contact me," she corrected. "He brought their spirits to talk to me, to tell me that everything was all right and that they loved me and were watching over me."

"And he did that at the church?"

"No, it was later, at his home. At the church I never got a message. But Ainsley did. Every time. The spirits were always talking to him." She smiled at the memory. "Some of the regulars at the church started to get jealous because the messages were always for Ainsley. It was as if the spirits were queuing up to speak to him."

"Then he took you to his home?"

"He had a lovely house. So big, with a huge garden. Bigger than this, with trees and flowers and a summer house. That was where he made love to me for the first time."

"And you got pregnant?"

"Not then. That was later. After my parents spoke to me."

"How did they do that, Rebecca? Did you hear their voices?"

"No," she said, shaking her head. "Ainsley knew how to use the Ouija board and they spoke to me through that. Every night they would talk to me. About why they had died, why I had to be strong, and why I should trust Ainsley and let him take care of me."

"Rebecca, was it your parents who said you should have a baby with Ainsley?"

She nodded fiercely. "They said they wanted grandchildren. They said I was their only child so it was up to me to give them a grandchild and that if I did they would be happy in heaven."

"But when the baby was born, you thought it was dead?"

She put a hand up to her forehead. "I don't know," she said. "I'm not sure." Her lower lip began to tremble. "I remember telling the nurse that I wanted to hold the baby and Ainsley taking it and saying that it was dead but I think it was breathing."

Nightingale closed the album. "You never saw him again, after you had the baby?"

She shook her head. "I came back from Blackpool and I went to his house, but it was empty, and everyone I spoke to said that it had been empty for years." Tears were running down her face but she ignored them. "Why did he leave me?" she whimpered. "Why did he take my baby?"

"I think you know," said Nightingale harshly. "I think you know what he planned to do right from the start. That's why he paid you. He paid you to have me, didn't he?"

"No!" she wailed. She grabbed at him with both hands, the fingers curled like talons. She grabbed the lapels of his suit and pushed her face up against his. He could smell the sourness of her breath and a sickly sweet perfume around her wrinkled neck. He tried to release her grip on his suit but her hands were locked rigid. Her face was only inches from his. "No!" she shouted and her spittle peppered his cheek. The photograph album fell onto the grass.

"Please, Rebecca," he said. "Calm down, it's okay."

He heard running footsteps and twisted around to see the male nurse running toward them, his white coat flapping behind him like the feathers of some demented bird. "What happened?" asked the nurse, as he gently pried the woman's fingers away from his suit.

"I don't know," lied Nightingale. "I was just talking to her about the pictures and she went off again."

The nurse sat down next to the woman and put a protective arm around her. "I think you should go," said the nurse.

"I think you're probably right," agreed Nightingale. He bent down and picked up the photograph album.

He stood up and put a hand on the woman's shoulder. "Take care," he said. She didn't react, she just stared at the stone birdbath, her cheeks still wet from her tears. She slowly reached up with her right hand and began caressing the crucifix again.

CHAPTER

38

Finding someone to buy the books from Ainsley Gosling's library was surprisingly easy. On Wednesday morning, before he showered or shaved, Nightingale made himself a mug of coffee and powered up his laptop. He put "shops selling secondhand books on witchcraft" into Google and it came back with more than six thousand sites. He added the word *London* and that brought it down to a little over five thousand. He scrolled down the sites and realized that most of them were regular bookshops, so he put a plus sign in front of the word *witchcraft* and tried again. He sipped his coffee as he looked at the list of sites. One on the second page looked promising—a store called Wicca Woman in Camden, close to Camden Lock market. He clicked through to the website. Wicca Woman apparently sold everything that a wannabe witch could need, from clothing to potions to magic wands, and it had a comprehensive list of books, including a secondhand section. The address of the shop was on the main page, along with a telephone number. Nightingale shaved and showered and put on his second-best suit before calling the number and asking to speak to the owner. Her name was Alice Steadman and she said that she would be delighted to see any books that he might want to sell, and that she would be in the shop all day.

Nightingale managed to find a parking space in a multistory car park a short walk from the Wicca Woman shop. It was in a side street, sandwiched between a shop that sold hand-knitted sweaters and a boutique that seemed to sell only T-shirts that promoted drug use. A bell chimed as he pushed open the door. A stick of incense was burning next to the cash register, filling the premises with a cloying, flowery fragrance. There were two pretty black teenagers in the shop, giggling as they looked at a display of love potions. The sales assistant was a punk girl with fluorescent pink hair, a stud in her chin, two studs in each eyebrow, and a nose ring. "Don't they set off metal detectors in airports?" asked Nightingale.

The girl grinned, showing perfect white teeth. "All the time," she said. She patted her groin. "But this is the one I have problems with."

"I bet," laughed Nightingale. "Is the boss in? Mrs. Steadman? I spoke to her on the phone, about some books." He held up the bag that he was holding as it proved his good intentions. It contained five books that he had taken from the basement in Gosling Manor.

"I'll get her for you," said the assistant. She disappeared through a beaded curtain and returned with a tiny woman in her sixties. Dressed in a long black shirt that reached her knees, black knitted tights, and black shoes that curled up at the toes, she looked like a pixie's shadow and had a birdlike, inquisitive face. Just like a bird she cocked her head on one side as she looked at Nightingale. "Mr. Nightingale?"

"Yes," said Nightingale.

"I thought you'd be older," she said. "You sounded older on the phone."

One of the girls held up a small cloth bag. "Here, do these fings really work?"

Mrs. Steadman tilted her chin up and fixed the girl with a steely glare. "My dear, everything in this shop works, providing you believe in it."

"But it'll make my boyfriend fall in love with me, yeah? And not look at any other girls?"

"That's what it says on the label, my dear, and that's what it'll do. But use it sparingly. No one wants a lapdog for a husband, do they?" She smiled at Nightingale. "Come on through, young man, and show me what you have."

She led him back through the curtain into a small room. There was a circular wooden table and three wooden chairs and above it a colorful Tiffany lampshade. A gas fire was burning and Nightingale took off his raincoat and draped it over the back of one of the chairs. "Would you like a cup of tea, I've just made a pot," asked Mrs. Steadman.

Nightingale sat down and placed the bag on the table. "Tea would be lovely, thank you," he said as he sat down.

Mrs. Steadman brought over a tray on which there was a brown ceramic teapot, two blue-and-white-striped mugs, and a matching milk jug and sugar bowl. "How do you like it?"

"Milk and no sugar," said Nightingale, as she poured tea into the mugs.

"Sweet enough?" she said, and giggled like a teenager. "So these books, they were left to you, you said?"

"Yes, by my father. His name was Ainsley Gosling, have you heard of him?"

The woman frowned. "Should I have done?" she finished pouring the tea and sat down.

"He was a collector of books on the occult. I wondered if he'd bought any from you."

"I don't recall the name," she said, stirring her tea. "And really I don't carry a huge selection of books. I deal mainly in spells and talismans."

"And you make a living from that?"

Mrs. Steadman chuckled. "Young man, I don't do this to make money. This is my life. This is who I am."

"Forgive me for asking, but are you a witch?"

Mrs. Steadman's eyes sparkled with amusement. "Just show me what you have in the bag, young man," she said.

Nightingale took the five books from the bag and put them on the table in front of her. She took a pair of reading glasses from the top pocket of her shirt and perched them delicately on the end of the nose. She picked up the first book, opened it carefully, and studied the first page which listed the date of publication and the publisher. "My goodness," she said.

"It's about witchcraft in the eighteen hundreds," said Nightingale.

"I can see that," she said. "This book I've seen before, but only reproductions. This is a first edition with the original illustrations. They were changed in later editions because some people found them…offensive."

"Is it valuable?"

"Oh yes."

"Would you buy it off me?"

She looked at him over the top of her glasses. "Young man, if I wanted to buy this I'd have to remortgage my house."

"It's valuable?"

"A second edition sold for fifteen thousand pounds last year. This is a first edition and it is in perfect condition."

"But you won't buy it?"

Mrs. Steadman sat back in her chair. "It's out of my league, young man," she said. "If you like, you could leave it with me and

I'll see if I can sell it for you. For a commission, of course. Say, ten percent."

"Sounds like a plan," said Nightingale. He took out his cigarettes. "Do you mind if I…?"

The woman patted her chest. "I'm afraid not," she said. "Asthma. And you know those things will give you cancer."

"Please don't tell me that I'm going to hell," he said. "That's the last thing I need to hear right now."

"There's a big difference between dying of lung cancer and going to hell," said the woman.

"Do you believe in hell?" asked Nightingale.

The woman fixed him with her eyes. They were so brown that they were almost black, Nightingale noticed. Glistening like pools of oil. "No, young man, I do not."

"There's no such place?" he sipped his tea. It was very strong, the way his mother used to make it. "Strong enough that the spoon stands up in it," was what she'd always said.

"How could there be? Fire and brimstone and such like."

"But I thought…" He was going to say "witches" but he caught himself just in time. "…people in your line were big believers in heaven and hell and devils."

"Young man, you have a very strange idea of what my line of work entails," she said. "I channel energy, I use the power of the natural world to make changes for good. What I do has nothing to do with God or the devil, with heaven or hell, and everything to do with the natural order of things."

"Love potions?" said Nightingale.

"Trinkets," said the woman. "We use the real power to help people, to cure sickness, or at least to ease pain and suffering. It has nothing to do with condemning people to eternal damnation." She picked up the second book. It was leather-bound, a history of the Salem witch trials of 1692. "This is nice," she said. "Not my sort of thing, but it should fetch a thousand pounds or so if you can find the right collector. It would probably fetch a higher price in America."

"Can you sell it for me, Mrs. Steadman?"

She nodded thoughtfully. "I know a lady in Boston would probably be interested," she said. She put it aside and picked up the third book. It was a Victorian book of natural healing that Nightingale had found open on a display cabinet. It was filled with watercolor paintings of plants and flowers and appeared to offer cures for everything from earache to bunions. "Now this I can definitely sell," she said. "I sold a copy over the Internet last month and I had several people chasing it. How does five hundred pounds sound?"

"Like music to my ears," said Nightingale. "Could you pay me now?"

"If you're happy with a check."

"Delirious," said Nightingale.

She picked up the next book and smiled. "This one too. It's one of the best books on pagan rituals there is, and I think…" She opened it and nodded enthusiastically. "Yes, it's a second edition. There's a market for this here in Camden, there's quite an active pagan community. Would you take three hundred for it?"

"Excellent," said Nightingale.

"Tell me, is there a reason you're selling them?"

Nightingale smiled. "I have a cash flow problem," he said. "And they're not really of any interest to me."

"Your father's books, you said. Was he a big collector?"

"I'd say so," said Nightingale.

"And if you don't mind me asking, why did you come to my little shop rather than trying an auction house?"

"I want to keep a low profile," said Nightingale. "I figured if they were in an auction there'd be publicity, and I don't really want that just now. My father only died a short time ago and I don't want newspapers trying to drum up a story."

"Why would that be a story?"

Nightingale smiled. Mrs. Steadman was as sharp as a knife and a better inquisitor than the detectives who had quizzed him after Simon Underwood had fallen to his death. "He killed himself, Mrs. Steadman."

The woman's eyes widened. "Oh, I'm so sorry. I didn't mean to pry."

"It's okay, we weren't exactly close. But at the moment I just want to sell a few of his books to raise some money, that's all."

"I quite understand," she said. She picked up the last book and smiled. "Now this one I will definitely buy, but I'm afraid it's not in the same league as the others," she said. "I sold a similar book just last week, here in the shop." It was a book of spells and seemed more like a coffee-table book than one that a witch would use, full of glossy photographs and recipes laid out as if they were in a Jamie Oliver cookery book. "It's only worth about twenty pounds, I'm afraid. Several thousand copies were published in the seventies."

"Twenty pounds is fine," said Nightingale. "I really wanted to know what you thought about that one. It says that anyone can work a spell, that you don't have to be in a coven or be a real witch. Is that right?"

"That's a difficult question, young man."

Nightingale pointed at the book she was holding. "But you believe in it, don't you? That if you light a candle of a particular color and use a particular incense and the right herb and you say the right words, that something magical will happen?"

"Would you like a biscuit?" asked Mrs. Steadman. "I rather get the feeling that you are going to be here for a while, so I think I should offer you something to nibble."

Nightingale laughed. "A biscuit would be wonderful, thank you."

Mrs. Steadman went over to a shelf and returned with a packet of Chocolate Hobnobs. "My weakness," she said, offering him one.

Nightingale took a biscuit, wondering if it had been a deliberate attempt to distract him, or if she was simply being hospitable. "I guess my question is, does magic work?" he said.

"Well, of course it does, young man," she said, taking a biscuit for herself and placing it on her saucer. "If it didn't work, people would soon lose interest, wouldn't they. If those young girls out there buy that potion and use it and it doesn't work, well, I'll have lost two customers and they'll tell all their friends and before long the shop would be out of business."

"But I thought you had to believe for magic to work."

"Well you could say that about medicine," said Mrs. Steadman. "With most illnesses, placebos work almost as well as the genuine article. Not for antibiotics, of course, but for the drugs that treat depression or high blood pressure or pain relief it's more a question of belief than of a true chemical effect. They believe that an aspirin will take away their headache so it does, when in fact a sugar pill would do the job just as well."

"You see, now you're confusing me," said Nightingale. "Is it what you're doing that works, is it the spells that do the business, or is it believing in the spells that makes them work?"

"Belief helps," said Mrs. Steadman, patiently. "It probably makes the spells more efficient, but even someone who didn't believe would get results. It's like cooking. You don't necessarily understand why yeast makes bread rise, but follow a recipe for bread and you'll get a loaf."

"And what about black magic?"

"The chocolates?

Nightingale laughed out loud. He was starting to like Mrs. Steadman, she had a sense of humor not dissimilar to his own. "I mean spells that perhaps aren't as well-meaning as the ones you sell in your shop."

"There's no such thing as black magic," she said earnestly. "There's no black magic and no white magic. There's just magic."

"But I thought—"

Mrs. Steadman silenced him with a wagging finger. "It's like electricity, young man," she said sternly. "You can use it to power a life-support machine or an electric chair. One saves lives and the other takes them, but the electricity itself isn't good or bad. It's just a power to be used."

"But stuff like selling your soul to the devil. Is that possible?"

Mrs. Steadman looked suddenly concerned. She reached forward and put her hand on top of his. "Is that what this is about? You want to sell your soul?"

Nightingale shook his head emphatically. "Absolutely not," he said.

"You swear, on all you believe in?" she stared deep into his eyes.

Nightingale met her gaze levelly. "I swear," he said quietly. "I just need to know, that's all. Is it possible?"

She pulled her hand back and sipped her tea, still watching him with her liquid black eyes. "There are spells that supposedly enable you to give your soul to the devil," she said eventually. "One I know is actually quite simple. You go to a churchyard at night. Any churchyard will do, but the older the better. You draw a magic circle on the ground, and within the circle you draw two crosses. You take a handful of wormwood in each hand and hold a Bible in your left hand. Toss the wormwood in your right hand up and the wormwood in your left hand down, taking care not to drop the

Bible. Then you say the Lord's Prayer backwards." She sipped her tea again.

"And that's it?"

"That's it. Bob's your uncle. On your way home, you leave the Bible on the steps of a church."

Nightingale frowned. It all sounded too easy. "So there's no contract? You don't do a deal?"

"It's a spell," said Mrs. Steadman. "Quite a simple one."

"And what if you change your mind? What if you want to take it back?"

"That's just as easy," she said. "You renounce Satan. Three times."

"That's it?"

"Did you expect something more dramatic?"

Nightingale reached for his cigarettes again, but remembered her no-smoking policy. "I thought there were contracts. I don't know, signed in blood or something."

"Ah…" she said, and winced as if she'd bitten down on a bad tooth.

"So there is more?" said Nightingale.

"You asked about making a pact with the devil. With Lucifer or Satan or whatever you want to call him. That's simple. But contracts with minor devils are a much more complicated matter. There are 66 princes under the devil, each with 6,666 legions."

"And each legion is made up of 6,666 devils," said Nightingale.

"You have been doing your homework," she said.

"I've been doing a bit of research," admitted Nightingale. "So to do a deal, you approach one of the devils?"

"Or one of the princes. But the devil himself can't be summoned by mere mortals."

"I know, I tried."

Mrs. Steadman's eyebrow shot skyward. "I do hope you're being flippant, young man," she said.

"I found a book, it had a spell or something, you recite the words and the devil appears."

"I think not," she said.

"Well, it didn't work anyway," said Nightingale. "But it is possible to summon a particular devil? One of the princes?"

"I wouldn't know, young man," she said archly. "Now you're talking about Satanism and devil worship, and that's as far removed from what I do as you can get. Wicca has nothing to do with the devil or devil worship."

"Do you believe in it, Mrs. Steadman?"

She shook her head. "No. I don't believe in hell and I don't believe that there is an entity called Satan. But I believe in good and evil. And I believe that there is a power in the earth that can be harnessed and used."

"But there are ways of selling a soul, aren't there? As opposed to giving yourself over to the devil."

"Mr. Nightingale, I'm not even sure that I believe in souls, not in the sense you mean. My beliefs are more that everything is connected, everything flows, that we are one with the earth."

"But for someone who did believe, there are things they could do to sell their soul? Or a soul?"

"In theory, yes," said the woman, but she was clearly uncomfortable with the way the conversation was going.

"Please tell me," said Nightingale. "I need to know."

"You are asking the wrong person," she said. "It's like asking a doctor how to commit murder."

Nightingale chuckled. "In my experience, doctors make the best murderers," he said.

"In your experience?"

"I was a policeman, in another life."

"So you believe in reincarnation? At least that's something."

Nightingale's laughed out loud. "I didn't mean that literally," he said. "Mrs. Steadman, please, how does one go about selling a soul?"

"Oh, Mr. Nightingale, what a question."

"Just hypothetically. What would one do?"

Mrs. Steadman sipped her tea, then put her mug down and held it with both hands. "Hypothetically then," she said. "You have to renounce God and the Church. You pay homage to the devil, drink the blood of sacrificed children, and strike your deal with whichever demon you summon. A contract is drawn up and signed with blood drawn from the left arm. Then your name is inscribed in the Red Book of Death."

"And if you wanted to sell the soul of a child, could you do that?"

Mrs. Steadman put her hands palms down on the table. "Why are you asking these questions? You seem like a nice man, a good man. What you're asking, it's not..." She shivered. "It's not right."

"Have you ever heard of a man called Sebastian Mitchell?" asked Nightingale quietly.

Mrs. Steadman stiffened. "You know him?"

Nightingale shook his head. "I have a book that he wrote. A diary."

"Burn it," said the woman, her tiny hands clenching into fists.

"It's handwritten. In Latin."

"Burn it," she repeated. "Go home now and burn it."

"You couldn't sell it for me?"

She shook her head emphatically. "The sort of people who'd want to buy a book like that, I wouldn't want to do business with," she said.

39

Nightingale was humming as he walked into the office. Jenny McLean looked up from her computer. "You sound happy," she said.

"I've come into some money," he said and dropped a check onto her desk. "Eight hundred and twenty quid," he said.

"Who did you kill, Jack?"

"Oh ye of little faith," said Nightingale, heading over to the coffeemaker. "I sold some of the books in the basement to a lovely little witch in Camden."

"You did not," said Jenny, picking up the check and holding it up to the light as if she suspected it was a forgery.

"I did so, and she promised to buy more. She has a shop and she sells on the Internet, too."

"Eight hundred and twenty pounds, that's brilliant," said Jenny.

"Should keep the wolf from the door. And there's more to come," said Nightingale, pouring himself a coffee. "She's going to sell a couple of the rarer books and she thinks she'll get top dollar.

I said I'd go back with a list of other books and she'll let me know what they're worth." He perched on the edge of her desk. "She wanted to have a look around herself but I don't think I should be showing visitors around Gosling Manor."

"You'll take me though, right?" said Jenny.

Nightingale raised his coffee mug to her. "You're different," he said. "You're family."

"You're so sweet."

"I know, I know."

He took a package out of his pocket and unwrapped it. It was a magnifying glass that he'd bought at the Wicca Woman shop. "Looking for clues?" she said. "It's very Sherlock Holmes."

"Yeah, and I bought the deerstalker hat and the pipe on eBay." He took the mug of coffee and the magnifying glass into his office and sat down at his desk. He pulled open the top drawer and took out his photograph album.

"What have you got there?" asked Jenny.

"Pictures of me as a baby," said Nightingale.

"No way," said Jenny. "Why've I never seen them before?"

"Because I never wanted you to see me naked," said Nightingale.

"Let me see!"

"You're shameless," said Nightingale. He pushed the album toward her. "Don't say I didn't warn you."

Jenny squealed and opened the album. "Oh my God, you were adorable," she said, looking at the first picture. She turned the page. "Oh look at that, you were so cute," she said. "Look at your smile, look at those chubby little cheeks." She turned to the next page and smiled when she saw the photographs of his parents. "They were so proud of you," she said. "You can see it in their eyes."

"Yeah, they were good people," said Nightingale.

Jenny nodded at the magnifying glass in his hand. "Seriously, what's that for?" she asked.

"You'll think I'm stupid."

"Heaven forbid," she said.

Nightingale pulled the album back across the desk and turned to the first photograph, the one taken when he was just a day old. "I'm pretty damn sure that I don't have a pentangle tattoo," he said. "I would have seen it at the gym or someone would have mentioned it over the years. I mean, I had four full medicals while I was with the Met, and the Met's doctors are bloody thorough. Not much gets by them."

"So?"

"So I was thinking that maybe it's somewhere where it can't be seen. On my head, maybe. Under my hair."

"You're right," said Jenny.

"I am?"

"Yeah, I do think you're stupid."

Nightingale smiled thinly. "Thanks."

"Well, at least checking your baby pictures with a magnifying glass beats shaving your head," said Jenny.

Nightingale put the magnifying glass over the photograph and moved his eyes closer. "There's nothing," he said.

"Of course there's nothing," said Jenny. "The whole thing is ridiculous."

Nightingale turned the page and began checking the rest of the photographs.

"Jack, give it a rest," said Jenny.

Nightingale opened his mouth to reply, but before he could speak the office door was thrown open by an angry woman. It took Nightingale a couple of seconds to realize who it was and that he'd last seen her through the lens of his video camera leaving the hotel where she'd met her lover. It was Mrs. McBride. Before Nightingale could react she rushed over and slapped him across the face. His mug fell from his hands and hot coffee splattered across the floor. "Hey!" shouted Nightingale.

He was off balance and before he could get off the desk she slapped him again. "You bastard!" she shrieked.

Jenny reached for the phone. "I'm calling the police," she said.

Mrs. McBride ignored her as she glared at Nightingale. "He killed himself, you bastard. Are you happy now?"

"Who?" asked Nightingale. "Who killed himself?"

"Who do you think? My husband. He killed himself because of you." She raised her hand to slap him again but then she burst into tears and slumped to the ground, her body wracked by sobs.

Jenny put down the phone and went around the desk to comfort the crying woman. At first Mrs. McBride shook her away, but eventually she allowed herself to be led over to the sofa. Jenny gave her a paper tissue and sat down next to her. "What happened?" she asked.

Nightingale picked up the mug and dropped a few sheets of copy paper onto the spilled coffee. It wasn't the first time that he'd been attacked by an angry spouse, and he doubted that it would be the last.

"He drowned himself," said Mrs. McBride. "In the canal. He left me a note." She dabbed at her eyes. "He said that he loved me and that he couldn't live without me." She looked up at Nightingale. "Why did you do it?" she asked tearfully.

"He was a client," said Nightingale. "I was working for him."

"You bastard," she said, but this time there was no venom in her voice, only despair.

"You were being unfaithful," said Nightingale quietly. "Your husband had a right to know."

"My husband was dead below the waist," said Mrs. McBride. "We hadn't had sex for five years. Five bloody years. What should I have done? Become a nun?"

"Mrs. McBride, I'm sorry, but that's not my problem. Your husband wanted to know where he stood."

"Ha bloody ha," said Mrs. McBride.

Nightingale flushed when he realized what he'd said. "You know what I meant," he said. "He suspected that you were being unfaithful. He wanted to know the truth."

"The truth? I'm his wife, that's the truth. I stood by him through all the time he was in the hospital. I stuck with him in sickness and in health. That's the truth."

"You were being unfaithful," said Nightingale.

"Jack…" said Jenny.

"I was having sex, that's all!" hissed Mrs. McBride. "I'm a woman, not a block of bloody wood. I needed sex and I found a man who'd give me sex and you went and told Joel. You bloody well told him and now he's dead!" She began to cry and Jenny put her arm around her.

"Mrs. McBride, I am sorry for your loss…" said Nightingale.

"It's your fault he's dead," she said.

"Did he say that?" asked Nightingale.

"He didn't have to. He said in the note that he couldn't live without me, and he said he knew that I was going to leave him." She looked up at him with tear-filled eyes. "Is that what you told him? Did you tell him that I was going to leave him?"

"I didn't tell him anything of the sort," said Nightingale. "I just gave him my report."

"He said in his note that he couldn't bear to live without me, but I was never going to leave him." She grabbed at Jenny's hands. "You have to believe me."

"I do," said Jenny.

She looked over at Nightingale with tears in her eyes. "When he told me that he knew I was glad, in a way. I'd been feeling as guilty as sin for weeks and wanted to tell him myself. But when he showed me the video you'd given him, I couldn't face him. I went to stay with my friend Lynn, to give him time to cool down. But then I was going to explain everything and tell him that I still loved him, that I still wanted to be with him. And now I can't because he's dead and that's your fault."

"Did he tell you about my investigation?" asked Nightingale.

"He showed me the video you gave him. And the phone records. But it wasn't until I found your name in his checkbook that I knew who'd done it." She dabbed at her eyes and looked at him. "How can you live with yourself, doing what you do?"

"It's my job, Mrs. McBride."

"You could have talked to me, I could have explained. I could have ended it with Ronnie. He's married anyway, you knew that, didn't you? His wife makes him sleep in the spare room, he just wanted some contact, to touch someone, to share a bed with them. Ronnie was never going to leave her and I was never going to leave Joel."

"There's nothing more I can say, Mrs. McBride, other than that I'm sorry for your loss."

"Sorry doesn't cut it," said Mrs. McBride. "You killed my husband, and you're going to hell."

"Your husband killed himself, Mrs. McBride. You know that and I know that."

"I don't know how you can live with yourself. You're scum, you make money from the suffering of others. You should be ashamed of yourself."

She burst into tears and Jenny gave her a box of tissues. Mrs. McBride threw the box at Nightingale and it hit him on the chest. "I don't want your bloody tissues, I want my husband!" she shouted.

Nightingale looked helplessly at Jenny. She waved for him to go. "I'll handle her," she mouthed. Nightingale did as he was told. He went outside and lit a cigarette. A lot of what the angry woman had said was just plain wrong, he knew that, but one thing she had said was definitely true. He was ashamed of himself.

CHAPTER 40

Six uniformed constables carried Robbie Hoyle's coffin to the grave, followed by Anna and Sarah. They were both dressed in black and carrying single red roses. The twins had stayed at home and were being looked after by Anna's sister.

More than three hundred people had crowded into the church, most of them police officers. Superintendent Chalmers gave one of the eulogies. He had talked about Robbie's career, but he also spoke about his family and his life outside work and told a couple of anecdotes about Robbie's early days on the beat that had the congregation smiling and nodding. Chalmers clearly spoke from the heart, and when his voice cracked a couple of times toward the end, the cynic in Nightingale wanted to think that Chalmers was faking it. But by the end of the eulogy Nightingale had come to realize that Robbie's death had hit the man hard.

Anna gave one of the readings and she was faultless, holding her head up and projecting her voice and smiling across at her daughter. Nightingale saw several tough CID detectives with tears in their eyes.

Nightingale was wearing a dark blue suit and a black tie, and Jenny had a black cashmere coat over a black dress and had tied her hair back with a black Alice band. They were standing on a gravel path, about fifty feet from the grave. The mourners had walked from the church to the graveyard, following a slowly driven hearse bearing the coffin. The six police officers somberly lowered the coffin into the ground as the vicar read from the Bible he was holding.

"When I die, I don't want to be buried," whispered Nightingale.

"You should say that in your will," said Jenny.

"I haven't got a will."

"Well draw one up," she said. "You've got your apartment in Bayswater and you've got Gosling Manor. You've got to leave it all to somebody."

Nightingale shrugged. "I don't care who gets it," he said. "My parents are gone and I've no kids." He grinned. "I'll leave it all to you."

"You will not," she said.

"There's nobody else close to me," he said.

"Find a charity then," she said. "I don't want to profit from your death, Jack. It's bad enough my parents always telling me that I'll be set for life when they pass away, I don't want that from you as well."

"I don't need a will, then."

"Yes, you do," she said. "Otherwise your assets get divided up according to some legal formula or other. If you're married, the surviving spouse gets it. If there's kids, they get it. And if there's no wife and kids then it goes up the line to the parents and if they're not around it goes to any relatives they have. Trust me, you need a will."

"Anyway, the will isn't the point. The point is that I don't want to be buried, okay?"

"Message received," she said. "Do you want to donate your body to medical science instead? I'm sure your liver would be worth looking at."

Nightingale flashed her a tight smile. "I'm not having bloody medical students poking around my innards," he said. "Cremation will do just fine."

"Cremation it is," said Jenny. "What shall I do with the ashes?"

"Whatever you like," said Nightingale. "Speaking of which, do you think it's okay to smoke in a churchyard?"

"I think legally you'd be okay but it's pretty bad form. How about an egg-timer?"

"A what?"

"I'll have your ashes put in an egg timer, that way you'll be one of the few men in the country that's actually useful in the kitchen."

The policemen finished lowering the coffin. The three men on the left dropped their end of the slings and the three on the right pulled them out. Anna dropped her rose onto the coffin and encouraged Sarah to do the same.

"Scatter them over the pitch at Old Trafford," said Nightingale.

"Are you serious?"

Nightingale nodded. "Yeah. I don't want to be in the ground, Jenny. I don't want to rot slowly, and I don't want a gravestone for people to look at."

"Jack, you're thirty-two years old, you've got years ahead of you. Provided you stop smoking and drinking."

"Unless Gosling was telling the truth. In two weeks' time I'm thirty-three. Two weeks today, in fact."

"Today's Thursday," said Jenny. "Your birthday's Friday the twenty-seventh."

"Yeah, but I figure that means my soul's up for grabs just after midnight on the twenty-sixth, right."

"I don't know how prompt demons are," said Jenny. "Anyway, it's all nonsense and you know it. Come on, we have to go to the reception."

"I can't face that," said Nightingale.

"Well at least let's say good-bye to Anna. You can't just leave without saying anything."

Anna was being comforted by Robbie's mother. "She's got enough on her plate," said Nightingale. "I'll call around tomorrow."

As Nightingale turned to go he saw Derbyshire and Evans, the two detectives who had called into his office. Nightingale went over and shook their hands. "Did you guys know Robbie?" he asked.

"Met him once on an interview course at Hendon," said Evans. "Never worked with him, though."

"Bloody nightmare," said Nightingale. "I still can't believe it. Anything happening with the taxi driver?"

The inspector shook his head. "The way things stand at the moment, we can't even do him for careless driving. He wasn't on his cell, he hadn't been drinking, he wasn't speeding. It really was an accident, plain and simple."

"What was the guy's name? The driver?"

Evans narrowed his eyes. "Why would you want his name?"

Nightingale faked a smile. "The Federation rep asked me if I'd give Anna a hand filling out the insurance forms. They need details of the accident, that's all."

Evans nodded. "Barry O'Brien," he said. "He lives out in Hammersmith. He was fully insured, clean license and everything, so I don't see there'll be any problems."

"How is he, the driver?"

"Physically fine. He was wearing his seat belt, so no physical damage, but he's really shook up."

"Yeah, well he should be," said Nightingale.

"No, I'm serious," said Evans. "He was in a right mess when we saw him. He's never had an accident before, and he's been driving a cab for over thirty years. He's taking it really badly."

Nightingale thanked the two detectives and then headed for the exit. Jenny linked her arm through his. "You just lied to him, didn't you?" she said. "There are no insurance papers."

"How do you know?"

"I just know. You can't go lying to the police, Jack."

"Yes you can, it's practically a national pastime," said Nightingale. "Everyone lies to the cops."

"But why do you want to know who the taxi driver was?"

"I want to talk to him."

"Because?"

Nightingale sighed. "Because he killed my best friend and I want to know what happened."

"They told you what happened. It was an accident. Robbie was in the wrong place at the wrong time."

"Yeah, well, cops don't always tell the truth," said Nightingale. "So I want to hear it from the horse's mouth." They walked out of the graveyard. "I can't work, Jenny, not today. Let's go and get drunk."

"I've a better idea," said Jenny. "Why don't you show me the house? Gosling Manor."

"You're serious?"

"Why not?" said Jenny. "I want to see if it's as big as you say it is."

Nightingale grinned. "Jenny, size isn't everything, you know."

"Actually," she smiled, "it is, pretty much."

CHAPTER

41

Jenny climbed out of the MGB and looked up at the house. "You weren't joking, it is a mansion," she said. "How many rooms has it got?"

"A lot," said Nightingale.

"I expected gargoyles and turrets and stuff but it's really, really nice," she said. "And the gardens are spectacular." She stood with her hand on her hips, admiring the house. "It's chocolate-box pretty, isn't it? Not the sort of house that you'd expect a Satanist to live in."

"It was built by the local squire, apparently."

"It's lovely, it really is. What is it, seventeenth century?"

"Sixteenth, the cops said. But it's been added to over the years. You should have a look around the back, there's a lake. And stables. So how does it compare to the McLean ancestral home?"

Jenny smiled. "Ah, now you're talking," she said. "My parents' place is a bit special."

"As special as this?"

Jenny shrugged. "I'm not playing the 'who has got the biggest house' game, Jack. But this is lovely, really lovely. You're very lucky to have it."

"Yeah, but I can't see that I'll be able to keep it," said Nightingale. He walked over to the garage, which was to the right of the main building. It was built in the same stone as the house with a pitched roof into which were set large skylights. There were four metal doors that opened upwards but all were locked. CCTV cameras at either end of the garage covered all the doors and the area in front of them.

"He was big on security then," said Jenny.

"Inside and out," said Nightingale. He walked around the far side of the garage. There were two windows there, dusty and covered with cobwebs. He peered through the first window but all he could see was a bare concrete floor, discolored from years of spilled oil. He moved over to the second window, cupped his hand over his forehead, and squinted through the glass. There was a long wooden work bench but no tools. A pulley and chains were hanging from a metal girder running the full length of the garage and there was a dark area at the far end which looked like it might be a pit.

"What are you looking for?" asked Jenny, joining him at the window.

"A Bentley," said Nightingale. "Apparently that's what Gosling drove. Or rather, that's what he was driven around in." He moved away from the window. "Empty," he said. "Just like the house."

"Maybe he sold it," said Jenny.

"Yeah, maybe he did," said Nightingale. "He seems to have sold everything else."

"Except the books," said Jenny.

"Except the books," agreed Nightingale. "Come on, I'll give you the tour."

They walked back to the front door and Nightingale unlocked it. He bowed and waved for her to go in first. Jenny walked into the hallway. "Wow, would you look at that chandelier," she said. "And this floor is Italian marble, right?"

"Only the best for Ainsley Gosling," said Nightingale, closing the door.

"And there's no furniture?"

"Just a bed and a chair in the master bedroom," said Nightingale.

"That's where he...?"

"Killed himself? Yeah. But you wouldn't know by looking at the room, it's been cleaned. Not a speck of blood." He waved his hand around the hall. "So, can you see the secret panel?"

"The what?"

"The secret panel. Gosling was the only one who knew how to get down to the basement."

Jenny walked slowly along the length of the hallway, running her hand along the wooden panelling. "How did you find it, if it's so secret?"

Nightingale waxed an imaginary moustache and did his best Hercules Poirot impersonation. "Because I am ze great detective," he said.

"Robbie found it, right?"

"It was a joint effort," said Nightingale. He pressed the panel that led down to the basement and it clicked open. He flicked the light switch. "Be careful, the stairs are quite steep," he said. "And keep a hold of the handrail."

He followed her down the stairs. "This is amazing," said Jenny. "There must be thousands of books here. Are they all witchcraft and devil stuff?"

"Seem to be," said Nightingale.

"Are you going to sell them all?" she asked as she pulled one out of the middle of a shelf and looked at the cover. "Ah," she said, before he could answer. "Perhaps not."

"What's wrong?" he asked.

She held up the book so that he could see the title. *Dissecting Humans.*

"No way," he said.

Jenny flicked through the book. "Complete with illustrations," she said. "I think it's a medical textbook. At least I hope it is." She put it back on the shelf and started walking through the display cases. "It's half library, half museum," she said.

Nightingale went over to Gosling's desk. He sat down and opened the top drawer. He pulled out a leather file. Inside were plastic folders holding business cards. Nightingale flicked through them. There were lawyers, businessmen, politicians, showbiz personalities, even high-ranking policemen. Ainsley Gosling had some very important friends.

"Have you seen these crystal balls?" asked Jenny. "Was he a fortune teller as well?"

"Get away from there!" shouted Nightingale, leaping out of the chair.

Jenny backed away from the display case, her hands in the air. "What's wrong?" she said.

Nightingale hurried over to her. "Just don't touch them," he said.

"Why, are they valuable?" she said. "Don't worry, I'll be careful."

"It's not that," he said. His shoe crunched on a piece of broken glass. "It's just…" He tailed off, not sure if he could explain what he was worried about without appearing to be a complete idiot.

"What's wrong, Jack?" asked Jenny.

"The last time Robbie was here, he saw himself, in one of the balls."

"His reflection, you mean?"

Nightingale took a deep breath. "This is going to sound crazy, but he saw himself being hit by a taxi."

Jenny's face hardened. "That's not funny, Jack," she said.

"I'm not joking," said Nightingale. He pointed at the shards of glass on the floor. "He was so shocked that he dropped it. Smashed it to bits."

"Jack, listen to yourself. You're saying that Robbie saw his future. You know that's impossible."

"I'm only telling you what he told me, Jenny. And if you'd seen the look on his face, you would have seen how serious he was."

"He saw himself being hit by a cab?"

"That's what he said."

"That's crazy," said Jenny.

"Everything about this is crazy," said Nightingale. "This basement is crazy, the DVD that Gosling left me is crazy, killing yourself in a magic circle isn't exactly a sign of sanity."

Jenny flopped down onto a leather sofa. "Are you okay?"

"In what sense?"

"You've just found out that your parents weren't your real parents, that your real father killed himself with a shotgun, your birth mother has spent most of her life in a mental institution, your uncle and aunt are dead, and you've just buried your best friend."

Nightingale lit a cigarette and sat down. "Yeah. It's been a stressful few days," he said sarcastically.

"And how are you going to deal with it all?"

Nightingale held up the cigarette. "Nicotine and alcohol, same as usual," he said.

"Do you want to talk about it?"

"With a therapist?"

Jenny laughed. "With me, you idiot."

"I'm okay," said Nightingale. "I'm in bits about Robbie, but I'm an adult, I can deal with it. The parents thing is confusing me a bit, but I'm not the first person to discover that they were adopted, and I can deal with that."

"And your mother?"

"She's not my mother, Jenny. She's…"

"She's what?"

Nightingale shook his head. "I don't know," he said. "Yes, she gave birth to me, I'm sure of that now. But she's nothing to me and never will be. My mother was Irene Nightingale and she's been dead almost fifteen years. And Bill was my father. Nothing will ever change that."

"And the DVD? Gosling's message to you?"

Nightingale shrugged. "The ramblings of a suicidal madman," he said.

She looked at him earnestly. "You're sure that's how you feel?"

"Why do you ask?"

"Because what you've been through, it's traumatic. Very traumatic. And you seem to be taking it all very calmly."

"I was a cop for almost ten years, Jenny, it takes a lot to faze me." He blew smoke up at the ceiling. "Trust me, I'm fine."

CHAPTER

42

When Nightingale woke up on Friday morning he lay in bed for almost half an hour staring up at the ceiling. He had acted on impulse when he asked the detective inspector for the name of the man who had killed Robbie Hoyle, but once he had it he knew that nothing would stop him going to talk to him. Nightingale wanted to know if Hoyle had died immediately or if he had lain dying in a pool of blood, begging and pleading to be saved. He wanted to know why O'Brien hadn't stopped or swerved, why he had just mown Hoyle down. Nightingale wanted to know what had happened, even though the knowledge wouldn't change anything. Hoyle's death didn't make any sense, but then in Nightingale's experience, few deaths did. He booted up his laptop and logged on to Tracesmart, an online service that provided access to the electoral rolls around the country. There was only one Barry O'Brien living in Hammersmith. He made a note of the address, switched off his laptop, and called Jenny to tell her that he would be in late. "I've things to do at Gosling Manor," he lied. "I'll be in during the afternoon. If there's anything important, I'll be on my cell."

Nightingale ended the call, feeling suddenly guilty. He didn't like lying to Jenny, but telling her what he was really doing wouldn't achieve anything and would only worry her. Nightingale had always been much more comfortable asking questions than answering them.

He got up and showered and shaved and put on a clean shirt and a dark blue suit that had just come back from the dry cleaners. He made himself a cup of black coffee, smoked a Marlboro, and then drove to Hammersmith.

O'Brien's house was on a terraced street and a black cab was parked in front of it. Nightingale found a space for his MGB about fifty yards from the house. He climbed out and walked over to the cab. There was no damage to the front, no blood, not even a scratch, nothing to show that the vehicle had ended the life of Robbie Hoyle. Nightingale wasn't surprised. A London cab weighed more than 1,600 kilograms, and flesh and blood was no match for hard steel moving at speed.

A middle-aged housewife walked by with a white poodle on a lead. She was holding a screwed-up plastic bag in her left hand and cajoling the animal to do its business. Nightingale flashed her a smile and she glared at him as if he were a child molester.

A flight of half a dozen stone steps led up to the front door of O'Brien's house. Nightingale rang the doorbell and he heard it buzz in the hallway. He went back to the sidewalk and looked up at the bedroom windows. The curtains were drawn. Nightingale wondered if O'Brien had worked through the night and was now sleeping. He rang the bell again. When there was no answer, he took out his cell phone and dialed the number that he'd been given by Directory Enquiries. He heard the phone ring inside the house.

He let it ring for a full thirty seconds then ended the call and put the phone back in his pocket.

He stood on the sidewalk with his hands on his hips, considering his options. If O'Brien was asleep, then he'd answer the door eventually. He obviously wasn't working because his cab was in the street. Maybe he'd taken the day off and had gone somewhere without his taxi. If that was the case then Nightingale was wasting his time.

He went back up the steps. There was a letter box in the middle of the door. Nightingale pushed it open and bent down to shout through it. "Mr. O'Brien?" The door moved forward. It was open. Nightingale frowned. He straightened up and pushed open the door.

There were half a dozen envelopes on the carpet, mainly bills, and several garish leaflets. Nightingale stepped inside. "Mr. O'Brien? Are you there?" There was no answer, though Nightingale could hear a soft buzzing sound, like an electronic hum, coming from upstairs. He pushed the door closed. He knew that he shouldn't be in the house, but he also knew that there was something wrong. People didn't leave their front doors open in London. He walked down the hallway and checked the living room and kitchen. There were dirty dishes in the sink and a half-drunk cup of coffee on the draining board. Nightingale touched the kettle. It was cold.

He went back into the hallway. "Mr. O'Brien? Are you upstairs?" A large bluebottle buzzed around Nightingale's head and he swatted it away. He headed up the stairs, peering up at the landing above. "Mr. O'Brien, is everything okay?"

The buzzing sound got louder as he went up the stairs. Two more large flies circled Nightingale's head. As he reached the top of the stairs he saw that the bathroom door was ajar. There were half a dozen flies on the wall by the light switch and as he moved closer to the bathroom more flew out through the open door. The buzzing was much stronger now, like a faulty electric circuit.

There was a bad smell in the air, an odor that Nightingale had smelled many times during his years as a police officer, a smell that was difficult to describe but which could never be forgotten. Before he even pushed open the bathroom door, Nightingale knew what he was going to find.

The man had been in the water for at least a day, probably longer, and had already started to swell up. There were deep cuts in both arms and the savage wounds were filled with flies. The flies were everywhere, feeding and laying their eggs, buzzing around Nightingale as if they resented his appearance at their banquet.

O'Brien had filled the bath with water and had cut his wrists with a Stanley knife. The knife was lying on the floor, its blade covered in blood. There were blood smears across the wall and the floor where arterial blood had sprayed, but most of it had gone into the bathwater. O'Brien's eyes were still open, staring up at the ceiling. The cuts were parallel to the arms and went right through skin, muscle, and blood vessels. Nightingale didn't know why Barry O'Brien had wanted to kill himself but one thing was for sure—it wasn't a cry for help.

Scrawled across the tiles at the side of the bath in bloody letters was the phrase that Nightingale had become all too familiar with. YOU ARE GOING TO HELL, JACK NIGHTINGALE. Dozens of flies were feeding off the blood.

Nightingale stared at the words in horror. "What the hell is going on?" he whispered to himself. He pulled a couple of feet of toilet tissue from the roll, swatted the flies away with his hands and then used it to wipe the tiles, then dropped the bloody tissue into the toilet bowl. He pulled off another long piece of tissue, wet it under the tap and wiped the tiles a second time, then threw it into the bowl and flushed. The tiles looked too clean now that he'd wiped them down, so he splashed bloody water from the bath over the tiles and then washed his hands in the sink. Flies buzzed around his hands as he washed them, and one got so close to his right ear that he flinched.

He dried his hands and went back into the hallway where he took out his cell phone and started to dial emergency. He stopped at the second digit. He cancelled the call and instead dialed the number of New Scotland Yard. He asked the switchboard operator to put him through to Inspector Dan Evans, and after a couple of minutes the inspector was on the line. "Dan, I thought I'd better tell you this before you hear it from anyone else," said Nightingale.

"That sounds ominous," said the inspector jovially.

"I'm at Barry O'Brien's house and he's killed himself."

There was a long silence. "I hope this is some sort of sick joke," said Evans eventually.

"He's cut his wrists. He's been dead for a while by the look of it."

"What the hell are you doing in his house?"

"I came around to talk to him," said Nightingale. "The front door was open."

"So you just walked in?"

"Like I said, the front door was open."

"You can't just go wandering around people's houses, Nightingale. You're not in the job anymore."

"I know that, but what's done is done. I was going to call emergency but I thought I'd better let you know what was happening."

"Do you need an ambulance?"

"He's definitely dead. Are you going to handle it or should I call emergency?"

"Have you any idea the trouble this is going to cause, Nightingale? You got O'Brien's name from me, right?"

"I've forgotten where I heard his name," said Nightingale. "And I doubt that I'm going to remember."

"Let's keep it that way," said Evans. "Where's the body?"

"Upstairs bathroom," said Nightingale.

"Wait for me downstairs, outside the house," said Evans. "And don't touch anything."

CHAPTER

43

They left him in the interview room for the best part of an hour, with just a cup of canteen coffee to drink. Nightingale had asked if it was okay to smoke and a sullen uniformed constable had said no. He hadn't been arrested so he was free to leave whenever he wanted, but there were questions that needed to be answered and Nightingale figured that the best thing was to get it over with. They hadn't searched him or taken his cell phone, so he rang Jenny and said that he would be later than expected. She wanted to know where he was. "It's complicated," he said. "I'll explain when I get back." Jenny started to press him for more details, but Nightingale heard footsteps in the corridor and then the door opened and in walked Superintendent Chalmers, in full uniform and holding a clipboard. Nightingale ended the call and put his phone away.

"Calling your brief?" asked Chalmers. Behind him were Dan Evans and Neil Derbyshire, both holding notebooks and ballpoint pens.

"I didn't think I needed a lawyer," said Nightingale. "They told me they just wanted a chat."

"A chat it is then," said Chalmers. He sat down opposite Nightingale. Evans took the chair next to Chalmers while Derbyshire moved the chair that was next to Nightingale and placed it by the door so that all three policemen were facing him around a metal table that had been bolted to the floor. On a shelf on the wall above the table was a digital voice recorder and in the far upper corner of the room a small CCTV camera was looking down at Nightingale.

Chalmers nodded at Evans, and Evans switched on the recorder. "Superintendent Ronald Chalmers, interviewing Jack Nightingale." He looked at the clock on the wall. "It is now a quarter past two in the afternoon on Friday the tenth and with me are..." He nodded at Evans.

"Detective Inspector Dan Evans," said Evans.

"Detective Constable Neil Derbyshire," added Derbyshire.

"If this is just a chat, why the recording?" asked Nightingale.

"It's procedure," said Chalmers.

"Can I smoke?"

"No, you can't," said the superintendent.

"But I'm not under arrest?"

"No, you're not," said the superintendent.

"I'm free to go whenever I want?"

"You're helping us with our enquiries into the death of Barry O'Brien."

"Just so we're all clear on that," said Nightingale. "I'm here to help."

"Date of birth," said Chalmers.

"What?"

"Your date of birth, for the record."

"I'm thirty-two, thirty-three on Friday the twenty-seventh. That's a week from today."

Evans and Derbyshire scribbled in their notebooks.

"Don't feel you have to get me a present," said Nightingale.

"What were you doing in Barry O'Brien's house this morning?"

"I wanted to talk to him."

"So you broke in?"

"The front door was open."

"You invited yourself in? Is that it?"

"The door was open. I pushed it and it opened. I went upstairs and found the body."

"Why did you go upstairs?"

"To see if he was there."

"But you'd already called his phone so you knew he wasn't in the house."

"I thought he might be asleep."

Chalmers sat back shaking his head. "So why didn't you just go away and come back another time?"

"I don't know," said Nightingale. "I just thought…"

"Yes? You thought what?"

"I thought that maybe something was wrong."

"So why didn't you call the police? Why did you break into his house?"

"I didn't break in," said Nightingale. "I already told you, the front door was open. Then I heard the flies."

"The flies?"

"He'd been dead for a while. He was covered with flies. I heard the buzzing from the hallway."

"And what did you want to talk to Mr. O'Brien about?"

Nightingale sighed. It was a difficult question to answer.

"You do understand the question, Mr. Nightingale?"

"Yes, I understand the question. I just wanted to talk to him."

"About what?"

"About what happened to Robbie."

"You're referring to Inspector Robert Hoyle?"

"Robbie Hoyle," corrected Nightingale. "Nobody called him Robert."

"You wanted to talk to Mr. O'Brien because he was responsible for the death of your friend, Inspector Hoyle?"

"I guess so."

"You guess so?"

Nightingale threw up his hands. "You make it sound like there was something sinister going on. I just wanted to talk to him."

"About what, specifically?"

"About what happened. How Robbie died."

"But there's no mystery as to what happened. It was a road traffic accident. What did you expect Mr. O'Brien to say? Did you want him to apologize, is that it? Did you want him to express remorse?"

"No," said Nightingale flatly.

"And when he wasn't remorseful, did that make you angry?"

"He was dead when I got there," said Nightingale.

"You're making a habit of walking in on dead people, aren't you?" said Chalmers.

Nightingale didn't reply.

"Come on, Jack, don't get all coy with me. You found your aunt and uncle dead, didn't you? Just a few days ago. Up in Manchester."

"He killed himself," said Nightingale. "He killed my aunt and then he hung myself. I was supposed to be having Sunday lunch with them."

"According to the Manchester cops, you smashed a window to get in. With a spade."

"There was blood on the cat," said Nightingale.

Chalmers looked confused. "What?"

"There was blood on the cat. And on the cat flap. So I knew there was something wrong. Then I saw my aunt through the window, lying on the kitchen floor."

"And again you didn't wait for the police."

"What do you expect?" snapped Nightingale. "I call emergency, and when and if I get through some civilian arsehole asks me a series of questions on his checklist before telling me that someone will be with me at some unspecified time, and then I sit on my arse and wait until they bother to show up? You know how piss-poor the police response times are these days? I saw blood on the door and I could see my aunt on the floor so I did what I had to do and I'm damn well not going to apologize to you or anyone else for that."

"And you don't think it's a bit coincidental, discovering three bodies in less than a week?"

"I don't know."

"Yes you do, Jack. You know there's something strange going on here. And I think you're not telling us the whole story."

"There's no story to tell."

"The thing is, you've always been a bit of a vigilante, haven't you? That's why you had to leave the Force."

Nightingale sat back in his chair and folded his arms. He knew that there was no point in rising to the bait, Chalmers was only trying to provoke him.

"You threw Simon Underwood out of his office window, didn't you? And got away with it without even a slap on the wrist. Is that what you think, Nightingale, you think you're some sort of masked avenger who can go around murdering at will?"

"Barry O'Brien committed suicide."

"And I suppose that Underwood threw himself out of his office window?"

Nightingale said nothing.

"Were you drinking before you went to see Mr. O'Brien?"

"Of course not," said Nightingale. "It was first thing in the morning."

"Because you do have a drinking problem, don't you?"

"Bollocks."

"You're due to appear in court on a drunk driving charge next month, aren't you?"

"I had a few beers and was stupid enough to drive," said Nightingale. "That doesn't qualify as a drinking problem."

Chalmers leaned forward and lowered his voice to a gentle whisper. "Look, Jack, I understand how you feel. I understand how you felt about Underwood, and I know there were no tears shed for him after what he did to his daughter. And I understand how you felt about Robbie's death. He didn't deserve to die. He was a husband and a dad and good cop, and some bastard who wasn't watching what he was doing ran him over. I understand that you'd be angry. Hell, I'm angry. And I could see that you'd want revenge, because we both know that the courts won't do anything. I can understand why you'd want to hurt O'Brien. Anyone could."

"It was an accident, you said."

"And you're okay with that?"

"Accidents happen," said Nightingale.

"They do around you, that's for sure," said Chalmers.

CHAPTER

44

The Australian nurse carefully cut the chicken breast into pieces so small that they couldn't be choked on. The potatoes were mashed and the carrots had been boiled for so long that they had turned to mush, so the chicken was the only potential threat. The plate was on a tray over Rebecca Keeley's lap. She sat with her hands by her side, a slight frown on her face as she watched him cut the meat.

"That must have been nice, seeing your son after all these years," said the nurse. The woman didn't reply. She hadn't said a word since Nightingale had left. The nurse wasn't even sure that she'd spoken to her son. "I hope he comes again, you could do with a regular visitor, it might get you out of your shell."

The woman said nothing.

The phone in the hallway started to ring and the nurse cursed. He looked apologetically at the woman. "Sorry about the language, Miss Keeley," he said. "It's just that it never rings when I'm not busy. Murphy's Law." He put the knife and fork down on the tray and went to answer the phone.

As the nurse closed the door, the woman reached for the knife with her right hand. For the first time she smiled, revealing her raw, ulcerated gums. She placed the blade of the knife against her left wrist, and splayed her fingers. She shuddered and began to recite the Lord's Prayer as she hacked away with the blade, sawing through the flesh, veins, and tendons. Blood sprayed across the bed as she continued to say the prayer and work the knife.

CHAPTER

45

Nightingale opened the door to his office and walked quickly over to his desk. He pulled open the bottom drawer and took out the bottle of brandy that he kept there.

"Jack, what's wrong?" asked Jenny, getting up from her computer.

"I've had a hell of a day," said Nightingale.

"And brandy is going to make it better?"

"It's going to make me feel better," said Nightingale. He unscrewed the top and raised the bottle to his mouth, then stopped. "Yeah, you're right," he said. "Booze has got me into more than enough trouble already."

"Coffee?"

"That would be great." He put the cap back on the bottle and the bottle back in the drawer.

"Where were you today?" asked Jenny as she went to get him a coffee.

"It's a long story," said Nightingale, dropping onto his chair and swinging his feet up onto the desk. "I went to see Barry O'Brien, the taxi driver."

"And what did he have to say?"

"Nothing. He was dead."

"What?"

"He killed himself. Sat in the bath and slit his wrists."

"My God," said Jenny.

"Must have done it a day or two ago. Maybe yesterday, while we were at Robbie's funeral."

Jenny brought over two mugs of coffee and gave one to Nightingale. "You think he felt bad about what he'd done? Couldn't live with himself?"

"Chalmers thinks I did it."

"He what?" She sat down on the edge of his desk.

"He had me in for questioning, along with the two cops who came to tell us about Robbie. Evans and Derbyshire. The three bloody musketeers. They were firing questions at me for hours."

"They can't seriously think you did it, Jack. Anyway, you were at the funeral or you were with me."

"They do have a point, though," said Nightingale. "You know what's been happening to me. My father, my real father, blows his head off with a shotgun. My uncle kills my aunt and then hangs himself. Barry O'Brien cuts his wrists before I can talk to him. It doesn't look good, does it? From their point of view. And that's before they even mentioned Simon Underwood."

"They're morons if they think that you had anything to do with any of those deaths." She sipped her coffee. "Sometimes people can be so bloody stupid," she said.

"Chalmers has always had it in for me," said Nightingale. "I don't think he seriously believes I killed O'Brien, he just wants to make my life difficult. And he's never forgiven me for the Underwood thing."

"They never charged you, did they? For what happened to Underwood?"

"They couldn't. There was no forensic, no witnesses, no CCTV. And I didn't tell them anything." He shrugged. "What could I tell them? That I'd conveniently contracted a nasty case of amnesia?" He flashed her his little-boy-lost smile. "I need you to do something for me, Jenny."

"I am here to serve, oh master."

"I'm serious," said Nightingale.

"So am I," said Jenny.

"I need you to find someone for me. A guy by the name of George Harrison."

"The Beatle? He's dead."

"George Arthur Harrison," said Nightingale. "He'd be in his early sixties now. He was a truck driver in the nineties. He lived in south London then, but he could be anywhere now."

"I'll get on it," said Jenny. "What's he done?"

"He killed my parents," said Nightingale flatly.

"Jack," said Jenny. "Are you sure you want to do this? It was a long time ago."

"I know that," said Nightingale defensively. "But it's unfinished business."

"Unfinished in what way?"

"I need to know what happened, Jenny. I need to know why my parents died."

"It was an accident, you know that already. You should let sleeping dogs lie."

Nightingale shook his head. "I should have spoken to him then, but I was too young. I was just a kid."

"Why, Jack? What on earth do you stand to gain by confronting him now?"

Nightingale ran his hands through his hair. "I just need to do it, Jenny. Can't you leave it at that?"

"It's because of Robbie, isn't it? And because of what happened to O'Brien."

"That's part of it," admitted Nightingale. "Bad things are happening around me, Jenny, and it's all to do with Ainsley Gosling being my father. If I can find out what happened to my parents, maybe it'll explain what's happening now."

"It was an accident, you said."

"That's what everyone said. But Robbie's death was an accident, too. Doesn't that seem a bit coincidental?"

"Coincidences happen."

"Sure they do. And people commit murder and kill themselves. It's just that it seems to be happening to people I know a hell of a lot recently. Maybe I'm the key. Maybe Gosling had my parents killed, have you thought about that? Maybe he paid this guy Harrison to kill them."

"And he paid O'Brien to kill Robbie from beyond the grave, is that what you think?"

"I don't know," said Nightingale. "But if I talk to Harrison, maybe I'll find out."

"You're starting to worry me, Jack." The phone rang and she picked it up. "Nightingale Investigations," she said. She frowned as she listened, then she placed her hand over the receiver. "It's Mrs. Fraser at the Hillingdon Home," said Jenny. "It's about Rebecca Keeley."

"Now what?" said Nightingale.

"Jack, she's dead."

CHAPTER

46

Mrs. Fraser was sitting behind her desk when an assistant showed Nightingale into her office. The Australian male nurse was also there, his arms folded across his chest, his face a blank mask. Mrs. Fraser didn't get up, and she waved for Nightingale to sit down.

"What happened?" asked Nightingale.

"What happened, Mr. Nightingale, is that after you visited her for the second time, your mother took a knife and slashed her wrists," said the administrator.

"What was she doing with a knife?"

"She was eating her dinner," said the administrator. "Your mother wasn't considered to be a danger to herself or to anyone else, so the use of cutlery wasn't an issue."

"Did she leave a note?" asked Nightingale. "Do you have any idea why she did it?"

"She did it because you upset her," said the male nurse. "She was fine before you came along."

"She was practically psychotic," said Nightingale. "According to you she never spoke. At least she spoke to me."

"And then she killed herself," said the nurse. "What did you say to her?"

The administrator raised her hand to silence him. "Darren, please, let me handle this."

"What's to be handled?" asked Nightingale.

"The thing is, Mr. Nightingale, as things stand we have no confirmation that you are in fact Miss Keeley's son."

Nightingale reached into his jacket pocket and took out an envelope. "Here's the results of the DNA test I told you about," he said. "It clearly shows that she was my mother."

Mrs. Fraser frowned as she took the report out of the envelope and read it. "I don't understand," she said. "How did you get a sample of her DNA?"

"I borrowed a hairbrush," said Nightingale. "The cells on the root of the hair are all they need these days."

"You stole a hairbrush?"

"I borrowed it," said Nightingale. "But as you can see, I'm quite definitely her son, so there's no problem at all in my visiting her."

"Your mother killed herself, Mr. Nightingale," said Mrs. Fraser. "Questions are being asked as to how that happened, and it might be that our level of care is called into question." She gave the forensic report back to him.

"My mother was upset, I don't see that anyone can blame you," said Mr. Nightingale.

"She died in our care, which means we are responsible," said Mrs. Fraser.

"Have the police been informed?" asked Nightingale.

Mrs. Fraser nodded. "Yes, but purely as a formality," she said.

"She died in my arms," said the nurse. "I was holding her while she bled to death." There were tears in his eyes.

"Did she say anything?" asked Nightingale.

The nurse shook his head.

"The point, Mr. Nightingale, is that it was clearly your visits that upset Mrs. Keeley," said Mrs. Fraser. "I think we are all agreed that prior to your visits she was calm, albeit uncommunicative. And afterwards…"

"I understand," said Nightingale. "I certainly wouldn't be in disagreement with you on that."

"That's good to hear, Mr. Nightingale," said the administrator.

Nightingale leaned forward. "I'm not looking to blame anyone, Mrs. Fraser, and I hope that's your position. My mother was obviously a very disturbed woman, and I know that you were giving her the very best care possible." He looked over at the male nurse. "I know that Darren thought a lot of my mother, and I could see that she really appreciated the way that he took care of her. I agree that my suddenly turning up had obviously upset her, but I don't think that anyone could have foreseen that she would suddenly harm herself."

Mrs. Fraser nodded.

They were more concerned about a possible legal suit or bad publicity than they were about the reason why Rebecca Keeley had killed herself, Nightingale realized. The meeting was about avoiding blame, nothing else.

"As to what I said to my mother, it was just family stuff. I showed her photographs of when I was a kid, and we talked about them. I don't know why she got so upset in the garden, but as soon as Darren asked me to leave, I did."

Mrs. Fraser nodded again, and even managed a smile. "Thank you for your understanding, Mr. Nightingale. You can imagine how upset we all are. One never likes to lose a resident, especially under such circumstances." She picked up a pen and began toying with it. "We have to begin making arrangements," she said. "For the funeral."

"What normally happens?" asked Nightingale.

"It depends on whether the resident has family or not," said the administrator. "If there's no family, we arrange a service at the local crematorium."

"Can you do that for my mother?" said Nightingale. "So far as I know I'm her only living relative, it would be a big help if you could make the arrangements."

"I'm happy to do that," said Mrs. Fraser.

"I'll pay, of course. Whatever costs there are just let me know."

"Mrs. Keeley's costs were paid for by the local authority, and they'll bear the cost of the funeral," said Mrs. Fraser. "Now, what would you like us to do with her belongings? Her clothes and such?"

"What normally happens?"

"If there are relatives then we obviously give them everything. Otherwise we clean any clothing and send it to charity shops. Along with electrical equipment and other articles that people might want. The rest we throw away." She grimaced. "It's sad, but most of our residents don't have much left by the time they come here."

"Charity shops sound like a good idea," said Nightingale.

"The crucifix," said the nurse. "Don't forget the crucifix."

"Oh yes, your mother always wore a crucifix," said Mrs. Fraser. "It was a great comfort to her. I think it might be the sort of thing you'd like to keep."

Nightingale looked over at the nurse. "Would you like to keep it, Darren?"

"Oh, that's not possible," said Mrs. Fraser quickly. "It's against company policy, I'm afraid, we're not allowed to accept bequests from our residents. Under any circumstances, I'm afraid. We had a bad experience a few years ago."

"I understand," said Nightingale. He took out one of his business cards and gave it to her. "You can send it to me here."

Mrs. Fraser studied the card. "I didn't realize you were a private detective," she said.

"For my sins," said Nightingale.

"That can't be a pleasant occupation," she said.

"It has its moments," said Nightingale.

CHAPTER 47

Nightingale was driving on autopilot, his mind more focused on the death of Rebecca Keeley than on the road ahead, which is why he didn't see the fox until a second before he hit it. The car slammed into the animal and Nightingale hit the brakes. The rear of the car started to spin and Nightingale pumped the brake as he desperately fought to control it. The road curved to the right, the sky overhead obscured by the drooping branches of the woodland that he was driving through. He straightened the MGB but realized that he was heading for a beech tree, and he spun the wheel to the right and the car skidded to a halt and then stalled.

Nightingale sat where he was, his heart pounding, gripping the steering wheel so tightly that his knuckles went white. He had chosen to drive back to London along B-roads rather than take the motorway because he wanted time to think, but his decision had almost cost him his life. He started the engine and carefully drove the car off the road, then climbed out and lit a cigarette with trembling hands. The MGB had stopped just a few feet from the tree. If he'd been going any faster or if he'd been a fraction slower braking, he would have slammed into the tree, and he was sure that the impact would have killed him. He inhaled deeply and then blew a plume of smoke skywards. The line between life and death was a fine one at the best of times.

He looked back down the road. There was no sign of the fox. He walked along the side of the road to where he'd hit the animal. There was no blood on the tarmac, no indication that there had ever been a fox there. He checked the vegetation at the side of the road but found nothing. Nightingale frowned. Had he imagined it? He shook his head, trying to clear his thoughts. There had been a fox in the middle of the road, he was sure of that, and he hadn't imagined the thud as he'd hit it. So where was it? Had it crawled off to die? He walked into the woodland, treading softly through the dandelions and nettles, listening for any sounds of an animal in pain, but all he could hear was the territorial chirping of birds high up in the trees.

He saw a church spire through the trees and he headed toward it. The church was surrounded by a dry stone wall, moss-covered in places, and a sign at the entrance proclaimed it as St Mary's. It was a small church, stone-built with stained-glass windows and a metal cross atop its spire. Nightingale walked toward the oak door and pushed it. The door opened silently despite its bulk, the hinges were well-oiled, and the wood had been polished until it shone. There were fresh flowers in the vestibule and the cloying smell of irises.

There were a dozen rows of hard wooden benches with an aisle down the center that led to a pulpit and behind it a stone font. Nightingale felt himself being drawn toward the font and he walked down the aisle, his hands in his pockets. The air was much cooler inside the church than it had been outside and he shivered.

The stone flags beneath his feet were worn smooth with the thousands of feet that had walked back and forth over the years, making the journey from the pews to the priest. There were thick oak beams overhead, and statues set into the walls depicting the agony of Christ's crucifixion. Candles flickered in alcoves, dripping wax onto the stone floor. Nightingale looked around but he appeared to be alone. To the left of the pulpit was a confessional box, the curtains on both sides drawn shut. Nightingale stopped and listened but he couldn't hear voices.

He walked slowly up to the font and looked down at the water. It was Holy Water, blessed by the priest. Nightingale smiled to himself. Holy Water was supposed to hurt vampires, and he wondered what it would do to a man whose soul had been promised to a demon. Would it burn his flesh, like it did in the movies? If he stuck in his hand, would it strip it to the bone, and would he run from the church, screaming in pain? He rolled up his sleeve and held his hand just above the surface of the water. "Our Father, who art in heaven," he whispered. He plunged his hand into the water. It was cold, colder than he had expected, and he gasped. He flexed his fingers, and then smiled to himself. At least he could still touch Holy Water, which must mean something.

"Can I help you?" said a voice behind him.

Nightingale jerked as if he'd been stung. He swung around to find an amused young priest watching him with unabashed amusement. "I was…" began Nightingale, but he wasn't sure how to finish the sentence. What exactly was he doing? Checking the potency of Holy Water?

"There is a washroom around the back," said the priest. He was in his late twenties with a shock of red hair and freckles peppered across his nose and cheeks. "You're welcome to use that if you want to wash your hands."

"I wasn't washing my hands," said Nightingale. "I just wanted to…to be honest, and I know it makes no sense, I just wanted to touch some Holy Water, that's all." He shook his hand dry and rolled down his shirtsleeve.

"You look distressed," said the priest.

"It's been a funny old day," said Nightingale. "I've just found out that my mother has killed herself, and I narrowly missed wrapping myself around a tree."

"I'm sorry for your loss," said the priest. "Was she a Catholic, your mother?"

"I don't know," said Nightingale. "She wore a crucifix, if that counts for anything." He took out his pack of Marlboros and tapped out a cigarette, but the priest wagged a finger at him.

"I'm afraid smoking isn't allowed on the premises," he said.

Nightingale grinned. "You can see the irony in that, can't you? What with all the candles and incense that you burn in here."

"Just one of the many regulations that makes our lives so much more complicated than they used to be," said the priest. "Don't get me started on refuse collections from our church. Would you class unused communion wafers as a foodstuff? Because our local council does. And heaven forbid they find their way into the recycling bin by mistake."

"Actually, I'd have thought that communion wafers would have been the ultimate in recycling, from bread to the body of Christ."

The priest chuckled. "I wish I'd thought of that," he said. "But they weren't consecrated, of course. Once they've been consecrated they have to be consumed. These had gone moldy so they had to be thrown away. But because they were edible they were classed as food and so they were in the wrong bin and some jobsworth decided that I had to pay a penalty or be taken to court." He waved at the door. "You can smoke outside and we can carry on our conversation there."

They walked together out of the church and over to a wooden bench at the edge of the graveyard. There was a small brass plaque fixed to the back. "IN MEMORY OF MARY, 1921–1998, MY SOULMATE." They sat on the bench and Nightingale lit a cigarette.

"Again, I'm so sorry for your loss," said the priest. "It's always difficult to lose a loved one, but the bond between a mother and son is the strongest of all, I think."

"Thank you," said Nightingale. The truth was that he didn't feel any sense of loss at all at the death of Rebecca Keeley, even though there was no doubt that she was his biological mother. She had given birth to him, but that was all, and he had no more feeling for her than for a total stranger. But he knew that the priest meant well so he nodded and tried to look as if his mother's death meant something.

"You're not a churchgoer, yourself," said the priest.

"I'm not a big one for churches," said Nightingale. "Do you mind me asking how old you are, Father?"

"I don't mind at all," said the priest. "I'm twenty-seven, so you can drop the 'Father' if that makes you uncomfortable. My name is Peter."

"That's young to be a priest, isn't it, Peter?"

"It is these days, that's for sure."

Nightingale offered the pack of cigarettes to the priest but he shook his head. "I've never smoked," he said.

"Do you drink?"

"Oh yes," said the priest. "Definitely."

"But no sex?"

The priest's eyes narrowed as if he suspected that Nightingale was being provocative. "That door is firmly closed," he said.

"I didn't meant to pry, it's just that I can't imagine why anyone would become a Catholic priest," said Nightingale. "You have to give up so much." He blew smoke, taking care to keep it away from the priest.

"But we get so much more back," said the priest.

"But wasn't it a hard decision to make, to turn your back on everything to enter the Church?"

The priest smiled. "You're looking at it the wrong way. I was turning to God, and that gives me everything I could ever want or need. There is no better way to love one's life than in the service of the Lord."

"And you have no doubts, no doubts at all?"

"I doubt the sanity of the idiots who run our local council, but no doubts at all about God."

"And you talk to God?"

"Of course, all the time. That's what prayer is."

"But does he talk back?" Nightingale took a long drag on his cigarette.

The priest chuckled. It was an old man's laugh, and he put up his hand to cover his mouth as if he realized that the laugh was at odds with his appearance. "I don't hear voices, if that's what you mean," he said. "It's not like Joan of Arc."

Nightingale exhaled smoke slowly. "But you have a conversation with God, that's why you believe in him?"

"It's complicated," said the priest.

"But he answers your prayers?"

"Of course."

"So if you prayed to win the lottery, he'd give you the winning numbers?"

The priest smiled and shook his head. "I wouldn't pray for that," he said.

"What about world peace? I'm sure that Christians around the world pray for world peace but the world is still a very dangerous place."

"You're asking why God doesn't stop all wars, why he doesn't create heaven here on earth?"

"I'm asking what is it that makes you believe in God, when all the evidence is to the contrary."

"Every day I see the evidence of God's hand, in the beauty of the world, in the people I meet."

"Yeah, well, I was a police officer and I tended to see less of the beauty and more of the dark side. And a read through any newspaper will prove that bad things happen to good people all the time."

"Again, it's perception. Maybe you should try talking to God. When was the last time you prayed?"

Nightingale dropped his cigarette butt onto the ground and stepped on it. "It's been a while."

"You should try it again," said the priest. "You don't even have to go to a church. Just find yourself a quiet place and pray."

"Our Father who art in heaven?"

"Not necessarily the Lord's Prayer, just tell him what's troubling you."

"And he'll talk to me? I don't think so."

"You won't know unless you try," said the priest.

Nightingale folded his arms and sat back. "Here's what I don't get," he said. "God wants us to obey him, worship him, and all that stuff. And church attendances are down because fewer people believe that he exists. So why doesn't he provide definitive proof? Why doesn't he let us know once and for all that he exists? If he did that, then the whole world would believe, right?"

"But he did that, didn't he?" said the priest. "He sent his son, and we killed him on the cross, and God brought him back to life. That was definitive proof at the time, and it still is."

"That was a long time ago," said Nightingale.

"A little over two thousand years ago," said the priest, "which in human terms is the twinkling of an eye. We can't keep asking for proof every twenty minutes. He gave us proof, and we have the Bible to remind us of that."

"But it's not enough," said Nightingale.

"For you perhaps. But have you read the Bible?"

"No," admitted Nightingale.

"And you're not a churchgoer, so how can you be expected to hear God's message?"

Nightingale sighed and stretched out his legs. "You are so sure, aren't you? You're sure that God exists, you're sure that you did the right thing becoming a priest."

"I am," said the priest. "Tell me, Jack, can you say the same about the decisions that you've made in your life?"

Nightingale grinned ruefully. "Fair point," he said. "What about the devil? You believe in the devil?"

"Without a doubt," said the priest. "And if it's proof you want, I'd have thought you were spoiled for choice so far as evidence of the devil is concerned."

"You believe that bad things are the result of the devil's work?"

"Don't you?"

"In my experience, bad people do bad things," said Nightingale.

"But what makes people go bad? You don't think there could be some influence at work?"

"And that influence is the devil. Is that what you're saying?"

"The devil. Satan. The Antichrist. Yes, I really do believe that. I believe that Satan wants people to act one way and God wants them to behave another. We have free will, so it's up to us to choose whom we serve."

"How are you on geography, Peter?" asked Nightingale.

"Geography?"

"I was talking with a vicar a few days ago, asking him about hell."

"Church of England?"

"I guess so," said Nightingale.

"Then you were asking the wrong guy," said the priest. "The Church of England isn't great on heaven and hell, they're more interested in race relations and gay marriages and women bishops. You want to know about hell, you talk to the Catholics."

"So you believe in hell?"

"Absolutely," said the priest. "And I believe that if you break God's rules you'll be punished."

"In hell?"

"In hell," repeated the priest.

"Fire, brimstone, devils with pitchforks?"

"Not necessarily, but a place where souls would be in eternal torment. The complete opposite of heaven."

"And Satan presides over hell and everything that happens there?"

"That's what the Bible says."

"And where is hell, Peter?"

The priest chuckled. "The geography question," he said. "Hand on heart, I don't know where hell is. But that's not important. What's important is that you don't get sent there."

48

Nightingale was making himself a coffee when his doorbell rang. He checked the intercom in the hallway and saw that Jenny was outside in the street, standing next to a brunette in a trench coat. He pressed the intercom button. "Not today, thank you," he said. "I gave at the office."

"Open this door, Jack Nightingale, or I'll huff and I'll puff and I'll blow your house down."

"You swear by the hair on your chinny chin chin, do you?"

"Jack, it's bloody cold out here, now let us in, will you."

Nightingale chuckled and pressed the button to open the door, then went into the kitchen and prepared two more mugs. When the inner door buzzed he went to open it. The girl with Jenny was in her late twenties, pretty, with dark green eyes and a splatter of freckles across her nose.

"This is Barbara, a friend from uni," said Jenny. "We're going to stay with my folks for the weekend but I wanted to see if you were okay first."

"I'm fine," said Nightingale. He shook hands with Barbara and took their coats. "Coffee's on in the kitchen," said Nightingale as he hung the coats in the cupboard where he kept his ironing board and hoover. He showed Barbara through to the sitting room and switched off his television. "So, was Jenny a suck-up at university?"

Barbara sat down on Nightingale's sofa and shook her head. "Actually she was one of those annoying students who never studied, she soaked up information like a sponge."

"That's so not true," said Jenny, carrying a tray of coffee mugs into the sitting room. She put the tray on the coffee table and sat down next to Barbara. "I studied, I just did it on my own." She sat down on the sofa next to her friend. "How did it go at the home? Did they say how she died?"

Barbara and Jenny looked at him expectantly and Nightingale realized that Jenny must already have told her friend about the death of his mother. He wondered what else she had told her.

Nightingale shrugged. "Everyone's in a state of shock. She was eating her dinner and just started slashing her wrists."

Jenny's jaw dropped. "She killed herself? You didn't tell me that."

"I didn't know until I got there."

"Jack, you should have called me."

"There wasn't anything you could do," said Nightingale.

She glared at him. "That's not the point," she said. "You should have told me. For God's sake, Jack, your mother killed herself. That's not the sort of thing you should keep to yourself."

"I'm sorry. She doesn't feel like my mother, she was just..."

"The woman who gave birth to you," she finished for him. "Which is what a mother is, actually."

Nightingale shook his head. "Irene Nightingale was my mother," he said. "The woman who killed herself was..." He shrugged. "I don't know what she was. Yes, she gave birth to me, but there's more to being a mother than that. She gave me away, Jenny, on the day I was born."

"But still…"

"Jenny, it meant nothing to me. I mean, I'm sorry she's dead, but I did my grieving when my mother died. My real mother."

"Did they say why she killed herself?"

Nightingale shook his head. "She's been on medication for years."

"At least you got a chance to talk to her before she passed away," said Barbara.

"I guess so," said Nightingale.

"Barbara's a psychiatrist," said Jenny. "I hope you don't mind but I did give her some idea of what you've been through recently."

"What I've been through?"

"Finding out that you were adopted, meeting the woman who gave birth to you, and then her dying. Finding your aunt and uncle. Robbie dying like that."

"I'm not denying it's been an eventful few days," said Nightingale. "But I'm dealing with it as best I can. This is just a social call, right, because I hope you don't expect me to lie on my couch and unburden myself."

"Would that be such a bad thing, Jack?" said Barbara.

Nightingale grinned at her. "With the greatest of respect, Barbara, I don't know you, and while any friend of Jenny's is a friend of mine, I'm certainly not going to strip myself bare in front of somebody I hardly know."

"Please God," said Jenny.

"Now you see, you wouldn't say that if you'd ever seen me naked," said Nightingale. "I've got nothing to be ashamed of in that department."

Jenny looked across at Barbara and gave her a knowing look. "Told you," she said.

"Told you what?" said Nightingale.

"Jenny mentioned that you might be a tad defensive," said Barbara. "It's understandable."

"We just popped around to see if you were okay, after what happened and all," said Jenny.

"I'm fine," said Nightingale. "There'll be an inquest, obviously, and you're both invited to the funeral."

"Jack!" said Jenny.

"It feels that you're more worried about her than I am."

"There was no bond, when you met?" asked Barbara.

"How could there be?" said Nightingale. "I'm almost thirty-three years old, and this week I met her for the first time."

"Sometimes when parents and children are reunited there's an immediate connection, as if the genes kick in and you recognize each other on a subconscious level."

Nightingale shook his head. "Didn't happen," he said.

"Did you tell her how you felt?" asked Barbara.

"I wasn't there for an exchange of emotions," said Nightingale. "I was there because I wanted to know why she gave me away."

"You wanted closure?"

"Barbara, please stop trying to psychoanalyze me. I didn't want closure, I wanted facts. Cold hard facts."

"And did you get them?"

"Not really."

"And how do you feel now, now that she's dead?"

"That's such a psychiatrist's question."

Barbara laughed and sipped her coffee.

"And that's an interrogator's trick," said Nightingale. "Leaving a silence and hoping the subject will fill it."

"You're not a subject, Jack. Or a patient. You're just a friend of a friend, that's all. We can talk about the weather if you'd prefer. Or sport. You're a Manchester United fan, aren't you?"

Nightingale smiled. She was good, all right. She had barely glanced at the photographs on his sideboard but had obviously spotted the one where he was with his father and uncle outside the Old Trafford stadium, all wearing team scarves. "I am indeed."

"I've always followed Liverpool. That's where I was born."

"You've lost the accent," said Nightingale. "I'd have placed you as Home Counties."

"Well, expensive private education does that for you," said Barbara. "Can I ask you about your memory loss?"

"My what?"

"Jenny said that you were having problems remembering things, things from your past."

Nightingale flashed Jenny a warning look. "And what else did she tell you?"

"Just that," said Jenny. "That sometimes your memory wasn't clear." She licked her lips anxiously. "That's all I said, Jack. I thought maybe Barbara might have some thoughts."

"Memory is a delicate thing," said Barbara. "You were a policeman, so you must have come across that. You can have a dozen eyewitnesses to the same event and they'll all see it differently. Even down to giving completely different descriptions of people and things."

Nightingale nodded. "Witnesses are the least reliable of all evidence," he said.

"Exactly," said Barbara. "And as the years pass, memories fade."

"I'm not going senile," said Nightingale. "Crazy maybe, but not senile."

"You don't seem in the least bit crazy," said Barbara. "A bit stressed, maybe, but that's hardly surprising."

"Considering what I've been through?"

"Jenny didn't tell me everything, I'm sure, but what she did tell me left me in no doubt that you could be suffering from PTSD."

"Post-traumatic stress disorder? I don't think so."

"It would account for the memory loss, Jack. Sometimes people under stress blot out those memories that would cause them more anxiety. It's the subconscious protecting the conscious."

"I'm fine," said Nightingale. "To be honest, I'm probably best not remembering."

Barbara leaned forward. "That's a very significant thing to say, Jack."

"I was joking."

"Jokes can be a window into our psyche, we often use jokes to make light of our real fears."

Nightingale laughed and threw up his hands. "I can't win with you, can I? You're determined to psychoanalyze me, no matter what I say."

"Jenny's worried about you, that's all. And sometimes a third party can offer a view that those close to the situation can't see. I think you are blotting something out, Jack. Subconsciously or consciously."

"And?"

"And if you wanted, I could perhaps help you remember. There are various relaxation techniques we can use that will open up your subconscious and allow you to get to those memories that you're repressing."

"You mean hypnotize me?"

"Not necessarily put you in a hypnotic state, but just a relaxed frame of mind where you're less anxious about remembering."

"Honestly, Barbara, if I need someone to talk to, I'll find someone."

"Like who, Jack?" asked Jenny.

"Don't worry, I'll sort that out. Really."

Jenny looked at her watch. "We should be going." She and Barbara stood up. "If you need me over the weekend, call me," Jenny said to Nightingale.

"I will, I promise," said Nightingale.

"And think about what Barbara said. Maybe she can help you remember. And if you do remember, then maybe things might become a bit clearer."

"Okay, I'll think about it," said Nightingale.

"I'm serious, Jack. I'm starting to worry about you."

Nightingale hugged her. He winked at Barbara over Jenny's shoulder. "I bring out her mothering instincts," he said.

"She was always rescuing stray dogs when she was a student," said Barbara. "I can see that nothing's changed."

CHAPTER

49

Nightingale walked slowly through the cemetery. There was a full moon overhead and the sky was cloudless so there was plenty of light to see by. A soft wind blew through the conifers that bordered the graveyard. Nightingale was smoking a Marlboro and holding a Threshers shopping bag. The earth had been shoveled back into Robbie Hoyle's grave and pounded down but there was still a slight curve of excess soil. Soil settled over time, Nightingale knew. He'd once been on a search team in the New Forest, looking for the body of a woman who'd been strangled by her husband seven years earlier. The guy had turned up at a local police station claiming that his wife had come back to haunt him and that she wouldn't leave him alone until he confessed and arranged for a proper Christian burial. The detectives who had interviewed the man didn't believe in ghosts, and neither did Nightingale, but they did believe in grief and guilt, and because the man was vague about where he'd actually buried his wife, more than fifty policemen in overalls and Wellington boots were dispatched to the forest.

Nightingale was with the group that found the remains, and there were two clues that pinpointed its location. There was a deep depression where the soil had settled, and the grass above the body was greener and lusher than the surrounding vegetation. Two hours before they'd found the murdered wife, another group had found the body of a child that had been in the ground for more than a decade. There was little more than a skeleton left, wrapped in a bloodstained rug, and the child was never identified. Again, it was the depression in the ground and the lush grass that gave it away.

There was no headstone on Hoyle's grave, but marble edging had already been put around the perimeter, white with dark brown veins. Nightingale flicked his cigarette butt away, spread his raincoat on the grass, and sat down on it. "How's it going, Robbie?" he asked. He smiled to himself. It was a stupid question. Hoyle wasn't going anywhere. He was in a wooden box six feet underground, his veins pumped full of formaldehyde, his best suit on and his tie neatly knotted, the way it never was when he was alive.

Nightingale opened the bag and took out a bottle of red wine. "I know you're a wine drinker, so I brought this," he said. He grinned as he held up the bottle. "I couldn't be bothered with a corkscrew so I got a screw-top bottle. The girl who sold it to me said it was a respectable red from Chile. Mind you, she was Romanian so I don't think she knows much about wine." Nightingale poured a splash of wine over the grave. "Cheers, Robbie," he said, then took a long drink from the bottle. He wiped his mouth with the sleeve of his jacket. "Respectable wine, long on the palate with a blackcurrant and raspberry aftertaste." He grinned. "Yeah, you got me, that's what it says on the label. Perfect for red meat and pasta.

What the hell do I know, I'm a beer drinker, right? Or whisky when there's serious drinking to be done."

Nightingale took another drink from the bottle, then poured more on the soil. "I know this is a bloody cliché, talking to your mate's grave and sharing a drink with him, but I couldn't think what else to do." He chuckled. "Actually, I did think of doing the glass and the letters trick but I'd feel a right twat if you told me to go and shag Jenny again." He shook his head. "And no, I haven't shagged her. Doubt that I ever will. Don't want to ruin what we have. Or I don't want to ruin what we don't have. Either way, we haven't. And probably won't." He raised his eyes skywards. "Yeah, I heard the 'probably', too. Freudian slip?"

Nightingale sniffed the neck of the wine bottle. "It's not bad, this, is it? But it doesn't give you the same warm feeling as a good whisky. Or a bad one." He took another drink. "My mum died, Robbie. My real mum. My genetic mum." He frowned. "I don't know why I said that because she doesn't feel like my real mum. She was just a sad woman who couldn't even feed herself, who got conned into having me by a guy old enough to be her father. She slashed her wrists with a knife. They're arranging her funeral as we speak. I don't think it'll be as well-attended as yours, mate. Did you hear Chalmers? Said some nice things, he did. For a moment I thought he'd turned over a new leaf, but then he had me in for a grilling because the moron that ran you over topped himself and Chalmers wants to put me in the frame for it."

Nightingale suddenly cursed vehemently. "Didn't anyone ever tell you to look both ways before you cross the road, you stupid bastard? How could you walk in front of a bloody taxi? And on Friday the bloody thirteenth. Another stupid cliché."

Nightingale drank again, then poured another slug of wine over the grave. "Right, so here's the thing, Robbie. Here's why I'm here. Here's why I'm sitting next to your bloody grave sharing a bottle of cheap plonk with you." He took a deep breath, then another drink. "I need a sign, Robbie. I need you to let me know that there's something after death, that you're still out there somewhere, that it's not…" Nightingale closed his eyes and cursed again. "What the hell am I doing?" he muttered. "This is mad. Crazy."

He opened his eyes. "Am I crazy? Am I sitting here talking to myself? Or can you hear me? I need to know, Robbie. I really need to know. I need something. Some sign. Something to let me know that death isn't the end. You know what's important, Robbie. You know why I need to know. Just give me a sign. Please."

A shooting star flashed overhead and vanished as quickly as it had appeared.

Nightingale laughed harshly. "Is that the best you can do?" he said. "A bloody meteor? One poxy bit of ice and rock? I need something real, Robbie. I need a bloody sign. I need to hear your voice or see you or feel your hand on my shoulder. It's not much to ask, Robbie, not considering all the years that we've been friends."

He took another drink of wine, and splashed more on the grave. "Someone else I know died the other day. Killed himself. Client of mine, he wanted me to follow his wife and when he found out she was having an affair he offed himself. He bloody well offed himself and now the wife's blaming me, calling me all the names under the sun and threatening to sue me." He drank from the bottle and wiped his mouth. "She won't, of course. It's just the grief and the anger talking. When you lose someone you want to lash out. I wanted to kill the driver of the black cab that hit you when I heard. But he was just in the wrong place at the wrong time. Same as you. Just one of those things. One of those stupid bloody things. If you'd stepped off the sidewalk a second later or he'd taken another route, or if he'd just been bloody well looking where he was going, then you'd still be here and…" Nightingale trailed off. He groaned, lay back on his raincoat, and stared up at the night sky, the bottom of the bottle balanced on his stomach. "He's dead, the guy that was driving the cab. He offed himself too. Slit his wrists down to the bone. God knows why. Grief maybe. Guilt." Nightingale sighed. "The thing about suicides is that they don't really think about death, about what it means," he said. "You know that, you did the courses. They think that what they're doing will prove something, or hurt someone, and because they're not thinking straight they imagine that they'll be around to see what effect their suicide has. They imagine that they'll be at their own funeral, seeing everyone crying and saying how sorry they are. If they really thought about what was going to happen, they'd hang on to every second of life because life is all there is, right? Tell me, Robbie, am I right?" He grinned. "You can't, can you, because if death really is the end then I'm wasting my time. You can't prove a negative, right? Or is the fact that you're not replying the answer to my question but I'm just too stubborn to hear it?"

An owl hooted off in the distance. Nightingale shook his head. "A bloody owl's hoot doesn't cut it either, Robbie. Give me something bigger. What about those nuns who see statues start to bleed or make the lame walk or hear voices? If they can hear voices, why the hell can't you talk to me? Just whisper to me, Robbie, no one else need know. And if it's against the rules then sod it, because you and I are the same, we can bend the rules when we have to if it's for the greater good. Just whisper my name, Robbie."

The wind picked up and the conifers swished back and forth, whispering like assassins.

"The trees don't count either, Robbie. Stop pissing around."

The wind died down and Nightingale closed his eyes and listened to the sound of his own breathing. It became deathly still. There was no wind, no traffic noise, no hooting owls or barking foxes. Just silence. Maybe that was what death was like, he thought. Just nothing. Perfect silence, perfect blackness, nothing for all of eternity. He took a deep breath and held it. No sound, no light, no feelings, no thoughts. Nothing. He slowly exhaled.

"I don't understand what's happening, Robbie. I don't understand why you died. I don't understand why my Uncle Tommy smashed his wife's head in with an axe and then hanged himself. I don't understand why my mother slashed her wrists. I don't understand any of it." He sighed. "So this is the way I see it, Robbie. If death is the end, if there is nothing beyond this life, then there really is no point, right? Death sucks, Robbie, you know that. Anna's in bits and it's going to be a long, long time before she's anywhere near okay. And what about your kids? The twins still think you're coming back, they've no idea what dead means. Shit, Robbie, all you had to do was to look both ways when you crossed the road. It's the Green Cross Code, for God's sake."

Nightingale opened his eyes and stared up at the moon. "If you could, you'd talk to Anna, wouldn't you? You'd tell her not to worry, you'd tell her to give the kids a kiss from you. And I'm sure my mum and dad would have done the same for me. But you didn't and they didn't, so that means you can't and the reason you can't is because you're dead and gone forever."

He closed his eyes again. "So, if dead is dead and there's nothing after it, then all this nonsense about Gosling selling my soul is just that. Nonsense. There are no souls to be sold. There's no God and no devil and no heaven and no hell, so I should just stop worrying about what Gosling did or didn't do because the only thing I really have to worry about is that one day, sooner or later, I'm going to be dead and buried the same as you." He smiled. "Well, not buried. I'll either be scattered across Manchester United's pitch or sitting in an egg timer in Jenny's kitchen. To be honest, Robbie, I don't know which is worse. To know that I'm going to hell, or to know that there's no such a place and that death is the end of everything."

Nightingale heard music. The Rolling Stones, "Paint It Black." It was his cell phone ringing in his coat pocket. Nightingale smiled to himself. "If that's you calling, Robbie, I'll be well impressed," he said. He groped around for the phone and pressed the green button to take the call.

"Jack? Jack Nightingale?"

Nightingale didn't recognize the voice but it definitely wasn't Hoyle. "Yeah?"

"This is Harry Wilde. I'm sorry to disturb you on a Saturday night and I'm sorry I didn't get back to you sooner, but I had a hell of a time trying to find my notebook. I'd left it at home and the wife had tidied it up, bless her."

Harry Wilde. The police sergeant he'd spoken to at Gosling Manor. "No problem, Harry," said Nightingale. "Any luck with the phone numbers?"

"The husband and wife lived in. They were given the day off the night that Gosling killed himself, but they turned up for work the next day and were interviewed at the house. There wasn't much they could say, obviously. They were paid their remaining salary a couple of days later and moved out, and I'm afraid we don't know where they went."

"No need, because it was open and shut, right?"

"Exactly," said Wilde. "Once it was clearly suicide everyone throttled back. I've got their names, though. Millie and Charlie Woodhouse. Millicent and Charles. I had more luck with the driver. He discovered the body so he was of more interest, but again it was obviously suicide so we were just going through the motions. Have you got a pen there?"

Nightingale fished a Parker pen from his pocket, along with a receipt from his local supermarket. "Yup," he said.

"His name's Alfie Tyler." Wilde gave him Tyler's address and cell phone number and Nightingale scribbled them down.

"I shouldn't be talking out of school, but Alfie was a bit of a gangster back in the day," said Wilde. "He used to work as a debt-collector for one of the North London mobs and did four years for GBH."

Nightingale thanked Wilde and put the phone away. "Bloody hell, Robbie, I need a real drink," he said. He stood up and poured the last of the wine over the grave. "Red wine always gives me a rotten hangover," he said, and tossed the empty bottle toward the conifers.

CHAPTER

50

Alfie Tyler's house wasn't at all what Nightingale had expected. It was a six-bedroom mock-Tudor house with tall chimneys on the outskirts of Bromley, with a double garage and a rock-lined pool in the front garden. There was a gleaming black Bentley parked in front of the garage. Nightingale had checked the electoral roll—there was no Mrs. Tyler, and from a cursory look at the house Nightingale was fairly sure there were no little Tylers in residence. He'd driven down on Sunday morning, assuming that it would be the best time to catch him at home.

Nightingale dropped the cigarette he'd been smoking onto the sidewalk and stamped on it. He'd phoned the landline and knew that Tyler was at home, and unlike Gosling Manor there didn't appear to be any CCTV cameras covering the building. The large black wrought-iron gates weren't locked and Nightingale pushed them open and walked up the driveway to the front door. The front door was painted black with a large brass knocker in the shape of a lion's head in the center and a brass bell in the brickwork to the right.

Nightingale pressed the doorbell and a music chime kicked into life in the hallway. It sounded like it might once have been classical. Then Nightingale heard footsteps on a wooden floor, and the door opened. "Who is it?" growled a man in a South London accent.

"Alfie Tyler?" asked Nightingale.

"Who wants to know?" asked Tyler, pulling the door wide open. He was a big man, at least three inches taller than Nightingale, and Nightingale was a little over six feet tall. Tyler had big forearms that strained at the sleeves of his polo shirt, and a trim but solid waist. There was a solid gold Rolex on his left wrist and a thick gold chain on his right, and a full sovereign ring on the second finger of his right hand. As he stood on the threshold of his two-million-pound house with his arms folded across his barrel chest, Nightingale caught a whiff of very expensive aftershave.

"Jack Nightingale," said Nightingale, speaking slowly and carefully and watching for any reaction. There was none, no sign that Tyler had ever heard of him.

Tyler just glared at him down his twice-broken nose. "Are you a cop?" he asked.

"No, not anymore," said Nightingale.

"Then get the hell off my property, before I throw you off," said Tyler. Tyler's graying hair and wrinkles around his mouth and eyes suggested he was in his fifties, but his body was more in keeping with a thirty-something boxer, and Nightingale was in no doubt that Tyler was more than capable of carrying out his threat.

Tyler started to push the door closed but Nightingale put his foot over the threshold. "I just need a chat with you, Alfie," he said. He took out his wallet and gave Tyler one of his business cards.

Tyler held the card between his thumb and first finger and scowled as he read it. "A private dick?" he said. "I'm going to count to five and if you haven't gotten the hell off my property I'm going to tear you a new arsehole," he said, and threw the card over Nightingale's shoulder.

"I'll take my car with me, shall I?"

Deep frowns furrowed across Tyler's forehead. "What?"

Nightingale gestured at the Bentley. "That's my motor," he said.

Tyler put a bearlike hand on Nightingale's shoulder and squeezed, digging his thumb into the pressure point near the socket. "You're starting to piss me off, private dickhead."

"I'm the sole beneficiary of Ainsley Gosling's estate," said Nightingale. "I've seen the will, Alfie, and there's no mention of you or the Bentley. So if I go along to the cops, the car will be back in my garage and you'll be back behind bars. Prisons are a lot more crowded than when you were last there, and I'm told the food's gotten a lot worse."

Tyler squinted at Nightingale. "How did you know I'd been in prison?"

"I don't care about your criminal record, I don't care about whose legs you did or didn't break, I just want to know about Ainsley Gosling."

"Mr. Gosling said the car was mine, after he'd gone."

"What, he came back from the grave to tell you that, did he?" said Nightingale.

Tyler frowned. "What?" He released his grip on Nightingale's shoulder.

"When did he tell you that the car was yours?"

"All the time. He knew how much I liked it, and he said I could have it. After…you know."

"So he told you he was going to off himself, did he?"

"What? No, he bloody well didn't. What are you trying to do here, you trying to say I had something to do with him killing himself, because that's bollocks." He put his fists on his hips and glowered at Nightingale.

Nightingale lit a cigarette. He saw Tyler's nostrils flare and offered him the pack.

"I'm trying to give up," said Tyler.

"One won't hurt," said Nightingale. Tyler shrugged and took a cigarette. Nightingale lit it for him. "Okay, here's the thing, Alfie. I'm not going to have much use for a car over the next year or two, and anyway I'm more of a fan of convertibles. I like the feel of the wind in my hair."

"What?"

"What I'm saying is I'm more than happy to let you keep the Bentley, free, gratis, whatever, but in return I want you to tell me what Gosling was up to in the weeks before his death."

Tyler's eyes narrowed. "What's the catch?"

"No catch, Alfie. I'll even sign a piece of paper here and now saying that the car's yours."

Tyler's brow furrowed again. "Give me another of them cards, yeah."

"Only if you promise not to throw it away," said Nightingale.

"What?"

"You say 'what' a lot, you know that?" Nightingale gave him another business card.

Tyler pursed his lips as he read the card. "Why did Mr. Gosling make you his heir?"

"It's a long story."

"Give me the short version, Nightingale."

"I'm his son."

"Mr. Gosling never told me that he had a kid."

"Yeah, well, I'm the family secret," said Nightingale. "But Gosling Manor's mine now. And so's the Bentley. So are you and I going to have a chat, or what?"

Tyler took a long drag on his cigarette and nodded. "Okay," he said. "What do you want to know?"

"It's going to take a while," said Nightingale. "Why don't you ask me in and we can talk over a drink. Or two."

Tyler sighted down his cue, smacked the white ball against the number five, and grinned as it shot into a corner pocket. "That's another tenner you owe me," he said, holding out his hand.

Nightingale took out his wallet and gave Tyler a ten-pound note. "That's the sign of an ill-spent youth," he said.

Tyler had built a bar in his basement, complete with a full range of optics and draught beer pumps, a pool table, a juke box, and half a dozen slot machines. On one wall were dozens of framed photographs of a younger Tyler with well-known villains, movie stars, and even a few members of the Metropolitan Police. Nightingale recognized two senior officers from the Flying Squad, both of whom had left the force on medical grounds and who now lived in palatial villas in Spain. Most of the villains pictured with Tyler had either retired or died, but as far as Nightingale could recall, none had served time behind bars.

"Not much else to do in prison," said Tyler.

"How long did you get?" asked Nightingale.

"I did two stretches, eighteen months and a four-stretch," said Tyler. "It was when I came out the second time that I started working for Mr. Gosling. He knew my probation officer and I went to see him and got on like a house on fire."

"Did you ever go down the basement in Gosling Manor?" asked Nightingale.

"Didn't know there was one," said Tyler, as he racked up the balls again. "How about twenty quid a game, give you a chance to win your money back."

"You conning me, Alfie?" he said.

"Wouldn't dream of it," said Tyler. He winked. "So, you're really Mr. Gosling's boy?"

"He had me adopted at birth," said Nightingale. "How long did you work for him?"

"Fifteen years, pretty much," said Tyler.

"And he paid you well, did he? Because this is one expensive place you've got here."

Tyler grinned. "I had this place long before I worked for Mr. Gosling. I was pretty productive during my glory days."

"So what were you doing driving for him if you weren't short of a bob or two?"

"He was a character, your dad," said Tyler, putting the white ball in position. He reached for Nightingale's pack of Marlboros and took out a cigarette. "Could charm the birds from the trees. And the people he knew. Film stars, businessmen, sportsmen. Everyone liked Ainsley Gosling. They were like moths to a flame. He was on first-name terms with half a dozen prime ministers. We had Mrs. Thatcher around three times at Gosling Manor. She was a real lady. Took a shine to your dad, she did."

"If he was that popular, why did I never read anything about him? And Googling him doesn't throw up a thing. There's never been a newspaper article written about him, there are no photographs, he's the original invisible man."

"He had a team of spin doctors who did nothing else but keep his name out of the papers. And if someone did start getting too close, well, let's just say that Mr. Gosling had a way of getting people to forget things."

"Now it's my turn to look puzzled and say 'what.' What do you mean?"

"You never met him, right?"

"I only found out he was my father last week," said Nightingale.

"He wasn't like other men, your dad," said Tyler. "He had a way about him. A strength."

"You know he was a Satanist, don't you?"

Tyler shrugged. "I'm not one for putting labels on people," he said.

"He studied the occult, he spent millions buying books on witchcraft and devil worship."

Tyler nodded. "Can't argue with that," he said.

"Did you ever see him do stuff?"

"Stuff? Like what?"

"Like summoning devils," said Nightingale.

"You on drugs, Nightingale?" asked Tyler.

"He was a Satanist. That's what Satanists do, right? They serve the devil."

"I never saw him do anything like that," said Tyler. "I was his driver, his personal assistant, his bodyguard. And I'd like to think that I was his friend, too." He hit the white ball and it shot into the triangle of numbered balls with the sound of a skull being cracked with a baseball bat. Two balls dropped into pockets and Tyler grinned.

"How did he make his money, Alfie?"

"He just made it. It came to him. I never saw anybody as lucky as Mr. Gosling. If he bought gold, it went up in price. If he bought oil, it went up. Any shares he bought went through the roof."

"Insider trading?"

"I don't think so. I think he was just lucky."

"Lucky?"

Tyler potted three balls in quick succession. Then he straightened up and rested the cue on his shoulder. "We went to a casino once. He had two girls with him, model-slash-singers or singer-slash-actresses, bloody fit, legs that went on forever, couldn't have been more than nineteen, either of them. He was always lucky with the ladies, was Mr. Gosling."

"Yeah, rich men usually are," said Nightingale.

"It wasn't about the money," said Tyler. "I mean, Mr. Gosling was a generous man, don't get me wrong, but I've seen women fall for him even when they didn't know who he was or how much he had. It's like he had a power over them, the sort of charisma that film stars have, you know. I mean, he was an old man and all but he had no problem pulling young flesh."

He bent over the table and potted another ball, then he picked up his pint of beer. "Anyway, the girls wanted to go to a casino so I drove them all to Leicester Square. Mr. Gosling won at every game he played. He sat down at the high-stakes blackjack table and he just won hand after hand. It's like he knew what cards were going to be dealt."

"Maybe he was a card counter?"

Tyler shook his head. "He was hardly even looking at the cards. He just sat there joking with the girls and chips kept piling up in front of him. Then they wanted to play roulette and he gave them thousands of pounds worth of chips and they lost it all. But pretty much every time he placed a bet, he won. It got so that a couple of the casino managers came over to see what was happening."

"Did they throw him out?"

Tyler chuckled. "You really don't know Mr. Gosling, do you?" he said. He sipped his beer. "Mr. Gosling just looked at them and smiled, in that way that he did, and they smiled and went away. Nobody ever gave Mr. Gosling any trouble, over anything. If a flight was overbooked, there was a seat for him in first class. If a restaurant was full, there was a table. He was like royalty, more often than not he didn't even have to ask. It wasn't money, it was…"

"Power," Nightingale finished for him.

"Presence is what I was going to say," said Tyler. "People just wanted to help him, to make his life easier, happier, whatever. That's why I stayed with him so long. Don't ask me why, I can't explain it."

"Probably a gay thing," said Nightingale. Tyler put down his pint and held his cue in both hands, his face tightening. Nightingale held up his hands. "Joke," he said.

"I'm not gay," said Tyler.

"I was joking," he said. "Trying to lighten the moment. Because what you're telling me is that Ainsley Gosling had power over people. And that's what I was told."

"By who?"

"Actually, by him. He left me a DVD, a sort of video last will and testament." He smiled, trying to show that he wasn't intimidated by Tyler's menacing stare. "Wasn't you that left the envelope on the mantelpiece, was it?"

"What?" said Tyler, his brow furrowing again.

"Someone left an envelope in Gosling Manor with my name on it. In the envelope was the key to a safe-deposit box and in the box was the DVD."

"And what did he say on this DVD?"

Nightingale shrugged. He was there to question Tyler, not open his heart to him. "Just the normal father–son sort of chitchat.

Basically apologizing for giving me up for adoption. He never mentioned me? Not once?"

Tyler shook his head. "Never."

"Or my sister? His daughter?"

"Never talked about kids, never mentioned having them or wanting them."

"I get the feeling that he was different, during the last few years."

Tyler nodded. He stopped using his cue as a club and picked up his pint. "He changed, that's true," he said. "Starting traveling overseas more, meeting some very strange people. Buying books by the dozen. Expensive books. Often in cash."

"Books about the occult?"

"I didn't get to see them all, but the ones I did see, yeah, witch-craft and stuff. And he started spending more time on his own. Then last year he started getting rid of the staff, one by one. Then he started selling his art collection, then his furniture. I asked him what was going on, but I don't think he ever explained to me what he was up to."

"You don't think? Don't you know?"

Tyler sighed. "You had to know him to understand what it was like. He had a way of, I don't know, looking at you that made you either forget something, or change your mind about something. Like I'd be really tired and I'd tell him, and he'd say something to me and it was like I'd just done a line of coke. Or I'd say that I couldn't work on such and such a day because I had to do some-thing, and the next minute I'd forget what was so important and agree to spend the day driving him around."

"He hypnotized you, is that what you're saying?"

Tyler shook his head. "Nah, I was never in a trance and he never did any wavy hand stuff or swung a watch." He sat down on a barstool. "It was weird though, sometimes he'd mumble something that didn't sound like it was English. But then he'd smile and I'd forget about it." He put a hand to his forehead. "Even talking about it sounds stupid. Like I was imagining it. But I'll tell you, Nightingale, I would have taken a bullet for Ainsley Gosling. Or a knife, or stepped in front of a train for him."

"But have you never asked yourself why you felt that way? How he inspired that sort of loyalty?"

"It was just his way," said Tyler.

"Charisma," said Nightingale.

"Yeah, charisma." Tyler put down his pint and potted the rest of his balls. He grinned and held out his hand. Nightingale sighed and gave him twenty pounds. "Double or nothing?" grinned Tyler.

"Yeah, why not," said Nightingale. He sipped his beer as Tyler set up the balls again. He'd asked for a Corona but the best that Tyler could provide was a bottle of Budweiser. "You were the one who found him, weren't you?"

"Yeah. One hell of a mess."

"He was alone in the house?"

Tyler nodded. "He'd given the Woodhouses the night off."

"The Woodhouses? That was the couple who took care of the house, right?"

"Millie and Charlie, they were with him even longer than I was. He had a big staff up until a few years ago but he let them all go."

"Do you know why?"

Tyler shrugged. "He was running out of cash, I think. Paintings started to go, then the furniture. He always paid me and he never seemed short of cash for books, but I think he lost a lot when the market crashed."

"How did you get into the house?"

"I had a key. I went to the kitchen like I always did for a coffee with Millie but she wasn't there. I waited until about ten and then I went up and found him."

"Was there a note?"

"No."

"You're sure? You're sure there was no note?"

Tyler looked up from the table. "You calling me a liar, Nightingale?"

"It's just that you and he were close, Alfie. Suicides usually want to explain themselves. To say why they did what they did. If he was going to say anything to anybody, it would have been to you, right?"

Tyler sighed and straightened up. "There was a letter, but it didn't explain anything."

"And you didn't leave an envelope for me on the mantelpiece in the main room?"

Tyler looked uncomfortable.

"Alfie, you might as well tell me everything. It couldn't have been anyone else but you. You found the body, and the police didn't see any envelope when they were there."

Tyler nodded slowly. "Fair enough," he said. "There was a letter for me and an envelope for you. In the letter Mr. Gosling told me to wait until the police and everyone had gone and to leave your envelope on the mantelpiece and lock up."

"And what did you do with your letter?"

"Burned it. That's what he told me to do."

"And what else did it say?"

"Said I could keep the Bentley, for one. Apologized for the mess. Told me to call the cops. And there was some cash for the Woodhouses."

"Where are they now?"

Tyler shrugged. "No idea. They just went. I think they had a place in the Lake District."

He finished setting up the table and picked up his cue.

"He was buying a lot of books over the year or so before he died, right?" asked Nightingale.

"Tell me about it," said Tyler. "He had me driving him all over the country and to and from the airport every week or so."

"Did you ever get to see any of the books he bought?"

"I saw packages, that's all."

"What about a diary written by a guy called Sebastian Mitchell? Did you ever see that? Big leather-bound book, written in Latin, back to front. I think it was the last thing he read."

"Like I said, he didn't show me his books. But I went to Mitchell's house a few times."

Nightingale's jaw dropped. "You met him?"

"Never met him, but drove to his house. Place up near Wivenhoe, in Essex. Big place, very heavy security."

CHAPTER

52

Nightingale drove up to a set of high wrought-iron gates set into a ten-foot-high brick wall. He climbed out of his MGB and walked up to the gates. There was a small brass speakerphone set into the gatepost on the left and he pressed it. It began to buzz, then there was static, but no one spoke. Nightingale leaned closer to the speaker grille. "Hello," he said. There was no reply, just static. There was a CCTV camera on a metal post on the other side of the wall, covering the gate. Nightingale grinned up at it and held up his driving license. "Jack Nightingale," he said. "I'm here to see Mr. Mitchell." He had no way of knowing if there was anyone watching him so he put his driving license away and went back to the speakerphone. "Jack Nightingale," he repeated. "I'm here to see Mr. Mitchell."

The static stopped abruptly, then a women spoke, her voice curt and official. "Mr. Mitchell doesn't see visitors. Please remove yourself from outside our property. Thank you." The speakerphone went dead.

Nightingale pressed the button again and the static returned. "My name is Jack Nightingale and I want to see Mr. Mitchell. Mr. Sebastian Mitchell."

"Mr. Mitchell does not receive visitors," said the woman.

"Can you tell him it's about the book he wrote. His diary."

"Mr. Mitchell never sees visitors," said the woman. "If you don't go away immediately, the police will be called."

There was more static. Nightingale leaned toward the speaker-phone. "Tell him my father was Ainsley Gosling." The static ended and there was only the sound of birdsong from the trees on the far side of the road. The lock buzzed and the gates swung open. He turned and looked up at the CCTV, threw it a mock salute, then climbed back in the MGB and drove through the gates. The drive curved to the right in front of a three-story concrete-and-glass cube. A flight of white marble steps led up to a white double-height door that was already opening as he got out of the car. Two men in black suits wearing impenetrable sunglasses walked down the steps toward Nightingale.

Nightingale knew instinctively that they were going to pat him down so he smiled amiably and raised his arms. One of the men, burly with a shaved head, slowly and methodically squeezed Nightingale's legs and arms, then worked his way down from his neck to his groin. He found Nightingale's phone and examined it carefully before handing it back. "Photo ID," he said. He wasn't English, Nightingale realized. Serbian maybe. Or Bosnian.

Nightingale gave the man his driving license.

"Business card," said the man, holding out his other hand. Nightingale took out his wallet and gave him a card.

The second man was walking slowly around the car, checking it inside and out. Nightingale smiled and nodded but the man ignored him.

The man with his ID went back up the steps where a woman had emerged from inside the house. She was wearing a black suit, the skirt ending just above her knees, a crisp white shirt and black high heels, and her blonde hair was tied back with a black ribbon.

As the man gave the driving license and business card to the woman, a gust of wind lifted up the back of his jacket and Nightingale caught a glimpse of a black automatic in a leather nylon holster. It looked like a Glock. The woman studied the license and card and then waved at Nightingale to come up the stairs. He held out his hand to shake but she just gave him his license and card. "My name is Sylvia, Mr. Nightingale. There are certain house rules that must be followed to the letter if you are to meet with Mr. Mitchell."

"I understand."

"No, you don't," she said primly. "You will do everything I ask or you will not be permitted to speak with him." She turned around and walked back inside the house. Standing in a large white-marbled hallway were two more men in black suits and dark glasses, their hands clasped over their groins. There were two stainless-steel CCTV cameras covering the hall and another covering the stairway.

There was a spiral marble staircase leading to the upper floors, and hanging from the center of the ceiling was a glass feature light that looked like a waterfall that had been frozen midflow. Off the downstairs hall led half a dozen jet-black doors with glossy white handles. Sylvia walked to the middle of the hall, her high heels clicking on the hard marble surface, and stopped under the glass waterfall. She turned to face him and pointed to a door. "In there is a bathroom. You will remove all your clothing and you will shower using the shower gel that is provided. You will use the same gel to wash your hair and you will wash your hair twice. You will use the brush provided to clean under your toenails and your fingernails.

There are no towels but there is an electric dryer in which you stand. When you are dry you change into the robe provided and come back here. Do not touch your clothes once you have showered. Do you have any questions?"

"Just one," said Nightingale. "I said I was the son of Ainsley Gosling, but my name is Nightingale. Yet you showed no surprise at the different names."

"Apparently Mr. Mitchell was expecting you," said Sylvia. She motioned at the door to the bathroom. "Please, if you will."

CHAPTER

There were two stainless-steel CCTV cameras in the bathroom, which Nightingale thought a slight case of overkill considering the men with guns in the hallway. He was sure that the cameras were being monitored but didn't bother trying to protect his modesty. There were white plastic hangers on a set of stainless-steel hooks and he stripped off his clothes and placed them on the hangers. A pristine white cotton robe was hanging on one of the hooks. Nightingale rolled up his socks and put them in his shoes, took off his watch, and then stood facing one of the cameras and held his arms out to the side. "Happy?" he said.

The camera stared back at him. He grinned and walked into the glass-sided shower. There were multiple jets all around the shower and when he turned the control dial water squirted at him from all directions. There was a soap dispenser to the right of the shower control full of a bright green gel. Nightingale rubbed the gel into his hair and lathered it over his body. It smelt of mint and tingled on his skin. There was a brand-new plastic nail brush on a wire tray under the soap dispenser, and he followed the woman's instructions and methodically cleaned his fingernails and toenails, then he rinsed off the lather and repeated the process.

The dryer was a stainless-steel box the same size as the shower with a rubber floor, and as soon as he stepped inside warm air started blowing all over his body, caressing him like a soft summer wind. Nightingale raised his arms and let the warm air play over his skin. In less than three minutes he was dry. He put on the robe. It reached down almost to his ankles. There was no comb or brush so he stood in front of a floor-to-ceiling mirror and tidied his hair with his fingers as best he could.

Sylvia was waiting for him in the hall, flanked by two of the men in dark suits. "Show me your hands," she said. He held them out and she scrutinized his nails, then she nodded. "There are procedures that must be followed at all times," she said. "If at any time you break any of the rules that I give you, the meeting will end."

"I'll be a good boy," said Nightingale.

She ignored his attempt at levity. "You will see that Mr. Mitchell is within a pentangle. You must not get within six feet of the perimeter."

"Because?"

"There is no because, Mr. Nightingale. There are only rules that have to be followed. If you make any attempt to get closer than six feet then my associates here will stop you."

"Stop me how?"

"By whatever means necessary."

"They'll shoot me if I try to get inside the circle?"

"By whatever means necessary," repeated Sylvia. "You must make no move to touch Mr. Mitchell. Or to give him anything."

"So no kissing, then?"

"This is not a laughing matter, Mr. Nightingale," said Sylvia disdainfully. "If you refuse to take this seriously then I will have to ask you to leave."

Nightingale's face hardened. "I don't think that's going to happen, Sylvia darling," he said. "Because the way I see it, you're the hired help here. You dance for Mr. Mitchell and Mr. Mitchell has decided that he wants to see me. When I was outside you were all for calling the cops and having me hauled away, but you changed your tune when Mr. Mitchell learned who I was. He told you to get me in here, which means that he wants to see me, which means you're not going to ask me to leave. So do your job and let me in to see him and stop playing the hard arse with me, because I have dealt with some very hard people over the years and believe me, you don't even come close."

Sylva's jaw tightened and if looks could kill Nightingale would have burst into flames on the spot, but he could see in her eyes that he was right. She didn't have the authority to keep him from the man he'd come to see. She walked past him, so close that he caught the delicate scent of her perfume. "Follow me," she said.

CHAPTER
54

Sebastian Mitchell was in a ground-floor room overlooking the gardens at the rear of the house. The floor was the same white marble that had been used in the entrance hall and the walls were painted white. He was sitting in a winged green leather armchair, an oxygen mask covering the lower part of his face and connected by a thin clear tube to a tall cylinder behind to his left. To his right was a heartbeat monitor connected to a sensor on his chest. He was an old man, at least ninety, with wisps of white hair and skin that was graying and speckled with liver spots. He was wearing a robe similar to the one that Nightingale had on, open at the front, and white cotton boxer shorts. There were pale blue slippers on his feet.

The room was large, almost as big as the main room in Gosling Manor. There were French windows leading out onto a stone-flagged patio which in turn led to well-tended lawns, as smooth as a billiard table. In each corner of the room stood a bodyguard. Unlike the men outside they had taken off their jackets but kept on their sunglasses. Two of the men had nylon shoulder holsters with Glock automatics, one had an Ingram submachine pistol in a sling, and the fourth was holding a shotgun across his chest. They were all staring impassively ahead into the middle distance.

Nightingale walked toward Mitchell, his bare feet slapping on the marble floor. Sylva followed him, her high heels clicking like an overwound metronome. "Not too close, remember, Mr. Nightingale," she warned.

There was a black circle etched into the floor, the edge of which bordered a five-pointed star. At first Nightingale thought that the design had been painted onto the marble, but as he got closer he realized that it was actually set into the white marble. There were other designs within the circle, strange markings and letters from an alphabet that Nightingale didn't recognize. At each point of the star there was a large white candle. The candles were burning but there was no smoke, just a pure yellow flame. The only other furniture in the room was a hospital bed and that was in the center of the circle, next to the armchair.

"Thanks for seeing me," said Nightingale.

Mitchell coughed, then slowly pulled the oxygen mask away from his face. "You have your father's eyes," said Mitchell. "And his jaw."

"I don't think anyone else sees a family resemblance," said Nightingale.

"He sent you?" asked Mitchell.

"He's dead," said Nightingale.

Mitchell's eyes narrowed and he put a hand up to adjust the oxygen mask. "How?"

"Suicide."

"How?"

"Shotgun to the head."

Mitchell began to laugh, but the laugh quickly degenerated into a cough. When he had the coughing under control he took a tissue from a box and dabbed at his lips. The tissue came away spotted with red. Mitchell screwed it up and dropped it into a steel wastepaper basket. "How old are you?" asked Mitchell.

"I'm thirty-three next Friday."

Mitchell nodded slowly, a cruel smile spreading across his face. "Today's the Lord's Day so five days to go," he said. "He was trying to get out of the deal, you know that?"

"I know. He left me a video, telling me everything."

Mitchell laughed sharply. "I hardly think he would have told you everything," he said. "But he was wasting his time. There was nothing he could do. And that's why you have come to see me, of course. But you are wasting your time as your father wasted his."

"He asked for your help?"

"I don't think your father asked for anything in his life. He demanded. He threatened. He bargained. But even if he had gone down on his knees and begged, even if I had wanted to help him, there is nothing that can be done. A deal is a deal." He leaned over and adjusted the oxygen flow, took several deep breaths from the mask, and then settled back in his chair. "You read my book?"

"Yes. Some of it."

"You read Latin?"

"A friend helped me."

"So you know what lies ahead for you?"

"I said I read it, I didn't say I believed it."

Mitchell coughed and removed his mask again to dab at his lips with a tissue. The blood-spotted tissue followed the first one into the wastepaper bin. "It doesn't matter if you believe it or not. A deal is a deal."

"Why my thirty-third birthday? Why didn't the devil take my soul straightaway, at birth?"

"A soul that hasn't lived is no prize," said Mitchell. "There are seven cycles each of eleven years. The start of the fourth cycle is the most precious, when the body is at its peak."

"And the deal would have been my soul for riches and power?"

"I don't know what your father asked for. But whatever it was, he regretted it. Eventually."

"And that's when he came to see you?"

"He kept coming. He was at my door every week. He knew I'd done a deal with Proserpine myself. He thought I could help him get out of the deal he'd done."

"Proserpine?'

"The demon who was promised your soul. A bitch of the first order."

"And you wouldn't help?"

"Wouldn't help, couldn't help, it amounts to the same thing. A deal is a deal and that's the end of it." He chuckled. "The end of you."

"Why did you give him your diary if you didn't want to help him?"

Mitchell chuckled drily. "Is that what you think? That I gave him the book? Your father stole it from me. He sent his people in at night and they killed two of my men and took it."

"Why? What is so important about your diary?"

"He thought it would show him a way to get out of the contract. But he was wrong. The book contains many things, but getting out of a contract with Proserpine is not an option."

"What about if I gave you the diary back?"

Mitchell stared at Nightingale. "That would be the honorable thing to do," he said.

"If I did," said Nightingale, "then what could you do for me?"

"What is it you want?"

"What I want, Mr. Mitchell, is to forget about all this and to get on with my life."

"I'm afraid that's not an option," said Mitchell. He began to cough and he bent forward and adjusted the oxygen flow again. He took several deep breaths to steady himself before speaking again. "Doing a deal with a devil, any devil, is easy enough. The information is out there. They want to be contacted, they want to deal, that's what they live for, to harvest souls. Even someone who is just dabbling in the occult will soon find out how to summon a devil. It used to be books that people turned to but now it's the Internet. Google will give you tens of thousands of sites that will tell you what to do. But once the deal is done, there is no going back. I told Gosling that but he kept asking, kept pushing. He thought the answer lay in my diary, but it doesn't. The diary tells you how to summon Proserpine and her ilk, but not how to rescind a deal."

"And what did you get? What did you bargain for?"

Mitchell sneered at Nightingale. "That's between me and her," he said.

"But you didn't try to back out of the deal?"

"I knew what I was getting in to," he said. "I wasn't like your father. He was too eager, he didn't think through what he was doing. I knew exactly what I was doing and I did a deal I was happy with."

"You sold your soul?"

"It's complicated," said Mitchell. "My soul is promised to a higher deity than Proserpine, though she would like to get her hands on it, I'm sure."

Nightingale nodded at the circle on the floor. "And what's the idea of the circle?"

"It's protection, of course."

"I would have thought the CCTV and the men in black suits would have been protection enough," he said.

"Then you know nothing of the occult," said Mitchell. "The circle is the only thing that keeps her from me."

"So you're just as scared as my father was," said Nightingale.

"Your father wasn't scared of her, she had no interest in him. She already had what she wanted from him—the soul of his first-born son, promised to her at the moment of birth. The sweetest of souls. And the soul of his only daughter. Once she had them, he had nothing else to offer her."

"But she wants you, is that it?"

"She wants my soul, yes."

"So what's your plan, to hide in that circle forever?"

Mitchell chuckled. "I'm not hiding, Nightingale. You can't hide from a devil. She knows exactly where I am, I'm sure of that. And forever isn't an option." He coughed again, then moved his mask and spat bloody phlegm into a tissue. He grinned up at Nightingale. "Cancer. I've a few months at most. Then I walk into hell of my own accord."

"But either way you're dead," said Nightingale.

"It's one thing to be dragged kicking and screaming into the eternal fire," said Mitchell. "If I walk in under my own steam, I take my place among the princes of hell."

Nightingale folded his arms. "So what are my options?" he asked.

"You have none," said Mitchell. "Enjoy what little time you have left, and say your good-byes."

"There are always alternatives," said Nightingale. "Options. Choices."

"Not in this case," said Mitchell. "Your soul is hers. Your father would have done the negotiation even before you were born. And at the moment of birth he would have carried out the ceremony. From that moment on, she owned your soul."

"What if I were to do what you're doing? Make myself a protective circle and stay inside?"

"She owns your soul," said Mitchell. "She wouldn't have to enter the circle to take it."

"What if I did what my father did? What if I stayed within a circle and killed myself?"

"You're thinking of suicide, are you?" chuckled Mitchell. He cleared his throat, slid his oxygen mask to the side, and spat into a tissue. "That would be ironic, wouldn't it? Father and son dying the same way. But you'd be wasting your time. Your soul is no longer yours, it has never been yours, it belonged to her before you were even born, and there's nothing you can do to stop her taking it."

Nightingale rubbed his chin. "In your book, you say that there should be a mark. A mark that shows that the soul has been sold."

Mitchell nodded. "A pentangle. Yes."

"I don't have a mark that looks anything like that."

"If your father sold your soul, then you do. You just haven't found it yet."

"And what if there isn't a mark?"

Mitchell chuckled. "Then you've got nothing to worry about, have you?"

CHAPTER

Nightingale followed Sylvia through the hall, flanked by two of the men in black suits. "How long's he been in the circle?" asked Nightingale.

"It's a pentangle," said Sylvia archly.

"Fine," said Nightingale. "How long's he been inside the pentangle?"

"Two months."

"And he never leaves it?"

"That's the point of the pentangle," she said. "If you leave, you are no longer protected."

"But I don't understand why he has to stay there. What's he frightened of?"

"I'm sure there are a lot of things that you don't understand, Mr. Nightingale," she said. She gestured at the bathroom. "Please get changed and we shall escort you off the premises."

Nightingale pushed his way into the bathroom. He took off his bathrobe and hung it on one of the hooks by the door. He caught sight of his reflection in the full-length mirror and instinctively sucked in his stomach. He stood facing the mirror, his head cocked on one side, and grinned at his reflection. "Not bad for a thirty-two-year-old," he said. Nightingale wasn't as fit as he had been when he was in CO19, the Met's armed unit. The training was rigorous and never-ending and fitness was a must, so he'd worked out in the police gym three times a week and taken regular runs. He'd stopped exercising once he'd left the force but his body was still in good condition, considering the amount he drank and smoked. He patted his abdominals. Not quite a six-pack but it wasn't a beer gut, either. And he still had all his own hair and teeth. But the one thing he definitely didn't have was a tattoo of a pentangle.

He turned around and looked over his left shoulder, then his right. No tattoo on his back. But he knew that. He knew every inch of his body and he had never seen a pentangle or anything like it. Neither had any of his girlfriends over the years, and a pentangle tattoo wasn't something that wouldn't be mentioned. As he looked at his backside he had a thought that at first made him smile and then brought a frown to his face. There were some parts of his body where you never looked, where nobody checked. He put a hand on each buttock and slowly pulled them apart as he twisted around trying to look at his reflection. He still couldn't see much so he tried with his legs apart and his head down between his knees, the pressure on his chest so tight that he had trouble breathing. There was nothing there, but then he had never expected that there would be. As he straightened up he saw the small red light flashing on the side of the CCTV camera opposite him and realized how ridiculous he looked. He winked at the camera. "Just checking," he said.

Nightingale put on his clothes and shoes and walked out of the bathroom. Sylvia and the two bodyguards were waiting for him and they took him outside and down the steps to his MGB.

Nightingale tried to engage Sylvia in conversation but she had given up all pretence of civility. There was a look of utter contempt on her face that left him in no doubt that she had been watching his contortionist's act on her monitor.

Nightingale climbed into his car and started the engine. He gave Sylvia a friendly wave as he drove off but she stared at him impassively, her eyes as cold and unforgiving as the sunglasses that her colleagues were wearing.

He headed for the road. The gates were already opening for him. He drove through then turned right. In his rearview mirror he watched the gates close behind him. He realized that his hands were shaking and he gripped the steering wheel tightly but that didn't stop the tremors. Two miles down the road was a pub and he pulled into the car park and climbed out of his car. He lit a cigarette. Beyond the car park was a stream and Nightingale walked down to it. He stood watching the water burble by as he blew smoke. The wind blew through the trees on the other side of the stream and they swayed like lovers slow dancing, and for the first time Nightingale realized that one day he would die, that the sun would still shine and the stream would still flow and the wind would still blow through the trees, but he wouldn't be there to see it.

Nightingale tried blowing smoke rings but the wind whipped them away before they'd even left his lips. The smoke rings were a good analogy for life, thought Nightingale, or a metaphor. He was never sure what the difference was. He smiled. Jenny would know, so he'd ask her next time he saw her. Whether it was an analogy or a metaphor, the smoke rings were like human lives. They came from nothing, they existed for a short time, and then they were gone. Gone forever.

Nightingale hadn't thought much about his own death before meeting Sebastian Mitchell. Death was something that happened to every living thing, he knew that much. It was part of the process.

You were born, you lived, and then you died. But even when his own parents had been killed in a senseless car accident, death had been something that happened to other people. He'd watched Sophie Underwood fall to her death from the apartment block in Chelsea Harbour, and he'd grieved for her, but it hadn't made him think about his own death. Robbie Hoyle's death had been a shock, but Nightingale hadn't for a moment imagined himself in his friend's place. During his years as an armed police officer, he'd been in positions where death was just a bullet away, but he'd never felt vulnerable. But Mitchell had shown what lay ahead for Nightingale even if he avoided bullets, looked both ways when he crossed the street, kept away from high places, and wore his seat belt every time he got into his car. If you lived long enough, you died anyway. That was the one simple fact about life. At some point it ended. Mitchell looked as if he didn't have more than a few weeks to live. Then he would die and that would be it. And as Nightingale had looked at the old man, gasping and wheezing and coughing up blood, he had realized for the first time that one day he too would die. It was a horrible feeling, like a cold hand gripping his heart and squeezing. He'd never see Jenny again. Never drink a bottle of Corona or a good malt whisky. Never enjoy the feeling of the wind in his hair as he drove his MGB with the top down.

He took a long drag on his cigarette and held the smoke deep in his lungs. He'd never smoke another cigarette, smile at a pretty girl, eat a bar of chocolate. The world would go on, nothing would change, but he wouldn't be part of it. And he wouldn't be dead for a week or a month or a year. It wasn't like illness where you went to bed and then you got better and got up and life went on. Death was forever. For ever and ever. Until the end of time, except that there was no end. You were dead forever and Nightingale didn't want to die and he didn't want to be dead.

He shivered and looked up at the clear afternoon sky, blue and cloudless. He didn't want to die, but it didn't matter, because no matter what he wanted it was going to happen, sooner or later.

He flicked what was left of his cigarette into the stream. He shivered again and turned up the neck of his raincoat. There was no solution to what was troubling Nightingale. All he could do was accept the inevitable—that one day he would die. He looked up at the sky again. All the talk of his soul being sold to the devil didn't really worry Nightingale. He didn't believe in the devil and he didn't believe in souls. But he did believe in death and that was what truly scared him.

He walked back to the pub. It was just after three o'clock and the lunchtime trade had gone. There were two pensioners in cloth caps sitting in a corner, one with a terrier asleep at his feet. Nightingale nodded at them as he went up to the bar. The bartender was a jovial fat man with slicked-back hair wearing a collarless shirt and red braces. "Afternoon, squire, what can I get you?" he asked.

Nightingale thought of asking for a Corona but decided against it. He wanted something with more of a kick. "A Bell's," he said. "With ice."

"On the rocks as our American cousins like to say," said the bartender. He pushed a glass up against the optic. "You're not from around here."

"Just visiting a friend," said Nightingale. The bartender pushed the glass against the optic a second time. "Just a single, I'm driving," said Nightingale.

"It's happy hour," said the bartender. "By one get one free. BOGOF as we say." He put the glass down in front of Nightingale. "Be happy."

"Do I look happy?"

"You look morose," said the bartender. "But everyone does these days. Four million unemployed, house prices halving, the pound in a slump, there's not much to smile about. Which is why we've got the happy hour. We're doing our bit."

Nightingale raised his glass to him. "Cheers," he said. He sipped his whisky. He reached into his pocket for his cigarettes and put the pack on the bar. "Every time I drink, I want to smoke. Reflex action," he said.

"Me too," said the bartender. "Still can't get used to not being able to smoke in my own bloody pub. I lost half my trade when the ban came in. The bloody nanny state, it is."

"And for what?" said Nightingale. "It doesn't save lives because everyone dies. Even if you never smoke a single cigarette your whole life, you still die."

"It's not about saving lives, it's about controlling the way we live," said the bartender. He helped himself to a brandy and clinked his glass against Nightingale's. "You know, if we're not careful, the bastards will be banning alcohol next. Then where will we be?"

"Do you ever think about the meaning of life?" Nightingale asked as he swirled the ice around his glass with his finger.

"It's the number forty-two, innit?" said the bartender. "According to that movie. *The Hitchhiker's Guide to the Whatsit*."

"The galaxy," said Nightingale. "Nah, forty-two was the answer to the ultimate question. It wasn't the meaning of life."

"Ah, well, now you're asking," said the bartender. "The meaning of life? It's got to be kids, right? That's all you leave behind, other than your debts. Your kids. Your DNA." He leaned forward. "My advice to you, have lots of sex and produce lots of kids. That Bin Laden chappie, you know how many kids he had? Twenty-six. Twenty-bloody-six. Doesn't matter who you are or what you do, good or bad, it's your kids that live on. Your kids and their kids and their kids' kids." He jutted his chin out. "I've got four myself, and three grandkids. Two of my lads moved to Australia and I don't see them much but that's not the point. They're the meaning of my life." His eyes narrowed. "You got kids?"

Nightingale shook his head. "Nah."

"There's your answer, then. That's why you're morose. Kids give your life meaning." He grinned. "Mind you, they also suck the life out of you, but that's another story."

Nightingale drained his glass and smiled. Maybe the bartender was right. Maybe children were the answer. But as it had been three years since he'd had a regular girlfriend, they weren't part of his immediate game plan.

"You're going to hell, Jack Nightingale," said the bartender, his voice cold and lifeless.

Nightingale's glass slipped from his fingers and smashed on the floor. "How do you know my name?" he said.

The bartender frowned. "What?"

"How do you know my name?"

"Squire, I asked if you wanted another drink, there's no need to start smashing my glasses."

"You said I was going to hell."

"You're hearing things. I asked if you wanted a refill but it looks like you've had enough to drink already."

Nightingale bent down to pick up the pieces of glass.

"Leave it, leave it!" said the bartender. "Health and safety. Customers aren't allowed to touch broken glass. The brewery would have my job if they saw you do that."

"Sorry," said Nightingale. He reached for his wallet. "I'll pay for the damage."

"Forget it," said the bartender.

Nightingale held up his hands. "I'm sorry," he said. "I've had a rough couple of days." He took a step back, then turned and left the pub. The terrier lifted its head and growled at him, then settled back on the floor.

CHAPTER

56

Jenny was tapping away on her keyboard when Nightingale walked into the office. "There are some sick bunnies out there, Jack," she said.

"Tell me about it," said Nightingale. He flopped down onto his chair and raised his eyebrows expectantly. "Coffee?"

"I'd love one," she said.

"I shall miss your sense of humor when I'm burning in hell."

"That's not very funny, Jack," she said.

"It's the best I can do this time of the morning," he said. "What did you mean about sick bunnies?"

Jenny nodded at her computer screen. "Do you know that you can buy a copy of *The Satanic Bible* on Amazon? With next-day delivery. And if you type 'Selling Your Soul to the Devil' into Google you get more than a hundred and forty thousand sites? What sad bastards would want to know how to sell a soul to the devil?"

"My father, for one," said Nightingale.

"Then there's Church-of-Satan-dot-com. The guys there certainly believe in the devil."

"There's a lot of rubbish on the Internet," said Nightingale. "Fifty percent is plain wrong and ten percent is malicious."

"Those are official statistics, are they?"

"I read it on Wikipedia," said Nightingale. "How's my coffee coming along?"

Jenny flounced over to the coffee maker.

"How was your weekend?" he asked.

"We had a great time," she said. "Bit of riding, bit of fishing, bit of shooting. Girl stuff."

"I hope I wasn't too rude to her. I just didn't feel like opening up to a complete stranger."

"Jack, you don't open up to anyone," said Jenny. "You're the original closed book, you are. But no is the answer to your question, she understood why you were so defensive and she wasn't offended by it. She's worked in Broadmoor, she can take care of herself."

"She seemed a smart cookie, that's for sure."

"Maybe she could help, Jack. You can't remember what happened with Simon Underwood. Maybe she could help you remember. And the other times when you heard people saying that you were going to hell. She could get you to relive those moments and find out for sure what they said."

"I'm not sure that I do want to remember," said Nightingale.

"Nonsense."

"Really? And what if she makes me remember that I actually did push Simon Underwood through the window? What then? Do I turn myself in? Maybe I'm better off not remembering."

Jenny didn't reply.

"And what if it turns out that I have been imagining all these people telling me that I'm going to hell? Then I'm crazy, right?

Crazy and maybe a serial killer to boot. Hand on heart, I think I'm better off not knowing."

"But she might prove to you that you didn't kill Underwood, have you considered that?"

Nightingale shrugged.

"Please, Jack, give Barbara a chance. She's very good at what she does, I promise."

"I'll think about it," said Nightingale.

"That means no," said Jenny.

"It means I'll think about it," said Nightingale. "Now, can we change the subject please?"

"Okay, fine," said Jenny. "So what did you get up to over the weekend?"

Nightingale explained about the phone call from Harry Wilde, meeting Alfie Tyler, and driving to Wivenhoe to meet Sebastian Mitchell.

Jenny put her hands on her hips and glared at him. "I can't believe you didn't tell me any of this."

"I'm telling you now."

"Jack…" Words failed her and she stood shaking her head. "You should have called me."

"Jenny, baby, I was on a roll. Wilde gave me Tyler's details and Tyler told me where I could find Mitchell. There just wasn't time to call you."

Jenny carried his coffee over to his desk and sat down. "And Mitchell talked to you?"

Nightingale nodded. "According to Mitchell, this devil is the real thing. Her name's Proserpine. He did a deal with her but somehow managed to piss her off. According to Mitchell, my father could well have sold my soul to her."

"That's nonsense, Jack."

"Mitchell says it's possible. But he says that if my father did sell my soul then I would have the mark, the pentangle. No pentangle, no contract."

"And you haven't, right?"

"I've checked and I've double-checked."

"You could shave your head."

"Yeah, so could you. I checked my head on the baby pictures, remember? Any tattoo would have been put there the day I was born."

"So you're fine. Even if there is a devil called Proserpine, and even if you can sell souls to her, none of that matters because there's no mark."

"That's what Mitchell says." He sipped his coffee. "My father might well have believed that he'd sold my soul, but the fact that there's no mark says otherwise. So it's bollocks. It's all bollocks."

"I was fairly busy myself," said Jenny. "In between riding and shooting I made a few calls." She pulled a piece of paper from the pocket of her jeans. "I tracked down George Harrison for you." Nightingale reached for the paper but she held it out of reach. "I want you to promise me something," she said.

"You can have a pay raise when the business picks up."

She shook her head. "I want you to promise me that you won't go and see him."

"I can't promise that, Jenny."

"Opening old wounds, it's not healthy," she said.

"Is that you talking, or Barbara?"

"It's common sense, something you seem to be short of at the moment."

"I have to talk to him, Jenny," said Nightingale. He tried to grab the paper but she moved it away.

"Jack, I'm serious..."

"So am I," said Nightingale. "Give me the address."

"If you go, and I don't think you should, but if you do I want to go with you."

"Deal," said Nightingale.

"Cross your heart and hope to die?"

"Yes to the first bit, no to the second. Dying isn't something I hope to do just yet. But I'll take you."

Jenny gave him the piece of paper. Nightingale looked at the address and phone number. "Battersea? He's in London?" He gave the piece of paper back to her. "I need you to phone him."

"And say what?"

"Ask him what cell phone service he uses, tell him a sales rep will visit him and give him a new iPhone for free, to test."

"You mean lie to him?"

"Just humor me," said Nightingale.

CHAPTER

57

Nightingale climbed out of the MGB and looked up at the block of apartments. "What floor did you say?" It was a drab council building, the concrete stained by years of pollution and pigeon droppings, the windows grubby and cracked. There was colorful graffiti on most of the walls. A pack of mongrel dogs watched them suspiciously.

Jenny grunted as she pushed herself out of the sports car. "There's no elegant way of getting out of one of these things, is there?"

"It's a classic," said Nightingale.

"I'm just glad I decided to wear jeans today."

"What floor?"

"Ninth. Are you going to leave your car on the street here? The wheels will be off by the time we get back."

"Like I said, it's a classic. People respect classics." He saw the look of disbelief on her face and laughed. "I'm serious. When was the last time you saw a classic motor vandalized? It doesn't happen.

They go for the flash cars, the ones owned by people with more money than sense. Plus they can see that I don't have a radio or CD player or anything worth stealing." He nodded at the entrance. There was a stainless-steel panel dotted with dozens of buttons, and there was a CCTV camera covering the door. "You should call him, tell him you're from the cell phone company."

"Why me?"

"Because you're a girl, and a pretty one to boot."

Jenny grinned. "To boot?"

"You know what I mean. A girl is less of a threat than a guy."

"Are you a threat, Jack? Is that what's happening here?"

"I just want to talk, that's all," he said. "Cross my heart."

CHAPTER

Nightingale leaned against the stairwell, his hand on the yellow metal rail that ran up the inside wall. "What floor are we on now?" he panted. There were piles of rubbish on every stairwell, cockroaches on the walls, and a strong smell of vomit and urine that got worse the higher they climbed.

"Seventh," said Jenny. "And you wouldn't be so tired if you didn't smoke so much."

"Smoking's good for you," said Nightingale. "It's packed with vitamins and minerals and has zero calories and fat." He gestured at the stairs. "It's exercise that's bad for you. Look what it's doing to me."

"You should go to the gym more," said Jenny. "Maybe start running."

"I don't need to lose weight," said Nightingale. He patted his stomach. "Not quite a six-pack, but I'm not fat. You show me a fat smoker and I'll show you a smoker who's not inhaling."

"What the hell does that mean?" asked Jenny.

Nightingale shrugged. "I have absolutely no idea," he said as he started to climb the stairs again. "I was just feeling defensive."

"When are you going to get over this elevator thing?"

"Never," replied Nightingale.

"Jack, elevators are just about the safest form of transport there is. You know how many people have died in elevator accidents in the UK in the last twenty years? None. That's how many."

"How do you know?"

Jenny grinned. "I don't, I just made it up. But you never hear about elevator accidents, do you?"

"That's because there's a conspiracy between the media and the big elevator companies."

"Nonsense."

"Can we just leave it that I don't like elevators? It's no big deal, Jenny. Besides, get stuck in an elevator here and you'd starve to death before someone came out to help you."

They reached the ninth floor and Nightingale held the door open to let Jenny go through first. The smell of vomit and urine was even stronger in the hallway. The floor was bare concrete and the pale green walls were streaked with dirt. A council notice warned residents not to leave their rubbish in the stairwell. "That's the apartment there," said Jenny, pointing at a door to their right.

"You knock on the door, check that it's him, then I'll step in."

"Jack, are you sure this is a good idea? We've lied our way into the building, he's not going to be happy to see us."

"Please, Jenny. Just do it."

Jenny walked over to the door and pressed the doorbell. Nightingale flattened himself against the wall. The door opened and Nightingale held his breath.

"Mr. Harrison?" asked Jenny.

"That's me," said a male voice. "You're from the phone company?"

"George Arthur Harrison?"

"I said already, that's me."

Nightingale pushed himself away from the wall and put his hand against the door so that Harrison couldn't close it. "Mr. Harrison, I need a few minutes of your time," he said.

Harrison was short and stick-thin, wearing a stained T-shirt that seemed to be several sizes too big for him and brown cargo pants that had been turned up at the bottom. It was as if he'd shrunk within his clothes. He frowned at Nightingale. "Who are you?" He was balding with a greasy comb-over that barely concealed his liver-spotted scalp. From behind him was the sound of a TV show, *Jerry Springer* or *Trisha*. The audience was howling and jeering.

"My name's Nightingale. Jack Nightingale."

Harrison's face hardened and he tried to push the door closed, but Nightingale was too strong for him. "I'll call the police," said Harrison.

"Jack…" said Jenny. "Maybe we should go."

"Just a few minutes, Mr. Harrison. Then we'll go. I promise."

Harrison continued to push the door but realized that it wasn't a contest he was ever going to win. He stepped back holding up his hands defensively. Nightingale saw that his nails were bitten to the quick. "Please, just leave me alone."

"You know who I am then?" asked Nightingale.

"You're the boy, the Nightingale boy. Of course I know. You think I could ever forget?"

"I want to talk about what happened to my parents," said Nightingale. "The accident."

Harrison's shoulders slumped and he turned and walked back down the hallway.

Nightingale looked at Jenny. "Do you want to wait outside?"

She shook her head fiercely. "I'm coming with you," she said.

"You don't have to."

"I want to."

Nightingale nodded and followed Harrison inside. The hallway was the same drab green as the corridor outside. A bare bulb hung from a frayed wire and there was a stack of unopened bills on a side table underneath a cracked mirror. As he went by the mirror, Harrison adjusted his comb-over. Jenny shared a smile with Nightingale.

The living room was a mess. There were two red plastic sofas, one piled high with magazines, most of which seemed to be pornographic, and the other was covered in old take-away cartons. The only item of value in the apartment was a large LCD television. Through an open door, Nightingale saw a filthy kitchen, a grease-covered gas stove, and a sink piled high with dirty dishes.

"How long have you lived here, George?" asked Nightingale. "What brought you to London?"

Harrison shrugged but didn't answer. He went over to a door that led out to a small concrete balcony that was filled with junk and pulled it open. A bicycle missing its front wheel was leaning against a box that was filled with empty vodka bottles.

Jenny stood watching the television. A young woman who must have weighed three hundred pounds was shrieking at a spotty-faced young man, accusing him of fathering a child with her sister as the audience screamed and shook their fists.

Harrison walked out onto the balcony and Nightingale followed him. The shabby council apartment had a stunning view of the River Thames, with the Houses of Parliament ahead of them and the London Eye to their right. It was a cloudless day and they could see for miles. High overhead, passenger jets were lining up to land at Heathrow in the west.

The wind ruffled Harrison's comb-over but he didn't seem to notice. He wiped his face with his right hand and shook his head.

"Why, after all these years?" he asked. "Why now?" His comb-over flapped in the air like a flag.

"I need to talk to you," said Nightingale. He took out his pack of Marlboros and offered it to Harrison. "About what happened to my parents."

Harrison shook his head. "I don't smoke," he said.

Nightingale lit a cigarette. "We're a dying breed, smokers," he said.

"You're going to hell, Jack Nightingale," said Harrison, his face a blank mask, his voice a dull monotone. He vaulted over the side of the balcony. Nightingale froze, the cigarette on the way to his mouth. He flinched as he heard the body slam into the concrete nine floors below.

Jenny appeared behind him. "My God, Jack, what have you done?"

Nightingale backed away from the edge of the balcony, the cigarette forgotten in his hand. "He just jumped," he said. "We were talking and he jumped."

"He jumped?" said Jenny. "Why would he jump?"

"He told me that I was going to hell and he jumped." He turned to look at her. "You heard him, right? You heard what he said?"

Jenny shook her head. "I didn't hear anything. I just saw him go over the edge."

"Jenny, he told me I was going to hell. You must have heard him say that? You were standing right there."

"Jack, I'm sorry…" She was shaking and she folded her arms across her chest. "I'm going to throw up," she said.

"We've got to get out of here, now," he said.

"You're not going to call the police?"

"And tell them what? That he took one look at me and jumped to his death? They're not going to believe that."

"But it's the truth."

"They'll assume that I pushed him to his death, Jenny."

"But you didn't."

"We have to go. We have to wipe everything we touched and then we have to go."

"What?"

"Forensics. We have to wipe everything we touched to remove DNA and fingerprints and we have to do it now, do you understand?"

Jenny stared at him blankly.

Nightingale grabbed her shoulders. "Jenny, I need you with me on this. We have to clean up and go, now."

She nodded. "Okay," she said.

CHAPTER

Nightingale waved the barmaid over. "A whisky, a double," he said. "With ice."

"Any particular brand?" she asked. She had a South African accent.

"Bell's. Teacher's. Anything."

"Jack, I don't see that a drink is going to help," said Jenny, putting a hand on his shoulder. They were in a pub close to the office. They had driven in silence from Battersea, too shocked to discuss what had happened.

"I need a drink," said Nightingale. "And so do you."

Jenny waved at the barmaid. "Make it two," she said. She put her head close to Nightingale's. "What happened back there, Jack?"

"You saw what happened."

"You were in the way, Jack."

"You didn't hear him tell me that I'm going to hell? Because that's what he said, Jenny, as clear as day. He said, 'You're going to hell, Jack Nightingale,' those were his exact words."

"The TV was on, I didn't hear him say anything."

"We were talking, on the balcony. You were right here."

"And he said you were going to hell?"

"That's exactly what he said."

"So think about it, Jack. Maybe it's your subconscious, maybe you were flashing back to what happened to Simon Underwood two years ago. Maybe you thought you heard him say that because the situations were so similar."

"Similar in what way?" asked Nightingale, his voice hardening.

"You know in what way," she said.

"You don't think I pushed him, do you?"

"Who?" she asked. "Underwood or Harrison?"

"Thanks a lot, Jenny. Thanks a bloody lot."

Jenny reached over to touch his hand but he pulled it away. "You don't want to get too close to me," he said. "I might push you out of the window."

"Don't be ridiculous, Jack," she said softly. "Of course I don't think you killed anybody. It's not in your nature. But Harrison couldn't have slipped, the railing was too high."

"I told you already. He jumped. He told me I was going to hell and he jumped."

"Why would he jump?"

"I don't know." He drained his glass and gestured for the barmaid to bring him another.

"Getting drunk isn't going to help," said Jenny.

"I'm not driving, if that's what you're worried about," said Nightingale. He handed her the keys to the MGB. "You can drive me home."

"I'm not your bloody chauffeur, Jack."

"No, and you're not my mother either."

His fresh drink arrived and he raised the glass to her, then sipped his whisky.

"You can be an arsehole at times," she said, sitting on a barstool.

"I'm sorry," said Nightingale. "I shouldn't have let you go with me."

"That's what you're sorry about? You're not sorry that a man died, that we saw him jump to his death?"

"You told me you didn't see anything."

"I saw him fall, I just didn't see if you pushed him or not." She raised her whisky to her lips, then put the glass down. "I'm not drinking this." She waved at the barmaid and mouthed, "Coffee, please."

Nightingale picked up her glass and poured the contents into his drink. "Waste not, want not."

"If the police come, it's not going to help if you're smelling of drink," said Jenny. "We should have stayed. We should have called the police and stayed."

"And said what? That he jumped to his death rather than talk about how he killed my parents? Chalmers already thinks I'm a vigilante killer after what happened to Underwood."

"The police will come, Jack. There were CCTV cameras, remember?"

"They might not check, not if they're sure it was a suicide." He drained his glass and waved at the barmaid. "Another whisky, darling," he said.

Jenny put a hand on his arm. "Jack, come on, you don't have to do this."

"Do what?"

"Drink like this. It isn't helping."

"It's making me feel better, and that's what counts."

"You should have stayed and talked to the police," said Jenny. "They would have believed you."

"Only someone who's never dealt with the cops would say that," said Nightingale. "Cops make mistakes like everyone else, and like I said, Chalmers is already gunning for me."

"You're not a killer, Jack. You couldn't kill somebody, not in cold blood."

Nightingale smiled thinly. "You don't know me, Jenny. You don't really know me."

"I know you couldn't deliberately kill somebody."

"I was in CO19, Jenny. I carried a gun. I was trained to kill people."

"There's a world of a difference between firing a gun as an armed cop and pushing someone off a balcony. The police would understand that."

"Maybe," said Nightingale.

"What's wrong, Jack?"

The barmaid put a fresh glass of whisky in front of Nightingale and he nodded his thanks. "I don't know. Maybe I'm just going crazy."

"You're not crazy," she said. "A bit confused, maybe. And knocking back double whiskies isn't helping."

"My father was crazy," said Nightingale. "Ainsley Gosling claimed to have done a deal with a devil and blew his head off with a shotgun. My mother, my birth mother, was in an asylum for most of her life and hacked her wrists over dinner. So I'm the product of two people who were both clearly deranged. With DNA like that, what are the chances that I'm going to be normal? Pretty bloody slim, I'd say."

"You're stressed out, that's all."

"People keep telling me that I'm going to hell, Jenny."

"It's an expression. It's just something that people say. They don't mean it literally."

Nightingale shook his head. "No, they say it but it's not them saying it. It's like someone is using them to get the message to me. And my uncle wrote the words in blood in his bathroom, and so did Barry O'Brien, and that night in the Chinese restaurant it was written in that fortune cookie." The words tumbled into one another and when he finished he drained his glass and it banged it on the bar.

"It's because Underwood said that to you, before he died," said Jenny.

"My subconscious, playing tricks with me? Is that what you really think?"

"What's the alternative, Jack? Messages from the grave? Spirits speaking through the living? The devil playing games with you?"

The barmaid looked over and Nightingale pointed at his empty glass.

"I'm starting to think that maybe Chalmers is right," he said. "Maybe it is me."

"What do you mean?"

"I went around to see Barry O'Brien and he's dead. I went to see my aunt and uncle and they're dead. Maybe..." He lowered his head, leaving the sentence unfinished.

"What, Jack? Maybe what?"

Nightingale sighed. "Maybe I did kill them," he whispered. "Maybe I killed them and blocked it out. Maybe two years ago I did kill Underwood. And maybe I pushed Harrison off the balcony and I'm blocking it now. Hysterical amnesia. Or my subconscious is just refusing to admit what happened. Look at it from Chalmers's point of view. Barry O'Brien killed Robbie so I'd want him dead. George Harrison killed my parents so I'd want him dead. My uncle and aunt lied to me so I'd want to hurt them. I've got the motive, and I had the opportunity, and I was at all three crime scenes. And it all started two years ago when Simon Underwood went flying through the window."

"Except you didn't do it, Jack. You didn't do any of it."

"But I don't know that for sure, Jenny. Don't you get it? The more I think about it, the more it feels like I might have done it."

"Are you saying that you remember killing them?"

Nightingale shook his head. "No. It's a feeling, not a memory. Like maybe I could have done it."

"Your mind's playing tricks on you. It's stress."

The barmaid came over with another whisky and ice. Jenny ordered two black coffees. Nightingale reached for his whisky but Jenny put her hand on his. "Take it slowly, Jack, please."

Nightingale nodded. "You know what I'm thinking, don't you?"

She nodded.

"Maybe I've done this before," he said. "Maybe what's happening now is a rerun of what I did to Simon Underwood. I get angry, I lash out, and then I block out the memories."

"I was with you today, Jack, remember?"

"But you don't know if I pushed Harrison or not."

"I know you're not a killer, Jack."

"You think I'm not a killer, that's not the same thing." He pulled his arm away and sipped his whisky.

The barmaid brought over two coffees and placed them on the bar. "You guys okay?" she asked.

"It's been a rough day," said Jenny. She waited for the barmaid to leave before putting her head close to Nightingale's. "It'll work out, Jack. I promise."

"Jenny, you don't know that. First rule of negotiating, don't make promises you can't keep. You don't know that it'll work out. Look, today's Monday and my birthday's on Friday. Maybe at midnight on Thursday night a devil is going to reclaim my soul, in which case I burn in hell for all eternity. Or maybe Gosling was just mad and I'm mad too and I'm going to spend the rest of my life in prison. Either way, it's not going to work out."

"You don't believe in this devil nonsense, do you?"

"I wish I did," said Nightingale. "Because at least that would explain what's happening to me. Because if it isn't the devil screwing with my life, then maybe I'm doing it myself."

"You're not a killer, Jack."

"I might be, Jenny. I might be. And that's what scares me."

60

"You're going to hell, Jack Nightingale," said Simon Underwood, his eyes blazing with hatred.

"How do you know my name?" asked Nightingale. "I didn't tell you my name. How do you know who I am?" Underwood was wearing a dark pinstripe suit that fitted so well that it could only have been made to measure. There was a gold Rolex watch on his left wrist and a gold signet ring on his right hand and a pair of designer glasses perched on the end of his nose. He was in his forties with a touch of gray at his temples and he was holding a cell phone and pointing it at Nightingale as if it was a gun. "How do you know my name?" repeated Nightingale.

Underwood turned toward the window behind him. It ran from the floor to the ceiling and gave a panoramic view of the tower blocks of Canary Wharf, home to some of the world's biggest financial institutions.

"No!" said Nightingale, knowing what was going to come next. "No!" he screamed.

The phone that Underwood was holding began to ring. It was a regular ringtone, an insistent bell, and it got louder and louder until the sound was deafening. Nightingale opened his eyes and groaned as he groped for the phone on his bedside table and squinted at his bedside clock. It was eight o'clock in the morning. "Mr. Nightingale, this is Alice Steadman, I didn't wake you, did I?"

Nightingale sat up, running his hand through his hair. His head was throbbing. He had drunk three double whiskies in the pub with Jenny and she'd driven him home where he'd finished off half a bottle of Macallan malt whisky. "Who, sorry?"

"Alice Steadman. From the Wicca Woman store in Camden."

"Right, sorry," said Nightingale.

"I did wake you, didn't I. I'm so sorry, I'm an early riser and I was asked to call you first thing to see if you'd be interested."

"Interested in what, Mrs. Steadman?"

"I'm sorry, I'm not explaining this well, am I? I've sold two of your books for you, Mr. Nightingale. For a very good price. And the gentleman concerned is very interested in another volume that Mr. Gosling has in his collection."

"Who is this mystery buyer, Mrs. Steadman?"

"An American gentleman," she said. "From Texas. His name is Joshua Wainwright. Like your father, he's a collector. And apparently he was at several auctions with your father and your father outbid him. Now he wonders whether you'd be prepared to sell at least one of the volumes to him. For more than your father paid, obviously."

"Obviously," said Nightingale. "Which book is it?"

"It's called *The Formicarius*," said Mrs. Steadman. "A first edition. Apparently your father bought it from a dealer in Germany."

"I've seen the receipt for it," said Nightingale. "Sure, I'll be happy to sell it to him."

"If you're agreeable, he'll fly over to meet you," said Mrs. Steadman. "And he'll pay you in cash."

"I'm certainly agreeable to cash," said Nightingale. "Tell him to give me a call when he gets here."

"Mr. Wainwright said that if you were prepared to sell, he'd fly over this afternoon."

"Tell him I'll have the book ready for him."

"And don't forget my commission, Mr. Nightingale."

"Heaven forbid," said Nightingale.

Nightingale put down the receiver and rolled over onto his back. His alarm wasn't due to go off for another fifteen minutes, and he was just wondering whether he was tired enough to doze off when the phone rang again. Nightingale sighed and reached for it, assuming that it was Mrs. Steadman again. It was Jenny.

"Jack…" Her voice sounded shaky as if she were close to tears.

"Jenny, what's wrong?"

"Jack, I'm at home, I've been robbed, can you come, please?"

"Of course," said Nightingale. "I'll be right there."

"They had guns, Jack. They said they'd kill me."

CHAPTER

61

Jenny lived in a three-bedroom mews house in Chelsea, just off the King's Road. The mews was quaintly cobbled and the house bedecked with flower boxes and outside the front door were two massive concrete urns containing six-foot-tall conifers. Nightingale parked his MGB in front of her yellow garage door and climbed out. Even after the property crash, Jenny's house must have been worth close to two million pounds. He had never asked her if it was hers or if she rented it, but either way he knew that she couldn't afford it just on the salary he paid her.

He pressed the doorbell and a few seconds later the door opened on a security chain. He caught a glimpse of unkempt hair and then she closed the door and unhooked the chain. She was wearing a dark green Cambridge University sweatshirt and baggy cargo pants and her eyes were red and puffy.

"Jenny, what happened?"

She ushered him into the hallway, closed the door, and then bolted it. "I was robbed, Jack. Three men broke in and took the diary."

"Mitchell's diary?"

"Of course Mitchell's diary. Do you think they'd break in to steal my bloody Filofax?"

"Big men, black suits, sunglasses?"

Jenny nodded. "Do you know who they are?"

"They're Mitchell's men. Bodyguards, protectors, his house was full of them. Jenny, did they hurt you?"

She went through to the sitting room and dropped down on a flower-print overstuffed sofa. "No, but they scared the life out of me."

Nightingale sat down in an armchair opposite her. "What happened?"

"I was leaving for work," she said. "I opened the front door and they were there. They just pushed me inside, one of them put his hand over my mouth and brought me in here, the other two looked for the diary. Not that they needed to do much searching, it was in my bag."

"Did they say anything?"

"Not while they were looking for the diary. But when they found it, one of them pointed a gun at my face and said that if I called the police they would come back and shoot me."

"I'm sorry, baby."

"It wasn't your fault, Jack," she said.

"I should have figured that Mitchell would try to get it back. I should have warned you. He told me that Gosling had stolen it from him." Jenny's hands began to shake. "I'll make you a cup of tea," he said. Jenny nodded.

Nightingale went through to her kitchen, all stainless steel with state-of-the-art German appliances. He made her a cup of tea, stirred in three sugars and a splash of milk, and took it to her. She sipped it and winced. "I don't take sugar," she said. "You know I don't take sugar."

"It's good for shock," he said, sitting down in the armchair again.

"I'm not in shock," she insisted.

"You are, you just don't know it," he said. "So do as you're told and drink it."

"Yes, sir," she said. She sipped her tea again. "What do you think, Jack? Should I call the police?"

"I'm not sure what they'd do, to be honest," said Nightingale. "There are no witnesses, no forensics, they'll be back in the Mitchell house and that's like a fortress, I doubt they'll open the gates without a warrant."

"They pointed a gun at me, Jack."

"I know. You want me to have them shot? I know people."

Jenny laughed uneasily. "You're crazy."

"Tell me about it." He stood up. "Leave it with me, Jenny. I haven't finished with Mitchell yet."

"I was so scared," said Jenny. Her hands began to tremble and tea slopped over the side of her cup and into the saucer.

Nightingale took the cup and saucer from her. "Are you okay to go to work? Or do you want to stay home? We don't have much on, work-wise."

"What are you going to do?" she asked.

"I've got to pick up a book from Gosling Manor and take it out to the airport later today. There's a buyer flying in from the States."

"You're really okay if I don't go into the office?"

"Not a problem," said Nightingale.

"I want to get a security company in," she said. "Get the locks changed."

"They won't be back. They got what they wanted."

"I'd just feel safer, you know?"

"I know," said Nightingale. "I'm sorry, Jenny. It's my fault, I should never have given you the diary."

"You couldn't have known," said Jenny.

Nightingale leaned over and kissed her on the top of the head. "I'll make it up to you."

"A pay raise?"

"I was thinking a bunch of flowers." He ruffled her hair and headed for the door. "Seriously though, put all the bills through the office. The least I can do is to pay for your locks. And an alarm if you want it."

"Thanks, Jack. But you know we're in the red as it is."

"Not for long, hopefully," he said, and winked. "Wish me luck."

CHAPTER

If you'd asked Jack Nightingale what he thought Joshua
Wainwright looked like as he climbed the stairs to the hatch in
the Gulfstream Jet, he'd probably have frowned and said that he
never prejudged people, but if pressed he'd have hazarded a guess
that the man would be old, wearing cowboy boots and a Stetson
and smoking a cigar, and like Sebastian Mitchell, probably with a
bodyguard or two in attendance.

He was wrong on all counts, except for the cigar. Joshua
Wainwright was smoking a foot-long Cuban that would have to
have been rolled on an especially large thigh, and was wearing a
New York Yankees baseball cap. He was sitting in a white leather
armchair with his bare feet on a matching leather footstool and
looked as if he were barely out of his twenties. And he was black.

Wainwright grinned when he saw the look of surprise on
Nightingale's face. "I'm guessing you were expecting someone
older," he said, his voice a lazy Texan drawl. "And maybe whiter.
That happens a lot." He waved at one of the chairs. "Take a seat."

"Just don't tell me that you're really two hundred years old," said Nightingale, sitting down and placing his briefcase on the table next to him. "Or that you've a picture slowly going bad in your attic."

Wainwright laughed. Standing behind him were two pretty blondes in matching charcoal-gray Armani suits. "Can I get you a drink, Jack?" drawled Wainwright.

"A whisky would good," said Nightingale.

"A man after my own heart," laughed Wainwright. He waved at one of the stewardesses. "Two whiskies, darling," he said. "Glenlivet." He looked at Jack. "Glenlivet's okay?"

"In my experience, any malt beginning with a G or an M can't be faulted," said Nightingale. "Ice in mine, please," he said to the stewardess. She flashed him a perfect gleaming-white smile.

The plane was sitting on the tarmac close to the private aviation terminal at Stansted Airport. A black stretch Mercedes limousine had been waiting for Nightingale airside, and a uniformed chauffeur had driven him out to the Gulfstream. The plane was expensively outfitted with four white leather seats the size of armchairs, a three-seater white leather sofa, a large LCD television screen on the bulkhead, and oblong picture windows.

"Can I offer you a cigar, Jack?" asked Wainwright.

"I'm a cigarette smoker," said Nightingale. "Is it okay to smoke in here?"

"It's my plane, we can do what we want," laughed Wainwright.

Nightingale took out his pack of Marlboros and lit one. The second stewardess placed a large crystal ashtray next to his briefcase.

"So you're Ainsley Gosling's son?" asked Wainwright. "How's that working out for you?"

Nightingale shrugged. "We weren't close," he said. The stewardess gave him his glass of whisky and another beaming smile.

"But he left you his library?"

"He left me everything," said Nightingale.

Wainwright jabbed his cigar at Nightingale's briefcase. "Is that it?"

Nightingale nodded. "It took some finding, I haven't worked out his indexing system yet. It's certainly not alphabetical." He put down his drink and cigarette and picked up the briefcase. Wainwright licked his lips as Nightingale opened the briefcase and took out the book. It was almost two feet long and eighteen inches wide and a good two inches thick, the pages yellowing, the white leather binding cracked and faded. It had taken Nightingale almost three hours to find the book in the basement. A lot of the books didn't have their titles on the spine so he had to take them down and open them one at a time.

Wainwright put down his cigar and took the book from him reverently, as if he was holding a baby. His eyes were wide and he had a faint smile on his lips. It was a smile of triumph, Nightingale realized.

"Awesome," said Wainwright. "Do you know what it is, Jack?

"*The Formicarius*," said Nightingale. "But that doesn't mean much to me."

"This is a first edition, printed in 1475," said Wainwright, stroking the cover reverentially. "Written by Johannes Nider. It took him two years to write and it was another eight years after he finished before it was published. It was the second book ever to be printed that discussed witchcraft. Before *The Formicarius*, everyone thought that it was only men who served the devil."

"And that's why it's so valuable?"

Wainwright shook his head. "No, it's not what's written inside the book that's so important. I have a second edition, and a third. I already have the words, it's the book I wanted. This book." He ran his fingertips down the spine and smiled to himself. "Your father knew, too. That's why he was so determined to get it." He looked across at Nightingale and grinned. "It was supposed to be mine, you know? The bookseller in Hamburg had agreed to sell it to me, but somehow your father got to him before I could wire the money. He was a very persuasive man, your father."

"So I'm told," said Nightingale.

"He paid a million and half euros, you know that?"

"I saw the receipt. So what is it about the book that makes it so special?"

"Are you sure you want to know, Jack?"

Nightingale nodded. "Why not?"

Wainwright smiled, relishing the moment, then he slowly kissed the front cover of the book. "This isn't leather," he said. "It's human skin."

Nightingale tried not to look surprised but he could see from the satisfied look on the American's face that he hadn't succeeded. "You don't say."

"Your father paid a million and a half euros, so how about I give you two?"

"Two sounds good," said Nightingale.

Wainwright smiled at one of the stewardesses and she pulled a small aluminum suitcase from a cupboard and placed it on the table next to Nightingale's chair. She opened it for him and then went to the rear of the plane. Normally Nightingale would have turned to look at her legs but he couldn't take his eyes off the bundles of banknotes in the case. "Wow," he said.

"You've got to appreciate the euro," said Wainwright. "That five-hundred-euro note makes moving cash around so much simpler. If I'd had to use hundred-dollar bills, we would have needed another suitcase."

"It's not a problem I'm normally faced with," said Nightingale.

"Well, it could be," said Wainwright. "There's a few other books in your late father's library that I might be interested in buying from you. When you get the chance, can you give me an inventory? There's not many volumes that I haven't got, but your father was buying books before I was born, I'd be interested to see what he has in his collection."

"No problem," said Nightingale. He was still staring at the money. Two million euros. He tried to work out how many years he'd have to work to earn that sort of money. Thirty years? Forty?

"Do you want to count it, Jack?" asked Wainwright.

"Do I need to?"

Wainwright laughed. "If it's short, give me a call. But it won't be."

Nightingale closed the case. "Can I keep the case? I don't think it'll all fit into mine."

"We'll do a swap," said Wainwright. He put the book back into the briefcase that Nightingale had bought with him. "Any objections?"

"I can always buy a new briefcase," said Nightingale.

The stewardess who had given him the case stepped forward with a clipboard and a pen. "I'll need you to sign an invoice and a receipt, and I've copies of both for you," said Wainwright.

Nightingale took the pen, a Mont Blanc the size of a small flashlight, and signed his name four times. He frowned when he saw that he was signing in red. "Please tell me that's not blood," he said.

"I like red ink," said the American. "It's a quirk of mine. Red is my lucky color, always has been. Humor me."

The stewardess took the pen and the clipboard from Nightingale, then gave him a copy of the invoice and a copy of the receipt.

"My cell-phone number is on there," said Wainwright, "and my personal e-mail address. Soon as you have an inventory, I'd like a look. I'll pay top dollar, cash on the nail."

Nightingale folded the papers and put them into the inside pocket of his raincoat. He nodded at the briefcase. "This stuff, it works, does it?"

"Some of it does, some of it doesn't. It's a process. It's something you become better at the more you do it." He grinned. "That's why they call it witchcraft. Because it is a craft."

"It just seems weird, sitting in a state-of-the-art jet with a suitcase of cash, but we're talking about magic."

"So?"

"So it's weird, that's all. Why didn't you fly over on a broomstick?"

Wainwright laughed. "You're thinking Harry Potter. Besides. Have you ever tried joining the Mile High Club on a broomstick?"

"I guess not," said Nightingale. "So flying broomsticks are bollocks?"

"Of course they are. But if I wanted to move around the world without the benefits of a Gulfstream, yeah that's doable. Astral projection. It's not easy and it takes a lot of practice, but I can do it. And remote viewing, seeing things at a distance. It's easier than astral projection, but not as useful."

"You're winding me up," said Nightingale. "Or shitting me, as you Yanks are so fond of saying."

"No, I'm serious," said Wainwright. "Let's say you're as good at astral projection as I am. We could arrange to meet somewhere, and at the appointed time we both go into a trance and meet on the astral plane, face-to-face."

"You've done that?"

"I've done that with your father, Jack. Many times. He was a master at it."

"So how does it work?"

"Now you're asking," said the American.

"I'm interested."

"I can see that." He swung his feet up onto the footstool and picked up his cigar. "You've got a cell phone, right?" He looked at his cigar and frowned as he realized that it had gone out.

"Sure."

"And you know how to use it, right?" He picked up a box of matches and relit his cigar.

Nightingale nodded, not sure what the American was getting at.

"So can you tell me how fifty people in a room can have fifty separate cell-phone conversations with fifty other people all around the world, and how those fifty people could get into fifty different cars and drive off in fifty different directions, all of the time continuing their conversations without a single overlap or lost word?" He sucked on his cigar and blew smoke without inhaling.

"I guess not," said Nightingale. "But you're not saying that cell phones are magic?"

"No, I'm saying it's technology, and we don't have to understand technology to use it. The occult operates on the same principle."

"And anyone can use it?"

"There are different levels," said the American. He patted the copy of *The Formicarius.* "This is a tool, and in the right hands, hands like mine or your father's, it can accomplish great things. But give it to a child and it's just a book. You have to know how to use the tools, and it's that knowledge that separates the greats from the wannabees."

"But how do you separate the wheat from the chaff, knowledge-wise?"

"You have to know your source," said Wainwright. He nodded at Nightingale's briefcase. "A book like that, you can rely on.

First editions are best because often there's information in the illustrations that gets left out if they go on to mass production. Handwritten books, illustrated manuscripts from the Middle Ages, that's the real gold."

"And what about talking to other..." He hesitated, not knowing what word to use. "How do I describe guys like you?" he said.

Wainwright grinned. "Young, gifted, and black," he said. "That works for me. And with a black man in the White House, it can only get better."

"I meant what you guys do," said Nightingale. "Satanist sounds a bit..." He shrugged. "I don't know. But I guess it's better than devil-worshiper."

"There are all sorts of descriptions," said Wainwright. "There are straight-up Satanists, theistic Satanists we call them, there are Luciferians, there are LaVeyans, there are Setians, Diabolotors, Demonolators, there's even the Slaytanists."

"The Slaytanists?" echoed Nightingale.

"Slaytanists," said Wainwright. "That's what we call the dabblers, the weekend Satanists who are more interested in the devil worship than the process."

"The process? What process?"

"The magik. And that's magik with a *k*, not the sort of magic you see on TV."

"So what do you call yourself?"

"I tend to avoid labels," said Wainwright. "They're so limiting."

"But do you guys talk to each other, share secrets and stuff?"

Wainwright chuckled softly. "Chefs don't give their recipes to other chefs, stage magicians don't go showing their tricks to their rivals. We guard our secrets, jealously. Why do you ask, Jack?"

"I need information about my father. What he did, what he was capable of, that sort of thing."

"You could try the Order of the Nine Angles," said Wainwright. "You know he was a member?"

"I know almost nothing about him," said Nightingale. "Who are they?"

"They're a Satanic sect, here in England. They're best known for saying that human sacrifice isn't necessarily a bad thing, which always guarantees them a bad press. And they're one of the groups that believe that Satan exists."

"You said angles, not angels?"

"A lot of people make that mistake," said the American. "They figure it's a group involved with rogue angels, but it's not. The name comes from their emblem, which has nine lines connecting the seven planets with the seven lower sefirot on the kabbalistic tree of life."

"You've lost me," said Nightingale.

"It's a complicated subject," said Wainwright. "Becoming adept can take a lifetime, which is why men like your father are always looking for shortcuts."

"And all these groups worship Satan?"

Wainwright shook his head. "Far from it," he said. "They don't all even acknowledge that Satan exists. You can believe in Satanic power without believing in Satan. It's the cell phone analogy again. It's not why it works that matters, it's what the effects are." He sucked on his cigar. "There are some practitioners who call themselves Atheistic Satanists. They believe that there is a dark force that uses entropy to destroy all things, and that the force can be used by us here on Earth. But they don't believe that Satan exists as an entity."

"And you, what do you believe?"

Wainwright grinned. "Me? In the words of the Monkees, I'm a believer."

"In the devil?"

"In God, in the devil, the whole nine yards."

Nightingale blew smoke. "I'm told that calling up a devil is fairly easy," he said.

Wainwright nodded. "It's Occult 101," he said. "Use any search engine and type in 'calling up the devil' and you'll get thousand of hits."

"And selling your soul is easy, too?"

Wainwright winced. "You've got to know what you're doing, Jack. You've got to make sure that you're protected and you have to know how to handle them. They're not lapdogs, they're the masters of hell. You make one wrong move and they'll rip your soul out."

"You've heard of Proserpine?"

"Of course. One of the greats. Definitely not amateur material. You wouldn't want to go calling her up unless you really knew what you were doing."

"And what about selling her the soul of an unborn child? Is that doable?"

Wainwright laughed, but his eyes had gone as hard as flint. "What's going on, Jack?" he said. "What is it you really want to know? You're dancing around it like a pole dancer on speed, whatever it is."

Nightingale smiled tightly. "Even saying it sounds crazy," he said.

Wainwright's cigar froze inches from his lips and he narrowed his eyes. "Gosling did it, didn't he?"

Nightingale said nothing. Wainwright's eyes bored into his and Nightingale had to look away.

"Ainsley Gosling sold your soul to Proserpine before you were born?"

"That's what he told me, yeah," said Nightingale. "He left me a DVD saying just that."

"You've got the mark? The pentangle?"

Nightingale blew smoke. "I don't think so."

Wainwright leaned forward. "If there's no pentangle, there's no contract," he said. "That's an absolute fact."

"I've looked everywhere" said Nightingale.

"Then you're okay," said Wainwright. "What happened to your father?"

"He killed himself."

"How?"

"Shotgun."

"But he was inside a protective circle, right? A pentangle."

Nightingale nodded. "How did you know?"

"Because that's the way I'd do it. Something quick and sure."

"And the pentangle?"

Wainwright sucked on his cigar. "So they can't get at you before you die, so that you can choose your own time."

"But you still go to hell, right?"

"That depends."

"On what?"

"On whether you've been naughty or nice. Bit like whether or not you get a gift from Santa." He laughed at his own joke.

"What I mean is, if you're going to hell and you die within the protective pentangle, do you still go to hell?"

"Yes, but you would be going in under your own terms."

"I don't understand," said Nightingale.

"I wouldn't expect you to," said Wainwright.

"You see, I can't work out why my father, my genetic father, went to all the trouble of protecting himself with the pentangle, and then he killed himself."

"Because he wanted it to be his decision," said Wainwright. "He wanted to choose the time and place of his passing. That's not unusual."

"And if my soul has been sold, what are my options?"

"Zero. But like I said, if there's no mark on you then your soul's your own."

Nightingale ran a hand through his hair and down the back of his neck. He could feel the tendons there, as taut as steel wires. "I need to talk to this Proserpine."

"No you don't, Jack. She's a devil. A demon. She'd eat you for breakfast."

A middle-aged man in a crisp white shirt with black and yellow epaulets opened the door from the cockpit. "We're about to fire up the engines, Mr. Wainwright," he said. "We're going to have to get our wheels off the ground within the next ten minutes or we'll lose our slot."

"Ready when you are, Ed," said Wainwright. He smiled at Nightingale. "Looks like our time's up, Jack," he said.

"It's starting to look that way," said Nightingale.

The pilot went back into the cockpit and closed the door behind him. Wainwright stood up and held out his hand. "Good luck," he said.

They shook hands. "Have a safe trip," said Nightingale.

"You too, man," said Wainwright. "But remember, if there's no mark, there's no deal, and you have nothing to worry about."

As Nightingale walked away from the plane toward the waiting Mercedes, he heard the stairs retract, the door thump shut, and the engines start to whine. The chauffeur already had the door open for him. "Shall I put that in the trunk, sir?" asked the chauffeur, nodding at the metal suitcase.

"I think I'll keep it with me," said Nightingale. He climbed into the back and put the case on the seat next to him.

CHAPTER

The bank manager rubbed his chin as he stared at the suitcase full of money. "Mr. Nightingale, this is very, very unorthodox," he said.

"Tell me about it," said Nightingale.

"You can't just bring in a suitcase of money like this," said Collinson. "There are money laundering regulations, customer identification protocols, procedures."

"I understand that, Mr. Collinson, but that's how the money came to me and that's how I'm giving it to you."

"But no one carries around two million euros in cash," said the bank manager, dropping down into his high-backed executive chair and patting his head to make sure that his comb-over was in place. "My head office is going to be asking all sorts of questions. You're not even a customer of the bank."

"But my father was, and I'm his sole heir. And I'm sure I don't have to remind you that I'm responsible for the mortgage on Gosling Manor."

Collinson pursed his fleshy lips, like a toddler about to burst into tears. "Very irregular," he said. "We're not even geared up for having this much cash on the premises."

"It's perfectly legitimate," said Nightingale. "I sold some of the books in my father's collection."

"For cash?"

"For cash," said Nightingale. "I was as surprised as you are." He reached into his jacket pocket and took out two sheets of paper. He gave them to the bank manager. "There's the receipt that the buyer gave me. And the invoice from the bookstore in Hamburg that sold the book to my father."

Collinson scrutinized both pieces of paper. He nodded slowly. "A substantial profit," he said.

"Especially when you consider how much the euro has risen in value," said Nightingale.

"You do realize that if you lodge these funds with our branch, we will be duty bound to inform the Inland Revenue?" said Collinson.

"I didn't, but I do now."

"There will probably be a capital gains tax liability, and you'll have to fill out a form explaining where the money came from."

"Not a problem," said Nightingale.

"So tell me exactly what it is you want to do with the money," said the bank manager, running the fingers of his right hand along the bundles of notes.

"I'd like to open an account with you, convert this to pounds, and pay it into the account. Then use that account to continue paying the mortgage that my father took out. Does that make sense?"

Collinson nodded. "It makes perfect sense," he said.

"I'll get my accountant to give you a call to arrange any paperwork."

"We'll need a copy of your passport, two recent utility bills, and a reference from your current bank," said Collinson.

"Easy peasy," said Nightingale.

"Will you be planning to sell more of your father's books, Mr. Nightingale?" asked the bank manager.

"Possibly," said Nightingale. "I'm going to draw up an inventory and see what there is."

"They must be very interesting volumes," said Collinson. "Perhaps you could show me sometime."

"They're an acquired taste, Mr. Collinson," said Nightingale. "I wouldn't have thought they'd be of much interest to you."

Next door to the bank was an optician offering free eye tests and fifty percent off all frames. Nightingale stood looking in the window. A young woman in a white coat with long black hair tied back in a ponytail was standing behind the counter, showing a range of frames to a housewife with two small children. There was a an eye-test chart behind the salesgirl and Nightingale had no problems reading the letters all the way down to the bottom line. He'd always had perfect vision. A buzzer sounded as he pushed open the door and went inside.

CHAPTER

64

Nightingale was already at his desk when Jenny McLean walked into the office. He had his feet up on the desk and his keyboard on his lap and was staring intently at his screen. "You're in bright and early," she said, then noticed the bottle of whisky next to his overflowing ashtray. "Or did you not go home last night?"

"Couldn't sleep," said Nightingale. "Are you okay?"

"I had new locks fitted to the doors and windows, and Banhams is putting in a motion-sensor alarm system later this week."

"They won't be back, Jenny. They only wanted the diary."

"I'd just feel more secure." She took off her coat and hung it on the back of the door. Nightingale picked up the bottle of whisky and took a long swig. "What's wrong, Jack?"

"Why should anything be wrong?"

"It's half past eight in the morning and you're drinking whisky."

"Do you believe in hell, Jenny?"

"Of course not." She sat down opposite him and moved the bottle of whisky out of his reach.

"Because?"

"Because how can there be a place called hell? Where would it be? We're mapping the universe, there's nowhere that hell could be. It can't be a planet or a star or a black hole."

"So you don't believe in heaven either?"

"As a place, of course not. Angels sitting on clouds playing harps. How ridiculous is that?"

"So when we're dead, we're dead, is that it? Just nothingness? The great abyss?"

"Life will go on, whether I'm here or not. So it's not blackness. What's wrong, Jack."

Nightingale shook his head. "I don't know. I guess I want to know what happens when we die, and it's the one question that no one can answer. That's the paradox, isn't it? We all die, it's the one thing we have in common, and yet no one knows what it really means."

"It depends on what you believe, Jack. Some people truly believe that when they die they go to heaven. Others believe they'll be reborn again, that our time here is just part of a process."

"Reincarnation?"

"I guess. Others, the atheists, think there's nothing. We're born, we live, we die, it's over."

"Which is pretty depressing."

"You think hell is a better alternative?"

"Oh Jenny, I don't know. I don't know what to think anymore."

"You think that it might be true? You're starting to believe that Ainsley Gosling sold your soul to the devil."

"To a devil. Proserpine. I'm sure that he did, yes. Or at least I'm sure he believed that he did. The big question is, do I have a soul to sell. Is the soul something tangible that can be traded? It's nonsense, right? There's no such thing as a soul."

"Are you asking me or telling me, Jack?"

"That's the thing, isn't it? We can talk about it until the cows come home but we'll never know. We'll never know for sure."

"That's what makes us human," said Jenny. "We're the only animal that knows it will die one day. No other creature thinks about death."

"But most of us do everything we can not to think about it," said Nightingale. "Because it's the scariest thing imaginable."

"Life is what you should be thinking about," said Jenny. "Enjoy it while you have it. Relish every moment. Every second."

"But one day it'll be over."

"Maybe."

"Maybe?" echoed Nightingale.

Jenny shrugged. "I don't know, Jack. I don't know any better than you. But I have a gut feeling that there's more. That's all it is, a gut feeling. What's wrong, Jack? What's brought this on? Has something happened?"

"You're not religious, are you?"

Jenny smiled. "No, I'm not. But religion has nothing to do with life after death, has it. You can believe in that without believing in God. Maybe we just move on to something else."

"Like what?"

Jenny sighed. "I have no idea, Jack. Nobody does. Who knows?"

"That's the point though, isn't it? If there was something else, wouldn't those that have passed on come back and tell us what lies ahead? Why didn't my mum and dad come back after they were killed? The last time I saw them they were on the doorstep, waving me off to university. Then *bang*, they're killed in a car crash. If there was life after death, wouldn't they have come back to say good-bye? Just one time, just to let me know that everything was okay?"

"Sometimes people do get messages from beyond, don't they? Or ghosts. Lots of people say they've seen ghosts."

"Have you?"

"No," admitted Jenny.

"And neither have I. And my parents died suddenly and violently, and so did my aunt and uncle, and if you believe what you read, those are the most likely circumstances to produce a ghost. I got nothing from them, Jenny. Not from my mother and father and not from my aunt and uncle. They died and that was the end of it." He sighed. "You know, when I buried my mum and dad I expected to feel their presence at the funeral, but there was nothing. Just the coffins." He reached for the whisky but couldn't make it.

"Maybe they couldn't come back, maybe that's not how it works," said Jenny, picking up the whisky bottle. "I'll make you a coffee."

"And what about my so-called genetic father? He died violently. It doesn't come more violent than a shotgun in the mouth. But I haven't seen him floating round. He left me a DVD apologizing for what he did, you'd think he might have come back and apologized in person. Or in spirit. And if there is life after death, don't you think he would get in contact and tell me what to do? And what about Robbie? Remember the message he left on my phone? He had something to tell me, something important."

"Maybe it's a one-way journey with no coming back. Like caterpillars."

"Caterpillars?"

"Caterpillars spend their lives crawling over leaves until one day they turn into a chrysalis and then the chrysalis bursts open and there's a butterfly. Now, does the caterpillar know that one day it'll be a butterfly? I doubt it. So far as the caterpillar is concerned, the chrysalis is death. The end of the caterpillar. And does the butterfly remember being a caterpillar?"

"Who knows?" said Nightingale.

"Exactly," said Jenny. "Who knows. But do you ever see butter-flies hanging out with caterpillars? No you don't. They've nothing in common. Maybe that's what happens when we die. Part of us moves on, and there's no looking back."

"Our spirit, is that what you mean?"

"They say that when you die, you lose twenty-one grams. It just goes. You weigh a person before they die and you weigh them afterwards and twenty-one grams disappears."

"Says who?" asked Nightingale.

"I did a philosophy course in my final year," said Jenny. "It was an American doctor who did the experiment, back in the nine-teen hundreds. Duncan MacDougall, his name was. He designed a special bed that was built on a set of scales and he had six dying patients who agreed to help him. By weighing the entire bed he was able to take into account sweat and urine loss, everything physical. With all six patients there was an immediate weight loss of twenty-one grams at the moment of death."

Nightingale narrowed his eyes. "And that's the weight of a human soul, is it? Twenty-one grams?"

"The weight of a hummingbird, give or take," said Jenny. "That was MacDougall's theory. He repeated the experiment with fifteen dogs. Tied them to the bed, drugged them, and then put them to sleep. With the dogs, there was no change in weight as the dogs died. His theory was that people had souls and dogs didn't."

"And why has no one done the experiment since?"

"What, weighing dying people? I'm not sure you'd get away with it these days." Jenny put a hand on his shoulder and squeezed gently. "What's wrong, Jack? What's brought all this on?"

"Give me the bottle and I'll tell you."

"Jack…"

Nightingale held out his hand. Jenny gave him the bottle.

"You know there's supposed to be a pentangle mark."

"If your soul is sold to the devil, yes. But you haven't got a mark, remember?"

"There was an opticians next to the bank in Brighton. I went there to deposit the money and the optician was offering free eye tests."

Jenny frowned. "You don't need glasses," she said. "Eyes like a hawk."

"I went to get my retinas scanned," he said quietly. "I figured it was one of the parts of the body that you never get to see."

"And?"

Nightingale slid a manila envelope across the desk. She opened the envelope with trembling hands and slid out the photograph inside. There were two images on it, retinal scans of his right and left eyes. On the left eye, down at the four o'clock position, was a small black pentangle.

65

"That's impossible," said Jenny, staring at the retinal scan in horror.

"Yeah, that's what the optician said."

"It's a pentangle."

"Isn't it just."

"On the back of your eye?"

"Apparently. He did the scans twice, thought there might be a problem with the machine."

"Jack…"

"I know."

"Oh my God."

"My thoughts exactly." He raised the bottle in salute. "Now you understand why I'm drinking. It's Wednesday morning. Tomorrow night at midnight…blah, blah, blah." He took another long drink.

"That's your plan?" said Jenny in disgust. "You're going to drink yourself to death?"

"My plan is to talk to Proserpine. I just can't work out how to do it. I've been trawling the Internet but there isn't much about her."

"Please tell me you're joking," said Jenny. "I'm making you a coffee whether you want it or not." She went over to the coffee maker. "Is that what you're doing, looking for an e-mail address for Proserpine?" She forced a smile. "Hotmail, probably."

"Ha ha," said Nightingale. "The guy I saw at the airport yesterday said that it's all true, that you can sell souls and that there are devils out there who'll buy them."

"Then he's a loony," said Jenny, sitting on the edge of his desk.

"A very rich loony, who gave me two million euros for one of the books in my father's library. And wants me to give him an inventory to see what else he wants to buy."

"Get out of here," said Jenny.

"I'm serious. I paid the money into the bank, here's the credit slip if you don't believe me." He held up a piece of paper.

Jenny went over and took it from him and stared at it with wide eyes. "Oh my God," she repeated. "Who is this guy?"

"According to Google, he doesn't exist," said Nightingale. "Young guy, looks like a rap star, flies around the world in a Gulfstream jet when he's not on the astral plane, and he reckons that if I have the mark, the pentangle, then my goose is well and truly cooked."

"Jack, it's nonsense and you know it."

"That's what I thought until I saw the pentangle."

"There are no such things as devils and demons, Jack. Same as there's no Father Christmas or Tooth Fairy. Waiting for a demon to come and claim your soul is as stupid as sitting by your fireplace waiting for Santa to bring your presents."

"I don't have a fireplace."

"Exactly."

Nightingale grinned. "Exactly? What exactly does my not having a fireplace prove?"

"This isn't about Father Christmas," said Jenny. "Stop changing the subject."

"You brought him up."

Jenny groaned in frustration. "As an example, as a way of showing how ridiculous you're being by even entertaining the idea that your father did a deal with the devil." She saw him opening his mouth to speak and held up a hand to silence him. "A devil," she corrected herself. "And a female devil to boot. It's all in Mitchell's diary, how he thinks he called up this Proserpine and did a deal with her."

"Yeah, it's a pity we don't still have it. The diary. Because I need to talk to her."

"I made notes," she said.

"They didn't take them? Mitchell's men didn't take your notes?"

Jenny went over to her desk and pulled open the bottom drawer. She took out an A4 ring-backed notebook. "They only wanted the diary. This was in my bedroom."

"You wrote down everything?"

"The bits that I'd read."

"Including how to call up Proserpine? You wrote that down?"

Jenny nodded. "There's a few words that I need to look up, but I got most of it."

Nightingale took the book from her and grinned. "You're a star, Jenny. An absolute star."

"It's nonsense, Jack. The ramblings of a deranged mind. Mitchell is as crazy as your father was."

"Does that mean that you don't want to help me?" asked Nightingale.

"Help you?" asked Jenny. "How?"

"Help me talk to Proserpine. Help me find a way out of this."

"Jack…"

"It's my only chance, Jenny." He tapped the scans. "This proves that my father was telling the truth. He did sell my soul. Tomorrow night at midnight a devil is going to come to claim it and I'm damned if I'm going to let that happen." He smiled without warmth. "Damned if I do, damned if I don't. Now will you help me or not?"

CHAPTER

Mrs. Steadman was dusting a display of crystals when Nightingale walked into her shop. She smiled brightly when she saw him. "Mr. Nightingale, so nice to see you," she said. "Did everything go all right with Mr. Wainwright?"

"Everything went perfectly," said Nightingale. He took an envelope from his jacket pocket and gave it to her. "I wanted to drop by and give you your commission. I hope a banker's draft is okay."

Mrs. Steadman took the envelope from him and opened it. She slid out the check and her eyes widened. She gasped and leaned against a display case. "Mr. Nightingale, this is a fortune," she said. "I can't accept this. I really can't."

Nightingale waved away her objections. "It's the commission that we agreed, Mrs. Steadman," he said.

"But this is…this is…I never expected…"

"It's fine, Mrs. Steadman. If you hadn't have put me in touch with Mr. Wainwright I wouldn't have sold the book, so you've earned that."

Mrs. Steadman shook her head and blinked. "I can't thank you enough, Mr. Nightingale," she said. She looked up from the check. "If there's anything I can ever do for you, please, just ask," she said.

"Actually Mrs. Steadman, there is," said Nightingale. "I want to draw a magic circle onto a wooden floor. Is there a special chalk or something that I should use?"

"Of course, I have the perfect chalk," she said. "I use it myself for making sacred circles."

She went over to a display of Tarot cards. Next to it were a dozen or so boxes about the size of cigarette packs, but instead of government health warnings they were adorned with stars and moons. "On the house," she said, giving him one of the boxes.

"And consecrated saltwater," said Nightingale.

"So this is a protective circle, is it?"

Nightingale nodded. "I'm told that a chalk circle reinforced with consecrated saltwater is the strongest defense."

"Defense against what, exactly?" she asked. "What are you planning to do?"

Nightingale ignored her questions. He took a list from his pocket and gave it to her. "There are a few other things here that I'm told I need, to open and close the circle."

Mrs. Steadman took the list from him and ran her eyes down it. Her lips tightened. "Oh dear, Mr. Nightingale. Are you sure about this?"

"I'm sure. Can you sell me those items?"

"Oh yes, they are all very straightforward. But I do hope you know what you are doing."

"So do I, Mrs. Steadman. So do I."

CHAPTER

Nightingale was mopping the wooden floor of the main drawing room when Jenny walked in carrying her briefcase. She smiled. "That's a first," she said.

"It's got to be clean," he said. "Any dirt will compromise the circle. That's what Mitchell wrote."

"You're not really going to go through with this, are you?"

"Tonight's the night," he said. "I spent all yesterday getting everything I need. I've got the special chalk and the consecrated saltwater, and the herbs that you said I needed. Mrs. Steadman sells all that sort of stuff."

"Did she ask you what you were planning to do?"

"I think she sort of guessed. Can you do me a favor, can you go down into the basement and bring up five of the church candles, the really big ones?"

Jenny handed him a small padded envelope. "This came in the post this morning," she said. "From the Hillingdon Home."

As Jenny headed down to the basement, he opened the envelope. Inside was his mother's crucifix and a handwritten note from Mrs. Fraser, repeating what she had said in her office, that she was sure his mother would have wanted him to have it. He put the chain around his neck. The crucifix nestled at the base of his throat.

Nightingale continued to clean the floor until Jenny returned with the candles. She put them by the door and watched as Nightingale got down on his hands and knees and dried the floor with paper towels. Jenny opened her briefcase and took out her A4 notebook. "Mitchell says that you can outline the circle with chalk, but for it to be really effective you need to inscribe it with a sword," she said.

"There are swords down in the basement," said Nightingale. "Lots of them."

"It has to be a magic sword," said Jenny. "That's what it says here. *Veneficus mucro.* Magic sword."

"How the hell am I supposed to know which of them are magic?" asked Nightingale. He gathered up the paper towels he had used and put them into a black rubbish bag.

Jenny ran her finger down the page of her notebook. "He says you can use the branch of a birch tree."

"Now that's more like it," said Nightingale. "We've got our own forest out there. Now please tell me that you know what a birch tree looks like."

"I'm a country girl, remember?" she laughed.

Nightingale put the black bag by the door. "One of these days I'm going to have to read your CV," he said.

68

Nightingale used the chalk he'd bought from Alice Steadman's shop to draw a circle in the middle of the room, about twelve feet in diameter. "Are you sure it doesn't have to be a particular size?" he asked.

Jenny looked up from her notebook. "Mitchell says it can be as big or as small as you want," she said.

Nightingale grinned up at her. "Funny that," he said, "because before you said size was important." He straightened up and used the birch branch that they'd taken from a tree in the garden to slowly outline the circle.

"Once you've gone around the circle with the branch, you draw the pentangle. A five-pointed star. Make sure that there are two points at the top of the circle and one at the bottom."

"Which is the top and which is the bottom?" said Nightingale.

"That's up to you," said Jenny. She frowned as she read her notes. "Okay, here it is. You have to draw a triangle around the circle. Once the demon has been summoned, it will be confined to the area between the circle and the triangle. And the apex of the triangle has to point north."

"Okay," said Nightingale hesitantly.

"So you make the apex of the triangle point north, and the two points of the pentangle should point north with one pointing south."

Nightingale looked through the windows and across the lawn, trying to visualize the way he'd driven to the house. He pointed across the lawn. "London is that way, so that's north," he said.

"I think we should be more accurate than that," said Jenny. "I saw some compasses downstairs, I'll get one."

As she headed back down the basement, Nightingale sprinkled consecrated saltwater around the perimeter of the circle.

Jenny returned with a brass compass. She stood at the edge of the circle and showed Nightingale which way was north.

"I wasn't too far off," he said.

"Well done, you," she said. She watched as Nightingale drew the pentangle inside the circle, and a large triangle outside.

When he had finished the triangle, he looked over at Jenny. "Now what?"

"Now you have to write in the three points of the triangle. You write MI and then CH and then AEL."

"Michael?"

"The archangel," said Jenny. "Don't blame me if it sounds ridiculous, I'm just telling you what Mitchell wrote in his diary."

Nightingale wrote the three sets of letters, then he put the chalk down and dusted his hands. "Is that it?" he asked.

"That's the circle done. When you're ready you put the candles at the points of the pentangle and you light them and you burn the herbs that you have."

"Okay," said Nightingale.

"Then you have to recite this." She showed him a passage in Latin that she had written in the book. "I'm pretty sure you'll have to say these words as they're written and not the translation. Then when you've finished you say, 'Bagahi laca bacabe.' And before you ask, I've no idea what that means. It's not Latin."

"And that's it?"

"According to Mitchell, once you've said those three words, Proserpine will appear. But then I've had enough Jamie Oliver recipes go wrong to know that sometimes it's not enough just to have the right ingredients."

He took the notebook from her. "You know what I don't understand, Jenny?" he asked.

Jenny sighed. "I could draw up a list, but it could take months."

Nightingale laughed. "Why do you stay with me?"

She frowned. "What do you mean?"

"You're way overqualified, the work isn't demanding, I'm an idiot most of the time."

"All true," she said.

"So why? Why do you work for me?"

She shrugged. "I haven't really thought about it," she said.

"You must have. You must think about changing jobs sometimes, everyone does."

"I like working with you, Jack."

"You know, I could never work out why you came for the job in the first place."

"It was pure luck," she said. "It's not as if I was looking for a job with a private eye." She ran a hand through her hair. "I never told you what happened, that day I came around for the interview."

"I thought you were a spy for the Inland Revenue at first," he said. "You seemed too good to be true."

"I was shopping in New Bond Street," she said. "I popped into Costa Coffee for a coffee. I was waiting to hear if I'd got a job that

I'd been interviewed for, assistant to the marketing director of a big advertising agency."

"Nice," said Nightingale.

"Yeah, well, I was sipping my latte and thinking that all was well with the world, then the director of human resources calls me and says that I didn't get the job, blah blah blah. As he's saying that, I'm looking at a copy of one of the free newspapers that someone had left on the table. He'd been doing the crossword but had screwed it up, big time. Couldn't even spell *Esperanto*. Anyway, under the crossword were the help-wanted classifieds, and yours had been circled. So as the human resources director is telling me that I wasn't quite right for the position, I'm looking at an advert asking me if I wanted a job that would never be boring."

"I wrote the copy for the ad," said Nightingale.

"I know," said Jenny. "But if I hadn't gone into that coffee shop, and if the paper hadn't been left there open at the page your listing was on…"

"Maybe my guardian angel wanted you with me," said Nightingale.

"Jack…"

"I'm serious, Jenny. If it wasn't for you, I'd never have known about any of this. I mean, who reads Latin these days?"

"It was serendipity, Jack. A fortunate set of circumstances."

"It's my clumsy way of saying thanks. Thanks for putting up with me, and thanks for sticking with me."

"Somebody has to," she said.

"Well, I'm glad it's you." Nightingale looked at his watch. "You have to go now, Jenny."

"No way," said Jenny.

"I have to do this on my own."

"I'm staying, Jack."

Nightingale folded his arms. "I don't know what's going to happen, but I do know that if it goes wrong I don't want you around." He smiled confidently. "I'll call you when it's over."

"They've got phones in hell, have they?" she asked.

Nightingale went to hug her but she shook her head and walked away.

CHAPTER

69

Nightingale stood looking out of the bedroom window. He saw Jenny walk toward her car, then stop and turn to look back at the house. She looked up and their eyes met. Nightingale gave her a small wave but she just shook her head sadly and turned away. Nightingale lit a cigarette as she got into the car and drove off.

He smoked slowly, then stubbed out the butt. He was in the master bedroom, the place where his father had killed himself. He slowly stripped off his clothes and walked through to the bathroom. There was a large bathtub already filled with water and he slid into it. He held his breath and submerged himself, sliding down the cold enamel and staring up through the tepid water. He stayed underwater until he felt his lungs start to burn, and then he pushed himself up and exhaled. He methodically scrubbed himself clean with a small plastic brush and a bar of soap. He washed and rinsed his hair twice, then climbed out of the bath and toweled himself dry. He put on clean underwear, socks, a pale blue polo shirt, and cargo trousers. He took his cigarettes and lighter from his suit and put them in one of the knee pockets in the cargo pants and put on a pair of brand-new Nike trainers. He looked at the padded envelope, then took out the crucifix and put it around his neck. Finally he combed his hair, checked himself in the mirror over the sink, and walked slowly downstairs.

He went through to the drawing room and used his lighter to light the five candles, then he stepped inside the pentangle. He took several deep breaths to compose himself, then used the birch branch to go over the chalk outline. He sprinkled more consecrated saltwater around the perimeter of the circle, then set fire to the contents of a lead crucible. The herbs and spices and bits of wood hissed and spluttered and filled the room with cloying smoke.

He picked up Jenny's notebook and began to read the Latin phrase she'd shown him, stumbling over the strange language. A wind blew through the room, even though the windows and door were firmly closed. The candle flames flickered and the smoke pouring up from the crucible began to form a lazy circle in the air. Nightingale coughed and continued to read, running his finger underneath the words so that he wouldn't lose his place. When he finished, he coughed again and said out loud, "Bagahi laca bacabe." He closed the notepad.

The room was thick with smoke, as dense as a pea-souper fog, sickeningly sweet but acrid enough to make his eyes water.

What happened next, Nightingale was never able to explain to anyone, not even to himself. He wasn't even sure that he remembered it properly. The only way his mind could even come close to interpreting what he'd seen was to picture it as space folding into itself, a series of flickering flashes, and then the air blurred and she was there, standing within the apex of the triangle. It was a girl, in her late teens or early twenties, white-faced and with heavy mascara and a black T-shirt with a white skull on it, and a black leather skirt and black boots, and she had a studded collar around her neck. She looked at him through narrowed eyes. "Jack Nightingale," she said, her voice a throaty whisper. "Are you in such a hurry to join me? You only have six hours left, why are you wasting them?" For the first time Nightingale realized that a second figure had folded out of the air. A dog, a black-and-white collie that sat down at the feet of his mistress.

"I know you," he said. "We've met before."

"Our paths have crossed from time to time," she said. Her eyes were black and featureless, the irises so dark that they merged seamlessly into the pupils. "I have an investment in you and I watch over my investments."

"Are you Proserpine? Princess of hell?"

"So formal," she said. She laughed and the floor shook. The dog at her side growled menacingly. She reached down and stroked it behind the ears. "Do you want to see my ID, Nightingale?" She laughed again and this time the whole building vibrated. "You expected what? Horns? A forked tail? The stench of brimstone? I can give you that, if that's what you want."

"But you're a girl," said Nightingale.

"I am what I am," she said. Her eyes narrowed as she looked at his neck. "Nice crucifix," she said.

"It belonged to my mother."

"I know," said Proserpine. She smiled. "You know I'm not a vampire, right? Crucifixes are only good against the undead."

"That's not why I'm wearing it," said Nightingale. "Did you kill her? My mother?"

"She killed herself."

"And my uncle? And Barry O'Brien? And George Harrison?"

"I always thought he was the weakest member of the band," said Proserpine. "I mean, 'My Sweet Lord.' What the hell was that all about?"

"You know what I mean," said Nightingale. "Did you kill them?"

"They killed themselves."

"What about Robbie?"

Proserpine shook her head solemnly. "A tragic accident."

"Uncle Tommy? Aunty Linda?"

"You have been unlucky on the relatives front, haven't you?"

"You killed them all, didn't you."

"Is this how you used to interrogate suspects when you were a cop?" she said. "It's not very subtle, is it?"

"Did you kill them?"

"No."

"I don't believe you."

"Ask them yourself," said Proserpine. She waved a languid hand and four figures appeared behind her, flickering at first and then becoming solid. Rebecca Keeley was on the right, wearing a long gray nightdress, blood dripping from her wrists, her eyes wide and staring. Next to her was Barry O'Brien, naked and soaking wet, his arms cut open to the bone. Blood and water dripped to the floor. Uncle Tommy stood next to O'Brien, his neck at a grotesque angle, his lips drawn back into a snarl. And just behind them was Aunty Linda, crawling along the floor, her skull in pieces with blood and brain matter trailing behind her.

Proserpine's hand moved again, forming a gnarled fist. Harrison appeared, the left side of his body all mashed up and bloody, one eyeball hanging from its socket. And next to him was Robbie, blood trickling from between his lips, a white bone sticking out from his left elbow, his right leg buckled and twisted. Robbie was staring at Nightingale, his shattered jaw moving soundlessly.

All six figures moved slowly toward Nightingale, reaching for him.

Proserpine looked over her shoulder and frowned. "We're missing someone," she said. "Who are we missing? Ah, of course..." She waved her hand again and Sophie Underwood appeared. Unlike the others, she didn't bear the marks of her death, she was exactly as Nightingale had seen her on the balcony of her apartment, her blonde hair tucked behind her ears, the Barbie doll clutched to her white sweatshirt. She looked at Nightingale, her lower lip trembling. "I don't like it here," she said. "I want to go home." She took a step toward the protective circle. "Please help me, Jack."

Nightingale forced himself to look away. He knew that she wasn't really there. Sophie was dead and buried and there was no way that she could be standing in the bedroom of Gosling Manor. "I want to go home, Jack," said Sophie, and she began to sob.

Nightingale glared at Proserpine. "Don't do that," he said.

"Don't do what?" asked Proserpine. She put a finger up to the side of her mouth and smiled girlishly. "Am I being bad? Do you want to punish me?"

"Don't use others to get to me," said Nightingale. "Fight your own battles."

Proserpine's eyes hardened and she waved her hand again. The figures vanished. She crouched down and slowly put a hand toward the chalk circle. "Consecrated saltwater," she said and nodded her approval.

"What are you? A devil? A demon? Are you here or am I imagining all this?"

"I am what I am, Nightingale," she said as she straightened up.

"I don't understand," he said, folding his arms. "I don't understand any of this."

"With respect, you're no Stephen Hawking, are you? Now there was a book. How can you write about the creation of the universe without discussing heaven or hell? And how can you get away with telling people that one moment there is nothing but the void and the next there is an expanding universe heading out to infinity?"

"I couldn't finish it," said Nightingale. "If there is a hell, then where is it?"

"Hell is everywhere, you just can't see it."

"And heaven?"

"The same."

"The same place?" Nightingale shook his head. "Maybe you're not even here, maybe this is all some sort of stupid delusion, brought on by the crap I burned in the crucible." He took out his packet of Marlboros. "Do you want a cigarette? I'm guessing cancer isn't one of your worries?" He took out a cigarette and slipped one between his lips. He held his lighter to the cigarette and was just about to flick it, but then hesitated. He looked at Proserpine with narrowed eyes. "Cigarette smoke's an impurity, isn't it? It'll weaken the pentangle."

Proserpine shrugged carelessly. "Maybe," she said. "Try it and see."

Nightingale slid the cigarette back into the pack.

Proserpine studied the pentangle, the candles, and the still-smoldering crucible. "Where did you learn this?" she said.

"I read a diary written by Sebastian Mitchell."

Proserpine's black eyes hardened. "And how did you come across the diary?"

"My father had it," said Nightingale.

"It won't do you any good," she said, putting her hands on her hips. "It didn't do your father any good, it didn't do Mitchell any good, and it won't do you any good either. Your father sold your soul to me on the day you were born. The contract is inviolable, written in his blood. And you bear the mark."

She stalked around the pentangle, occasionally moving closer to him but never touching the chalk mark. It was as if she were testing his defenses. Nightingale kept turning so that he was always facing her. She looked like a punk teenager but she was a demon from hell and not to be trusted. "Deals can be broken," said Nightingale quietly.

Proserpine threw back her head and laughed. The noise was like a thousand wolves howling, a bloodcurdling scream that chilled Nightingale's blood. The sound went right through him and he shivered. The dog sat up and stared at Nightingale. The animal's eyes were as black and featureless as the girl's. "Not this one," said Proserpine. "Your soul is mine. There's nothing you can do to change that."

"Why do you want my soul?"

"It's what I do. I take souls."

"Why?"

"The why doesn't matter. It's what I do."

"But what good is my soul to you?"

"It's how we keep score," said Proserpine.

"It's a game?"

She shook her head. "No, Nightingale, it's not a game. It's a struggle between the dark and the light, between good and evil."

"Between God and Lucifer?"

"Whatever," she said.

"If you're a demon, or a devil, or whatever you call yourself, why do you look as if you've just walked out of Camden Market?"

"It's my style, it's what I'm comfortable with."

"But you don't really look like that, is that what you're saying?"

"I do and I don't," said Proserpine. "I'm here and I'm not here. You're never going to understand it, Nightingale. Energy, matter, light, it's all connected. You're human, you only see a small part of it. I see everything. Me trying to explain it to you would be like you explaining nuclear physics to an earthworm."

"And why me, why my soul?"

"Because it was offered to me, by your father."

"But that's not fair. It's my soul, what right did he have to trade it?"

Proserpine laughed, her voice louder and deeper than any sound Nightingale had ever heard. "Fair?" she said. "You want fairness? Nothing in life is fair. Haven't you learned that yet?"

"So anyone can sell a soul, is that what you're saying?"

"Your soul was promised to me by your father before you were born. Before it was yours."

"And there's nothing I can do to stop you?"

She shook her head. "Nothing."

"Mitchell seems to think that you can be beaten."

"Mitchell is wrong."

"He says that so long as he stays within his pentangle, he walks into hell under his own terms."

Proserpine smiled. "Yeah, well, the fat lady hasn't sung on that one yet." She nodded at the pack of Marlboros. "Maybe I will have a cigarette."

Nightingale threw the pack to her and she caught it one-handed. She tapped out a cigarette, tossed it high in the air, and then caught it between her lips. "Got a light, mister?" she asked in a singsong little girl's voice. She winked and held out her right hand. It burst into flames and she used it to light the cigarette. She blew smoke at the ceiling and shook her hand. The flames vanished.

"I saw a conjuror do that once," said Nightingale.

"I shall miss your sense of humor," she said.

"When I'm in hell?"

"When your soul is in hell," she said. "You'll be dead."

"I've a question for you," said Nightingale.

"This isn't phone-a-friend, Nightingale. You can't summon demons simply to question them."

"Actually, I'm pretty sure I can," said Nightingale. "The spell means that you have to appear and that you have to stay between the circle and the triangle. And you have to stay until I release you."

Her face hardened. "So that's your plan, is it? You think you can keep me trapped here? Well that may be right, Nightingale, but you're trapped too. And I reckon I can go a lot longer than you without food or water. And it won't make any difference anyway because at midnight your soul is mine, pentangle or no pentangle."

"I didn't do this to trap you," he said. "And what I have in mind won't take long. I just want to ask you a question. Why is Sebastian Mitchell so scared of you?"

"He said that? He said he was scared of me?"

"He's sitting in a magic circle waiting to die because he knows that if he sets foot outside it you'll drag him down to hell, so I sort of inferred it. What did he do?"

"He cheated me," said Proserpine.

"Cheated a demon? How?"

"It doesn't matter how," said Proserpine.

"Just humor me," said Nightingale. He looked at his watch. "In a few hours you're supposed to be condemning me to eternal damnation, the least you can do is satisfy my curiosity."

"I don't owe you anything, Nightingale."

"I know that," he said. "What did he do that's got you so riled up?"

Proserpine glared at him, then slowly smiled. "Are you planning to write a book, because I have to point out that you probably don't have enough time."

"I just want to understand the situation I'm in," he said.

"Mitchell promised me four souls," she said. "Young girls. Virgins. They were novices at a coven of his. He promised me their souls, but then he went behind my back and gave them to someone else."

"Another demon?"

Proserpine nodded. "He was leading them along the path, getting them ready to offer themselves to me. But then he negotiated a better deal." She smiled thinly and took a drag on the cigarette. "What he thought was a better deal."

"But why does that matter? Are you in competition with the other demons, is that it?"

"You wouldn't understand, Nightingale. He made me look... incompetent. He made me look like a fool, like I wasn't in control."

"So you want revenge?"

"They were my souls," she said. "Promised to me. But he reneged. I can't let him get away with that." She took another long drag on her cigarette and then flicked it away. It bounced off the wall and hit the floor, still glowing. "Just get on with it, Nightingale."

"With what?"

"Begging for your soul. I assume that's why you summoned me. To plead for me to leave you alone, to allow you to continue your miserable existence."

Nightingale smiled. "Actually, you're wrong," he said. "I didn't call you here to beg."

Proserpine frowned. "Why then?" she said. "Why did you summon me when you have so little time left?"

"To do what I do best," said Nightingale. "To negotiate."

CHAPTER

Nightingale climbed out of his MGB and looked at his watch. It was eleven o'clock. One hour to go before midnight. He pressed the speakerphone button. It buzzed and he waved up at the CCTV camera covering the gates. The buzzing stopped. "Mr. Nightingale, if you do not leave the property immediately we will have no choice other than to call the police."

Nightingale bent down to talk into the speaker. "Nice to talk to you too, Sylvia," he said. "Tell Mr. Mitchell it's important. Tell him I know how to deal with Proserpine. Tell him I have the answer to all his problems."

"You're wasting your time, Mr. Nightingale. He doesn't want to see you."

"Just give him the message, Sylvia." Nightingale straightened up. The moon was full and dark clouds moved slowly across its face. "Nice night for it," he muttered to himself. The gates buzzed and began to open. Nightingale grinned and climbed back into his MGB.

When he arrived at the house Sylvia was waiting for him with four of Mitchell's heavies. Nightingale got out of the car and walked around to the boot. He opened it and took out the metal suitcase that Wainwright had given him.

"We'll need to check that," said Sylvia, holding up her hand.

"It's locked," said Nightingale. He handed it to Sylvia. "You can keep hold of it until I need it." He smiled at her look of apprehension. "If it was a bomb, sweetie, I'd hardly have been driving it around in an old banger like my MGB, would I?"

Sylvia looked at him coldly, then turned on her heel and walked up the steps to the entrance. The four heavies moved aside to allow Nightingale to follow her, but he stayed where he was. "Which one of you scumbags pointed a gun at my friend?" he asked.

The four men stared back at him, their eyes hidden behind impenetrable lenses. One of them drew back his jacket to reveal a submachine pistol in a nylon sling.

"Cat got your tongues?" said Nightingale, looking at them one by one. "You were very chatty when you were scaring a young woman, but now you're all coy, aren't you? When this is over, we're going to have a chat about what you did to her and I'll explain the error of your ways." He smiled brightly. "Right, let's go and put the world to rights, shall we?" He jogged up the stairs after Sylvia.

She took him into the hall and pointed at the bathroom door. "You know the procedure, Mr. Nightingale."

CHAPTER

71

When Nightingale walked out of the bathroom wearing just the robe, Sylvia was waiting for him with two of the heavies. They escorted him to Mitchell's room. He was in exactly the same position as he was when Nightingale had last visited, though this time he was wearing royal-blue silk pajamas. Sylvia made Nightingale stop ten feet away from the edge of the pentangle. Nightingale nodded at Mitchell. "You got your diary back, then?" he said. "You only had to ask, you know. I would have given it back to you."

Mitchell pulled the oxygen mask away from his face. "What do you want, Nightingale?"

Nightingale grinned. "I get asked that a lot these days," he said.

"Haven't you got better things to do? You've got what, an hour before she comes for you?"

"That's what I wanted to talk to you about."

"There's nothing I can do, Nightingale. I told you that already." He began to cough and he pressed the oxygen mask over his mouth.

"I've found a way," said Nightingale. "I've found a way to stop Proserpine."

Mitchell shook his head, still coughing. He regained his composure and took the mask away from his mouth. "She can't be stopped. She has too much power."

"Do you know Joshua Wainwright? American guy, I get the feeling he's embraced the dark side."

"I've heard of him," said Mitchell.

"Wainwright owes me a favor."

"I doubt that," said Mitchell.

"I sold him a book he's wanted for years. My father snatched it from under his nose but I got it back to him." Nightingale grinned. "I made a tidy profit, but he was still grateful. Grateful enough to help me."

"No one can help you," said Mitchell. "One minute after midnight and it's all over for you."

"Not according to the book that Wainwright has loaned me."

Mitchell began coughing again. He dabbed at his lips with a tissue, then threw it into the bin by his side. "What book?" he said.

"It was written by an Iranian Satanist, back in the eighteenth century, but he only showed it to a few people. When he died it went missing, but it turned up in Paris in the 1930s and was translated into French. There are only three copies in English, and Wainwright has one. And he's loaned it to me."

Mitchell frowned. "This book, what's it called?"

"It has no name, no title," said Nightingale. "But it has a chapter on killing devils."

"You can't kill a devil," said Mitchell.

"Not so much kill, as destroy," said Nightingale. "There is a spell that ends them."

"Nonsense," said Mitchell. He coughed again and spat bloody phlegm into a fresh tissue. "Proserpine sits on the left hand of Satan, she's beyond all attacks."

"The book tells of a spell that weakens a devil's power. Then you can use a dagger. A dagger that has been given but not thanked for."

"And where did you get the dagger?" asked Mitchell.

"Have you heard of the Order of the Nine Angles? Nasty little group that goes in for human sacrifice? My father was a member."

"The Order gave you a dagger?"

"And I didn't say thank you. How rude was that?"

"So why are you here? Why not just do it?"

"I need your help," said Nightingale.

Mitchell shook his head. "I'm not leaving the circle," he said.

"You don't have to," said Nightingale.

Mitchell coughed and put the oxygen mask over his mouth. He continued to stare at Nightingale with unblinking eyes as his chest heaved.

"Here's the thing," said Nightingale. "I can't summon Proserpine to do this. That won't work. For the spell to be effective, she has to come of her own accord and she has to be in human form. And at midnight, she's going to come for me."

"How do you know she'll come in human form?"

"Because I've already summoned her."

"And she came?"

"My assistant, the girl your heavies terrorized, she made notes from your diary. Including the section on summoning Proserpine."

Mitchell chuckled. "And you performed the spell?"

"Couldn't find a magic sword, but we made do with a birch branch."

"And when she came, what form did she take?"

"A girl. With a dog."

Mitchell nodded. "The dog is always with her. Her protector."

"Seemed like a regular sheepdog to me."

"They choose their appearances, Nightingale. But she came to you the same way that she appeared to me."

"But don't you see? That's her weakness. She appears as a human, and when she's in human form, she can be killed. With the dagger."

"So why are you here, Nightingale? Why don't you just do it?"

"Because when she comes, she's going to be focused on me, which means I won't get the chance to get close to her. But you'll be a distraction. And when she's distracted, I can get to her."

"I'm not leaving the circle," said Mitchell.

"I already told you, you don't have to," said Nightingale. He pointed at the terrace outside the French windows. "I'll do it there. She'll come at midnight. You keep the lights off, until you see me reading the spell from the book. As soon as I close the book, you turn on the lights. She'll see you, and that's when I'll do it."

Mitchell coughed. "You're mad," he wheezed.

Nightingale shook his head. "No, I'm not mad," he said. "I'm desperate."

CHAPTER

Nightingale walked out of the bathroom. He had changed back into his suit and had on his raincoat. Sylvia was waiting for him, holding the metal suitcase. Two of Mitchell's heavies were standing behind her. "If you do anything to compromise Mr. Mitchell's security, you will be dealt with immediately," she said.

"Don't worry, Sylvia, I've his best interests at heart," said Nightingale. "Once I've dealt with Proserpine, he can go back to living a normal life."

Sylvia flashed him a cold smile. "Mr. Mitchell's life has never been normal," she said. "We will walk around the house to the patio," she said. "Mr. Mitchell says that I am to give you anything that you need."

Nightingale grinned and patted the suitcase. "I've got everything I need right here."

They went outside and around the house, flanked by the two heavies. The gardens were illuminated by floodlights, and by the wall Nightingale saw another heavy walking with a Rottweiler on a leash.

When they reached the terrace, Nightingale put down the case and lit a cigarette. Sylvia looked at her watch. "It's half an hour until midnight," she said.

"I know," said Nightingale. "But I figure that the condemned man deserves a last cigarette."

CHAPTER

73

Sebastian Mitchell kept the oxygen mask against his mouth as he took deep breaths, his eyes on Nightingale. Nightingale was slowly chalking a pentangle on the stone slabs. There was a clock on the wall and Mitchell squinted at it. Eleven forty. Twenty minutes before Proserpine was coming to take Nightingale's soul.

Sylvia walked into the room, her high heels clicking on the wooden floor. "I've stationed extra men around the house, and we have three dogs in the garden now, sir."

"Thank you, Sylvia," wheezed Mitchell. "But there's no danger for us, it's Nightingale she wants."

Nightingale placed the metal suitcase in the center of the pentangle. He took out an ornate gold dagger and held it up. It glinted in the spotlights covering the terrace. He waved the knife over the five points of the pentangle and then slid it into the inside pocket of his raincoat. "You're wasting your time, Nightingale," Mitchell muttered. "Knives are useless against demons."

Nightingale took a piece of branch from the case and slowly went over the chalk outline with it, then he sprinkled water from a small bottle around the perimeter. "Consecrated saltwater," Mitchell wheezed. "But it will do you no good. It will keep her out but you will still lose your soul."

Nightingale put the branch and the bottle of water back into the case, and took out a small leather-bound book. Mitchell frowned. "What is that? Sylvia, can you see what book he's holding?"

Sylvia walked over to the French windows and peered through the glass. "I can't see, sir," she said. "There doesn't appear to be a title but it looks old."

"What are you up to, Nightingale?" muttered Mitchell.

Nightingale sat cross-legged in the center of the pentangle with the book in his lap, staring out over the garden.

"Now what's he doing?" said Sylvia.

Mitchell looked up at the clock on the wall. "He's waiting," he said. He looked back at Sylvia. "Turn the lights off," he said. "We might as well give him a chance."

CHAPTER

Nightingale could feel his pulse racing and he tried to slow his heart, keeping his breathing slow and even. Behind him, the lights in the drawing room went out. The spotlights around the terrace were still on and he was bathed in a clinical white light. There were lights around the perimeter wall, too, casting long shadows from the trees that dotted the garden.

He didn't have to look at his watch to know that there were still ten minutes to go. There was nothing he could do to speed up the process. Proserpine would come exactly at midnight because that was the time when his soul would be forfeit. There was no point in trying to summon her, all he could do was wait until she showed up of her own accord.

An owl flew overhead, its wings beating silently in the still air. Then it swooped down into a patch of grass under an oak tree and grabbed something small and furry in its claws and then flew up toward the roof.

Nightingale closed his eyes. He could hear a far-off rumble of traffic but other than that the night was silent. There was no sound from the house behind him but he was sure that Mitchell was watching him. He tried to visualize Mitchell sitting in his chair, the oxygen mask pressed against his mouth, staring out of the window. Sylvia would be there, too, close to Mitchell's protective pentangle, watching and wondering.

The seconds ticked by. Then the minutes. A breeze blew from the north, ruffling Nightingale's hair. He opened his eyes. The trees were swaying in the wind, their shadows writhing on the grass like living things.

Nightingale's knees cracked as he got to his feet. He held the book against his chest and licked his lips, desperately wanting a cigarette but knowing that it was impossible.

A mist had gathered around the lawn, patchy at first but soon thickening, and the security lights around the walls became glowing balls that grew dimmer with each second that passed. A dog barked in the distance but the sound was cut short as if its leash had been pulled harshly.

Nightingale stared ahead. He could no longer see the wall surrounding the garden, or the trees. He could see the terrace but only a few dozen yards of lawn before it was swallowed up in the mist. Then it happened, the air in front of him seemed to cleave apart, then fold in on itself, then shimmer, and then she was there, standing about twelve feet from the pentangle, a sly smile on her face. Her eyes were dark pits, her lashes thick with mascara, her lips black and glossy. She was wearing the same black skirt and boots as the last time he'd seen her, but she had on a different T-shirt, black with a gold ankh cross on it. Her collie dog circled around her, its eyes continually watching Nightingale, its tail twitching from side to side. Proserpine grinned at him. "Time to pay the piper, Nightingale," she said.

Nightingale ignored her. He had already marked the page that he was to read. He opened the book. It was Latin, and he read the words slowly and precisely, his eyes fixed on the page. The wind was getting stronger now and he held on to the book tightly, fearful that it would be whipped out of his grasp.

"You're wasting your breath," said Proserpine. She took a step toward the pentangle. "It's midnight, time for me to take what is mine."

CHAPTER

Mitchell took the oxygen mask away from his face. "What's he doing?" he croaked. "No spell can stop her, she's too strong."

"What's going to happen, sir?" asked Sylvia.

"She'll take his soul, that's what's going to happen," said Mitchell. "Nightingale's got balls all right, but he's as good as dead."

He pushed himself up out of his seat to get a better look at what was happening on the terrace. Proserpine was moving closer to Nightingale. She was saying something to him but Mitchell couldn't make out what it was. Nightingale was being buffeted by a strong wind, his hair in disarray, his coat whipping around his legs like a living thing, but Proserpine was totally unaffected by it.

Nightingale was reading from the book, his head down as he concentrated, ignoring the demon that was now only feet away from the pentangle.

"He's wasting his time," muttered Mitchell. "It's over."

"The lights, sir," said Sylvia. "Nightingale said we should turn on the lights."

"It won't make any difference," he said. He dropped the oxygen mask onto the chair. Proserpine was next to the pentangle now, her black eyes glaring at Nightingale, her fingers curved into talons, bent forward at the waist like a wild animal preparing to spring.

Nightingale stopped reading and he closed the book. He held it out to Proserpine.

"No, never allow contact!" said Mitchell.

"The lights, sir," said Sylvia.

"Yes, okay," snapped Mitchell. "Put the lights on, but it won't make any difference." He stared at Nightingale, who was still holding the leather-bound book out to Proserpine.

Sylvia's heels clicked on the wooden floor as she hurried over to the light switches. She placed her hand against the panel and flicked the three switches together. The room was flooded with light.

Proserpine's head jerked and she stared at the French window, snarling when she saw Mitchell standing there. "Mitchell!" she screamed, so loudly that the glass rattled. Mitchell took a step back and his leg banged against the chair behind him.

Nightingale dropped the book and the dagger was in his right hand. He brought it down in an arc toward Proserpine's chest. There was a flash of lightning and then another and then a howl from Proserpine as she staggered backwards. There was black blood gushing from the center of the golden ankh, pulsing out in a stream that splashed over Nightingale's legs. The lightning flashed again and then there was a clap of thunder so loud that the ground shook.

Nightingale stepped out of the pentangle and stuck the knife in her chest again and again, his face contorted into an angry mask. He was screaming at her but the wind was tearing the words from his mouth and ripping them away.

"No…" said Mitchell, holding on to the chair for support. "It can't be."

Proserpine's dog ran away, its tail between its legs, its ears flat against its head, keeping low to the ground as if it hoped to escape unnoticed.

Proserpine fell back, her arms flailing. Lightning flashed again and again and there were simultaneous booms of thunder. Nightingale straddled her and used both hands to slam the knife down into her chest.

She bucked and kicked and then went still.

"I don't believe it," whispered Mitchell. "He's done it." He looked up at the clock. It was barely two minutes after midnight. He looked back at the terrace. Nightingale was standing up, the dagger in his right hand, the wind tugging at his coat. "Sixty years I've studied, sixty years, and I couldn't have accomplished that." He looked over at Sylvia, who was still standing at the door, her hand on the light switches. "Nightingale, he's worked a miracle. Did you see that, Sylvia? Did you see what he did?"

"I saw, Mr. Mitchell."

"He killed a demon. He killed a demon from hell." He stood with one hand on the armchair, shaking his head in bewilderment.

CHAPTER 76

Nightingale stood looking down at the body, his ears ringing from the thunderclaps. The knife dropped from his nerveless fingers. His body was drenched in sweat and it felt as if the strength had drained from his legs. Lightning flashed and the earth shook with another rumble of thunder.

He heard the French windows open behind him, but he didn't look around. "You did it, man!" shouted Mitchell.

He heard Mitchell step out onto the terrace, and only then did Nightingale turn. Mitchell was standing there, his blue silk pajamas rippling in the wind. Sylvia was standing behind him, her hands clasped together as if she were in prayer, and behind her were four of Mitchell's heavies, guns at the ready.

"I wouldn't have believed it if I hadn't seen it with my own eyes," said Mitchell. He walked unsteadily across the flagstones and grabbed Nightingale by the arm, his fingers digging into him like talons. "You killed her. How did you do it? How in God's name did you do it?"

"God had nothing to do with it." The voice was a deep growl that came from behind Nightingale.

Mitchell stiffened. Nightingale stepped away from him, leaving Mitchell standing alone with his arms outstretched. They both stared down at Proserpine. She was smiling. As they watched, she pivoted upright, the wounds on her chest vanishing.

Mitchell took a step backwards, his mouth working soundlessly, his hands clutched to his chest.

"Nice to see you, Sebastian," said Proserpine in her little girl's voice. "It's been a long time. But not as long as you're going to burn in hell."

Mitchell threw up his hands to cover his face. "You set me up," he hissed at Nightingale.

Nightingale shrugged. "I did a deal," he said. "Your soul for mine."

"You bastard!" screamed Mitchell.

"Sticks and stones," said Nightingale.

Mitchell started to turn. Proserpine laughed and waved her hand. Mitchell's feet sank into the stone slab he was standing on. He swayed unsteadily as he stared down at his feet in horror.

"Where do you think you're going, Sebastian?" asked Proserpine.

"Shoot her!" screamed Sylvia. The four heavies behind her fanned out across the terrace. The one on the left holding a machine pistol was the first to fire. Bullets smacked into Proserpine but she just smiled. She made a motion with her left hand and a bolt of lightning hit the man in the chest and he fell back, smoke belching from a gaping wound.

The other three men started to fire their guns. Nightingale heard a growl and he turned to see the collie running across the grass out of the mist toward the terrace. It leapt into the air, and as it did it rippled and doubled in size. It was as big as a tiger, and its fur had become hard and scaly. Its four massive paws hit the terrace and it sprang into the air again, passing so close to Nightingale that he felt the rush of wind as it went by. It had three heads now, doglike but with massive fangs and forked tongues, and there were bony spikes down its spine. It hit the flagstones and now it was the size of a large car, and two of the heads bit into one of the men and the third ripped off an arm of the other. The last remaining heavy turned to run but the dog or whatever it had turned into leapt onto his back and ripped him into a dozen bloody pieces.

Sylvia screamed but Proserpine made another motion with her hand and the woman fell silent. "Am I going to have a problem with you, Sylvia?" she asked.

Sylvia shook her head.

"What do you think, Nightingale, does she live or die?"

Nightingale shrugged. "It's up to you," he said. "None of them means anything to me."

Proserpine looked at him suspiciously. "Are you trying to play me, Nightingale? You think if you pretend not to care then I'll spare her?"

"I'm not the devious type," he said.

"Where's your chivalry then? She's a woman. You don't care if she lives or dies?"

"I think you've made up your mind already," Nightingale said quietly. "I think that nothing I do or say matters anymore, I'm just a spectator. So do what you have to do and have done with it."

"Die then," said Proserpine flatly. She made another motion with her left hand and Sylvia burst into flames. She screamed and ran off the terrace toward the garden but barely made half a dozen steps before she fell on the grass in a smoldering heap.

The dog had reverted back to a collie and was sitting at Proserpine's feet, its tongue lolling out of the side of its mouth.

Proserpine walked toward Mitchell, her hands swinging, her head up. "I have a deal," said Mitchell, his voice a raspy croak. "I can get you whatever you want."

"I have what I want," said Proserpine. "I have you."

"I can get souls for you, all the souls you want." He coughed and bloody spittle frothed between his lips. "Just listen to…"

Proserpine waved her hand and Mitchell fell silent. His mouth kept working but he made no sound. Proserpine smiled. "Go to hell, Mitchell," she said.

There was a ripping sound and the air behind Mitchell split apart and folded in on itself. Figures moved in the air, rippling like dark mirages. Mitchell screamed and coughed up more blood, and things, things with scales and red eyes and tails and claws reached for him, things that smelled of decay and death and sweat and fear, things that hissed and growled and grunted, and then Mitchell was dragged away, screaming and crying, and then the air folded again and it was as if he had never been there. Proserpine turned to look at Nightingale. She smiled. "I do hate long good-byes," she said.

"This was all planned from the start, wasn't it?"

She shrugged carelessly. "It worked out all right in the end, didn't it?"

Nightingale nodded. "You got what you wanted."

"And you got your soul back. So all's well that ends well." The collie dog made a soft woofing sound. "Yes, baby, soon," Proserpine whispered to the dog. She patted it on the head as she continued to smile at Nightingale.

"You used me, to get Mitchell," said Nightingale.

"It was your idea, Nightingale. Remember? You summoned me. You negotiated."

"Which is what you intended, right from the start? All those people telling me I was going to hell. To put the frighteners on me. Then anyone who might be able to help me, they die. Except for

Tyler. Because Tyler pointed the way to Mitchell, and Mitchell is what you wanted all along."

"I'm just glad you're a better negotiator than you are interrogator," she said.

"The key to a good interrogation is only to ask questions that you know the answers to."

"But doesn't that rather defeat the point?"

"All those people dead," said Nightingale. "My aunt. My uncle. Robbie. What about my parents? Did you kill them?"

"Do you want to deal, Nightingale? How about you offer me your soul and I'll tell you everything?"

Nightingale stared at her but didn't say anything.

"Many happy returns, Nightingale." She blew him a kiss and turned to go.

"Wait!"

She stopped and looked at him over her shoulder. The dog growled, its hackles rising. "Do not try my patience, Nightingale," said Proserpine, her voice deeper now and more menacing.

"My sister?"

Proserpine shook her head. "Not my problem."

"My father sold her soul, too."

"Not to me."

"To who, then?"

Proserpine laughed. It was a deep, booming laughter that echoed off the house and reverberated around the garden. Nightingale shivered. "Who gets my sister's soul?" he shouted.

Proserpine grinned and winked at him. "Unless you want to put your eternal soul on the table, you've got nothing left to bargain with, Nightingale. We're done. Catch you later."

She walked away, the dog following in her footsteps. She waved without looking back and then reality shimmered and bent in on itself and she and the dog vanished. The wind gradually died down and the trees stopped whispering. The mist had cleared and he could see the gardens again. Two of Mitchell's heavies were standing by a willow tree close to the perimeter wall, scratching their heads. One of them was holding a leash but there was no sign of his dog.

Nightingale took out his pack of Marlboros and lit a cigarette. He held the smoke deep in his lungs and relished the feel of the nicotine entering his bloodstream, letting him know that he was still alive. He blew a smoke ring toward the moon, and smiled to himself. "That went well," he muttered to himself. "All things considered."

CHAPTER

77

There were five candles spaced around the circular table and Nightingale lit them one by one. "Very romantic," said Jenny.

"If you don't take this seriously, I'll do it myself," said Nightingale.

"How can you use a Ouija board yourself?" said Jenny scornfully. "The whole point is that it's a joint effort."

Nightingale went up the stairs, switched off the lights, and came back down into the basement. He had found the Ouija board in the bottom drawer of Gosling's desk. It was made of oak that had cracked with age, the words YES and NO in the top corners and the letters of the alphabet embossed in gold in two rows across the middle of the board. Below the letters were the numbers zero to nine in a row, and below them the word GOODBYE.

The planchette was made from ivory or bone, cool to the touch and as smooth as marble. He had put the board on a circular table in the middle of the basement with a crystal vase containing freshly picked flowers and a crystal glass containing distilled water.

He had placed the five large church candles around the table. He took a small bowl of sage and sprinkled it onto the burning candles, then smudged some of it on the board and the planchette. He had also prepared bowls of consecrated salt and lavender and he sprinkled them over the board before taking two high-backed wooden chairs and putting them together at one side of the table. He waved for Jenny to sit down. "Are you sure this is a good idea?" she asked.

"We won't know until we try it," said Nightingale, taking his seat. "Come on, sit down. It won't bite."

"I wish I had your confidence," she said, and sat down. She looked at the candles. "Shouldn't we have a protective circle or something?"

"This isn't about raising demons," said Nightingale.

"That's right," said Jenny, "all we're doing is talking to the recently departed."

"Relax," said Nightingale.

"That's easy for you to say," said Jenny. "Why the salt and herbs and stuff?"

"It's what you're supposed to do."

"And the flowers and the glass of water?"

"Spirits love flowers and water."

"What about the ones with hay fever? Or the ones that died of rabies?"

Nightingale looked at her sternly. "You've got to take this seriously or it won't work," he said. "The table has to be free of all negative energy or the spirits won't come."

"It's a kid's game, Jack."

Nightingale shook his head. "I've read some of Gosling's books on it, and it's deadly serious," he said. "Over the years it became a game, a bit of a laugh, but the Ouija board is a genuine way of conversing with spirits." He reached over and took her hands in this. "Close your eyes," he said.

"You've got to be joking."

"Jenny, just do as you're told. If nothing else, do it to humor me."

Jenny closed her eyes. Nightingale closed his eyes and began to speak, clearly and loudly so that his voice echoed around the basement. "In the name of God, of Jesus Christ, of the Great Brotherhood of Light, of the Archangels Michael, Raphael, Gabriel, Uriel, and Ariel, please protect us from the forces of evil during this session. Let there be nothing but light surrounding this board and its participants and let us only communicate with powers and entities of the light. Protect us, protect this house, the people in this house, and let there only be light and nothing but light, amen."

He gently squeezed her hand. "Amen," she said.

They both opened their eyes. "Now, this bit is important," said Nightingale. "You have to imagine that the table is protected with a bright white light. First you imagine it coming down through the top of your head and completely surrounding your body. Then push it out as far as you can go. Can you do that?"

"I'll try," said Jenny.

"Good girl," he said. "Now we both put our right hands on the planchette. If anything goes wrong, we move the planchette to GOODBYE and we both say, 'Good-bye' firmly and then I'll recite a closing prayer."

Jenny took her hand off the planchette. "What might go wrong?" she said.

"A malicious spirit might try to come through, that's all."

"Oh, that's all," she said.

"Jenny, it'll be fine, just trust me. Now put your hand back."

Jenny slowly reached out with her right hand and touched the planchette.

"Now visualize the white light. Okay?"

Jenny nodded.

Nightingale took a deep breath and looked up at the ceiling. "We're here to talk to Robbie Hoyle," he said.

The candle flames flickered.

"Robbie, are you there? Please, talk to us."

Jenny looked around the basement, then back at Nightingale. "Jack…" she said.

Nightingale ignored her. "It's Jack, Robbie. And Jenny. Are you there? We need to talk."

He took another deep breath, then exhaled slowly.

"This is a waste of time," said Jenny.

"I have to try," said Nightingale. "He said he knew something about my sister."

"He's dead, Jack. Robbie's dead."

"I know that."

"So this isn't going to help."

Nightingale glared at her, then looked up at the ceiling again. "Robbie? Robbie, are you there?"

Jenny shook her head. She was just about to take her fingers off the planchette when it twitched. Her mouth opened in surprise. "Jack…" she whispered.

Nightingale smiled. "Robbie," he said. "Is that you?"

The planchette slid slowly across the board until its point was resting on the word YES.

THE END

ABOUT THE AUTHOR

Stephen Leather was a journalist for more than ten years on newspapers such as *The Times*, the *Daily Mail*, and the *South China Morning Post* in Hong Kong. Before that, he was employed as a biochemist for ICI, shoveled limestone in a quarry, worked as a baker, a petrol pump attendant, a barman, and worked for the Inland Revenue. He began writing full-time in 1992 and his bestsellers have been translated into more than ten languages. He has also written for television shows such as *London's Burning*, *The Knock*, and the BBC's *Murder in Mind* series. You can find out more from his website, www.stephenleather.com.

MORE JACK NIGHTINGALE FROM STEPHEN LEATHER

Jack Nightingale's harrowing and hellish adventures continue in:

Midnight (September 2012)
http://www.amazon.com/Midnight-ebook/dp/B005J61F22

and

Nightmare (coming soon).

Plus, there are many more dark roads to travel with Jack at
www.jacknightingale.com.

Be sure to let us know your thoughts on the Nightingale series
at www.amazon.com/47North, and you can see more of the
author's work at www.stephenleather.com.